W9-BZP-462

BY

ALEXANDER GORDON SMITH

THE DEVIL'S ENGINE

HELLRAISERS

THE
DEVIL'S
ENGINE

HELL

RAISERS

ALEXANDER GORDON SMITH

FARRAR STRAUS GIROUX
NEW YORK

Farrar Straus Giroux Books for Young Readers
175 Fifth Avenue, New York 10010

Printed in the United States of America
Designed by Andrew Arnold
First edition, 2015
1 3 5 7 9 10 8 6 4 2

fiercereads.com

Library of Congress Cataloging-in-Publication Data
Smith, Alexander Gordon, 1979– author.
   The Devil's engine : Hellraisers / Alexander Gordon Smith. — First
edition.
       pages cm.
   Summary: Marlow Green is a high school boy in New York who is
always in trouble for vandalism and acting out, until one day he stumbles
into the middle of a battle with a demon, and learns about the Devil's
engine—an ancient machine which can grant anything you wish for, in
exchange for your soul.
   ISBN 978-0-374-30169-9 (hardcover)
   ISBN 978-0-374-30171-2 (e-book)
   1. Demonology—Juvenile fiction.   2. Monsters—Juvenile fiction.
3. High schools—Juvenile fiction.   4. Science fiction.   5. Adventure
stories.   6. New York (N.Y.)—Juvenile fiction.   [1. Science fiction.
2. Demonology—Fiction.   3. Monsters—Fiction.   4. High schools—
Fiction.   5. Schools—Fiction.   6. Adventure and adventurers—Fiction.
7. New York (N.Y.)—Fiction.]   I. Title.   II. Title: Hellraisers.

PZ7.S6423Dh 2015
[Fic]—dc23

                                                    2015007190

Our books may be purchased in bulk for promotional, educational, or
business use. Please contact your local bookseller or the Macmillan Corporate
and Premium Sales Department at (800) 221-7945 ext. 5442 or by
e-mail at MacmillanSpecialMarkets@macmillan.com.

FOR LUCY
FOR AVALON
FOR JELLYBEAN
(SORRY, WE DON'T KNOW
WHAT YOUR NAME IS YET!)

THANKS TO ALL OF YOU
FOR MAKING ME A VERY PROUD
AND VERY HAPPY DAD!

PART I
NEW WORLD

HELLRAISER

That was the trouble with being a hellraiser.

Sometimes you got burned.

Marlow Green knew this better than anyone. How many times had he heard it? From his teachers, when he got kicked out of class. From the principals, when he got kicked out of *schools*. From his mom, over and over. *You set fire to the world and you run, Marly.* And he did. Not literally—hellraiser, yes; arsonist, definitely not—but he lit up the world around him, started wildfires that burned through bridges, that sent his friends and his family packing, that spat and roared into his future, destroying it before he could even get there. Then, when it got too hot, he turned and bolted.

One of these days you're gonna start a fire that can't be put out, his mom had told him. *One you can't ever run fast enough to escape.* And he'd always wondered when that would be, always wondered what he'd have to do to ignite an inferno of that magnitude.

Turned out the answer to the first question was now. And the second? Yeah, that would be carving a certain part of the male anatomy into the paintwork of his principal's car.

They came for him during class. They didn't knock, just barged in through the door like they were raiding a meth lab instead of math. Half the kids were dozing off, staring out the dirty windows at the blazing June sunshine that drenched Staten Island. The sight of three school cops and the principal flooding into the room like a dark, cold current made everyone jump.

"Green!" growled the principal, Mr. Caputo, a scarecrow of a man drowning in his cheap suit. He pointed a blade-like finger at Marlow. "That's him."

Oh, crap.

The biggest of the three cops pushed his way through the desks. Everyone called him Yogi because he was always confiscating kids' lunches, then scarfing them. That and the fact he was a major fat-ass. His eyes were two raisins drowning in the doughy flesh of his face and he smiled wickedly at Marlow with sausage lips.

"Got you."

Marlow blew out a long sigh and sat back in his chair, feeling the heat on his cheeks. He chewed the skin of his knuckles the way he always did when he was stressed. His windpipe was already starting to crackle, like static, and he wondered whether he should use his inhaler now before things heated up. He decided against it, not wanting to look weak in front of the class.

Another cop swept between the desks with an expression like murder. The third cop stayed by the door, her holster open, hand on the butt of her pistol.

"For the love of . . ." Charlie Alvarez sat at the desk next to him, running a hand through his mess of dark hair and popping gum. "Dude, what did you do now?"

"Me?" Marlow smiled at his best friend—his *only* friend—coughing to clear his throat. "Absolutely nothing. I'm being framed."

Yogi stepped in front of the window, blocking the sun and

making the room feel ten degrees colder. He reached out and grabbed a fistful of Marlow's shirt with his free hand.

"Get your flabby hands off him, Yogi," yelled Charlie. "He didn't do nothing."

"This isn't your business, Alvarez," Caputo said, turning to Marlow and doing his best to stab him to death with his eyes. "Too far, Mr. Green," he spat, flecks of spittle spraying like gems against the sun.

"I'm sorry?" Marlow replied, as innocently as he could.

"You've gone too far. There's no way back from this."

"I'm not sure what you think I did," Marlow said, feeling his windpipe tighten and cursing his asthma for making him so weak. He snatched in a breath. "I'm just sitting in class, minding my own—"

"Get him up," Caputo said. "Take him outside."

Yogi obeyed, hauling Marlow out of his chair so hard that it toppled over behind him. Charlie was out of his just as quick, squaring up to the cop even though he was half his size.

"That's assault," he said. "You got no right."

"I said drop it, Alvarez," the principal replied. "This shi— This *idiot* isn't worth ruining your life for."

"Yeah, kid," said Yogi. "Sit down."

"Or what? You gonna eat me?"

The whole class laughed at that, somebody lobbing a crunched-up ball of paper at the cop's big, bald head. Yogi glanced at the other two cops but they just shrugged. Marlow laughed. He didn't blame them. Charlie was tiny, but he was scary as all hell when his blood was up.

"I'm glad you find this so amusing," the principal said. "But I can assure you, you won't be laughing for long. Move."

Yogi yanked his shirt and he started walking, coughing hard to release the pressure in his windpipe. Somebody in the class was clapping, and by the time he'd reached the door there was a full-on round of applause going on, complete with cheers and whistles. He turned and bowed to his audience before being bundled out of the room so abruptly he lost his footing. Yogi and the other two cops hoisted him up and it was like Marlow was penned in a prison of black cloth. Somehow the wiry principal managed to squeeze between them.

"You have no idea how much trouble you're in, Green," he squawked.

"I still don't know what I'm supposed to have done."

"So it wasn't you who scratched the hell out of my car?"

"Your car?" Marlow shook his head, trying to hold back the grin that wanted to explode across his face. "I didn't even know you had a car."

"Green Prius, out in the lot."

"You just admitted to driving a *Prius*?" came Charlie's voice, although Marlow couldn't see him past the circle of cops.

"The one that now has . . . has something scratched into the hood. Something obscene." He showed Marlow a snapshot on his cell phone.

"It looks like a rocket ship to me," said Marlow. "And it definitely wasn't my doing."

"Really?" The man leaned toward him, his fists clenched so hard that his knuckles were white. "So the fact that it says 'by M. Green' underneath is a lie, then?"

The laugh punched up from Marlow's throat so hard he couldn't hold it back. The truth was he'd done it that very morning, with his keys, while waiting for Charlie to turn up. It wasn't like Caputo didn't deserve it, he'd been on Marlow's case ever since he arrived at Victor G. Rosemount High School.

The principal looked ready to start swinging punches, but instead he turned on his heels and walked briskly down the corridor.

"Bring him to my office, we have paperwork to fill out."

That could only mean one thing. Marlow chewed his lip, feeling his heart drop into his sneakers. Yep, raise enough hell and you got burned—he knew that better than anyone. This was his third school in eight months, after all.

They climbed the short flight of steps that led to reception, crossing the foyer, past the security gate with its metal detectors. It had been the same in every other school, the long walk. Like he was being marched to his execution down the green mile.

The only difference this time was the police escort.

"Green," said the principal over his shoulder. "I don't know why you're so determined to ruin your life before it has a chance to begin. You're fifteen years old and about three short steps away from incarceration. You do understand why you're here, don't you? At this facility?"

Yeah, he did. Victor G. was the last stop on the road to Loserville. It was the place you went when you'd been chucked out of every other remedial high school in the city, when you'd incinerated every other option. Marlow felt the familiar pressure in his chest, the storm there starting to rage. He coughed up some phlegm, swallowing hard, then clawing in a breath.

"You're a coward, Green. You run away from every shred of responsibility in your life, you burn every bridge. Cowards are not welcome here. If VGR doesn't want you, nowhere else does. And you can be damned sure that VGR *does not want you.*"

Marlow's blood was boiling too fiercely for him to find a reply. Yogi was holding his shirt so tight that it had become a noose around his neck, making it even harder for him to breathe. Charlie trotted along beside them, looking genuinely concerned now.

"You okay, dude?" he said. "You're going blue."

"I'm fine," he wheezed. But that was a lie. He was about as far from fine as it was possible to get. He sucked in some air through the straw of his windpipe, knowing that as soon as he got into the principal's office it would be over. He'd be given his marching papers, told to scram. Then it would be home to his mom, confession time again.

"Get back to class, Alvarez, unless you want to go down as an accessory," the principal said. "There will be criminal charges, this time, Green. You hear me?"

Marlow tugged at his collar. Where the hell was all the oxygen? He eyed the main doors, the glorious sunshine beyond, twenty feet down the hallway, and all he wanted to do was run. Get the hell out of here. Escape while he still could. Charlie had backed off but caught his eye and shook his head. He knew him way too well.

They reached the door to the office and the principal pushed it open, disappearing into the darkness. Yogi shoved Marlow in after him. The room beyond was small, barely enough space for a desk and a couple of filing cabinets. It was dark, too, the window boarded over from where somebody had lobbed a brick through it a couple of weeks ago. It was too cramped in here, not enough air. The panic was like a punch to the lungs, paralyzing them. Marlow took a breath and nothing happened.

Don't seize, he ordered himself, the panic like an acetylene torch behind his eyes. *Please, not an attack.* He couldn't handle the terror, the ambulance, the rush to get the nebulizer, not on top of everything else.

"You do understand what this is?" the principal asked. "You do understand that you're finished here?"

8

Marlow ignored him, taking a step back toward the door. He reached down to his pocket, for the inhaler, and Yogi grabbed his hand.

"What you got in there, kid?" he asked.

Nothing, Marlow tried to say, producing a sound like a broken accordion. He tried to shake his hand free but Yogi's grip was a python's, made his bones feel like snapping. He could hear the cop talking, telling him to calm down, but his heartbeat was loud enough to bring down the walls of the office. He felt like he was being held underwater. Panic made him act before he even knew what he was doing, his hands darting out and slamming into Yogi's chest. The man was made of solid oak but he was unprepared, the push catching him off balance. He staggered back, letting go of Marlow, arms cartwheeling wildly. He crashed into the desk, sending papers flying.

Marlow didn't wait to see what happened next. He turned, shouldering past another of the cops, his lungs running on empty. He burst back out into the sun-filled hallway, skidding toward the metal detectors standing sentry just inside the doors. A quick look behind him let him know that they were in pursuit.

Charlie stood farther down the hallway, back toward the classroom. He waved his arms frantically, mouthing *Go!* Marlow nodded to him, then turned, bolting out one of the doors and across the parking lot. He dug the inhaler from his pocket as he went, squeezing off a few shots and feeling his lungs loosen up, the relief of being able to breathe again so good that he almost didn't hear the doors open behind him, the principal's voice screaming out: "You're expelled! Green, you hear me? Run all you want, there's no coming back!"

Marlow did just that, sprinting past the Prius with its brand-new decoration. He spun around as he went.

"Nice car, *dick!*"

And even though he was well and truly burned, even though he could hear his future being flushed, even though it was probably the worst comeback in the history of comebacks, he was grinning as he fled.

SLAUGHTERHOUSE

"We're in trouble."

Pan didn't need anyone to tell her that. It was pretty damn clear that they were in trouble. *Big* trouble. They were barreling down the Cross Island Expressway at eighty miles an hour, the truck roaring like a jet plane. Most of the cars on the road had the good sense to swerve out of their way, but a couple had been shunted off the tarmac by the Ford F-650's custom grille guard. Pan hadn't looked back to see what happened to them. There were more important things at stake.

Her life, for one.

She checked her watch. There was no time on the display, just a line of bright red numbers. *00:00:32:21.* There were way too many zeroes there for her liking. Thirty-two minutes, counting fast. Thirty-two minutes until they came for her. She checked her black Kevlar body suit, designed to withstand a close-range shot from a .44 Magnum. Not that it mattered. It wouldn't last five seconds against what was coming.

"Serious trouble," said the guy sitting next to her. His name was Forrest, although Pan didn't like to think of him as something with a name. It made it too difficult. You didn't name cattle when you sent them to the slaughterhouse. His skin was a nasty shade of gray, coated in sweat, and it wasn't surprising. He'd made his contract ten minutes before her so he'd have ten minutes less on his countdown. He wiped his brow, then sat forward in his seat looking like he was going to puke. It was Forrest's first mission and the Lawyers were cutting it fine.

Way too fine.

"Hold it together, guys," said the other man in the back of the truck. Herc. He was mission commander but he'd commanded *jack* on this particular mission. The whole damn thing had gone wrong and if the Lawyers didn't hurry up, then all he or anyone else in the van was good for was a mid-morning snack for hell's hungriest. He rubbed a hand through the grizzled stubble on his chin. "Take the next exit, we gotta get out of sight. And rack 'em up, we're gonna need 'em."

Herc pumped a shell into his combat shotgun and Forrest fumbled with his. They were the best defense they'd found against the demons. *Kind of like saying a toothpick was the best defense against a rabid bear,* she thought. Pan didn't have a gun. She reached down, felt the crossbow at her feet. Even that wouldn't do much good. Not unless the Lawyers found a way to end her contract. What the hell was taking them so long?

"Ostheim," she said into the radio attached to her armored suit. There was a permanent open link between her and her employer, Sheppel Ostheim. "You guys any closer? We don't exactly have a lot of time here."

There was a hiss of static, followed by a voice with a trace of a German accent.

"They're going as fast as they can, Pan. This is a tricky nut to crack. Just stay alive, they'll get there."

Pan spat out a bitter laugh.

"Stay alive? You finally developed a sense of humor, Shep? Any chance of backup?"

"*Nightingale and Truck are inside the Engine, everyone else is airborne. Until then you're on your own.*"

Great.

Everyone jolted in their seats as the truck made contact with something else. The sour stench of fear filled her nostrils, making her want to gag. She and Herc had done this before but Forrest had only heard stories—the way the world is torn open, the way they swarm out from behind the paper-thin shell of reality. He had a hand over his mouth, his eyes wide and white, the brightest things in the truck. She didn't offer him any words of comfort. What would be the point? Chances were that in less than half an hour the only evidence he'd ever existed would be his entry in the *Book of Dead Engineers.*

Right next to her own.

"Hang on!" yelled the driver, wrestling with the wheel. The truck lurched off the expressway, thumping into the side of the road hard enough to jolt them all off their seats. Pan was pushed back by an invisible hand as they accelerated, her stomach trying to punch its way out past her spine, the world flashing by outside the tinted windows too fast to see. It didn't matter how fast they were going. They couldn't outrun them. They couldn't escape, they couldn't hide. The only thing that mattered was finding cover, where nobody could see what happened next.

"*Get off the street,*" Ostheim said, reading her mind. "*By my calculation . . .*" He swore. "*Twenty minutes, Pan, and counting, fast. Get out of sight.*"

The world cannot know. It's the only thing that counts, it's more important than your own life. Ostheim had drilled that into her on day one. And every day since.

So why the hell were they heading right into the heart of Staten Island?

"Out of sight, goddammit!" Herc yelled, grabbing the seat as they smashed into the back of an SUV, sending it spinning out toward the side of the road.

Too late, Pan thought as the driver steered them around a wide bend, so fast that the world outside was just a blur. The screeching tires threw up smoke, and for a second the driver almost lost it. There was a wet retching sound as Forrest puked over his trousers but Pan ignored it. There was something else in the air alongside the smell of vomit. A thick, heavy, sulfurous scent that she knew all too well.

Their smell. The stench of hell.

"Twenty minutes, Pan," Ostheim repeated, like she hadn't heard him the first time.

Twenty minutes. Twenty minutes between her, Forrest, and an eternity of agony. Twenty minutes before they dragged her kicking and screaming down to hell.

"Those Lawyers better shift their asses," she yelled at Ostheim, cursing herself—for the hundredth time at least—for ever accepting his offer.

The Engine.

The goddamned Devil's Engine.

She'd always known it would be the death of her.

BREATHLESS

Marlow had jogged a block and a half before he dared to slow down. Crossing the street, he tripped into the alley that ran down the back of the expressway, crashing against a fence. He took another couple of puffs of his inhaler for good measure, feeling the last of the blockage shift from his windpipe. His lungs still ached, though, like he'd breathed in a lungful of pepper spray and run a marathon, not a few hundred yards.

He spat out a wad of phlegm and wiped the sweat from his brow. Only here, in the sudden quiet—just the distant rumble of the city and the eerie wail of a siren—did the events of the last few minutes sink in.

What the hell were you thinking?

He was screwed. Not only had he been expelled from the last school that would take him, he'd also committed vandalism and assault—on a *cop*. There was probably an APB out on him by now; the siren he could hear would be a squad car blazing up the street. This was Mariners Harbor, they'd shoot him on sight.

His palms stung from where he'd pushed Yogi, and he rubbed them on his pants, trying to work out a plan. The best thing would be to turn around, head back to the school with his tail between his legs, offer to pay for the paintwork to be redone or something. He could get down on his hands and knees, kowtow his way back to his math class like nothing had ever happened.

Yeah, right.

There was more chance of him sprouting wings and flying into Harvard. He wiped the sweat from his face, sweat that had less to do with running and more to do with the terror of not being able to breathe. He'd been lucky this time. His asthma was a constant threat, always doing its best to kill him.

When he'd been a kid, lying in his bed, writhing back and forth and going blue while his mom called for the ambulance, he'd seen it as a monster, something that wrapped invisible fingers around his throat, whose tongue wormed its way into his windpipe, sealing it tight. Even though he was fifteen now he still carried that beast around with him; it was always on his back, waiting to attack. When it was bad, *really* bad, it was a battle to the death. The inhaler lost its power. Even the nebulizer he had at home didn't work. It had been close today. A couple more minutes, maybe, and the principal would have been calling 911 and giving him mouth to mouth.

Maybe that would have been better. You couldn't exactly expel somebody who was dying on your office floor.

Marlow shook his head. What was he going to tell his mom? *Please, Marlow,* he heard her say, as clear as if she were standing next to him. There had been enough Bacardi on her breath that day to make his eyes sting. *Please, just this once, be good. I can't stand it, I can't stand the trouble. I need you to do this for me, stay in school.*

And he had been, he'd been doing okay. It was just that douche bag principal, riding him every day. This was all Caputo's fault. Maybe he should go back and teach the man a proper—

Footsteps, hard and fast, rising up from the end of the alleyway. Marlow pushed himself off the wall, fists clenched.

16

Please, not the school cop. He'd half turned, not sure if his lungs could stand another sprint, when Charlie's face appeared. When he saw Marlow he flinched. Then he broke into a sweaty grin, skidding to a halt with his hands on his knees. Marlow swore.

"Jesus, Charlie, where'd you come from?"

"They were all so busy chasing after you, I couldn't resist slipping out behind them."

Then they were both laughing, sniggering nervously, just in case somehow the cops could hear them half a mile away. "Man, you should have seen it back there, it was utter chaos. I can't believe you punched Yogi!"

"I didn't punch him," Marlow said. "His fat ass just fell over. What happened?"

"It sounded like all hell had broken loose in there, I had to go look. Yogi was on the desk and the desk was on the *floor*; the whole thing had snapped in two. He was rolling around like a turtle, funniest thing I ever saw. Then they were after you." Charlie had to stop to catch his breath he was laughing so hard. "Best part is, Yogi came out of the office so hard he nearly knocked me over, ran straight into one of his guys and ended up flat on his face. And he was rolling around all over again. Took the other cops and Caputo to pick him up. Man, I almost died laughing."

"They come after you too?" Marlow asked.

Charlie shook his head. "Nah. Don't exactly look like a threat, do I?"

Understatement of the century. Charlie was a year older than Marlow but five foot three and stick thin. The phrase "can't punch his way out of a wet paper bag" was invented for him, although anyone who thought that would be wrong. Charlie was a pit bull. He wouldn't just tear his way out of a wet paper bag, he'd shred it, set fire to it, then stamp the ashes into

17

oblivion. Spending three-quarters of your life in foster care would do that to you.

"Besides, Caputo loves me. I'm one of his model students, turning my life around, getting back on track. They used me in the brochure, remember? You, though . . ." Charlie shook his head, sighing. "Pretty stupid thing to do, Marlow, even for you. What made you scratch *that* on the principal's car?"

"It was a rocket ship," Marlow muttered.

Charlie cracked a smile, but it slipped off his face after a second or two. "Seriously, dude, what are you going to do now?"

Marlow didn't answer, just turned and walked down the alley. Best thing to do to a question like that, turn your back on it.

Charlie scampered after him, his feet kicking up gravel. "Marlow, I'm not kidding, you got to start facing up to things."

"I am," Marlow said. "I hated that place anyway."

"So you're bolting again? You're running out of places to go. Gonna be prison or the army at this rate."

Not the army. No way. Marlow closed his eyes, thought of Danny. He barely even remembered his brother, but he saluted his yellowing, fading photo—full combat gear, bleached in desert sun—on the kitchen wall every single day. Had done ever since he was five years old and his brother hadn't come home. Once upon a time all he'd ever wanted was to be a marine like Danny. Maybe that way his mom would look at him the same way she did that photo, with love.

Then he thought of the empty coffin. The flag draped over it, folded by the honor guard and handed over to his mother at the funeral. *Cowards can't be soldiers,* his brain said, and he stared up at the sun to try to burn the words away.

"They're hiring up at the concrete plant," Charlie said, kicking a crushed can into a section of fence. "Not great but at least it'll keep you out of trouble." He snorted. "Though trouble always seems to find you." He snorted. "Picking a fight with Yogi Bear."

"I've seen you do worse," Marlow said, looking at his friend. The first time he'd met Charlie the kid had been in a fight with two college jocks over in Tottenville. He'd been out-numbered and outgunned but he'd been giving as good as he got. They'd both ended up bolting, holding their bloodied noses. Charlie probably would have chased them halfway across the state if Marlow hadn't stepped in to hold him back. He'd almost gotten a black eye for his trouble.

"I'm the very definition of sweetness and light," Charlie said. "Where we going now?"

Marlow pulled his cell from his pocket and checked the time. It was nearly eleven. He half thought about calling his mom, telling her on the phone. It was better than seeing her face crumple, watching the tears fall. But he couldn't face her, not even on the phone. It wasn't the anger that worried him, he dealt with that all the time. No, it was the disappointment.

He needed some Dutch courage before he spoke to her.

"Gonna go celebrate my newfound freedom," he said, flashing a bitter smile at Charlie. "No more school, man. Just sunshine and partying. Wanna join me?"

"Getting hammered before lunch? That's your big plan?"

They exited the alleyway onto Park, a solid line of traffic bleating like robotic sheep and pumping out fumes. Marlow coughed, feeling the tickle again, the beast slipping its fingers around his throat. Man, he hated this city, hated the cars, hated the schools, hated the people.

"Marlow?" Charlie said, reaching out and grabbing his shirt. "You don't want to end up like your mom. Like my old man."

He shrugged loose, the anger burning up inside him like the sun.

"I'll be fine," he said, walking off so that Charlie wouldn't see the fire reach his face. "Just go back, do your thing, live your life."

Push, push, push. It's all he seemed to do sometimes.

"Yeah, real fine," said Charlie. "Go have a morning cocktail, Marlow, run away like you always do."

There was the sound of scuffing heels as he made his way back into the alley, then his voice again.

"You know, Caputo is right about one thing. You're too scared to face up to anything. Do yourself a favor, Marlow, grow some *cojones.*"

Then he was gone. Marlow stood there, wanting to chase after him but standing his ground.

Sometimes people don't push back. Sometimes you push them so hard they fall right out of your life.

"Who cares," he muttered to himself. "I'll be fine."

But it was starting to dawn on him that maybe he wouldn't.

COLLATERAL DAMAGE

00:00:22:21.

Twenty-two minutes.

Pan checked her watch again, swore time was going twice as fast as it should be. She even tapped the watch face, like it was broken.

You wish. It was a custom model—waterproof, bombproof, bulletproof.

The only thing it wasn't was demonproof.

The truck lurched, ripping her back into the real world. They were off the expressway and smashing through traffic like a demolition derby. Too many people watching them with eyes like pickled eggs, too many CCTV cameras picking them up. Pan could hear sirens rising over the growl of the engine. That was bad.

Really bad.

The driver reached the end of the road and wrenched up the hand brake like he was trying to rip it off. The truck skidded to the left, vibrating hard enough to shake them all to pieces. For a second it lifted onto two wheels, the whole thing on the verge of toppling. Pan swore, clutching her seat to stop herself from sliding into Forrest. The driver flicked the wheel and the truck leveled with a bump.

They had to get into hiding, *fast.* The consequences of

staying in plain sight were bad. Worse even than the thought of what would happen to her in twenty-two minutes.

She checked her watch.

Twenty-one.

She swore, leaning forward, scanning the road ahead. There was nothing but apartment blocks, rising on both sides like tombstones. The truck was doing seventy, bludgeoning its way past the traffic.

Come on, come on, give us a break.

"They're going to crack it, right?" asked Forrest. The kid was covered in his own puke and shaking hard. He was the same age as her—seventeen—but right now he looked half that, a little boy who's suddenly found himself miles away from home with no idea how he got there. She didn't know much about him, other than his name. It was the way she liked it. In this business, people died. Simple as that. It was easier if they were strangers.

"You need to focus," she said. "Let the Lawyers worry about the contract."

"Seriously," Herc growled at the driver, "if you don't get this hunk of junk into cover *right now* I'm gonna throw you out the door."

"Just remember, you're a soldier, a Hellraiser," Pan said to Forrest, "you can fight them, the demons. You traded for strength, right?"

He nodded.

"Then just punch the crap out of them."

It would be like fighting a tide. They'd keep coming. Nothing could stop them. But at least this way he'd have hope.

She lifted her crossbow to check that it was ready to use. The weapon was over three hundred years old but it was still as good as new. The bolt in the chamber was iron, taken from the Engine itself. Not as intimidating as a shotgun, but it was loaded with something far older and more powerful than buckshot.

The demons were coming to collect, sure. But that didn't mean she was going to pay up without a fight.

"You need me to . . . to speak to anyone?" Herc asked. It was the last thing she wanted to hear. Herc knew better than anyone that there was nobody for him to speak to. She ignored him, focusing on the road, on the endless barriers of buildings on either side. The truck was doing fifty now, slowed down by the thick stream of traffic clogging the street. The grille guard was doing its job but sooner or later it was going to run into something bigger than it and that would be that, they'd be stranded in the middle of America's most densely populated city.

"Pan? Your mom? I can find her. I can tell her—"

She reached out and slapped her gloved hand over his mouth. There was no need, because the glare she shot at him would have shut him up by itself.

"Herc, stop talking. I'm not planning on dying today."

00:00:19:23.

Her watch had other plans.

"What about you, kid?" Herc said to Forrest. The boy looked back, his wide eyes full of terror.

"You told me this wouldn't happen," he said, his quiet voice almost lost beneath the roar of the engine. "You said the Lawyers could crack it."

"They will," said Pan, trying to give him a reassuring look. She caught a glimpse of his watch. Less than ten minutes. She keyed the radio. "Ostheim, we could really do with some help right now."

"Not long, Pan, they've almost got it."

The truck thumped up onto the curb, somebody screaming as they dived out of its path. It rammed into a hydrant, water blasting up into the sun and filling the street with rainbows. Rainbows that flickered with red and blue light.

Ah, crap.

"Cops!" yelled the driver. Sure enough the rear window was filled with light, a blue-and-white squad car blazing up behind them.

"Get the caltrops out!" Herc roared, and when nobody responded he plowed his way to the back of the truck. He grabbed a duffel bag and unzipped it, kicking open the rear doors and lobbing it out. The mechanism inside the bag activated, unleashing a string of razor wire and sending it spinning out across the asphalt. The cop car braked but not before it tore across the wire, all four tires exploding. Then it was on its side, rolling hard, bouncing into the parked cars along the edge of the road.

Pan turned back to the front, part of her wondering if the cops inside were still alive, part of her trying not to care. *Two lives are nothing compared to what might happen if the world finds out about us,* she forced herself to think. *Collateral damage, just collateral damage.* If she kept saying it, then it had to be true.

"We have to get off the road!" Herc said, his eyes almost popping out of his head. "We have to find—"

The wall of buildings on the left-hand side of the road split, plunging them back into the sun. Pan squinted, seeing a bigger building behind a screen of trees. There was a gate there, and beyond it the road swept down into the mouth of a tunnel. An underground parking lot. It was their only shot.

"There!" she said, pointing over the driver's shoulder. He panicked, turning the wheel too early, blasting a gatepost to brick dust as the truck slammed through. Then they were in the shade, swallowed whole by the tunnel.

Pan's ears popped, a change in pressure that had nothing to do with being underground. A spark ripped across the inside of the truck, so bright that it left its mark on her retinas, made her short hair stand on end. The sulfurous smell was stronger here, a haze of smoke already pooling around their feet. The truck skidded down the spiral ramp, scraping the concrete walls, and spat out into the first level of the parking lot. The driver slammed on the brakes and they screeched to a halt.

The lights on the ceiling were flickering wildly, more sparks tearing the air around them. The whole building shook and groaned like a sinking ship. The demons were always powerful, but this time there were two souls on the table, and they were hungry. They would demolish half of New York trying to collect.

"Go go go!" she yelled.

Herc kicked open the doors at the back of the truck and hopped down, his shotgun at the ready. Even though Pan had been in this situation countless times she still felt like screaming, fear turning her whole body hollow. She fought it, grabbing the seats and literally hauling herself toward the doors.

The lights in the parking lot gave up, exploding into sparks and flooding the world with darkness.

"Tubes!" she shouted, ripping a light stick from her belt and lobbing it out the doors. It flickered on, burning fiercely, making the parking lot swim like it was at the bottom of an ocean of blood.

"You two," said Herc, pointing a finger inside the van and flashing them both a warning look, "stay here."

He turned, slotting spare shells into the shotgun and pumping one into the barrel. It was getting hot down here—*really* hot—the air shimmering like they were inside a furnace.

She glanced at her watch again, barely ten minutes left to live if the Lawyers didn't get their asses in gear. Ten minutes, then she was worse than dead.

Collateral damage.

"Listen to Herc," said Ostheim's voice in her ear, the signal broken up by the layers of concrete overhead. *"Do not leave that vehicle."*

"Yes, sir," she replied. Then she checked her crossbow, took a deep breath, and threw herself out of the doors into the nightmare of blood and fire.

DROWNING SORROWS

Charlie was right. For someone who couldn't jog ten paces without reaching for his inhaler, Marlow did a hell of a lot of running.

Not sprinting, not jogging, not running a marathon. No, his kind of running was the other kind. He never ran toward anything, he ran away from *everything*.

It's what cowards do, said his head. He'd been five when Danny had died, so he couldn't remember what his brother's voice sounded like. He was pretty sure this was him, though, the big brother whose ghost lived in his mind.

"Shut up," he whispered to him. "You ran away as soon as you were old enough to enlist."

Needed to get the hell away from Mom, came the reply.

Marlow put his head down and engaged autopilot. He didn't know where he was going. He didn't care. As long as he kept moving he didn't have to think about anything. Didn't have to think about what he was going to tell his mom, didn't have to think about what he was going to do with his life. He crossed the street, the sunlight boring holes in his skull, blinding him. A truck tore past, close enough to touch, cocooning him in exhaust fumes. Its horn bellowed, deep and loud, making his bones tremble.

What are you going to tell her? Danny asked.

He had no idea. It wasn't like she gave a happy crap what he did with his life—she spent all day in her rum-and-Coke bubble. All she ever talked about was how proud she was of Danny, how much she missed him, how Marlow could never fill his brother's army boots no matter how hard he tried—not that he was interested in trying.

No, better to run, better to keep your head down, your ears closed, your mouth shut. Run and find a good place to hide. His mom had found a home in a Bacardi bottle, Marlow was pretty sure he'd be comfortable there too.

He looked up, no idea where he was. There was a main road up ahead, though, and he marched toward it. He turned left, weaving between the crowds of kids skipping school and moms with strollers. An auto center, a nail parlor, a pizza joint, and there, so small he almost missed it, the faded green canopy of a corner bodega.

Perfect.

He started to cross, pulling back when an ambulance barreled past, siren screaming. Another followed. They skidded right up ahead, disappearing behind the buildings. Now that he was tuned into it he could make out more sirens, the air swimming with them. Not that it was unusual, of course. This was New York City. It was the day you didn't hear any sirens that you knew you were totally screwed.

The traffic broke and he jogged across the street. The bodega looked more like a prison than a store—bars tight against the windows and half a dozen cameras aimed down at the sidewalk. There was a huddle of guys smoking cigarettes outside and they eyeballed him hard enough to make him stop, think about turning around. Then one of them laughed at something and they looked away, and Marlow stomped the last few paces and crashed through the door.

Inside it looked even more like a prison: a single chest-high shelf running to the back of the store, teeming with rows of dusty canned goods; beat-up refrigerators against the walls stocked with juice, soda, and beer; the aisles crammed with flimsy displays loaded with chips and other junk; up front, a small deli area, and behind the Plexiglas, a counter with lotto tickets, cigarettes, candy within an easy snatch of the cash register. It took his eyes a while to adjust to the gloom, the window bars keeping the sunlight out but trapping the heat and dust inside. It was like a sauna in here and he had to ease his inhaler out of his pocket, firing off a blast to stop his lungs from rattling.

He grabbed a forty-ounce bottle of malt liquor from one of the coolers. But he could feel somebody watching him, and he was suddenly aware of how he looked—stooped and pouting like a sulky child.

He straightened up to his full five ten, clearing his throat, jangling the coins in the pocket of his sweatpants the way he'd seen older guys do. He strode as confidently as he could to the front of the store, stopping at the newspaper rack to pick up a copy of the *Daily News*, figuring it would make him look older.

Gradually a face became visible behind the glass, a woman who had to have been around when they signed the Declaration of Independence. She was so small she could barely see over the counter, but she had fire in her eyes and right now she looked like she was trying to make Marlow spontaneously combust. He coughed nervously and put the bottle and the newspaper in the hatch. The old lady didn't move.

"Just these please," he said, sounding like a church mouse. He looked at the counter, at the wall, at the ceiling, at his shoes, then finally at the old lady.

"Sure, kid," she said with a thick accent that he couldn't place. "Why don't I grab you some smokes and a lotto ticket, make it a party."

"Um . . ." Marlow felt every liquid ounce of blood rise to his face. "It's not for me, it's for my . . . wife. She asked me to pick it up on the way home from my . . . job."

He thought for a moment that the woman was going to choke to death from laughing. She wiped her eyes with a leathery hand.

"Oh, right, we wouldn't want to disappoint the *wife*," she said when she had recovered herself. "What's her name?"

Marlow reached into his head for a name and found nothing there. He stared at the front page of the paper, an article on Rio.

"B . . . Brazil," he stuttered. "Brazilia."

"Brazilia," she said, nodding. "She sounds beautiful. Where did you meet?"

"At . . ." Marlow struggled again. "Look, I'm in a hurry, it's been a bad day. Can I just pay for these and get going?"

The chime above the door rang out and the woman's head jerked up, her hand reaching under the counter. She probably had a bat or something under there, although Marlow had no idea what good it would do her, she was surely too small to lift it. She quickly relaxed and Marlow glanced over his shoulder to see a couple of women walk inside, chatting furiously in Spanish. Through the open door he could hear more police blazing past on the street, sirens shrieking.

"Trouble outside," said the woman, shaking her head. "Always trouble."

"Yeah," he said, tugging his wallet out of his sweats. It was black and red, and when he pulled apart the Velcro fastener he felt like he was ten years old. There was a twenty inside, and a bunch of ones. He took the twenty and slapped it down in the hatch. "This cover it?"

"Sure, kid, wanna pull your ID outta there while you're at it?"

Marlow looked at his wallet, then back up at her.

"It's . . ."

"In your other wallet?" she said, folding her arms across her chest. Marlow opened his mouth to answer but she cut him off again. "The dog ate it? It's in your *wife's* handbag? Aliens abducted it? You left it at—the office?"

"All of the above?" Marlow said with what he hoped was a charming smile. He thought the woman might have fallen for it, but the distant roar of an engine filled the room, a crunch of metal, squealing brakes. Was that a scream, muffled by the walls of the store? She looked over his shoulder, shaking her head.

"Better not be your trouble, kid," she said.

Marlow shook his head, standing aside as the two women walked to the counter and bought gum. He half thought about just turning and bolting with the bottle. It wasn't like the cashier would be able to catch him. His lungs had already taken a beating, though, and by the time he was even half-way to working up the courage the women had gone and he was alone with the clerk again. He pinched the top of his nose, an ache brewing in his skull.

"Look, it's been a real bad day. I wanna forget it."

"Kid, you're young, you're healthy, you wouldn't know a bad day if it bit you on the ass. No ID, no booze. I'll sell you that newspaper and a bag of Skittles and you can count yourself as lucky as the angels. Deal?"

He looked at the bottle, licking his lips as he imagined the peace that lay inside.

"Lady, please."

"Lady?" the woman. "You call me a *lady?*"

She leaned in toward the glass, and this close her wrinkled face seemed to take on a more masculine appearance.

Oh crap.

"Sorry, man, it's—"

"Go on!" the little guy yelled, banging a gnarled fist on the glass. "Get out of here before I—"

Something outside exploded, not so much a sound as a tremor that rocked through the store and into Marlow's bones, almost knocking him clean onto his ass. He gripped the counter hard, doing his best to clamp his jaws around a scream. The shock wave punched open the door, a roar like thunder pouring in from the outside world. One of the windows imploded in a spray of sun-drenched shrapnel. Behind the glass the cashier almost fell off his stool.

"Holy Jesus Christ," he grunted, propping one hand on the counter and reaching under it with the other. When he came up again it wasn't a bat he was holding, it was a shotgun, sawn off and double-barreled. He pointed it right at Marlow, finger on the trigger, everything shaking.

"Hey," Marlow said, hands over his head, his heart jack-hammering against his ribs. His ears were ringing. There was a smell in the air, not smoke but something worse, something that smelled like old eggs and acid.

"You better tell me what the hell's going on," the bodega guy said, his eyeballs practically bursting out of their sockets. His greasy hair was defying gravity, stretching up toward the ceiling like it was trying to make a getaway. Marlow could feel something on his skin, some kind of electric charge. "I swear to god I'll cut you down right here and make your imaginary wife an imaginary widow."

Another sound was filtering through the chaos, the *pop pop pop* of gunshots.

"It's nothing to do with me," Marlow said again, staring into the big, empty eyes of the shotgun. He wondered if bullet-proof glass worked both ways. "I swear, I have no idea. I just wanted a drink."

"Yeah? Some coincidence that. Go on, get outta here."

Marlow backed away. Another siren wailed past outside, louder now that the door was open. The dust was aggravating his asthma, shutting everything down again. He tried to cough open his windpipe, reaching down for his inhaler.

"Uh-uh," the man said. "Hands where I can see 'em until you're out the door."

Marlow backed off, arms stretched out to his sides. He'd made it four feet when another explosion rocked through the store, this one powerful enough to knock him to his knees. His vision flashed white, so bright that it felt like a physical force against his retinas. He used a shelf to pull himself up, lumps of ceiling smashing down around him like hail. The cashier opened his mouth, seemed like he was going to shout something at Marlow, but he never got the chance. The ceiling above him split in an avalanche of plaster and beams. One second he was there, the next he was buried.

Marlow waved the dust away, ignoring the pain in his lungs, running to the counter. There was a door to the side, knocked ajar by the blast but wedged tight with rubble. He shouldered it open. There was no sign of the clerk except for a hand and a leg beneath the debris. Marlow reached out, a jagged spark of electricity leaping from the man's flesh to his own, but he felt no sign of a pulse.

Oh god.

Marlow held the man's limp hand for a moment more,

trying to will him back to life. The remains of the ceiling groaned. At this rate the whole building was going to collapse, so he clambered onto the bar again, retreating only when he remembered the shotgun. He dived down, snatched it up, spying a box of shells behind the bar and tipping as many as he could into his pockets. If things were as bad as they sounded, then he was going to need all the firepower he could get.

Marlow took one last look at the dead clerk's hand. *That could have been me.* Then he sprinted across the empty room, slipping on the dust and rubble, once again running as fast as his sneakers would let him.

DO YOUR WORST

The world was coming apart.

Literally.

Pan propelled herself away from the truck, knowing that if she stayed still she was finished. Not dead, but something infinitely worse. The air above her was sparking wildly, fingers of sulfurous white lightning ripping past close enough to burn her skin. The parking lot was a mess of fire and noise and smoke and there was something up there, in the darkness between the steel beams. Something that thrashed and squirmed.

"I told you to stay in the truck!" yelled Herc. He didn't wait for an answer, pulling the trigger on his combat shotgun. The ceiling exploded into concrete dust. Forrest was there too, his shotgun clenched in one white-knuckled hand but his bulging eyes fixed on his watch. She didn't have to see it to know that the display read *00:00:00:00*. The demons were here. His time was up.

Pan hefted her crossbow, scanning the space around her, everything drenched in red, liquid light from the glow sticks. Other than the truck there were maybe half a dozen cars down here, two SUVs, a Corvette that had seen better days, a—

Halfway across the parking lot, she spotted a red Ford. Tongues of fire licked across the vehicle, fierce enough to shatter the windshield. One of the tires hissed, then popped, the car bouncing. But Pan was looking at the hood, the way it seemed to be peeling away from the rest of the car. A thin strip of metal curled up, followed by another, and another, then the bulk of a body, like a camouflaged spider, was finally revealing itself. It stretched, a living sculpture of red metal and engine parts, then ripped free from the rest of the car.

"There!" Pan said.

"Pan, wait!" yelled Herc behind her, his voice lost in the thunder of gunfire. She ignored him, sprinting toward the Ford. The creature pounced, landing on the floor with a crunch, its metal legs skittering. It stretched up to its full height, all four feet of it. The metal folded and refolded like it was paper, jaws opening and snapping shut, lined with scalpel-like teeth. It had no eyes. It didn't need them. It knew exactly where to find its prey.

"Protect Forrest!" she yelled at Herc, but he was already by the boy's side pumping another shell into his gun. The demon opened the bear trap of its mouth and shrieked, a noise that grated down her soul, making her want to curl into a ball and cry. Instead she ran, flicking the safety off the crossbow. The demon moved too, its clumsy legs finding their form, picking up speed, demolishing the distance between them. Twenty yards, fifteen, five. It leaped, the force of it punching holes into the concrete floor.

Pan pulled the trigger. The demon might have been made of steel but the bolt that flashed from the bow was forged out of the heart of the Engine itself. It slammed into the beast like a wrecking ball, stopping it dead. The creature crumpled to the ground, slashed at its own metal skin. It had time for one hellish scream before the bolt exploded like a grenade, sending both halves of the demon spinning across the car park.

"Move!" yelled the driver, running her way. Both halves of

the demon were wriggling, trying to reassemble themselves. The driver aimed his shotgun at the head end and fired, blasting it into metal splinters, filling the air with shrapnel. Its movements slowed, pieces of broken metal moving like jumping beans as they clung on to life. He fired twice more. Then, just like that, it was still.

"Got to—" he said, then his mouth opened in horror, unleashing a scream that almost deafened her. By the time Pan had worked out what was going on the driver was staggering back, his left foot missing. The floor where he had been standing had opened up like a mouth, barbs of concrete gnashing and grinding at the air, slick with his blood. The ground split as the new demon pulled itself free. Its body was a chunk of masonry, the white lines of the parking bay still etched over it. It tried to find its balance on five stunted concrete legs.

Pan stepped back, jamming the crossbow on the floor in order to reload it. The weapon was powerful but it was just about the most awkward thing Ostheim could have given her. She wound the handle, yelling as she did, "Somebody shoot it!"

The driver was on the floor now, jets of blood spraying from the stump of his leg, his eyes rolling back in their sockets. But Herc was there, jabbing the end of his shotgun against the bulk of the concrete demon and pulling the trigger. Pan threw up her hands, feeling shards of floor embed themselves in her face, the pain lost in the thunder of the adrenaline. She finished winding the bow, fumbling for a bolt and jamming it into the gutter. Herc pumped, fired again, and the demon was gone, just a concrete shell left behind.

"*Hang in . . . re . . .*" said Ostheim through her earpiece, his words faint and in pieces. "*They've al . . . broken . . . contract. Five min—*"

Five minutes. That was an eternity. She scanned the parking

37

lot. The metal demon and the concrete one were both gone, and a pile of rubble by the side of the truck made it clear that Herc had finished off another. But the air was still full of sulfur. She could almost see that paper-thin line between this world and theirs straining, the countless demons that teemed on the other side, all trying to break through. All trying to get to her.

But where the hell was Forrest?

Herc swore, pointing up the ramp.

"Kid's doing a runner!" he roared. "Goddammit! Forrest!"

Stupid. Really stupid. You couldn't run from them. There was nowhere to hide. Pan opened her mouth to call the boy's name but it was too late. Something wrenched itself from the wall that formed the side of the ramp, a dog-like shape with concrete skin and a steel spine. Forrest never even saw it coming. It pounced onto his back, crushing the boy in a spray of blood and jelly. Even past the howl of the demon Pan heard him scream, a rasping, desperate, haggard cry that echoed off the walls.

Turn away, something in Pan's head told her. *You don't want to see.*

But she kept looking, seeing the floor beneath the dead boy grow soft, melting like licorice. The air began to shimmer, the way it does over a barbecue, and with a soft *pop* Forrest's clothes ignited. The whole ramp was growing red, dissolving in the heat, but the dead kid was still howling—even as his hair caught fire, even as his skin bubbled.

She didn't look away. She didn't blink. Not even when she felt Herc's hands on her, trying to pull her around. The demon's head snapped forward like a viper's and Forrest's head exploded, scraps of bone and brain skittering across the molten ground. But she could still hear those screams as the boy's twitching body started to sink into the ground.

He'd be screaming for the rest of time.

Forrest vanished slowly, as if he had fallen into a tar pit. Then the demon crumpled to the floor, like its batteries had run out. Through the smoke and the haze Pan watched the ground start to heal, cooling.

Not for long, though.

She looked at her watch. Less than a minute and she'd be pulled under too, the fast track to hell. She felt Herc's hands on her again, pulling her close.

"We'll do what we can, Pan," he said, his voice shaking like a leaf. "I . . . I'll try."

She shrugged him away. She didn't need his pity. She knew what she was getting into. *You play the game, you take the pain.* She checked her crossbow, choking on that gut-churning stench of sulfur seeping out between the cracks in reality. There was another smell too. She looked back at the Ford, seeing gasoline spurting from the ruptured tank, pooling around the tires.

She checked her watch.

Five, four, three, two, one . . .

It emitted a soft, chirping alarm. Somehow it didn't quite have the gravity she expected it to—an air-raid Klaxon would have been more appropriate. She lifted the crossbow, the whole thing shaking.

Here they come.

"The wall!" Herc yelled, and she followed the barrel of his gun to see a shape pull itself free from a pillar. This one was bigger, almost human shaped, exploding outward in a plume of dust. The whole parking lot groaned, cracks appearing in the ceiling, the weight of the building above threatening to crash down, bury them all alive.

Herc lifted his gun and fired, the demon pushing through a hail of buckshot. It swiped a huge fist before Herc could reload, sending him flying. Pan fought her panic, lifting the crossbow and firing. The creature twisted at the last second, the bolt burying itself in the wall behind. Pan swore, slamming down the crossbow and winding the handle.

It pounced, its fingers gouging trenches in her armor, knocking the air from her lungs and the crossbow from her fingers. Herc appeared by her side, shoulder charging the demon, forcing it back. He raised his gun and fired, again, again, each blast punching the demon across the parking lot. Too late Pan noticed where they were heading.

"Herc, no!"

The demon slipped and fell into the puddle of gasoline from a car's ruptured fuel tank, Herc firing one last shot. The world went white, burning like a supernova, a silent explosion that lifted Pan up and hurled her backward. By the time she'd hit the floor the noise had caught up, a wave of rolling thunder that felt thick enough to drown in. She fought against the heat, against the boiling tide of smoke and vaporized blood, feeling like she was drowning.

"... *zzzttt* ... *okay?* ... *ing hell, Pan!*"

She tried to push herself up onto her elbows, her whole body made of pain. Everything was red, glowing, and she realized her eyes were closed. It seemed to take an age for her to remember how to open them. The parking lot was a lake of fire. Everything danced in the heat, nothing quite real. It was almost as if the fire were a living thing, lumbering toward her ...

Oh no.

The burning demon was made up partly of a charred corpse, partly of something that might once have been a car seat. The whole thing was an inferno, but it wasn't slowing it down. These were demons, after all. Fire was like silk to them. It lurched through the wreckage, bounding right for her.

Pan grunted, ignoring the agony as she lifted herself up. Her leg wasn't working properly, and when she looked down she saw a shard of bone poking from her shin. She stumbled, crunching against a pillar. Where the hell was the crossbow? The demon was halfway across the lot when another parked car exploded, the force of it lifting the Corvette up and crunching it against the ceiling. Pan ducked behind the pillar, feeling the fist of the shock wave buffet past her.

She hobbled around, flanking the demon. There, a dozen yards away, her crossbow. She pushed herself away from the pillar, limping toward it, hearing the howl of the demon on her tail. She collapsed next to the weapon, swinging it around just as the creature was reaching for her. The wire twanged and the bolt buried itself in the creature's eyeless face. It had time to grunt, almost like it couldn't believe its luck, then it exploded into dust.

A shotgun blast behind her. Herc calling out a word that might have been her name. Pan turned to see him limping her way, clouds of smoke billowing around him. His face was a mess, smeared with angry burns. She couldn't see what he was shooting at, the truck was in the way. At least *part* of the truck.

Part of the truck that unfolded into a demon the size of a grizzly; which opened its mouth and roared.

Pan swore, lifting the crossbow even though it wasn't loaded. One of the demon's long front legs curled around her chest. It squeezed and she heard a rib snap, a supernova of pain detonating inside her. The crossbow fell, clattering to the floor.

Herc's gun roared again, the creature's head tinkling like a tuneless music box. Clouds of shot tore past her, stinging her skin. The demon didn't even seem to feel it, lifting another leg, angling its bladed foot in her direction. Its head was made up of part of the bumper and the license plate—SKI

UTAH!—serrated teeth still pushing themselves free of the metal. Even though it had no eyes it seemed to look at her, and she knew exactly what it was thinking.

Finally, after all these years, we can collect.

She almost felt the relief of it, until she remembered what would happen next.

"Pan!" Herc cried out, too far away, too slow. The creature squeezed again, her bones splintering. Pan closed her eyes, hoping it wouldn't be as bad as they told her, hoping that Ostheim had been wrong when he'd said she'd be begging for death if they ever caught her. She'd be begging for death for the rest of eternity.

"Go on, then," she spat, half words, half blood. "Do your worst."

And it did.

COWARD'S WAY OUT

First he was expelled. Now the world was ending.

Talk about a day from hell.

Another dull explosion shook the bodega, hard enough to rattle Marlow's bones. He grabbed the door handle, sucking in a lungful of hot, smoky air. The shotgun was heavy, threatening to slide out of his sweaty hand, and he gripped it hard enough to make his fingers ache.

What was he doing?

Sirens rose up over the echo of the explosion, wailing like mourners at a funeral. There was a smell in the air like nothing he'd ever experienced, something that was almost volcanic. He wondered if it actually was the end of the world out there, if he'd step out of the store to see lava running down the streets of Mariners Harbor.

Staying here, though, wasn't an option. The rest of the ceiling was coming loose, threatening to crush him like it had crushed the cashier.

He eased open the door, squinting. There was no lava but plenty of people, all of them panicking. A few looked his way, double-taking when they saw the shotgun clenched in his hand. The guys hanging out in front of the store had scattered.

He half thought about dropping the gun but he had no

idea what was out there. Could have been a terrorist attack or a full-on gang war, in which case he might need it. Not that he was planning on shooting anyone, but it might give him the time to run. The air outside was thick with smoke, tendrils that snaked into his lungs, choking him. He coughed them out as best he could, reaching for his inhaler with his free hand, sucking in a couple of blasts until the pressure on his chest loosened.

Where was he? He didn't recognize any of the buildings but every window in sight had been shattered. The explosions were coming from behind him, which meant the best way to move was forward.

He jogged across the street, clutching the shotgun to his chest, hoping the thing wouldn't self-detonate and blow off his head. He'd only made it a few paces when he saw a shimmer of light up ahead, a cop car screeching around the corner.

"Hey!" he yelled, then suddenly pictured himself charging down the street with a lethal weapon. *Great move, Marlow.* The cops around here shot first and asked questions never. He turned and bolted the other way, in the direction of the smoke and thunder.

Are you insane?

All that mattered was not being caught. He was in enough trouble as it was.

He was wheezing bad by the time he passed the store, seeing what looked like a hospital up ahead. There was a ramp for an underground parking lot, smoke churning out of it like an upturned waterfall. It rose up into a sky that was too dark for this time of day, the sun just a greasy smudge. The air was full of something sharp, almost electric, that same charge that made his hair stand on end, which pricked his skin with gooseflesh.

A car engine behind him, revving hard. He glanced over his shoulder to see the cop car looming up. Another cop car was approaching from the right, a couple of hospital security guards to the left. He heard the squeal of tires behind him and the pop of a car door being opened. Putting his head down, he went the only way he could, right toward the ramp. Whatever was going on down there, he might be able to find a way out. If they arrested him now, god knows what they'd charge him with.

He ran, tripping over the soft ground, the weapon rattling in his grip. The cops were yelling, the guards pushing their way past the flocks of people in pastel scrubs and billowing hospital gowns that were scattering from the building. Marlow ignored them, pushing forward into the darkness of the ramp and doing everything he could to catch his breath.

He peeked down, seeing a whole lot of nothing through the smoke. Something was glowing there, though, like the heart of a volcano. *Pop pop*, then a scream that didn't sound human, that sounded more like shredding metal. He tried to take a step but his body wouldn't obey, locked tight in protest. Maybe he should just surrender, try to explain himself.

Yeah, and what's the going rate for a weapons charge? Five years? Ten?

He took as deep a breath as his crappy lungs would let him, then he set off, propelling himself down the ramp. He ducked low but the smoke still found him, clawing its way down his throat, as solid as a dead man's fingers. He coughed, again and again, each time feeling like he was going to spit up a lung. The glowing embers up ahead grew brighter and he saw the passage leading into the first level of the parking lot. It looked like it had been sculpted out of clay by a child—the floor covered in huge bumps, the ceiling drooping. The parking lot beyond was framed by fire, and through the shimmering haze he could see at least two cars blazing, the floor a lake of flame and the ceiling a storm of smoke.

The bark of a gun rang out from somewhere in the chaos, startling him. He squinted into the flames. Was that somebody up there? A man dressed in black, his hair singed away. He was holding a rifle of some kind, or a shotgun maybe, firing it into the churning heat of one of the exploded cars. Marlow raised his own gun, so much heavier than it had any right to be. Was the man one of the good guys or the bad guys? Should he pull the trigger now, cut him down? What if he called out and the guy turned around, shot back before Marlow had a chance to defend himself?

Marlow had taken half a dozen steps into the garage when he heard a crunch behind him. He swung around to see something that had to be an illusion caused by the heat, that couldn't be real.

The armored truck that stood at the end of the ramp was coming to life.

Literally coming to life. Something was pulling itself out of the vehicle, a shape made up of the wide grille and the license plate. One of the tires exploded, a shard of lightning slicing up from the floor into the ceiling hard enough to knock loose chunks of concrete. Still that shape came, looking like a bear, its legs made of long strips of metal, its huge, bulky body half engine, half chassis, its face a twisted knot of license plate, the Ford medallion where one eye might have been.

It's not real, it's a trick of the light, it's something poisonous in the smoke, it's . . .

The creature slipped free, crunching to the ground, shaking itself like a wet dog and spraying sparks across the garage. Then it started to run on all fours, its clumsy feet slipping, claws churning up concrete like the floor was made of butter. Marlow had swung the gun up before he even knew what he was doing, wrenching at the triggers, both of them, as the creature loomed up before him.

Nothing happened.

The creature slammed into him as hard and fast as a truck. He was thrown back, spinning, landing hard enough to knock away the last scraps of oxygen. He rolled onto his back, seeing the lumbering metal shape canter away into the smoke, heading for a pillar, toward a silhouette there. And surely that had to be another hallucination, because even though Marlow had no air left to give, the girl he saw there still managed to take his breath away. She was beautiful, despite the blood and bruises on her face. It was a hard kind of beauty, her brow folded into a frown, her lips a thin, grim line, her eyes chips of flint, utterly focused, like she was ready to head-butt her way through a stone wall and not give a damn about the consequences. And as for her body . . .

Are you serious? Focus!

He shook his head. The girl was carrying an old-fashioned wooden weapon—a *crossbow*?—but she was obviously hurt bad because she was struggling to lift it. A bone jutted from a broken leg. The guy with the shotgun was advancing, firing shot after shot, but the truck-thing was relentless, crunching forward, heading right for the girl. It reached out for her with a long, metal limb, curling it around her chest, lifting her up. She screamed, the crossbow falling from her hand.

Marlow pushed himself to his feet, ignoring the pain as he searched the floor for his gun. By the time he'd picked it up the creature had raised another limb, this one tipped with a wicked shard of steel. He still didn't know who the good guys were, but out of a guy and a girl and a monster he figured the odds had to be on his side. He sprinted toward them, this time remembering to slide off the safety catch. He reached the girl at the same time as the man in black. The guy flicked him a glance—his face half scar and half grimace—then he lifted his weapon and fired.

They were ten feet away from the creature, and the blast from the man's shotgun was so fierce that it made its metal flesh ripple. Marlow gritted his teeth, pulled both triggers on his own gun. It barked, bucking hard enough to rip itself free of his fingers. A bolt of pain licked up his shoulder into his neck, making him cry out. The creature didn't react, bringing its limb back like a scorpion tail, the girl hanging before it, kicking pathetically.

"Pan!" the man cried, pumping the mag, firing again. He threw the weapon aside and leaped, grabbing the creature around the neck, trying to wrench it away. Maybe two hundred pounds of flesh against half a ton of metal. It didn't end well, the creature lashing out with another of its metal limbs and sending him spinning away. He slid across the floor, groaning wetly, lying still.

Marlow scrabbled for his gun, working shells from his pocket, dropping them, panicking, unable to breathe, the air too thick. The darkness that was creeping into his vision had nothing to do with the smoke.

"Go on then," he heard the girl say, her words choked with anger. "Do your worst."

A scream, maybe human, maybe not, so full of violent glee that Marlow fell on his ass. He looked up, saw the creature's limb flick back, then dart forward. It punched through the very center of the girl's chest, right through her heart, appearing from her back in an eruption of blood and bone.

Her face knotted up in agony and defiance, her teeth gritted, like she was trying to hold back death with sheer force of will. Then everything went slack, her legs dangling, her arms slapping against her sides, her face falling, like meat sliding

48

off the bone. Her eyes were the last, flicking away from the creature, finding Marlow, holding him for an instant that could have been an eternity. He couldn't move, couldn't have drawn a breath even if he had been physically able to. He just sat there on the warm concrete, the heat of the fire on his skin, until the last trickle of life drained away and her gaze moved off toward some different horizon, some place that only the dead could see.

No.

There was still time to save her. He grabbed the gun, snapping it open and ejecting the used shells. The creature slid its limb free from the girl, flicking it hard enough to spray blood into the fire, sending jets of pink steam into the air. Marlow jammed shells into the barrels, cranked the gun shut, walked right up behind it, and pulled one trigger. This time he kept a solid hold, bracing the stock against his shoulder, shifting his weight against the recoil. The force of the explosion shattered the back of the creature's head, scattering lethal shrapnel. It dropped the girl, turning. Marlow didn't wait, just pulled the second trigger, ripping another chunk of metal away from the creature's body.

It staggered, weakening, its metal limbs squealing as it flailed. Marlow retreated, reloading, each attempt at a breath like he was trying to lift a dead weight off his chest. He clawed them in, his wheezes even louder than the roar of the fire, even louder than the crunch of the beast's feet as it advanced. He shunted two more shells into the holes, held his ground until the creature was close enough to touch. Then he pulled both triggers, blowing a hole right through the center of the thing. It stood still for a moment, as if trying to figure out what was wrong, before collapsing.

Marlow reached for his pockets, the world suddenly spinning, not enough oxygen. He reeled, glancing off a pillar, dropping like a ton weight. And it hit him, just as hard, the knowledge that he was going to die in here. He tried to breathe, his windpipe no wider than a hair, refusing to let anything in or out. Kicking at the ground, grasping at his pockets, finding his inhaler and bringing it to his lips. Where was the damn end of it?

Something loomed up in front of him, the truck beast with its ragged wound of cables and splinters. There was another shape to the side, Marlow's vision so blurred that he could almost convince himself that what he saw there wasn't a living creature made of concrete, its mouth a jagged, saw-toothed scar across its body, big enough to swallow him whole. They closed in, smelling his fear, his blood.

He sucked on the inhaler, pressing randomly, nothing. Lifting it, he saw that it was a shotgun shell, and his heart seemed to give up alongside his lungs. He wheezed, not even enough air for a cough, his hand slapping down to the floor. At least the asthma would get him first. Better to suffocate than to be torn to pieces by . . . by whatever the hell those things were.

They prowled toward him, almost lazily, their eyeless faces somehow burning right into the very core of his soul. Close enough now that he could see the way the metal bent like plastic when they moved, concrete as malleable as Play-Doh but still hard enough to crush his bones to powder. The rock-like one reared up, that vast maw opening.

"Thought you'd finished with me, did you?" said a voice.

There was a soft twang and a metal bolt plowed into the neck stump of the truck beast. There was a blazing wave of light and a booming explosion, like a concussion grenade, and the creature was reduced to a mound of rubble. What stood behind it was surely impossible. The girl's chest was caved in, firelight visible through the gaping hole where her heart should have been. Even now, though, the wound seemed to be closing, flesh knitting back together. The ugly tears on her arms and neck and face were sealing, too, as if time were going backward, white smoke drifting up from her skin. She was gritting her teeth against it, the pain etched into every line of her face, every jutting tendon in her neck.

The concrete creature saw her and uttered a noise that could have been a building collapsing, a feral, industrial roar. It bounded past, running right for her. And over the thunder of its feet he heard the girl say, "I'm whole. End the contract."

The beast pounced, so heavy that Marlow felt the tremor as it left the ground. The girl just stood there, empty crossbow by her side, those dark eyes never blinking. Then, like it had hit some kind of invisible wall, the creature dropped, landing with a crunch, exploding into dust. It twitched once, then lay still. The truck thing simply froze. There was another metallic bang from the other side of the garage, Marlow squinting to see a figure formed from a fire door and a section of wall fall over like a felled tree. Then there was silence, other than the subdued whisper of the flames and Marlow's desperate, choking breaths.

He almost had time to feel relieved before he remembered he was still dying.

He clutched at his throat with one hand, slapping his empty pockets with the other, his back arching. The girl scanned the lot, a look of bored contempt on her perfect face. Only then did she look at Marlow, not a trace of gratitude or kindness in those perfect features. Her injuries had stopped healing, some of the nicks and scrapes still dripping blood. But there was no sign of the puncture wound in her chest other than a thick, leathery scar. Her uniform, though, had been unable to repair itself. It flapped open, revealing a black bra underneath.

Not such a bad way to go, his brain told him, and for once in his life he had to agree.

51

The girl noticed where he was looking, but made no effort to cover up, just opened her mouth and spoke.

"Done?"

Marlow couldn't have answered even if he'd known what she was asking. His lungs were completely empty. There may as well have been a tank parked on top of him. He tried to shape his mouth around the word *inhaler*, tried to jab a finger at his throat, screaming inside his head, *Please, find it for me, get help.*

"You cut that one too close, Ostheim," she said, and he realized she was talking to somebody else. "We lost Forrest, and Herc."

"Not quite," said another voice. Marlow saw the man he'd been fighting alongside earlier, walking over, barely an inch of skin not drenched in blood and smeared with filth. He stood stooped next to the girl, panting, but she didn't even acknowledge his presence. They both looked at Marlow.

"None," the girl said in answer to some unheard question. "No other survivors."

The man glanced at her.

"What about him?"

"What about him?" she replied, her voice the coldest thing Marlow had ever heard.

"Saved your life."

"No, he didn't. The contract did. Remember the rules, Herc. Nobody knows."

Marlow could no longer hold his eyes open and he fell into darkness. He could almost hear his lungs screaming, the loudest thing in the world. Squirming on the floor. It was a coward's way out.

"Hellraisers don't grow on trees," he heard the man say. "We need more Engineers. He can fight."

"Look at him. He can't even breathe."

"Pan."

Marlow made out the scuffing of feet, the sound of somebody walking away.

"Pan!"

And that was it. One last squeaking, pathetic, airless breath. Marlow wished his last thought could have been of his mom, of his brother, of the things he loved. Instead, the very last bubble of oxygen he would ever breathe was expended wishing he could tell a girl whose life he had just saved to go screw herself.

ICE QUEEN

"Pan!"

She turned away, partly so she could scan for an exit, partly so Herc wouldn't see her face. It was taking every ounce of strength she had to stay upright, her body a broken engine on the verge of stalling. Everything hurt. *Everything.* Especially her chest. Although *hurt* was the wrong word. It wasn't pain so much as a grinding, awful sense that this time she'd gone too far. Her heart pulsed weak and wet and the vertebrae in her spine scraped together. There was a trapped nerve in there, and it felt like somebody jabbing her repeatedly with a scalpel. She wasn't taking in enough air because one of her lungs hadn't fully reinflated. Her contract had worked, but only barely. A few more seconds, maybe, and they'd have had her.

The underground parking lot was hell on earth, literally. The scattered remains of the demons lay beside the corpse of the driver, identical only in the absence of life. The truth was he didn't know how lucky he was, to be dead, to be cold. There were far worse places the living could go when their hearts stopped beating and their bodies started cooling. She'd almost found out exactly how bad those places were.

No time for that. No time for what-ifs. There would be a SWAT team down here soon, and she didn't want to be around when they started firing bullets or questions at her. She couldn't take the exit ramp, the whole world would be watching by now. But there was an access door in the far wall. Half a door, anyway, with a demon-shaped hole in one side where something had pulled loose. It hung off its hinges, swinging in the currents of heat that circled the parking lot, beckoning her like a finger.

"... *zztt* ... *oing?*"

The earpiece was history and she plucked it out, chucking it. She walked toward the door, going as fast as the wreck of her body would let her. The molten heat of the adrenaline was cooling into solid metal in her limbs, weighing her down, the reality of the situation bleeding back in. Had she died back there? She rubbed the scar on her chest, the mottled skin completely numb. The thought frightened her. It *terrified* her. Because for an instant, when the demon's blade cut through her heart, she'd felt the world dissolve, felt something take hold of her soul, wrench her down through the fabric of reality into whatever waited for her below. Only an instant, then the contract had kicked in. But it had been close.

It always was when you traded for the big one. When you traded for invulnerability.

She stepped over the dead driver, her foot almost slipping in a puddle of blood. She didn't even know his name, even though he'd been working with them for weeks, even though she'd shared a Wendy's breakfast sandwich with him that very morning. *Not a man, not a human, just a corpse. It's all he ever was.* And better to think of it that way, better to stay cold than to burn in the fire of regret and guilt and shame.

Forrest, though. He was different. Not a driver, not a bodyguard like Herc. He'd been an Engineer, the same as her. She could still see him being dragged into the molten ground, screaming even though his head had been obliterated. She could still hear him. She would hear him for the rest of her life—him and all the others. Just one more name in the *Book of Dead Engineers.*

"*Sorry*," she said, then regretted it. It wasn't her fault. He'd known what the risks were when he'd made the deal. He'd known the price he would have to pay. If she took responsibility for him, then she'd have to take responsibility for the rest of them, and then she'd be buried by guilt, her soul as tormented as theirs.

Ostheim should never have let them get so close to the end of the contract, though. This was his fault.

Behind her she heard shuffling, a grunt, a pathetic wheeze, and she didn't have to look back to know what was going on. She did anyway, if only to scowl at Herc as he lifted a hunk of plastic between his fingers, inserted it into the kid's mouth. An inhaler. He pressed it a few times, massaging the boy's chest. Then he hefted the unconscious body over one shoulder. He fired a look right back at her, one that said, *What you gonna do about it?*

He was right. They needed Engineers. They needed them all the time, the way a butcher needs a yard full of chickens. The kid, he'd appeared out of nowhere, had maybe—*maybe*—distracted one of the demons long enough to let her ruined flesh knit itself back together. But he was still just a boy, and a dying one at that, if his pitiful breathing was anything to go by.

But that was always Herc's problem, his big, stupid, bleeding heart.

Pan reached the door, pushed through into a concrete stairwell, a haze of smoke making her eyes water. There was a choice of down or up, but the thought of heading even deeper beneath the earth after what she'd just felt made her stomach want to explode out her mouth. She headed up, running for a couple of steps before her battered heart slowed her to a walk.

"Place should be big enough to make us invisible," growled Herc behind her. "Cops'll be setting up a perimeter outside, but we should pass as civvies." He coughed. "You might wanna lose the crossbow, though."

"Yeah?" She doubled around the bend, snatching in breaths as she continued up. "I lose the bow, you lose some teeth."

"Just saying," he replied. "Nothing quite says crazy like a big-ass seventeenth-century weapon hanging off your back."

She ignored him, reaching the door to the ground level. There was an alarm going off, she realized, and she could hear footsteps and screams from the other side. A stampede. Perfect. She opened the door a crack, peeking past to see a corridor, people flowing out of wards, bare feet slapping on the floor. A few orderlies and security guards were doing their best to herd them toward the back of the hospital. Herc was right, the bow was a little conspicuous. But there weren't more than a dozen of these things in existence, and Ostheim only owned three.

She grabbed the collar of her tattered Kevlar shirt and pulled, the Velcro tearing. Shrugging it off, she wrapped it tightly around the bow, leaning on it like it was a walking stick, standing there in nothing but her bra.

"Well, that'll take their minds off the crossbow if nothing else," said Herc, his eyes scrolling over every inch of the stairwell except her. Even past the blood and dirt she could see him blush.

"Perv," she said, pushing through the door into the crowd. It didn't take one of the guards long to pick her out, his eyes widening as he executed the perfect double take. She didn't need much help looking like a patient, coughing violently as she was swept along with the tide. Another guard was standing at the end of the corridor, ushering everyone to the left. Pan used her crossbow to hold herself up, limping around the corner to see a big double door up ahead, splashed with sunlight. The sight of it almost brought tears to her eyes. Probably would have done if the heat of the fire hadn't singed her tear ducts shut.

There was a line of cops outside, beady eyes assessing everyone who left the building. Pan did her best to look the way normal people probably looked when they saw death, her face crumpling, her hand covering her eyes, her shoulders lurching like she had broken down into sobs. It wasn't exactly an Oscar-worthy display but it must have done the trick because they waved her on toward a posse of waiting ambulances and first responders.

Pan ducked between two trees at the side of the road, hopping over a low metal fence onto the street beyond. There was a rustle of leaves and Herc appeared, trying to maneuver himself over the iron spikes, the boy still slung over his shoulder.

"Little help?" he said.

"Your new boyfriend," Pan replied. "You love him so much, you carry him."

"Do you always have to be such an icy bitch?" He stumbled, almost fell, clutching the kid like a sack of potatoes. A couple of teenage boys walked past holding skateboards, both of them ogling her, oblivious to everything except her exposed bra. She pulled the shirt off her crossbow, gave them something else to ogle, sent them skittering. They were on a side road, a couple of cars parked next to the curb. They weren't exactly flash, but they'd do. She made for the closest one, used the butt of the crossbow to shatter the driver's-side window.

"Do you always have to be such a miserable old git?" she replied as she popped the lock, the central locking clunking.

"Do you always need thirty seconds to come up with a riposte?"

Herc opened the rear door, slid the kid inside. Pan waited until the big guy had straightened before shaking her head at him.

"That's a lot of effort for a skinny kid," she said. "You should have left him up there, with the paramedics. Saved yourself some bother."

"He's seen us, Pan. Seen *them*. Can't take the chance he won't talk."

"Left him to die, then," she offered. "Not like he'd be the first. Hell, we've lost a dozen Engineers in as many months, what's one more corpse for the cleaners to bag up?"

This time Herc's eyes narrowed, his face turning to stone. He didn't reply, just stared at her. If looks could kill, and all that. She had to turn away, her own cheeks heating, suddenly ashamed. She hissed out a humorless laugh to cover it.

"I'm glad you find this so funny, Pan," Herc said, pushing past her, his disgust oozing off him in waves. He folded his body into the driver's seat, slammed the door, and started ripping out wires from the dash. She stood there a moment longer, chewing on the stew of emotion that bubbled up from her stomach, wanting to punch Herc in the face, wanting to scream her lungs out at the sky, wanting to curl up beneath the car and cry and cry and cry. And it was only because she couldn't work out which of those feelings scared her more that she walked robotically to the other side, opened the creaking door, and clambered in.

Herc fired up the engine, revved it.

"You had to pick a goddamned Honda?" he said, and it was

almost an apology. "Come on. We need to get hold of Ostheim before he sends the whole Pigeon's Nest down here looking for you."

Pan didn't answer. She just stared out the windshield, watching the world start to roll past, happy to be cold, to be hard, to be made of ice.

CALL THEM CHOICES?

"He's coming around."

Marlow rose from a dream of demons and dead things, clinging to the voices like they were a life raft. He wrenched open his eyes, felt like he'd been punched in the brain by the bright white light, screwed them closed again. When he took a breath he heard the familiar rattle and clank of his lungs. He eased his eyes open again, seeing blurred shapes there, two of them. He tried to sit up but found that he was in a narrow hospital bed, rows of thin plastic straps holding him tight. He was almost angry until he remembered his last thought—that he was never going to wake up again.

"What the hell?" he said, his mouth dry, his tongue getting stuck to his teeth. He blinked the two figures into focus. One was the big guy from the parking lot, cleaned up now but still covered in bruises, grazes, burns, and scars. He was sitting on a metal chair to the side of the bed, and when he heard Marlow speak he stood up, running a hand through what was left of his gray hair.

"So," he said, his voice a low rumble, "you're back. Wasn't sure you were gonna make it for a while there. How's he doing?"

"Good," said the other figure, stepping up to the man's shoulder. She was a woman in a red overcoat, in her fifties maybe, white-blond hair pulled back in a severe ponytail. She held a clipboard in her hand, one page lifted. "Couple of lumps and bumps." She let the paper drop, looked at Marlow with an easy smile. "Nothing that won't heal."

"Maybe I'll heal a little quicker if you loosen these up a bit," he replied, struggling to lift his arms.

"Just a precaution," said the man. "You . . ." He seemed to chew on the words. "You saw a few things, back there. Things we don't really want you sharing."

Creatures, made of rock, concrete, metal, dead flesh. A girl who died, who had a hole punched through her heart.

A girl who came back.

Marlow looked past the man and woman, seeing a huge room, easily a hundred feet each way. There were windows on all four sides, flooding the space with sunlight. He squinted, trying to see anything through the golden haze. Was that the *Chrysler* out there?

The man followed his gaze, then shared a look with the woman that Marlow couldn't quite place. She nodded and walked away into the giant space. There were other people there, just a handful, milling between various stacks of boxes and complicated-looking pieces of equipment. One thing in particular caught his eye, something that looked like one of those huge machines they used in hospitals, like a giant tube you slid into. An MRI scanner or something, emitting a loud hum. It was on the other side of the room, but he could make out a pair of legs stretched from it, toes flexing. Was that a scar on the shin? *An injury, bone sticking through the flesh.* And his heart flipped like a pancake when he realized who it was.

This time, when the man saw where he was staring, he grinned. Just about the most terrifying grin Marlow had ever seen, with his lips chapped and burned and one of his upper front teeth missing.

"Kid, don't even go there."

"Who is she?" Marlow said, breathless again. The machine was spitting out light as it did whatever it was supposed to do, but those bare legs still stretched into darkness.

"Her name's Pan," said the man.

"Pan?" Marlow craned his neck up, trying to get a better look. "Kind of a name is that?"

"Pandora," he went on. "Best you don't ask why. I'm Herc."

"Herc?" Marlow managed to tear his eyes off those legs, looked at the man. "Kind of a name is *that*? Short for Hercules?"

"Not quite. Herman. Herman Cole. Got called Herc one day when I started here, by mistake, kind of stuck."

"Here," said Marlow, chewing on the word. "A hospital, right?"

It had to be, didn't it? With this bed, and all the equipment. That explained a lot. Explained why he'd imagined the world coming to life and trying to murder him. Explained why he'd seen somebody return from the dead. He stretched his mind back, trying to put the chaos of his memories in some kind of order. The school, the store.

"It's all real, before you ask. What you saw. I'd love to tell you otherwise but that would make me a liar. And say one thing for me, I'm not that."

Real. Marlow shook his head.

"No way," he said. "No way." As if repeating it might make it true. He tugged at the straps, grunting with frustration, his mouth drier than ever. "Think I could get something to drink?"

"In a minute," said Herc. The big man winced, his injuries obviously painful. "Got some choices to talk over first."

"Choices?" Marlow frowned, didn't like the expression on the man's face.

"I'll keep it simple. What you saw back there was never meant to be seen. Not by you. We have a protocol here. The first law. The world cannot know."

"Know what?" Marlow said, feeling the panic start to claw into his lungs, the asthma a claw around his throat. He coughed again, wheezing as he drew breath, trying to work out where his inhaler would be.

"Well, that's the problem, ain't it?" Herc said. "I can't tell you, because then you'll know. Why don't you start with what you *think* you saw."

Marlow frowned, his mind slipping back into the fire, into the chaos.

"Those things," he said. "They were made of . . . They were . . . What were they?"

And too late he figured he should have said, *I didn't see anything, everything is a blank, was I in a car accident?*

"I mean, I don't remember," he stuttered.

"Nice try." Herc sat back, sighed, the chair creaking under his bulk. "Okay, so you saw them. That limits what choices you get, and they were a limited bunch of choices anyway. Pick door number one, you come work for us."

"Work for you? As what?"

"An Engineer," Herc said, grunting when he saw Marlow's expression. "A soldier, really. Of sorts. Good work, great pay, we look after your family too."

When you die. He didn't need to say it, it was right there in the way his eyes never left the floor.

"I'll pass, thanks," Marlow said. "Whatever you guys are into, you're welcome to it. I don't want any part of it."

The hum of the MRI machine faded, making the room seem deathly quiet. Marlow looked over as the tray slid free from the machine. Pan rolled off, as graceful as water, dressed in her underwear, her hands fluffing up her short hair. There was still a scar over her heart but it looked ancient now, like it had healed years ago. She caught him staring and scowled, snatching up a dressing gown and marching behind a curtain.

"You sure?" Herc said, reminding Marlow that he and Pan weren't the only two people in the world. "*She's* behind door number one."

"I thought you said don't go there?"

"Just saying," Herc said. "There are other perks too."

"Yeah? Like what?"

"Like anything you want," Herc said with another gruesome smile. "*Literally* anything."

Marlow shook his head, trying to shuffle his thoughts into some kind of order. He snatched in a breath, caught the stench of smoke wafting off Herc. And suddenly he was right there again, in the heat of it, his lungs full of fire and burning flesh. He closed his eyes and all he could see was the world tearing itself apart, a creature made of concrete and metal rearing above him, ready to stamp him into mud.

"No," he said before he even knew he was talking. "No way. Door number two. I'll take it."

"Door number two," said Herc, almost sadly. "Door number two and you'll never know. Door number two and you'll always wonder about what happened. That's the thing about secrets. They're like a hole in your life."

"Yeah? Better a hole in my life than a hole in my heart."

He shrugged his arms beneath the straps, waiting for Herc to release him. Herc showed no sign of moving, though.

"You fought well, kid. Came outta nowhere, shotgun blazing. What were you doing down there anyway? Pretty heroic."

Ha! Marlow grinned without humor. Yeah, real heroic. Taking a gun to save himself, trying to run away. The only reason he'd been down there was because the cops had herded him that way. Yeah, Marlow Green, real hero.

"Just . . . just thought I could help," was what he said, staring at the ceiling.

"Well," Herc said, "that's a rare thing, kid. And you saved our asses in there, whatever *she* might say."

Marlow glanced over to the curtain, disappointed that Pan was still out of sight. He took the time to chew on Herc's words. A soldier. Like Danny. So he could be dead, like Danny. But there was *something* about these guys, something that tugged at him.

"Who are you anyway?"

"Need to know," Herc replied, tapping the side of his nose with one finger. "Pick that first door and you get to find out."

There *was* an itch inside his skull, the need to know. After all, it wasn't every day that everything you thought you knew about the world turned out to be a lie.

No. Better to forget. Better to run. It's what he did best.

"Look," he said, "it was just a fluke. I wasn't thinking. If I could do it all again I'd have run the other way, okay? Just get me the hell out of these things and let me go."

"Let you go?" said Herc.

"Yeah, door number two, I just wanna go home."

Herc shook his head.

"Sorry, kid, if only it were that simple. Door number two is . . . Like I said, you've seen things. Things the world can't know."

Marlow let his head crash down onto the pillow. Herc didn't have to say any more. It was pretty clear what he was driving at.

"So, door number one, I join you, fight those things, probably get my head ripped off. Door number two, I never leave this building, right?"

Herc shrugged. Marlow swore beneath his breath.

"And you call them choices?"

YOU GOTTA LAUGH

No sooner had Herc left his bedside, a guy and a girl took his place. They were young, maybe early twenties, both dressed in black Kevlar bodysuits with a big, black pistol holstered on one hip and a bowie knife on the other. Their expressions looked just as lethal, each of them wearing a scowl that made the big guy look like the happiest man on the planet. Marlow tugged and strained but the plastic straps did their job well.

"Wait," he said. "What are you going to do?"

They didn't answer, the man popping the stud and sliding the bowie knife free of its sheath. It glinted in the blinding glare from the windows, stabbing Marlow's eyes with sunlight. He winced, wanting to shut his eyes but too afraid that if he did so he would never get the chance to open them again.

"Wait!" he grunted, struggling, his whole body held tight. His windpipe was shrinking, fast, and he had to suck in his next breath, so little air that he could barely get the words out. "Wait, I'll go for door number one. Door number one, dammit."

"Too late for that," said the guy. He had a long face that reminded Marlow of a moose. "You had your chance. No room here for maybes, buddy. Hold him."

The girl moved in, pressing down on his chest and head. She was freakishly strong, his ribs feeling like they might snap beneath her fingers. Marlow snarled, a noise from deep inside his throat. It was the sound a dog made when it was cornered, knowing it was about to die. He swore at them, curse after curse. The knife rose, hanging there, then it plunged down like a guillotine blade. Marlow winced, every muscle tensing, waiting for the fire. But the blade simply sliced through the first plastic strap.

"Wait, *what*?" wheezed Marlow. The guy did the same with the other straps and suddenly the only things holding him down were hands. He took as big a breath as he could manage, his throat the size of a juice carton straw. The guy slid the knife away, then pulled on the sheet, lifting it up. Marlow's body lay beneath, so many bruises and bandages there that it took him a second to realize he was only wearing his boxers.

"You gonna make this difficult?" the knife guy asked. Marlow shook his head. "Then get up. Slowly."

They stepped back to let him past. Marlow snatched in a thimbleful of air, struggling to sit up, every muscle creaking. He hopped down onto the cold floor, flexing, the joints in his neck and back sounding like somebody popping bubble wrap.

"What now?" he said, still alert. Herc had given the impression that it was either sign up or sign out—*permanently*—but the knife guy just gave him a gentle nudge, steering him toward the middle of the giant room.

"Now we show you out," he said. "And we never see your scrawny ass again. Clear?"

Marlow didn't reply. There was no sign of Herc, or Pan, but there were a couple of other people in the room and they looked at him like he'd just spat in their coffee. The fear he'd felt seconds ago was fast becoming something else, something much worse. Shame. They all knew what he was. They could see right through the skin of his chest into his cowardly heart. He hated them for it.

He hated himself more.

He lifted a hand and chewed on his knuckles as he walked, keeping his eyes on the floor. *Screw them.* What the hell was he supposed to have done? Joined up with a bunch of weirdos to fight against things that couldn't possibly be real?

There was an elevator in the middle of the room, the doors open.

"Get in," the girl snapped. The moose man shunted him forward and he staggered into the car, the whole thing wobbling. He spun around, doing his best to look angry, to look tough, feeling like a sheep that's suddenly found itself in a room full of wolves. The girl and guy walked in beside him. The man grabbed the outer set of metal doors and hauled them shut, then did the same with the inner ones. The girl stood there, her eyes running up and down, making Marlow feel more self-conscious than ever. His knuckles hurt from where he'd bitten them.

"When do I get my clothes back?" he said, coughing out phlegm. Each breath was a struggle. "My inhaler."

Neither of them answered. The man pressed one of the big brass buttons and the elevator began rattling slowly downward.

"Hey," he said. "Clothes?"

They didn't answer, just glanced at each other. He almost didn't see the mutual nod, it was so subtle. But it was there, and when they both suddenly lunged at him he was ready. He stepped back, spinning his body to avoid the flailing hands. The man tripped on his own feet and Marlow gave him a powerful shove, sending him clattering into the wall. The elevator rocked, groaning, and Marlow staggered. By the time he'd found his balance the girl was coming right for him, something shining in her hand.

A knife.

"Wait!"

She stabbed the blade toward him and he only just managed to get a hand up, slapping her arm away. It felt like he'd deflected a baseball bat in full swing. He lashed out with his fist, hit thin air as the girl ducked beneath him. The blade flashed as it slashed his way again, scraping his skin. He let loose a gargled scream, backing away.

Something grabbed him from behind, a bear hug that could have popped his rib cage. The guy and the girl were closing in and Marlow tried to look over his shoulder to see who was holding him.

There was nothing there.

What?

The invisible arms tightened, lifting him up and slamming him into the ceiling. Then they were gone and he fell, crashing back to the floor. He kicked out with his legs, not aiming for anything in particular, just trying to keep them both away. There was a meaty crunch as the heel of his right foot connected with the guy's face, a gargled scream. Marlow propelled himself up, seeing the man on his knees, hands to his face, blood pouring through his fingers like somebody had turned on a faucet. The girl had gone two shades paler, the knife gripped in shaking fingers. They all stood there for a moment, catching their breath, nobody sure what should happen next, the elevator grumbling steadily downward.

"I don't want any trouble," said Marlow, his voice paper-thin. "Just let me go, okay? You'll never see me again, I promise. I won't tell a soul."

Neither of them responded, the girl looking nervously at the man, the man on his knees, clutching his broken face like he was worried it might slip right off. Marlow sucked in an airless breath, coughed it out again, his lungs feeling like they were full of water, like he was drowning. It didn't make any sense. Why didn't they just kill him when he was trussed up like a turkey? Why wait until he could fight back? The elevator counted down the floors, *ding, ding, ding*.

The man's hand darted forward, so fast that it sprayed a line of blood across the wall and floor. An invisible force connected with Marlow's chest and he thumped back against the side of the elevator, the breath snatched from his lungs. He tried to push himself away but the force was too strong, pinning him there.

"Do it!" the guy yelled.

The girl moved, that blade flashing as she stabbed it down toward his neck. Marlow twisted but he still felt it punch into his flesh, no pain just a cold heat. He screamed, threw himself at the guy, his fist catching the man in the middle of his face, crunching broken nose bones. Moose guy dropped like a ton of bricks, the girl stepping away, hands in the air.

Empty hands.

Marlow lifted a trembling finger, felt something sticking out of his neck. He plucked it free, his eyes swimming, the whole elevator starting to spin around him. It wasn't a knife after all. It was a hypodermic needle, empty, the tip slick with his blood. It came loose and he threw it to the floor. Everything was swinging back and forth like he was on a ship.

"'Chu do to me?" Marlow said, trying to remember how to form a sentence. He jammed himself into the corner of the elevator to stop himself falling over. The girl showed no sign of moving, the guy shuffling back across the floor holding his face.

He heard the slowing of gears, felt his stomach sucked into his feet as the elevator slowed. There was a final *ding* and they came to a halt—although it felt like the elevator was still moving in every direction at once. He had to feel his way across the cab, unable to take his hands off the wall for fear of falling flat on his face. All the while he waited for a shot behind him, a bullet in the back, or those phantom hands. But he didn't care anymore. He couldn't even recall why he'd been in the elevator in the first place.

Something about monsters, he thought, and it was so absurd that he was laughing as he tugged and wrestled with the doors. He managed to get them open, swaying out into a small lobby, all marble and bronze. It was empty, and he weaved his way left and right toward the doors. It was like being on a fairground ride, one of those ones where the floor lurches back and forth. That thought made him laugh even harder, great whooping snorts.

He moved toward the light, barging into the doors, spilling through them and onto the busy street. He was in a canyon of tall buildings. The people around him were a blur, yelling and shrieking as he stumbled through them. He caught a glimpse of himself in a window—nothing on but his underpants—and he was howling with laughter now. He spun, crashing back and forth, car horns blaring at him as he fell onto the street. He slapped the hood of a cab, blurting out meaningless curses. Then he tripped on his own bare feet, sprawled onto his face.

And there he lay, lips against the warm asphalt, laughing, laughing, laughing.

LOOK AT HIM GO

"Christ on a bike, what the hell happened?"

Herc's voice boomed across the giant space like thunder. Pan twisted her head around, a bolt of pain dancing through the tendons, to see him striding toward the elevator. Bullwinkle and Hope were walking out. Staggering might have been a better word for it, though. They looked like they'd just fought ten rounds against a rhino in there. Bullwinkle's face—never a pretty sight at the best of times—was stained red, his nose twisted at a funny angle. Hope was as pale as he was bloody, teetering across the room with a limp.

"Where is he?"

Herc's growling voice stopped them both dead. He towered over them like a parent over two frightened children, looked for a moment like he was about to cuff them both around the head.

"Tell me you stuck him, at least."

"Yeah," said Hope. "I got him."

"Well thank heaven for small mercies." Herc grunted, shaking his head. "Two fully charged Engineers against an injured lamb, what is the world coming to? Go, clean yourselves up."

Pan followed him across the room, wincing every time she put weight on her broken leg. The wounds had healed, the bone knitted back together, but it still felt like she had razors sewn into her flesh. The scan had shown she was all clear. Her heart had a new layer of scar tissue—"The scars are the only thing holding it together," Betty had joked—and her left lung would probably never fully inflate again. She was alive, though. She was still here.

"Problems?" she said when she was close enough. Herc was standing by the window, big hands clutched behind his back. He was staring at the street thirty stories below. Pan swallowed the sudden rush of vertigo, squinting down to see that traffic had ground to a halt. A crowd had gathered, surrounding a naked shape sprawled on the ground. Among the bloom of yellow taxis was a blue-and-white cop car, lights flashing. Two officers pushed through the onlookers. Now that her eyes had adjusted to the blazing sunlight, Pan could see it was Marlow, writhing around on the street, legs and arms paddling like he was trying to swim upside down. She almost smiled before she remembered herself.

"Look at him go," she said. "How much did you give him?"

"Enough," said Herc. Then, a heartbeat later, "To floor a goddamned bear."

He snorted, and the laugh spilled out of her before she could clamp her teeth shut. They coughed together, both of them trying to cover up their giggles. Man, was it good to laugh, though. In this line of work, you never knew which joke was going to be your last. That thought made her remember Forrest, laughing at some joke about a penguin the night before the mission. Had he known he'd never laugh again? She swallowed loudly.

"I'm sorry, Herc," she said, croaking out the reluctant words. "About yesterday, about what I said. I . . ."

I what? An apology wasn't going to bring the boy back to life. It wouldn't bring any of them back. They were down there now, drenched in the eternal fire of hell. Couldn't she hear them screaming?

"Suck it up, Pan," he replied, watching her out of the corner of his eye. "There's no room here for sorrys, not anymore. You do what you do, you are what you are."

A kid, she thought, suddenly feeling her age, not even old enough to drink and yet here she was driving events that could change the world.

Or end it.

How long had it been, now? Four years? Almost. And how different would things have been if Ostheim had never sent Herc to her cell that day, if he'd never offered her the chance to start again? She'd be locked up tight, thirty years at least. Maybe even death row.

That's what happened when you took a life.

"We need you," Herc said, seeing the expression on her face. "Not many people can do what you do, remember that. We need you. *They* need you." He gestured out of the window with a broad sweep of his hand. "Things are heating up, Pan. The Circle's attacks are growing bolder. They don't give a crap about the rules anymore. Something big is coming. So stop apologizing and get back in your ice cube."

Herc was right, things really had been heating up. And they were paying the price, too. Eleven Engineers dead this year alone. She used her fist to smudge away the breath from the glass. The cops were trying to heft the kid up from the road but he was squirming and flopping like a landed fish. Everyone had their phones out, snapping away happily. Even in the deranged carnival that was New York you didn't often see a half-naked guy drunk off his face trying to fight off the police.

"This is gonna be everywhere," she said. "Twitter, Instagram, you name it."

Herc shrugged, and she looked at him.

"*The first law,*" she quoted. "*The world must not know.* Funny way of going about it."

"Desperate times," Herc said.

She looked down again to see the cops manhandling Marlow into their car. It swept away, siren bleeping.

"You better go get Ostheim on the comm," Herc said when it was out of sight. "We're gonna have to move soon."

"No rest for the wicked, eh?" she said, snorting another laugh, this one with absolutely no humor in it.

"No rest for them, no rest from them. What'cha gonna do."

"What about the other Engineers?"

"Truck and Nightingale are en route," Herc said, checking his watch. "The jet should land in a couple of hours. Hope and Bullwinkle have ten days left on their contracts, nothing to worry about."

Unless Ostheim leaves it to the last second again, she thought but didn't say.

"I need to get back to the Engine," she said, feeling the familiar itch in her gut, her bones, her soul. It was always this way. Once the Engine got inside you it was an addiction. You couldn't go without it for long—even when it almost cost you everything. She scratched at her skin, hard enough to hurt, to take her mind off the ache. "I need to make a new contract, I have to be there."

"Not up to me, Pan. It's Ostheim's call."

And Ostheim was the last person she wanted to talk to. She'd failed her last mission and the aftermath had destroyed a hospital. She'd pretty much broken every rule in the book and her employer wasn't going to go easy on her.

"Don't look so worried, kid," Herc said. "Cover-up team is in full swing. The world won't know. Ostheim's already planted evidence that it was a Middle Eastern terrorist cell; the video'll be on CNN within the hour."

"You think the kid will talk?" she asked. Herc turned to her, cracking his knuckles. His burned, scarred face twisted into something that was probably a smile.

"He'd better," he said. "This whole operation is counting on it."

Pan frowned. "What?"

"Nothing." Herc coughed, scratching at an invisible fleck of dirt on the glass.

"What operation?"

"Operation, um, Live Bait, I guess is the best way of describing it." He must have seen the look Pan threw at him because he shrugged. "Ostheim's idea, not mine. Anyway, it's not like you actually liked the kid."

True, Pan thought. But not liking him was one thing, and throwing him to the wolves was something very, very different.

0.37%

"Oh sweet merciful Alabama cheesecake, would you look at this—it's off the chart."

The detective held up a Breathalyzer printout, shaking his head so hard his thick gray eyebrows looked in danger of falling off. Marlow was so exhausted he could barely keep his head up, feeling like he'd downed a whole crate of Jim Beam. He'd puked three times already, twice in the back of the cruiser, apparently, again inside the holding cell. He didn't really remember how he got here, only something about an elevator, tall buildings, then he'd been facedown in his own drool. He'd been expelled from school, way back, but everything between then and now was just salt in water, impossible to see but leaving a nasty taste in his mouth.

"Kid, you have to be the drunkest skunk I ever seen. Point three-seven blood alcohol level?"

They were sitting in a small interview room, Marlow's hands cuffed to the table, one wall filled up by a mirror that was actually a window. The entire room was filled with a haze of booze and BO. The fat old detective dropped the printout on the table, looked over his shoulder at the uniformed cop behind him. She was in her thirties, maybe. Cute.

"You ever seen anyone this drunk, officer?" he asked her.

"Not outside of St. Patrick's," she replied. The detective sat back, rubbing his hairy chest through the opening on his sweaty shirt. He coughed, reached into his pocket as if going for a cigarette, then pulled his hand back and stroked his white-flecked lips instead. Marlow shifted uncomfortably in the orange jumpsuit they'd given him. His head was starting to pound, a demolition ball swinging between the two sides of his skull.

"Since when," he started to say, then coughed, trying to clear his throat. The paramedic who'd accompanied them to the station had given him a couple of puffs on an inhaler when he'd asked for it, but his windpipe showed no sign of reopening. "Since when has it been illegal to be drunk?"

The detective smiled, showing a row of crooked, tobacco-stained teeth.

"Oh, it ain't illegal to be drunk, kid," he said. "If it was, then I'd be locked up every Friday night and not let out until Tuesday morning." He laughed at his own joke. "But you, you were drunk *and* disorderly. The old Double D."

"I—"

"Criminal damage to a city vehicle," said the detective, counting off on his chubby fingers.

"Come on—"

"Assault on a police officer."

"I puked on him, I didn't—"

"Conspiracy to deploy a terrorist weapon on the city of New York."

This one shut Marlow up like a punch to the gut. He sat there, his jaw just about hitting the table.

"Conspiracy to *what*?"

"That's what I want you to tell me, kid," the detective said, craning forward as much as his belly would allow. "Back in the cruiser you had a hell of a lot to say for yourself."

"I did?" Marlow said, trying to think back. He couldn't even remember being in the car. "Look, I can't—"

"'Touch me again,'" the detective said, lifting another sheet of paper and reading from it, "'and I'll kill you.' There's more after this, but I don't really want to have to read it in front of Officer Settle here. You've got quite a mouth on you, kid." He cleared his throat, scanned down the page. "Aha, this is the interesting bit. 'You want to say that again, you *bleeping bleep*? I'll tear you a new *bleep*hole like I did to those things back in the hospital. I'll shoot your *bleeping bleep* off and make you eat it, I'll blow up your car and your house and your dog. I did it before, just today, I'll do it again, just you wait, you horse— *bleeping bleep*.'" The detective gently laid the paper down, clearing his throat. "There's quite a bit more, all lovingly transcribed by the officers who carted your drunken ass off the street. But the gist of it is pretty damn clear. You were there, yesterday."

"Yesterday?" Marlow said, his head reeling. He lifted his hands to rub his temples but the cuffs snapped tight, rooting them to the table. He swore under his breath. What was his mom gonna think? She'd have been waiting for him last night. She'd be worried sick.

"That tells me all I need to know," said the detective. "How the thing that surprised you was the date, and not the 'there.'"

"The what?" he replied, trying to get his brain around the conversation. "Where?"

"Where indeed," the man said, dirtying the water even further. Marlow lowered his head until his chained hands could reach it, massaging his temples. There was something in there, now that he thought about it, a place full of fire, of screams, of gunshots, of exploding cars, of monsters. But that couldn't be right. He pressed his fists against his eyes until his vision was a snowstorm of color.

"The hospital, right?" he said a moment later, looking up. "Staten Island. The parking garage."

The detective and the cop shared a look, the woman's hand straying down to her holstered weapon as if to check that it was still there. When the man looked back at Marlow there was nothing nice or welcoming left in his expression.

"So, you *were* there."

"I . . ." *Tread carefully, Marlow,* said his brain. "It was a bad day. I was trying to buy something to drink."

"Tell me something I don't know."

"I live on the island. I'd just . . . just been kicked outta school. Was planning on drowning my sorrows, y'know? Then I heard the explosion."

"You weren't there when it went up?" the detective asked.

"No," Marlow said, his thoughts becoming clearer. "No, I was inside a store. Clerk had a shotgun, I grabbed it. Thought it was, I don't know, terrorists or something."

"And?"

"And . . ." *And what? Girls coming back from the dead? Walls and floors that moved.* "Look, this is going to seem weird." He coughed, both of the cops leaning in close. "The parking garage was full of . . . There were these things. They were alive, but not . . . Look, you kinda had to be there."

"You wanna start making some sense, kid?"

"They were . . . monsters," he said, the word out of his mouth before he could stop it. And it was like a locomotive, dragging everything else behind it. "They were made of stuff, like walls and cars. But they looked like . . . like animals. They had claws, and teeth. I fought one that was part of a truck, and some floor maybe. So there were other people there, dressed in black like soldiers. I think they were dead, apart from one, this big old dude, like really ugly. He had a gun, he was shooting these things. And a girl too, she was . . . Well, y'know, she was pretty cute, but she had a crossbow, and she was . . ."

He realized the detective had raised a hand and his words slowed to a halt. The man released a spluttered sigh.

"You for real?" he said.

"Yeah, I'm telling you the truth." Marlow sat forward, hands out as far as they could go. "Seriously, it's what happened."

"Mr. Green," the man said, and Marlow was shocked to hear his name. With no wallet on him, or phone, how did they know? "I'm not gonna waste your time anymore, and I'd appreciate it if you didn't waste mine. You've been with us before." *Ah, that was how.* He'd been arrested a couple of times before, nothing major, just being tanked up and loudmouthed. "Both times off your trolley. You're getting into some bad habits."

"I swear," said Marlow. "I didn't actually get around to drinking. These people, they took me. That's where I've been all day. I mean all two days. They injected something into me, it must have been alcohol. *They* did this."

"Yeah, and the only reason I get wasted on the weekends is 'cause Officer Settle here keeps spiking my coffee with rum. That right, Settle?"

"Yes, sir."

"Funny how my wife don't believe that story neither."

"But I can show you where they—"

"But nothing." The detective stood up, flattening his hands down his creased shirt. "You were drinking, I believe that much. We found the store, one dead guy, crushed by a collapsing ceiling. So you saw what was going on, a ton of people witnessed the hospital going up in flames. But let me tell you something, kid." He slammed his hands down on the table, his greasy face looming in, his breath full of coffee and cigarettes. "We drag you in here again, you ever make a threat against one of my

82

officers again, you puke within twenty goddamned yards of a city vehicle again, then you'll be wearing a jumpsuit for real, and not just because you left your pants at home. Clear?"

"I—"

He smashed his palms against the wood, hard enough to shunt the table into Marlow's chest.

"Clear?"

"Yeah," he wheezed. "Yeah, I got it. No more drink."

The detective eyeballed him for a moment more, then turned on his heels and smacked on the door. A second later a bolt was pulled back on the other side and it squealed open, the sound grating down Marlow's spine, reminding him of the screams of the creatures. He shook it off, waited for the police-woman to walk over and unlock his cuffs.

"If you want to collect your possessions you have to go to the front desk," she said as he massaged the blood back into his wrists. "But given that all you had on you is your undershorts, I'm guessing you're good to go." Marlow stood up, muttering his thanks. She glanced at his jumpsuit and smiled, and it was the first kind expression Marlow had seen since this whole thing started. "But maybe go anyway, we might be able to sort you out something better to wear."

WHO THE HELL
IS STEELY DAN?

It wasn't exactly what Marlow would have called "better." A pair of baggy green shorts. A white T-shirt that was three sizes too big for him, the front plastered with the name STEELY DAN in big red letters. He had no idea who or what Steely Dan was but he was pretty sure it wasn't the sort of thing he wanted to be seen in. To top it off—or bottom it out—the only footwear they had in his size was a pair of leather sandals that had been worn so often they had somebody else's footprint permanently mushed into them. They were surprisingly comfortable, but *seriously*—he figured he'd have more street cred walking home in his underwear.

Where do they even get this stuff from? he thought as he made his way out of the station, hopping down the steps with a hand up to shield himself from the glare. They probably kept the worst bits and pieces of clothing from the drunks and the dead guys just so they could pass it over to people like Marlow.

He looked left and right, not quite sure where he was. Somewhere in lower Manhattan, he figured, where the jumbled streets weren't numbered and there were lots of storefronts with Chinese lettering on their signs. It was quiet for the time of day, just a scattering of people, all of whom looked like they'd rather be cooling down in an air-conditioned apartment or office right now. Only one of them caught his eye—a girl fifty yards away—and Marlow's heart did a cartwheel in his chest. She was familiar, his age, dressed in jeans and a sweatshirt and a coat, of all things. She had to be dying in there.

Marlow turned away, trying to work out where he'd seen the girl before. At school, probably. So why was there a feeling in Marlow's gut? Like he'd just been kicked hard. He glanced back. She was there, still as a stone, unblinking eyes locked on Marlow.

Twenty yards away.

He hadn't seen her move and Marlow suddenly felt as if he were on a roller coaster car that had reached the top of the slope, that quiet moment before the drop. He reached out, placed a hand on the nearest tree just to stop the world from spinning. Something was wrestling with his intestines, discomfort radiating out from the very center of him, making his spine tingle.

He clamped his eyes shut, and when he opened them again the girl was gone.

You're going mad, Marlow.

He pushed himself off the tree and started walking, no idea where he was going. The sun was right overhead, beating down on the city like a hammer on an anvil, and he was sweating after half a block. The air—as fresh as it ever got in New York—was good, though, helping to clear his head. The world was still spinning, but slower now. He didn't know what they'd shot him with, but it must have been strong. He peeked over his shoulder. No sign of the girl.

He waited for a truck to rumble past, followed by a couple of honking cabs, before crossing an intersection. The whole thing felt like a dream now, because of the alcohol, fading away like the last few scraps of a nightmare. Here, in the sun, in the melting pot of the city, surrounded by people going shopping, going to work, going to school, the thought of monsters and soldiers seemed ridiculous, impossible.

But *she* was still there. Pan. He could see her now, like she was standing right in front of him, and he wasn't sure whether the ache in his stomach was because he liked her or hated her. She'd left him for dead, after all. Treated him like dirt. All the same, though, she was hot.

Leave it be, said Danny. *Girl like that, she'll be the death of you, literally.*

"You're one to talk," he muttered. "Didn't you sign up to the marines so you could impress Marcie Jones?"

No . . . said his brother. Danny had never been much good at lying, his mom had told him. *I signed up to serve my country. Marcie had absolutely nothing to do with it. Besides, she worked at Walmart. She didn't run around with a crossbow, killing things.*

"Fair point," he said, earning a suspicious look from a couple of old ladies walking past. Marlow clamped his mouth shut, keeping his eyes down. He already looked like a crazy bum, talking to himself wouldn't help. He crossed onto the next block, sunlight flashing off the windows of the apartment buildings, everything drowning in the liquid heat, sounding muffled but perfectly clear in that weird way things always sounded in summer. Yeah, Pan was real, no doubt about it.

And if she was real, so was everything else.

He swore, reaching the end of the block. There was a whole bunch of green up ahead, a park or something, but halfway down to his right were the steps to the subway. He jogged down them, happy to get out of the sun, less happy to be back underground. He kept expecting something to explode, a creature to wrench its impossible body from the walls and lumber toward him. Keeping his head down, his fists clenched, he shouldered his way through the thin crowd toward the turnstiles. He didn't have any money on him but it had never stopped him before, and he checked that the coast was clear before leaping the barrier and sprinting to the downtown platform.

It was a cattle train, rammed tight with sweating livestock, and Marlow clung on to the handrail as it tore beneath the city. As hot as it was down here, it felt good to be moving. Moving away from the police, away from the place where he'd been held prisoner. Away from his attackers, who'd filled his veins with poison. It's what he did best, after all. He ran.

Now that he had some distance, it kind of made sense. They'd dosed him up so that nobody believed his story. It was a madman's tale anyway, he figured, but making him a drunken madman had to help. What was it they'd said? The first rule or something, that the world couldn't know.

"Steely Dan!" yelled a voice, right in his ear, almost making him jump out of his skin. He looked up, saw a guy with a huge belly and an even bigger beard breaking the cardinal rule of the subway—under no circumstances acknowledge any other passenger—in order to give him a rocker's salute. Marlow smiled nervously at him and edged down the train, stopping only when that same thumping discomfort began to creep into his guts, vertigo making the whole train feel like it was tilting upside down.

He grabbed for the handrail, closing his eyes against the rush. When he opened them again and stared through the crowd he could have sworn he saw the same girl there, that stab of familiarity. Their eyes met for a second before the train rocked around a bend and she was lost in the swaying bodies.

Losing it, he told himself.

With any luck, the fact the police had let him go meant they were done with him. Nobody would believe his story, nobody would investigate it. He could just get on with his life. He sighed, loudly. His amazing, fulfilling, fantastic life. Now the churning in his gut was something else, something that might have been disappointment. It was making him feel hollow, like part of him was missing. *Secrets are like a hole in your life,* Herc had said. And he was right. Marlow would have to live with the not knowing for the rest of his days.

It doesn't matter, he told himself. *Just forget it.*

He screwed his eyes shut, feeling the motion of the train, imagining the city far behind him, fading fast. The memories would be the same. They had to be. If he kept moving, then they'd vanish, in time. Yeah, it was good to be moving.

And he almost smiled, until he remembered where the train was taking him. South, to the ferry terminal. Back toward Staten Island. Back into the nightmare.

"Mom?"

Marlow hovered on the steps that led up to his front door, shuffling his feet. It was a decent enough place that he'd lived in since he was born, although it had seen better days. The blue paint had all but peeled away, like leprous skin. The filthy windows, too, were like eyes dulled with cataracts. The only new thing on the whole building was the satellite dish that spoon-fed his mom her stories day in, day out. He could hear the TV now, the dull roar of applause from some game show.

He eased the door open a couple of inches, his face pressed into the gloom beyond. It was dark inside, the way it was always dark inside, even on a day like this when the sun seemed hot enough to burn a mile underground. His mom had closed the curtains on the day of Danny's wake and the shadows had never left.

"Yo, Mom, it's me."

There was a scrabbling of claws, a soft bark, then Donovan came trotting around the corner. The old mongrel—part Doberman, part English sheepdog, maybe part dalmatian, nobody really knew—slipped and slid on the wood, his tail beating so hard that his ass was almost ping-ponging off the walls. Marlow crouched down and ruffled the dog's fur, that big, wet tongue slobbering over his face.

"Yeah, yeah," Marlow said, holding Donovan's massive paw. "I know, I missed you too, boy. Where's Mom?"

There were noises in the kitchen, the clink of a glass.

"Mom?"

"Marly?" His mom's face appeared around the corner, smiling, and he walked over and wrapped her in his arms, feeling like he couldn't hug her too hard or he might break her. She was a bag of bones wrapped in a velour jumpsuit, her hair unbrushed, her skin too loose on her face. A badly made doll. But she hugged him back as hard as her skinny arms would let her, her glass slopping booze over his T-shirt. When he finally let go she smiled at him again.

"I was worried, sweetheart. You weren't answering your phone. Where you been?"

"Nowhere," he said, patting the dog as it limped in behind him. "Just out with Charlie. I crashed at his place. And I lost my phone."

"You're lying to me," she said, walking across the tiny kitchen. There were bottles on the counter and it took her a couple of attempts before she found one that wasn't empty, topping up her glass. His mom's drunk wasn't the kind that you could really notice—she never fell over, never started shouting and screaming, never really even slurred her words. But it was there, quiet, patient, like a parasite that controlled its host without them knowing.

"No, Mom, I—"

"Charlie stopped by, yesterday evening," she said, leaning on the counter and taking a sip. She swallowed, grimacing. "Said he was looking for you."

"Yeah, um," Marlow tried to find an excuse inside the storm of his head. "Well, we had this school thing, we were supposed to be working on together, research and stuff, and—"

"And I got a call, from your principal."

Oh crap.

"Mom, it's not my fault."

"I don't want to hear it, Marlow," she said. "You promised me."

"He had it in for me, I could have been the model student and he still would have kicked me out."

"So you didn't scratch a . . . a nasty picture onto his car?"

Marlow chewed his knuckle, shuffling uncomfortably. The dog whined, his tail hanging between his legs, his eyes big and wet and sad. Marlow tickled his ear, more to cover his shame than anything else.

"It was a rocket ship," he muttered, too low for her to hear.

"Marlow, you're nearly sixteen. Why do you insist on acting like a child? This was your last chance. Your *last chance*. What about that was hard to understand?"

She took a sip of her drink and smudged a tear away, her tiny body shuddering.

"I don't know what to do, Marly," she said. "I don't know what to do. I wish Danny was here, I wish your brother was here. He'd know."

It was like a slap to the face, and Marlow couldn't help but turn to the photo on the wall. Danny grinned at him through his shades, his skin thick with dust, his teeth the brightest thing in the kitchen.

"Mom, please, it will be okay, I promise," he said, his throat swelling—not asthma this time but tears, ready to explode out of him. He clamped down, feeling the sting in his eyes. "I promise."

"You promise?" she said, tipping back the glass and emptying it in one swallow. "Promises and lies, Marlow. I can't stand it. You sound just like *him*."

She didn't have to say who. She was talking about his dad, a man he'd never even met but whose every shortfall he seemed to share. The accusation turned his tears to anger.

"I told you, it's not my fault."

"Yeah," his mom said, fixing him with just about the coldest look he could imagine. "That was his line too. Right before he ran away."

He opened his mouth to reply, found nothing there to say. He spun around, clenching his teeth against the wave of dizziness and nausea. Somehow he made it out of the living room, up the stairs into his bedroom. It was brighter in there, syrupy light seeping in through the filthy glass. But it still took everything he had not to run to the window and drop headfirst to the street where he wouldn't feel that unbearable weight on his shoulders, like the whole house was resting there, the whole big, dark, screaming world.

Instead, he stripped off the clothes, slung on a fresh tee and some sweatpants and his old sneakers. He grabbed his spare inhaler, then bolted past his sad, old dog for the door.

FAST EXIT

They moved out as quickly and as smoothly as they had moved in. Like a rising tide, Pan thought, each wave so small and so quiet that you didn't notice them creeping up the beach until your feet were soaked. Nobody said much as they traipsed out of the building. There wasn't exactly much to talk about. Nothing good, anyway. And it was nice to get some peace and quiet.

Pan had almost managed to shut the elevator doors when Herc's scarred hand slid through the gap. Her sigh of relief became a splutter of frustration as the big man clambered inside, slamming the gates behind him. He stood on a streak of fading blood that stretched along the floor, his boots squeaking as he spun to face her.

"How you holdin' up?"

"Worse now than I was a second ago," she grumbled. The doors closed and the cab rocked as it started to descend. She sighed again, not enough left inside her to have this conversation. She lifted a hand, placed it against her chest, against the scar she could feel beneath her tee. It was like a lump of hot coal had been stitched there, her body trying to repair a wound that it couldn't even understand.

"You talked to Ostheim?" Herc asked, knowing full well what the answer was.

Pan felt her whole body slump. She closed her eyes, listened to the whining gears of the elevator.

"He needs to speak with you, Pan," Herc said, and the rush of anger that rose from her gut was so fierce it scared her. She bit down on it, trapping her response behind her teeth, taking a deep breath through her nose.

"I know," she hissed. The elevator growled, then thumped home. Herc snatched the gates open, let her out first. The building was an empty office tower, abandoned when it was only half-finished by an insolvent developer—one of an endless list of deserted buildings they'd already used that year. She marched through the empty lobby, just wanting to be out in the sun, wanting to leave all of this behind her. *Keep walking, keep walking, keep walking.*

"Pan." Herc's voice was like a choke chain around her throat, stopping her dead. She looked back, saw him lob a cell phone her way. She snatched it out of the air, fought the instinct to throw it back like it was a live grenade. Herc stood in the flickering fluorescent light of the elevator, shrugged his big shoulders. "He's on now."

She punched through the doors into the noise and heat of the street, clutching the cell so hard she thought it might splinter into pieces. *No such luck.* She barged past the people, swearing at the ones who didn't get out of her way, ducking into the nearest alleyway. For a second or two she stood in the muggy shadows, took a couple of breaths of exhausted air. She could almost feel her employer there, a presence at the end of her arm, and she wondered if somehow he could see her, if he'd hacked into the phone's camera, or a nearby CCTV camera, or a even a satellite. She glanced nervously up at the white-blue sky. There wasn't much that Ostheim couldn't do. She lifted the cell.

"Ostheim."

"And here's me thinking you'd left off without so much as a letter of notice," he replied, that familiar accent that was half German, half somewhere even farther away. She'd never been able to place it, and as she'd never actually met Ostheim, or so much as seen a photo of the man, she had no other clues as to his whereabouts. "But it's good to hear your voice, Pan. For a second back there, I thought we'd lost you."

"For a second, you did."

"So I heard. How was it?"

"Death?" Pan swallowed, her throat parched. She could still feel it, invisible hands reaching through her skin, through her bones and muscles, grabbing hold of something even deeper, ready to rip it away and drag it down to wherever it was they came from. She wrapped her free hand around her stomach as if to hold in her soul, worried that now it had been wrenched loose it might simply fall out. It was almost too much, and she leaned back against the warm bricks, sliding down into a nest of old newspaper.

"Pan?" She'd almost forgotten he was there, his voice making her jump.

"I'm okay," she said. "I don't want to talk about it."

"Fair enough," he replied, as bright as always. "But you know I'm here if you need me. Just a phone call away. I've been doing this a long time, Pan, I know what it's like."

To feel the very essence of you almost torn away? I doubt it.

"Anything you need, you just let me know. Anything at all."

"How about a reference for a new job?" She spluttered a humorless laugh at her own joke.

"You know you can get out any time. All you've got to do is say the word. We'll set you up, you'll never have to worry about anything again. Is that what you want?"

Yeah, and then what? A job at McDonald's? Sharing a small

apartment with a roommate and a poodle called Herc? She wasn't sure if the thought made her want to laugh again, or just weep. This was all she knew. And a life without the Engine, without the things it gave her . . . that was no kind of life. No, she wasn't going back.

"All you got to do is—"

"Shut up, Shep," she said. "I told you, I'm fine. What's next?"

She could almost hear him smiling, like he'd known exactly what she was going to say. He probably had, the smug bastard. Ostheim knew everything.

"Next is you tell me what went wrong."

"Hasn't Herc already debriefed?"

"He has, but I want to hear it from you."

Great. Pan pushed herself up, pacing down into the darkness of the back of the alley. Behind her she heard car horns and children shouting, somebody barking out a laugh loud enough to echo off the walls. She tried to tune it out, thinking back, back past the tower, back past the hospital, back past the van as it barreled down the expressway, back to yesterday morning.

"It went wrong," she said, knowing even as she spoke that it was the most pointless statement in the history of statements. "The target, he wasn't there."

Their objective had been simple: to infiltrate the suspected home of a guy called Patrick Rebarre. He was an Engineer who worked for the other side, a creep whose sole purpose was to bring about the end of the world. He'd deserved to die, and she'd been more than willing to do it. That was a soldier's job, right? Take out the enemy.

The only problem was he hadn't been there.

"We breached the house, Ostheim," she said.

"And . . ."

"And somebody had beaten us to it. His security team was dead, three bodyguards left on the floor like . . . like dog food."

She could see them now. Not just killed but turned inside out.

Literally.

"You found his body?" Ostheim asked.

"Rebarre?" Pan shook her head. "No, he'd gone."

No corpse, no clues, no nothing.

"You think somebody warned him?"

"I think . . ." She swallowed hard to keep down the boiling contents of her stomach. "I think *he* did."

Mammon, said her brain before she had the chance to stop it. She glanced behind her, just in case thinking about him somehow managed to conjure him. Stranger things were possible, after all. But there was just the alley, and the world beyond, oblivious to the knowledge that monsters walked in their midst. She rubbed her churning gut, forcing herself to speak.

"It was a trap. I knew something was wrong as soon as we breached. There was something in the air, something that shouldn't have been there. You've been around the Pentarchy, Ostheim, you know the stench they leave behind."

The Pentarchy. The Five. They'd be considered gods if they weren't already devils.

"But you didn't actually see him?" Ostheim asked.

"I didn't need to. He was there."

"Then we have to assume he followed you," Ostheim said. "Or at least tracked you. There was no sign of him at the hospital?"

"No. I think we lost him."

"You didn't," Ostheim said. "Just stay alert. You know I don't have to tell you how dangerous this could be. Out of all

96

of them, he's the worst. He can tear your soul apart with far greater efficiency than the demons can."

She wrapped her free hand around herself, holding her shaking body as tight as she could. She needed to be whole again, needed to be protected, needed to be immortal.

"I need the Engine, Ostheim," she said. "Send me back."

"In time," he replied. "Take this chance to recover. I'm sending Nightingale and Truck to your location."

"They won't be enough," Pan said. "Not if *he* shows up. Please, Ostheim, I need it."

"I need you to find Rebarre. We cannot afford to let him live. Not with what he knows. I don't need to remind you what's at stake here. If the Circulus Inferni find out the location of our Engine, then that's it, game over."

Understatement of the century, she thought. *It's why they had that name, why they'd had it for thousands of years. Circulus Inferni, the Circle of Hell. If they won this war, then it would be hell on earth.*

And that wasn't just a metaphor.

"Pan?"

"Yeah, yeah, I know. We'll find him."

She heard Ostheim sucking his teeth, like he was deep in thought.

"Good. See that you do. What about our bait?"

"The kid? Shep, I have no idea what you're planning but—"

"It's what we need to do, Pan. We have to draw them out somehow, position them where we can get to them. What better way?"

"They'll kill him," she said.

"And here's me thinking you never had a heart," he said, laughing. "We'll be there. We'll get to them before they get to him."

Yeah, right.

"And, Pan . . ."

"What?"

"I meant what I said. If you sense Mammon, if you feel him in the air, if you so much as break into gooseflesh or get a shiver down your spine, you start running. Okay?"

"Shep, I'll be fine."

"What he will do to you is worse than an eternity in hell, you hear me? Listen to my words. If you sense him, you run. Run, and never look back."

And with that he was gone. Pan listened to the dead line for a moment, hearing the echo of his words in the hissing static.

Run.

Yeah, like she really had a choice.

GHOSTS

Marlow stood outside Victor G. Rosemount High School in the sweltering heat, trying to work out why he felt so lost.

Because you've got nowhere to go, his brain told him. *Nobody wants you.*

The words stung, but only because they were true. This place had kicked him out, and his mom would happily trade him in for the son she'd lost ten years ago. Danny may have been dead, but Marlow was the ghost. Even here people streamed past him like they couldn't see him, nobody so much as acknowledging his presence.

Except one—the merest glimpse of a familiar face, the same girl half-lost in the crowd, then gone before Marlow could make sense of it.

Hold it together, man, he told himself.

He wanted to find Charlie, if only to prove that he still existed. He needed someone to talk to, to try to make sense of everything that had happened. Things may have been about as crap as they could be but Charlie would crack a joke and they would laugh and at least he'd feel like a real person again. Besides, however bad his life was Charlie's had been worse, and there was nothing like perspective to make you feel a little less sorry for yourself.

With no cell, though, he needed to fetch him in person. He pulled his inhaler from his pocket and squeezed two shots into his mouth, grimacing against the bitter taste. His lungs crackled and he rubbed his chest until they eased. Then he walked across the road to the locked gates. He jabbed his thumb against the intercom button. Seconds later the school receptionist answered.

"It's, um . . . I'm late, sorry, need to get in."

"Name?"

"Mar—" he started, then, "Charlie Alvarez."

There was a pause, then the gates buzzed and he pushed his way through. He decided against the lobby and cut around the side of the main building. He entered through the fire door that never latched properly, clattering up the stairwell and along an empty corridor. He had to peer into three classrooms before he found the right one. Charlie was sitting in the middle of the room, lost in a daze, pen between his teeth. Marlow knocked softly, then pushed open the door. Everybody turned to him, and Charlie's eyes just about popped free of his head.

The teacher—Marlow couldn't remember her name—folded her arms across her chest.

"You're not supposed to be here," she said.

"Yeah," he replied, scratching his head. "About that. You don't have to worry, it's all sorted. Mr. Caputo apologized to me, actually commissioned me to decorate the rest of his car."

"Nice try," she said. "Now leave. You know what happens when you're on school premises without permission."

By the time she'd finished Charlie was out of his seat and halfway across the room.

"I'd better go see what the trouble is," he said as he reached the door.

She protested some more, but Charlie just flashed her one of his grins and closed the door behind him.

"What the *hell*, dude?" he said, grabbing Marlow's arm and hauling him down the corridor. "Where have you been?"

"You wouldn't believe me if I told you," he replied, leaning in close and keeping his voice low. Charlie reeled back, waving his hand in front of his face.

"Wouldn't believe you? Jesus, Marlow, I can *smell* it. You could fuel a goddamned power station with those fumes."

"It's not . . ." Marlow covered his mouth self-consciously. "It's not what it looks like, Charlie. I was drugged."

"*What?*"

"By these guys. They injected me with alcohol." He shook his head to try to clear his thoughts. Nothing was making sense up there, the last couple of days a storm of dream-like half-memories. Charlie's eyebrow just about shot off the top of his head.

"They injected you . . . with *whiskey?* You okay? Did they . . . ?"

Marlow realized what he was asking.

"No! No way, dude. It's because I saw something. I was there, at the hospital."

"The one the terrorists blew up?" Charlie said.

"What?" Marlow said.

"It's all over CNN, man. The cops got there before they could do too much damage. Some wacko cell is claiming responsibility. You saying terrorists made you get drunk?"

"No, wait." Marlow looked back, saw the demons ripping themselves from the walls, the girl with the hole in her heart. "That's not what happened. They weren't terrorists."

He heard a door opening, the hammer of distant footsteps.

"There were these people, and these . . . I don't know, creatures I guess."

"Creatures?" Charlie actually took a step back. "Listen, Marlow, I don't know what you've been on but—"

"I'm not *on* anything," he spat back.

Charlie spluttered out a sigh.

"Look, I get it, Marlow. This is how you deal with things. You burn up and take off. But you got to get it under control, dude. I'm serious, you sound crazy."

"I'm not crazy," he started, and would have said more if the intercom hadn't fizzed to life.

"Please listen carefully," said a voice that Marlow recognized instantly as the principal's. "The school is currently in lockdown. We request that all students remain inside their classrooms. Staff, this is a code orange. Please ensure that all doors are secured."

"What's going on?" Marlow said. "What's a code orange?"

"I have no idea," Charlie replied. "But I'm guessing it's you."

"*Me?*"

The sound of footsteps grew louder and the door at the end of the corridor exploded outward, the giant shape of Yogi lumbering through as fast as his fat legs would let him. It only took him a second to see Marlow, and when he did he started fumbling at the Taser on his belt.

"Yeah," said Charlie. "I'm pretty sure it's you."

"Stop!" Yogi roared, ripping the weapon from its holster. His other hand held a radio. "He's in east wing, level two. No weapon in sight."

"Weapon?" Marlow said, frowning. Yogi was jogging toward them, everything jiggling. "What's he talking about?"

"I have no idea," Charlie replied, backing away. "But if I were you, I'd start running."

He didn't need to be told twice, sprinting after Charlie toward the far end of the corridor. They burst through the double doors, skidding around the corner into the stairwell.

Caputo must have seen Marlow entering the gates, probably thought he was here for payback. He didn't blame him. Victor G. Rosemount was the kind of place where payback could be brutal.

"Where are you going?" he asked Charlie, feeling the monster start to squeeze its fingers around his throat. "And why are *you* running?"

Charlie grinned back at him.

"Gotta be more exciting than geography, right?"

They punched through the doors at the bottom of the stairs, running out into the main school corridor. Yogi was still behind them, grunting like an injured bear, and Marlow took the lead, splitting right, heading toward the way out. He smashed through the final set of fire doors into the lobby, the sun so bright there that it was like a flashbang going off in his face. He slammed into something big, spinning to a halt and panting for breath.

Two school cops stood between him and the way out. They weren't as big as Yogi—*nobody* was as big as Yogi—but there were Tasers in their hands and murder in their eyes. Marlow froze, lifting his arms over his head in surrender. Charlie flapped to a halt beside him, his sneakers squeaking on the floor. Yogi appeared behind them, growling, at the same time that Caputo stepped out of his office door.

"You shouldn't have come back, Marlow," the principal said, hovering behind one of the guards. "You have just violated your contract with the school and broken the law. The city police have been notified."

"Whoa," he said, coughing out phlegm. "Don't give yourself an aneurism, I just came to see him." He tipped his head at Charlie.

"Yes, sure." The man sneered. His lips moved as he carried on speaking but Marlow didn't hear it, his head suddenly full of noise. It was a sound like breaking china—as though some-body was walking across broken glass. He clamped his hands to his ears, gritting his teeth against it.

What is that? he said, or maybe didn't. Caputo's face was turning red, the principal jabbing a finger at him, his words drowned out by that infernal noise. Behind him the school doors opened. Marlow glanced up, squinting against the pain, against the light, to see the girl walk in—the one he'd seen outside the cop shop, the one who had followed him here. A girl he didn't know, but who seemed so familiar.

"Hello, Marlow," she said, smiling right at him.

And that's when all hell broke loose.

CRAZY STUPID

"We've got definite fluctuations in the reality continuum."

Pan sighed, looking over her shoulder at Herc. He was sitting at a bank of computers in the back of the van, his scarred forehead furrowed as he focused on a stream of data on one of the monitors. She put her hands behind her head, struggling to stay awake in the stream of golden light that poured through the windshield.

"You know, Herc," she said, "the fact that you say stuff like that is one of the reasons nobody likes you."

"I thought everybody liked me," he said, pouting. "I'm the life and soul of the party."

"You couldn't be the life and soul of the party if the party was full of demons," she said. Then, when he didn't reply, "You know, because demons don't have lives or souls."

"Pan, it isn't really a joke if you have to explain it," he said, smudging a palm across the screen as if he could somehow change what was written there. "Seriously, though, we've got a hit. What do you think?"

Pan reluctantly got to her feet, and moved to the back of the van. She sat next to Herc, staring at the lines of code and trying not to go cross-eyed. It was hopeless. She could read ancient Egyptian hieroglyphics better than she could read the data pumped out by the Lawyers.

"I have absolutely no idea, Herc," she said.

She knew what he'd found, though. Tiny inconsistencies in the fabric of the world—*cracks in the code* is how the Lawyers always described them—that were a sign an Engineer was close by. When you used the Engine it basically took a sledge-hammer to physics, smashing a great big hole into reality. Those holes were like a homing beacon, if you knew how to look for them.

"How many?" she asked.

"I can't tell," Herc said. "The data's off. Two, maybe. Possibly more."

Great. Two enemy Engineers, at least. That could be bad. The trouble was you never knew what their powers were until you saw them—or *didn't* see them, if that's what they'd traded for. Invisibility was always popular. You didn't know whether you'd be facing up to superstrength, supersonic speed, the ability to blow fire out of your ass. Or the big one, of course: invulnerability. But the contract for that was a nightmare to break, so only idiots and crazy people went for that.

Yeah, and which one are you?

"Shut up," she told her brain.

"What?" said Herc, pouting again.

"Nothing." She stood up, yawning as she paced the length of the van and back. She felt like she could sleep for a week, and she would have if someone could guarantee that there would be no nightmares. "This is a bad idea anyway. Why would they even care about him?"

"Marlow? Because he's seen us. Because they think he'll be able to lead them to Ostheim, give them something to work with."

Pan snorted. Ostheim was way too clever for that. They were always moving, always hiding. This war had been raging for decades and they'd never been found. Marlow could tell them everything he knew, everything he'd seen, and it wouldn't do the Circulus Inferni any good. All they'd find is an empty high-rise in Manhattan.

"And remind me again why *we're* here?" she asked, examining her filthy fingernail.

"See if we can't lure some of them into a trap, take out a couple of the enemy, even up the odds a little."

Tit for tat, just like always. You kill some of the enemy, the enemy kills some of you, and the demons just sit there waiting for a chance to drag everybody down to hell. Maybe she *should* have taken Ostheim's offer of escape.

"They're never going to show up," she said. "The kid's not a big enough target."

The words were barely out of her mouth before the radio squawked and Truck's voice boomed through. He and Nightingale were three streets up, on lookout duty.

"We got movement here. By the school."

"Yeah?" Pan said. "You getting some fluctuations in the reality continuum of your bowels?"

"No joking, Pan, got a bad feeling. I think something big's about to go down."

Your fat ass, she wanted to say, but before she got the chance a squealing hiss of static erupted through the speakers. She clamped her hands to her ears as Herc wrenched the volume down.

"Truck? You there?"

Just static.

"Goddammit."

Herc clambered behind the wheel and fired up the engine. Pan just had time to grab hold of the rail before it roared up the street.

"We're eyes-only on this one, Pan, hear me?" Herc said.

It was good advice. Without a contract she'd be as vulnerable as it was possible to be out there. An Engineer could crack her open with just a thought.

"I mean it. Do *not* do anything crazy or anything stupid."

She reached back with her spare hand, felt the crossbow there, praying she wouldn't have to use it but knowing she would. *Crazy or stupid, Pan?* she asked herself as they skidded around a corner, accelerating hard.

Probably both.

WHEN ALL HELL BREAKS LOOSE

The girl smiled again and Marlow almost screamed. It was a friendly smile, like they were old friends, like they were the only two people in the room. But there was something just beneath it, something sharp and dangerous, like a razor hidden by icing sugar. She was still dwarfed by her huge jacket, her mousy hair falling in tangled curls. Even in the dazzling light of the lobby her eyes seemed to glow, too big, too bright.

Marlow's gut tightened, that same wave of nausea bubbling up from deep inside him. Something felt wrong.

Something felt *really* wrong.

The girl walked across the lobby, pushing past the guards and the principal like they didn't exist. Caputo frowned at her.

"Excuse me, what do you think you're doing?"

She didn't reply, those big, moon-bright eyes never leaving Marlow. Caputo reached out, grabbed hold of her coat.

"You have no right, I'm asking you to . . ."

The words dropped from his lips in clumps, his eyes bulging like something inside his skull was pushing them out. He put a finger down his collar and tugged at it as if he were standing inside a furnace.

"You," Caputo said, gulping. He was shaking now, like he was on the verge of a seizure. "You you you . . ."

"Hey, Vince," said Yogi, "you okay?"

Caputo didn't reply, just collapsed against the wall, shaking like a broken machine, saying that one word over and over. Yogi and the other guards had run to him, one of them calling for help on his radio. The girl ignored them, still smiling at Marlow. His guts did another somersault with every step she took, like she'd unraveled them and was using them as a red carpet. Charlie must have sensed something too because he grabbed Marlow's arm.

"Dude," he said quietly. "This is weird."

"I said hello, Marlow," said the girl. She took another step forward and the air around her seemed to shimmer, giving the illusion that her feet weren't touching the ground. It had to be the heat, right? But could the weather be blamed for the way her words seemed to ricochet around the room like bullets, making his ears ring?

"I know you?" he said.

"I've been looking for you," she replied. She didn't so much as blink as she walked across the lobby, but her smile grew even wider. Her teeth looked small and sharp. It was a shark's smile.

"Lady, you're going to have to go through my secretary," he said, but he took a step back as he did so, hitting the wall.

This won't hurt, she said, and her words buzzed inside his ears like there was a wasp trapped in there.

"What won't?" Marlow asked.

She sailed closer, still moving without really walking. Her eyes were growing alongside her smile, becoming as fat and bright as headlights. His headache was growing more painful by the second, needled feet walking across the flesh of his brain. His mouth was full of the taste of copper.

"Marlow?" Charlie's voice was quiet, as though he were speaking from the other side of the school, or Marlow had cotton wool in his ears. "Dude, your *nose*."

Marlow put his fingers to his face and they came away red, blood pattering down onto his T-shirt, onto his sneakers.

Relax, the girl was saying, or not saying. *I'm just going to open you up, see what's inside. You have something we need.* She was a dozen yards away now, still gliding. Her hands flexed in the air in front of her, and each time one of her fingers moved Marlow felt like a blasting cap had been detonated inside his head. Visions flashed up with each explosion, too bright and too real—the hospital parking lot, the demons, and *her,* Pan. Marlow groaned, putting his hand to his head, feeling like his mind was about to start slopping out of his nose along with the blood.

"Hey!" yelled one of the cops. "What the hell's going on? Get away from him!"

Marlow felt Charlie's fingers tighten around his arm, tugging. He let himself be pulled, taking a step down the corridor toward the fire doors.

Where are you going, Marlow? the girl said. She reached out and took hold of his shirt, pulling him close, those eyes burning more fiercely than the sun. He struggled against her, hearing the police demanding to know what was going on, hearing Charlie shout his name. But all of it was drowned out by the girl's voice in his head, those bone-breakingly loud whispers. *Don't be afraid, Marlow, the pain will be over soon, it will all be over soon.*

The memories flashed by without his permission, as if he were watching a movie inside his head. He saw things he didn't even remember: staggering out of the office tower, so drunk he couldn't stand straight; looking up at the window where he could almost make out Pan's face watching him go, vomiting over a police car as they tried to bundle him inside. The girl's eyes flicked back and forth like she was watching it all, like she was reading his mind. It was too much, too much.

"No!" Marlow cried, lashing out, shunting the girl away. She grunted, the visions in his head vanishing so fast that for a second he couldn't see anything at all. Something in her expression dropped away like a mask, her eyes suddenly normal, her smile wiped clean.

"That's enough!" yelled Yogi, moving toward the girl. "What are you doing here?"

The girl closed her eyes, scrunched up her face, put her fingers to her temples like she was trying to remember where she'd left her keys.

"You need to get the hell out," Yogi said, reaching out for the girl with one fat hand.

Then Caputo started screaming.

It was a noise unlike anything Marlow had heard, a savage, brutal shriek that filled the entire lobby. Everybody turned to the principal as he pushed himself up from the wall, his movements jerky. He screamed again, spraying spittle, and started to run toward Yogi, building up speed.

"Hey—" was all the big guy had a chance to say before Caputo leaped on him, his wiry arms clamped onto the cop's big, bald head, his legs wrapped around his waist. Yogi staggered, trying to wrestle the man off him, but Caputo looked possessed. He raised a hand and punched Yogi, right in the side of the head. The noise was like somebody shooting a watermelon, a wet crack that echoed off the walls. He punched him again and this time his knuckles came away red.

"Christ!" yelled one of the other school cops, running into the fray. Yogi and Caputo looked like they were locked in some kind of dance, then the big guy's legs gave out beneath him and they both crumpled to the floor. Caputo was still punching, staving in the side of Yogi's head, blood and bone spraying across the lobby. He was grinning like a madman, shrieking with glee as he bent down and bit into the gaping wound. Marlow heard the clack of teeth against bone and he almost screamed too. One cop shot his Taser, the principal's entire body shuddering, blood spraying from his mouth. He lay there, out cold, twitching. The other cop was trying to yell something into his radio.

Nearly there, said the girl, and Marlow felt as if she had an ice-cream scoop inside his head, digging into the tender meat of his brain. *Just a little more.*

"Screw this," Charlie almost shrieked, and suddenly the girl was staggering back again, holding her nose. Charlie bounced on his heels, his small fist bunched. He moved in for another punch but the girl opened her mouth and shrieked:

"Patrick! I need you!"

The entire lobby shuddered, as though an earthquake had just hit. The windows imploded, a crack tearing its way across one wall. A cloud of dust billowed down from the ceiling, diffusing the sunlight and making the air swim like an ocean of gold. Marlow grabbed hold of Charlie to stop himself toppling. The room shook again. It was filled with so much dust that it took Marlow a second to notice there was one more person in the lobby.

A guy stood right next to the girl; late teens maybe, blond hair, dressed all in black. The third cop leveled his Taser at the new guy and pulled the trigger, the two electrified wires burying themselves into the boy's neck. They sparked once, but the guy didn't even seem to feel it. The wires glowed red-hot, a bolt of electricity snaking into the cop's hand and sending him flying into the wall. The Taser dropped to the floor and erupted into flame, the plastic bubbling. Smoke curled upward and suddenly the school was full of noise as the fire alarm triggered.

Marlow tried to run but he couldn't move. The dust and smoke was aggravating his lungs, making each breath a long, panicked wheeze. He felt Charlie pulling his arm but nothing was responding the way it should.

I haven't finished with you yet, said the girl's voice in his skull. She reached out and he could feel her fingers there, plunging into his memories, filling his thoughts with pain. He tried to shake her away but he was rooted tight, like he was a puppet and she had hold of his strings. All he could do was watch as the guy in black lifted his hand once again. The cop vanished with a concussive thump, the whole lobby shaking with the force of it.

The policeman on the floor was back on his feet and he swung a punch at the boy. There was another *pop* and the kid vanished. The cop's punch hit nothing but air and the man spun around in a circle, tripping over Yogi's body and landing on his face with a meaty crunch. Then Patrick was there again, blinking back into existence. He twitched his fingers and the man's flailing body exploded in a blinding flash.

Where are they hiding? the girl asked, pulling Marlow's attention back to her. Her eyes were big and bright once again. *Tell me.*

"I don't know what you mean," Marlow said, feeling like his whole body was bound by invisible ropes, his lungs full of sawdust. "I don't know anything."

The door at the far end of the lobby opened, a stampede of students spilling out, heading for the fire exits. Those at the front took one look at the chaos and tried to stop. The girl flinched, her attention wavering as she looked over. Marlow felt the chains loosen, just a crack but enough to let him move. He ripped his mind free, turning and bolting. His legs were like jelly, like this was the first time he'd ever used them, and he almost fell, but Charlie was by his side, hauling him along.

No! came the girl's voice, and he felt her fingers inside his head again, felt his body start to seize up. Then they plunged into the crowd, drowning in a river of limbs. Even past the screams Marlow could hear her.

"Patrick, we can't lose him!"

There was another *thump*, a channel of warm air flowing over them, screams. The flow of people changed, everyone pushing back the way they'd come and dragging Marlow with them. He lost sight of Charlie, called his name, but all he heard in return was the girl.

Marlow, she said, her voice distant now, like a badly tuned radio. *Marlow, don't you dare run . . .*

Then she was gone. Marlow passed an open door and he plowed through the crowd toward it, squeezing into a classroom. There were half a dozen younger students there, cowering in the corner. Somebody had opened a window and was halfway out, casting a nervous look back before disappearing.

"Go!" he wheezed at the rest, scattering them.

He looked back at the crowd raging past the door. Charlie was there, pushing and punching his way through the melee until he was close enough to hold out a hand. Marlow grabbed it, hauling him in like he was dragging him out of quicksand. They staggered into the classroom together, Charlie panting and Marlow gasping.

"What the hell is going on, Marlow?" Charlie asked. The room trembled, an aftershock strong enough to send chairs and tables skittering across the floor. "Seriously, dude, what the hell?"

"I told you, some weird stuff went down yesterday," Marlow replied. He pulled out his inhaler, using it four times and feeling the panic subside as the hot, dusty air was channeled into his lungs. The relief didn't last long. The room shook again, the windows shattering. Marlow shielded his head with his arms, feeling blades of glass embed themselves in his skin.

"Marlow!"

When he snapped his eyes open the boy called Patrick was right in front of him, wrapping a gloved hand around Marlow's throat. He leaned in, snarling.

"My sister has one way of interrogating people," he said. "I have another."

Patrick grunted in pain as a chair exploded over his back. Then Charlie's scrawny arms were around the guy's neck, dragging him away. Marlow didn't hesitate, throwing a punch. It was badly aimed, glancing off Patrick's cheek. He threw another, this one connecting with the boy's nose. There was a brittle crack and Patrick gargled in pain. Charlie was raining blows down onto his head and neck, trying to knock him down onto the floor.

"Run!" he yelled at Marlow. "I got th—"

There was a dull explosion and Charlie was gone, the dust billowing in crazed circles as the air rushed into the space he'd just occupied.

"No!" Marlow said, just a choked cry. "Charlie? *Charlie!*"

Patrick straightened his jacket, smudging blood over his face as he walked leisurely toward Marlow.

"Where is he?" Marlow asked, backing away and bumping into a desk. "What did you do with him? I swear to god if you've hurt him."

"You'll what?" Patrick said, advancing. "You'll run to Mommy?"

Patrick's grin grew even wider. His was a shark's smile too, and Marlow could suddenly see the resemblance to the girl, his sister. They had to be twins.

"I'll fu—" he started, but Patrick's viper hand snapped out, fingers squeezing tight around Marlow's throat.

"That's enough," he growled. "Time to talk."

Something outside seemed to catch his attention and he swore. There was a blinding flash of darkness, like an inverse starburst. Marlow again felt like he was on a roller coaster, his stomach almost ripped out of his throat. He screwed his eyes shut against the sickening force of it, too scared to even scream. Then the world re-formed around him, his body too heavy, like he was conscious of every bone, every muscle.

He opened his eyes to see Patrick. The boy's face was worn and lined, his eyes pale, like he'd aged fifty years in a flash. Behind him was the big, blue sky, no classroom in sight. Marlow glanced left, then right, realizing that he was on the roof of the school building. And when he peered over his shoulder there was nothing but air between him and the parking lot forty yards below. Vertigo hit him like a punch to the solar plexus and he gulped air like a fish out of water. Only Patrick's hand around his throat was stopping him from falling and he grabbed the boy's arms, holding them tight.

"Last chance," Patrick said, the wind whipping his blond hair into a frenzy. "Tell us what you know."

"About what?" Marlow said.

"About *them*."

"I don't know anything," he said, and Patrick straightened his arm, pushing Marlow farther over the edge. "I don't, I swear, they gave me something, I don't remember any of it."

"Then you're no good to me," Patrick said.

"No, wait!" Marlow yelled.

There was the sound of a door opening, the pop of a gunshot. Then Patrick was gone, and Marlow was falling.

SAFETY'S OFF

The van screeched to a halt so fast that Pan almost flew through the windshield. Outside, the school was in chaos, a hundred kids or more scrambling out of the gates and swarming to safety. Even from inside the van, over the panicked cries, Pan could hear the ringing of an alarm. There was smoke, too, rising from the main door.

"There are definitely two Engineers inside, and they're powerful," Herc said, his eyes still glued to the monitors. "Where the hell is Truck?"

"Probably taking a nap," she replied.

Something hammered on the van door and Pan wrenched it open. A familiar fat face glowered back at her.

"Truck, nice of you to turn up," she said.

"Wish I could say the same," he grunted, squeezing his obese frame halfway into the van, the whole vehicle tilting with his weight. "Herc, we got two agents inside and they're blowing the place to hell. Do we engage?"

"Engage," said Herc, nodding. "Of course you should engage, you dufus. We got a chance to kick the Circle where it counts here. Try to take one alive, okay?"

Truck nodded, his chins jiggling, then he pushed away hard enough to make the van rock on its suspension. Pan watched him go. He didn't look like much, for sure, but she could almost smell the Engine's power inside him—blood and iron, age and power. He would have gone for strength, the way he always did when he forged a contract. It was a safe bet, the Lawyers had brokered that one so many times they could break it with their eyes closed.

The big guy reached the gates, the kids backing away from him like they could sense something different, something *wrong*. A small figure danced up beside him, casting a nervous look back and lifting a hand to Pan in greeting. *Nightingale*. Pan didn't wave back, just nodded at her. Night would have gone for something else, speed maybe. It was impossible to tell until Pan saw her in action.

She sat down, then pushed herself up again, pacing like a caged animal. God, she hated being out of contract, being *human*. The word caught in her craw, making her feel like choking. When she was human she was weak, fragile, pathetic. The Engine made her whole, made her real. With the Engine, she wasn't human at all, she was something so much more.

Being human didn't mean she had to sit here like a lemon, though.

"Don't," Herc said, squinting suspiciously at her.

"Don't what?"

"Don't do whatever it is that you're thinking about doing," he said. "Let Truck and Night handle it, kiddo, you'll be like a sitting duck out there. A duck with no legs or wings or . . . superpowers."

"That's probably the worst analogy I've ever heard," she muttered back, sliding the crossbow out of the pouch on her back. She'd lost three bolts in the hospital parking lot but she had two left, each one forged from the Engine. They were designed to stop the demons in their tracks, but they did a pretty good job of putting holes in Engineers too.

"Pan, I'm serious, Ostheim wouldn't want you out there."

"Ostheim can kiss it," she said. "You want to take down the enemy, you're gonna need more than a fat guy and his shadow. Give me that."

She nodded at the pistol holstered at Herc's waist. He shook his head, but it was more in resignation than denial, because he popped the stud and held it out.

"Safety's off," he said.

"Just the way I like it," she replied, grinning. Then, before he could say another word, she was out of the van. The sun was fierce, drumming on her skull as she ran across the street. People pushed past her but she ignored them, crossing the parking lot, the pistol cocked in her right hand and the bow held tight in her left. There was a soft explosion, a set of windows to her left detonating into shrapnel. She jogged toward them, seeing a classroom drenched in shadow. It was so dark inside that she could only make out an outline. No, *two* outlines, next to each other.

"That's enough," she heard one of them say. "Time to talk."

She lifted the gun, finger on the trigger. The man who had spoken saw her—his eyes glinting in the dark—and a second later both figures vanished, blasting out a shock wave of heat and air. Pan swore, jamming a finger to her collar radio.

"Contact, we've got a 'Porter. It's Patrick Rebarre. I lost him."

She looked right and left, waiting for them to reappear. Teleporters never went far, it was too draining, especially when they were carrying a passenger. There was another *whump* above her and she backed away, staring up the huge brick tower that made up the corner of the school. There, at the top, over the clockface, a figure dangling precariously over the edge. Pan swore again, clambering through the window into the school, blinking the last of the sun out of her eyes. She bolted across a classroom into the corridor beyond. To the right was the lobby and she could hear shouts inside, Truck's voice booming. She ignored it—the big guy could handle himself—cutting up a flight of steps, then another. The halls were deserted now, the fire alarm still screaming. She reached the top floor, her injured heart beating like a hummingbird's.

"Come on, come on," she growled, running one way then doubling back, finding a door with CLOCK stenciled on it. It was locked, but she aimed the pistol and fired off four shots, splinters of wood exploding. A solid kick forced it open and she ran up three more flights of stairs, bursting through the door at the top.

Patrick and Marlow were there, dark silhouettes against the day. She squeezed the trigger, the pistol bucking in her fist. Too slow. Patrick blinked out of sight with another concussive thump, leaving Marlow hanging there, his arms cartwheeling manically, his mouth open in an expression of terror as gravity reached up and grabbed him.

Leave him, her brain said. *He's trouble, he knows too much.*

But before she could even acknowledge what her head was saying she was halfway across the roof, diving like a fielder as the boy tumbled over the side. She skidded on her stomach, stretching as far as she could, thinking she'd missed him before his hand caught hers. He felt like an anchor, his momentum pulling her over. She dug in everything she could, the nails of her other hand gouging into the dust and filth of the roof, catching the bricks and holding her.

She screamed, the boy hanging from her arm, heavy enough to rip it from the socket like a turkey leg at Thanksgiving. Beneath them people swarmed like insects, so far down. Marlow struggled, swinging back and forth, his sneakers scuffing the brickwork as he tried to pull himself up. She couldn't hold him, no way. *Stupid stupid stupid,* she told herself, knowing that if she didn't cut him free he was going to drag them both to their deaths. But his hands were on hers now, clinging like barnacles. He looked like he was having trouble breathing, his face turning purple.

"Let go," she grunted.

"No way!" Marlow shot back. "Pull me up!"

She tried, the fingers of her left hand slipping on the roof, her body sliding closer to the edge.

"I *can't,* you have to let go."

Pop, a current of warm air. Pan looked back to see Patrick reappear on the roof. He tucked a strand of long blond hair behind his ear and grinned at her.

"That was stupid, Pan," he said.

Pan tried to shake Marlow loose but his fingers were a vise around her wrist. She scanned the floor. The crossbow was by the stairwell door, the pistol closer, but she had no hands to reach with. Patrick knew it, too, walking closer, never taking his eyes off her.

"The irony is we wanted him"—he nodded over the edge at Marlow—"to get to you. We thought he might be able to lead us to where you were hiding. You're so damn good at hiding."

He squatted down next to her, picking up the pistol and studying it like it was the first time he'd seen one.

"But here you are, you plonked yourself right in the palm of my hand." He sniffed the air. "And you don't even have a contract. Killing a kitten couldn't be easier."

"You'd know," Pan spat, fat beads of sweat dripping down her forehead, into her eyes. She didn't blink, though, didn't want to give him the satisfaction of seeing that she was afraid. "What are you waiting for, anyway? Not got the guts to pull the trigger?"

"Oh, I don't want you dead," he said, pointing the gun at her stomach. "That would be a waste of an asset. I know how much information you've got in that pretty little head of yours."

This was bad. *Better to die than let them take you,* she told herself. *They'll torture you, then kill you anyway. Let go, just drop. Three seconds, four at most, then it will all be over.* She was out of contract. If she died now, then the demons could never take her.

But she'd been too close to death too many times, and that gaping absence scared her almost as much as hell did. She tightened her grip on the bricks, the pain sharpening in her cramping fingers.

"Where's Ostheim?" Patrick asked, pushing the barrel of the gun into her ribs.

"With your mom," she said.

The boy laughed but there was no humor in his cold, blue eyes. He pushed the gun in farther, his finger twitching on the trigger.

"Not good enough," he said.

"Yeah, that's what Ostheim said."

"Last chance, Pan."

She laughed. Not because it was funny but because she wouldn't be able to tell him even if she did know. She had no idea where Ostheim was. Nobody did. Not even *Ostheim* knew where he was half the time. He traveled on a remote unit, never stopping for more than an hour, never broadcasting his location. It had been like that for as long as she'd been a Hellraiser. She'd never even met Ostheim. None of the Engineers had. What better way to protect the guy at the top than to keep the whole operation blind?

"Fine," the boy said, all trace of a smile now wiped clean. "You don't deserve to live anyway. One less piece of vermin in the world. Just remember, you—"

A streak of light blazed past and Patrick's head lurched back with a *crack*. He toppled onto his ass, spitting blood, the gun clattering away. There was another splintering crunch as something hit Patrick in the mouth. The blur skidded to a halt, taking the slim shape of Nightingale. She was panting, out of breath, which wasn't surprising, really, given she'd been running too fast to see. The boy was groaning, clutching his broken teeth. He lifted a hand and Pan felt the air twist and bubble as he prepared to teleport Night—probably into the middle of a tree, or a hundred yards into the air.

"Night!" Pan shouted, and the girl became a blur again, running in a circle around the roof and blasting up a whirl-wind of dust. With a look of pure fury, Patrick snapped out of existence. Night reappeared as she stopped running, staggered, looked for a moment like she was about to pass out, then walked to the edge of the roof. She grabbed Pan's arm, pulling hard. Pan grimaced, swinging Marlow up. The kid reached for the roof, missed, but on the second attempt he caught hold.

She almost didn't have the strength to pull herself up, but Night's skinny arms helped. She hauled her body onto the bricks and lay there for a moment, everything aching, feeling like she'd been stretched on the rack.

"Chu okay?" Night asked in her thick Spanish accent.

"Yeah, fine," Pan said, pushing herself up with arms that felt like tissue paper. "Thanks."

"*De nada,*" Night said, bouncing back and forth from one foot to the other. Nightingale couldn't stay still for more than a millisecond. "Where'd the *hijo de puta* go? 'Porters, always cowards."

"Anyone want to tell me what's going on?" said Marlow. He was sitting on the floor looking like he'd just gone ten rounds with Truck, his face drenched in sweat, his whole body trem-bling. He had his inhaler in one hand and was squeezing off shot after shot into his mouth. "You drugged me, right? This is . . . this is just some joke."

"Ha, ha, yeah, you got us. So funny!" she replied, deadpan. She turned to Nightingale. "Where's Truck?"

"Downstairs, other one's a Reader but he knocked her out cold."

A Mind Reader. They were brutal if they wanted to be, could control your thoughts, could make you strangle your own mother, then run under a bus. Pan set off across the roof, picking up the crossbow as she headed for the stairwell.

"That douche has probably 'ported down there, we'd better go help." She jammed a finger on her mic. "Hey, Truck, you there? I think the 'Porter's heading your way."

There was a hiss of static in her ear, then Truck's voice— *"You think?"*—almost lost in the rumble of an explosion. Pan could feel it in her feet, like the whole school was about to collapse. She broke into a run.

"Hey, what about me?" Marlow yelled behind her.

"Stay here if you want," she shouted over her shoulder. "But if you're planning on living out the day, I suggest you follow me."

FIGHT! FIGHT! FIGHT!

Marlow scrabbled to his feet, wondering for a moment if his lungs had fallen out while he'd been hanging over the roof. He'd pumped seven shots of his inhaler but he was still struggling to breathe. Some situations were so bad that even Ventolin couldn't help. *Yeah, like being thrown off the school tower by a guy who can teleport and then being saved by a girl who's just come back from the dead.* His mind must have fallen out, too, because he was pretty sure he'd lost it.

He wasn't crazy enough to stay here by himself, though. The girl might have looked like she wanted him dead, but she had risked her life to save him. The guy called Patrick had been about to homicide his ass.

He set off after the girl—*girls*, although the petite one seemed to have vanished again. He stumbled into the stairwell, clutching the banister hard because he didn't trust his shaking legs to hold him. By the time he reached the deserted ground floor hallway he could hear noises spilling out of the lobby, shouts and something that might have been a gunshot or an explosion. He turned, ready to flee, only to thump into somebody running the other way.

"Hey!" he yelled, panicking until he recognized Charlie's face. The relief of seeing him alive was almost overwhelming and before he even knew what he was doing he'd thrown himself at the boy, hugging him tight.

"What happened?" Marlow asked once Charlie had squirmed loose. "You disappeared."

"I have no idea," he replied. "One minute I'm kicking the crap outta that guy and the next I'm all the way up in the art room. Man, I black out or something?"

"Something," Marlow replied.

With an almighty crack the lobby doors blew off their hinges, tearing through a bank of lockers and cartwheeling down the hallway. Marlow dived out of the way, looked up to see that all hell had broken loose in there. The lobby looked like it was burning up, flames licking the walls and an upside-down flood of thick, black smoke billowing out. There were shapes in the chaos, forms that swept back and forth so fast and so erratically that they could have been made of shadow and smoke.

"Come on," said Charlie. "We gotta get out of here."

A burst of light burned its way into the hallway and suddenly Patrick was there, just yards away, engulfed in a ball of fire. He managed to shrug off his coat before a blurred shape streaked out of the lobby and thumped into him. They crashed into the wall hard enough to crack the plaster. Through the dust Marlow could make out the girl from the roof sitting on the guy's chest, her fists as fast as a pneumatic drill. Patrick managed to get a hand up but the girl was too fast, disappearing into a fizzing silhouette of light. The wall behind her vanished as if somebody had willed it out of existence. With a groan like a dying whale the ceiling cracked and drooped, the windows blowing out in a hail of glass.

Patrick struggled to his feet, barely sparing Marlow a glance. He ran for the hole in the wall but the girl blazed in front of him, tripping him and sending him sprawling. Then she was on his back, those hammer blows pummeling his face into the floor. Patrick growled and vanished, reappearing an instant later behind the girl. He looked exhausted but he had enough strength to grab her around the neck, choking off her cry. She pushed herself back, sending them both flying into another bank of lockers, caving a hole in the metal. But he didn't let go, squeezing so hard her face was turning blue.

"Hey!" Marlow shouted. "Get off her!"

Patrick didn't even hear him. Marlow started toward them, not sure what he was planning to do but knowing he had to do something. The smoke from the lobby curled into his lungs like fingers.

"Marlow," he heard Charlie behind him, "you crazy? Come on!"

There was another explosion from the lobby and Marlow turned to see a man bulldoze his way out of the fire. He was huge, like bigger-than-Yogi huge, and he had a face like a bulldog that had swallowed a mouthful of bees. He bowled down the hallway, gaining momentum with every step. The big guy reached out with a fist the size of a catcher's mitt, engulfing Patrick's face and hoisting him into the air. He threw the man like he was a rag doll, hard enough to punch him through the doors at the far end. Then he crouched down beside the girl, who was recovering her breath.

"You okay, Night?" he asked in a voice that rolled like thunder. She nodded, letting him help her up. Both the guy and the girl turned and looked at Marlow, dismissing him in a way that made him feel relieved and disappointed all at once. "I'll get Patrick," the guy said. "Go make sure Pan's all right."

They split up, but only for a second. After a couple of steps the big guy stopped walking, putting a hand to his head like he was in pain. He staggered, collapsing against the wall. Then he turned, lurching back the way he'd come. There was something different about his face, his mouth drooping, his eyes unfocused. And the way he walked reminded Marlow of the old zombie films. It was almost comical, until he drew level with Night and wrapped his tree-trunk arms around her in a bear hug. She screamed as he lifted her off the floor, struggling against him.

"Truck! Stop! What are you doing?"

"Not . . ." the big guy grunted. His nose was leaking blood. "Not . . . me . . ."

The girl was wriggling so furiously that she was just a blur again, like the guy was holding on to a mirage. It was making Marlow's eyes hurt just to look at it. He backed off a step, feeling Charlie's hands around his arm, tugging him.

The blond girl emerged from the lobby. Her face was bruised but her eyes were colder and more focused than ever. She was weaving her fingers in front of her, like before, whispering something under her breath. What had Pan said, up on the roof? That the girl was a *Reader*? Each movement of her hands held an invisible string, like she was a puppet master and the big guy was her plaything. He squeezed and something inside Night cracked like a pistol shot.

"Kill her," the girl was saying. "Kill her kill her kill her."

Marlow shook Charlie loose, grabbing the first thing he could see—a fire extinguisher. He wrenched the pin out of the handle like it was a grenade, then fired it. A white plume of carbon dioxide jetted out of the end and filled the corridor. He tried not to breathe it in but there was nothing he could do, the acrid taste filling his mouth, scouring his damaged lungs. He fired it again, marching forward and directing the flow right at the girl.

She coughed, using a shoulder to wipe her watering eyes. But her hands were still working away, pulling Truck's strings.

Marlow hefted the fire extinguisher above his head and charged at her, ready to KO her out of the equation.

He never got the chance.

The girl suddenly cried out, collapsing onto one knee. She put her fingers to her shoulder and Marlow could see some kind of arrow sticking out of her uniform, slick with her blood. Pan strode out of the lobby, reloading her crossbow as she went.

"Truck, you okay?" she said as she walked, lifting the bow and aiming it at the mousy girl's head. Truck was looking at his hands like he no longer trusted them, the girl called Night now lying in a puddle of quivering limbs at his feet.

"Yeah," he said. "Sorry."

Patrick's sister was trying to get back to her feet, one hand rising up, trembling like it belonged to an old woman. Marlow felt a pang of agony lance across the front of his head, realized he was staggering down the corridor toward Pan, somebody else at the wheel.

No! He barked the order at his brain and felt the girl's telepathic hold waver—not by much, but enough to let him wriggle free of it. He swung the extinguisher. It was a lucky shot, catching her in the temple and knocking her to the floor. She lay still, only the soft rise and fall of her chest letting him know he hadn't just become a killer.

His weapon hit the floor with a clang and he reached for his inhaler, shaking it. There wasn't much left. Another bout of vertigo hit him and he had to sit down on the ledge by the window to stop the world doing cartwheels. Charlie perched next to him, his face a mask of shock and disbelief, as if he'd just been pulled out of a car crash. Marlow guessed his own face looked exactly the same. Only it wasn't a car that had crashed, it was reality.

Pan reached the girl and toed her with her boot to make sure she was unconscious. She grabbed the crossbow bolt and tugged it free with a spurt of blood. Wiping it on her trousers, she slid it into her pocket, then held a hand out to Night.

"You good?" she asked, hauling the smaller girl up.

"I'm fine," Night wheezed, her voice a crone's cackle. She coughed, looking up at the big guy. "Not the first time he's got a little too friendly, right, Truck?"

"Hey," he said with a sheepish shrug. "What can I say, I'm a hugger." He looked over his shoulder toward the far end of the corridor. "We still got one loose, and he'll be . . . Yeah, I thought so."

All eyes turned to see Patrick stagger back through the doors. He looked like he'd been hit by a train, one arm hanging by his side—too loose, probably dislocated—the other feeling its way along the wall. Pan stepped to the front of the group, aiming her crossbow at him. It would have to be a good shot from here, maybe twenty yards between them.

"Let Brianna go," Patrick said, spitting out something that might have been a tooth. "Don't you dare . . ."

"Dare what?" Pan said, swinging the crossbow back until it was pointed right at the girl's head. "Kill her? Why not? You were going to kill me, kill us."

Patrick staggered forward a few more paces, grimacing. His good hand was flexing but whatever magic he had possessed before seemed to have dried up. He stopped halfway down the corridor.

"She's my sister," he said, almost pleading. "Give her back and we'll go, I promise."

"Too late," Pan replied. "You play the game, you take the pain. You can go. But she stays with us."

"Please," he said.

Pan tilted her head, like something had buzzed into her ear. She brushed at it with her free hand. Marlow could feel it too, a soft hum deep inside his skull, like when you could hear the subway rumbling through the grates. He shook his head, trying to ignore the sensation of something crawling inside his brain.

"You got three seconds," Pan said. "Get out of my sight or I swear to whoever built the Engines I'll put a bolt right through her head. One."

Patrick must have seen something in her expression because he straightened, his eyes so full of hate that they didn't look human. He pointed a finger at Pan and she shook her head in a warning.

"Uh-uh," she said, her head still twitching in discomfort. "That's two."

"Brianna, I'll come back for you, I promise," he said, almost in tears. Then, to Pan, "And you'll pay for this."

She snorted a bitter laugh.

"Yeah, we'll all pay for this. Goddammit what *is* that?"

The sensation was getting stronger, a tremor that seemed to fill up the whole corridor. What little glass was left in the windows was rattling, the rest trembling across the floor like a river of ice. It was more like a subway than ever, like there was a train hurtling their way. Only whatever was coming was worse than a train. Marlow could feel it in his gut, a sickness born of fear, some primal instinct demanding that he run, run and never stop. Everybody seemed to be feeling it, whatever it was, Pan and her friends casting nervous looks at each other. Marlow glanced at Charlie but he was wearing a thousand-yard stare, lost in the horror of the last twenty minutes.

Patrick started to back away, then his hands shot up to his head, clutching it like he was trying to stop it popping off his shoulders. He seemed to go three shades paler in as many seconds.

"No no no no," he muttered, staggering back. "No no please no no not yet no no no."

He looked back at Pan and this time his expression was one of pure horror.

"Get my sister out of here, *please*," he yelled. He turned so quickly he almost tripped on his own feet, pushing through the doors, his shrieks echoing back to them down the corridor.

"He's coming. He's coming. *He's coming!*"

His fear was contagious, Marlow's skin growing cold, his scalp tightening. He stood up, turning to Pan. She too was shaking her head, and when she looked back at him her eyes were wide and full of fear.

"Herc," she said, speaking into a radio on her collar. "Please tell me he's wrong."

She listened to a reply and collapsed against the ruined bank of lockers. The whole school seemed to be shaking now, like a giant steamroller was about to crush the building into dust. There was more buzzing inside Marlow's skull, a thousand bluebottles feasting on his brain.

"What's going on?" he asked. "Pan?"

She pushed herself off the lockers, stumbling away, her eyes never leaving Marlow's.

"He's coming," she said, her voice that of a child who hears something beneath her bed in the middle of the night. She looked about half her age, a little lost girl. "Oh god, he's coming."

"Who?" asked Marlow. The ceiling cracked overhead, filling the corridor with billowing clouds of dust, like it too needed to find a way out fast. "Pan, who?"

"*Him*," she said, the word just a sob. "*Mammon.*"

MAMMON

Pan had never felt fear like this before. Not even her first time in the Engine, sinking into the infernal blackness of the pit and not knowing whether she'd make it out alive. Not the first time she'd seen *it*, the creature that lived inside the machine, the one that craved her soul. Not the first time she'd seen the demons, hefting their bulk from the shattered remains of the world they possessed. Not even when she was a kid, watching her parents arguing, seeing her drunken father bunch up his fist and unleash his fury on her and her mother.

This fear was something else, something so unfamiliar that it was almost alien. It was a physical thing, a cold fire inside her stomach, a painful tickle like somebody's dirty fingers were burrowing between her vertebrae. Her head was a mess of white noise.

He was coming.

She forced herself to put one foot in front of the other, but even that was a struggle. Her body—her mind—was on the verge of a complete breakdown. All it wanted to do was lie down and die, because anything—literally anything—was better than seeing *him*. Her vision went dark, hallucinations of moldering flesh flashing up against the ruin of the corridor.

She tried to ignore them. Ostheim had warned her it would

be like this, if she was ever close to one of the Five. The Pentarchy were freaks, monsters who had used the Engine too many times. They weren't human, not anymore. They weren't Engineered, and they weren't demons. They were something horrific that lay in between. And Mammon was the worst, a force of utter wickedness who corrupted everything he touched. All he had to do was smile at you, Ostheim said, and your soul would rot.

Mammon.

Just thinking his name made the corridor shake more violently, the floor vibrating so hard that she almost lost her footing. She braced herself against the wall, screaming when she felt something soft and wet there, something *moving*. The plaster was crumbling away, a solid mass of maggots squirming beneath, like the building was made of them. She recoiled, watching as more of the façade fell away, unleashing a torrent of insects and spiders that poured to the floor. More dropped from the ceiling, pattering down onto her head like big, fat drops of rain. Something squirmed its way down the back of her suit and she almost gagged. It couldn't be real and yet it was—the Five made a mockery of physics.

"Pan?" A voice behind her, but she was panicking too much to care who it was. Herc was barking into her ear but the line was drenched in static. She ran, spiders crunching beneath her boots. The floor was growing soft, as if it was melting beneath the weight of so many moving bodies. Her feet began to stick and she had the awful feeling that she was trapped inside a nightmare, that soon she would be completely paralyzed.

"This way!" A hand under her arm, pulling her so hard that she was lifted off the ground, swung toward the window. It was Truck, with Brianna unconscious over one shoulder. A bead of blood wound its way down from his eye. "Move, Pan!"

He gave her a shove that almost catapulted her through the broken glass. She jumped onto the dying grass. It was too hot out here, the paint on the window frames blistering.

Somebody was screaming close by, an unbearable, endless shriek. She didn't blame them, whoever they were. The world was literally crumbling, dissolving. The school building was falling into pieces around them, bricks toppling from the tower, walls caving in like cardboard in a rainstorm. The ground was changing, creatures that might have been worms or leeches oozing up from the grass, from the soil, even from the concrete, wriggling pathetically as they roasted.

Pan.

Something said her name and the force of it almost knocked her to her knees. The word conjured up more visions of dead things, cadavers that lifted their skeletal fingers to point at her. She recognized her dead, the ones she had killed, or left to die, and she covered her face with her hands. It was too much, too much.

A hand on her back, guiding her. She opened her eyes to see Marlow there, and his friend. They ran, soft bodies erupting into pus beneath their feet. They turned the corner of the school—now nothing more than a column of crumbling brick—to see Herc there, standing beside the van waving them on manically.

"Do you want to die?" he yelled, and there was a madness in his eyes—a lunatic terror—that was somehow even worse than her own fear.

Why are you running, Pan? His voice, Mammon's, injected into her ears by a long, sharp needle. It was disjointed, the voice changing pitch from an adult's to a child's, a man's to a woman's, like a hundred people were speaking to her. *We have so much to talk about, you and I.*

"No," she said, digging her fingers into her temples. The

pain was good. Better to have a head full of agony than a head full of *him*.

"Ignore it," said Herc, running forward. He and Marlow hefted her into the van and she collapsed into a seat. The vehicle was shaking, the whole street rattling. "Get in, *now!*" Herc bellowed, waiting for the others to scramble inside before sliding the door shut. He jammed his foot on the gas and the vehicle lurched, the tires screaming on the asphalt.

The van didn't budge.

There's no need to hurry, said the voice, louder now, like it was whispering into her ear. Pan had to swivel around in her chair to make sure Mammon wasn't right behind her. She was almost relieved until she looked out of the rear window.

The street that led up to the school was changing, *widening*, like an invisible force was pushing the buildings to one side. No, not an invisible force. She could see something there in the center of it, a ball of blinding darkness that ground slowly up the street. There was a silhouette inside it, the vague shape of a man. And even though his face was obscured by impossible light, she could still see it, burning into her retinas— a cruel face, a joker's grin, and two lunatic black eyes overflowing like toppled ink pots.

There's nowhere to run, he said, that voice like a record being played at the wrong speed. *Come to me, I have so much to offer you.*

"Herc," she said, tasting blood in her mouth. "We need to go. *Now.*"

"Take off the parking brake!" Truck boomed, the van shaking but still rooted to the ground as the tires spun.

"It's off!" yelled Herc. He was crying, his foot stamping on the gas like he was trying to kick a hole through the bottom of the van. He swore, smashing his hands on the steering wheel.

137

Pan looked back. Clouds of black smoke plumed upward from the burning tires but through them she could see Mammon, so much closer now, hauling himself up the street like a leviathan. The buildings seemed to step out of his way, as if they would rather shake themselves into oblivion than block his path. Windows shattered, bricks exploding as they were forced sideward, the sidewalk shaking to dust and rippling like water. The sight made Pan think of an icebreaker shattering its way through reality.

There is nothing I can't do, he said, and there were sounds in her head, somebody licking their lips, a burst of insane laughter, a scream, a baby crying, all played at once like some sadistic sound track, threatening to deafen her. *There is no need to run.*

"Herc, please get this van moving," she said.

The engine was howling, threatening to blow. Through the back windshield Mammon was closer, that orb of light taking up the entire street. Somebody ran past the van, bumping into them, then staggering off into the cloud of dust. He had no eyes, Pan saw, just two holes in his head where they had been gouged away. She looked around her, saw the terror inside the van—Marlow and the other boy clawing at their own faces, trying to get Mammon out of their heads. Night was curled up into a ball beneath one of the chairs, sobbing. Truck was sitting there looking like he was about to have an aneurism, his eyes bulging, blood dripping from both of them.

"Herc, please!" she said. Because if they didn't start moving, then Mammon would be on them, and it would all be over. Ostheim was right: he could rip their souls apart with a touch, send them to the deepest, darkest parts of hell. Compared to him, the demons were old friends, almost gentle in their mindlessness. Mammon was pure, undiluted evil. Pan realized she was crying. "Please, Herc. I can't stand it."

I am your savior, Pan. You may not know it yet but you will. You will come to me.

"No! No!" she screamed into her hands, clutching her face and wishing wishing wishing for them to move. She heard feet, felt something pull at the harness on her back. When she opened her eyes she saw Marlow there, fumbling with her crossbow. He pushed past her, using the butt of the weapon to smash a hole in the rear windshield. Then he thrust the bow through, taking aim.

He was too low, it would fall short.

She reached out, slapping his arm up just as he took the shot. The bolt soared out and up, looked for a second like it was going wide. Then it punched through Mammon's bubble. Just a sliver of iron, no bigger than a pen. But the metal had been harvested from the Engine itself and it was powerful. There was a sudden flare of negative light, everything going black, like the sun had been turned inside out.

The van lurched forward, throwing Pan off her chair and into Marlow, both of them crumpled into a heap. The acceleration took her breath away and she held on to him as they skidded around a corner, then another, the van groaning as it shunted smaller vehicles out of the way.

You can't run forever, said Mammon, a hundred voices screaming from a madhouse. *I'll find you.*

They barreled around another corner and the voice faded, burned up by a burst of static.

I'll find you, and you will burn . . .

She burrowed her face into Marlow's chest, felt his arms lock tight around her, his chest heaving, wheezing, both of them sobbing into each other as they left the madness behind, that voice just an unbearable, whispered echo in the very center of her brain.

You will burn . . .

FRESH KILLS

Marlow didn't know how much later it was that the van shuddered to a halt. It might have been minutes, it felt like days. He lifted his head, the world gradually coming into focus. Pan lay beside him, her head resting on his chest, and she stirred too, blinking like she'd just woken. It only took a couple of seconds for her expression to harden and she scowled as she pushed him away. She looked in shock, though, her whole body trembling, her chattering teeth the loudest sound in the sudden quiet.

Marlow struggled up, groaning. He felt like he'd just run an Ironman race, every single muscle aching. He eased his head left, then right, the tendons so tight they might snap. He couldn't make out much from down here but he could see blue skies and he could hear seagulls, the soft lap of waves. Warm, musty air seeped in through the van's broken windows and he inhaled deeply, doing a good impression of bagpipes. He reached for his inhaler, pressing it until the tightness began to ease. How many shots were left? Ten, twenty at a push.

"Everyone okay?" Herc said softly, like he didn't want to give anyone a fright. He looked around, his pale face catching the light that streamed in through the windshield.

"Yeah," spat Pan. "I'm great, just dandy."

She pushed past the others, grabbing the handle and

pulling hard. The van must have taken a beating on the drive because the door was wedged tight.

"Truck?" Pan said. "You think you might want to make yourself useful for a change?"

The big guy didn't reply, just stared at something only he could see, his eyes crusted with dried blood, making it look like he was wearing clown makeup. Pan kicked him, and not gently.

"Hey, *Truck*, I'm talking to you."

He snapped out of his trance and it seemed to take him a moment to work out where he was. He lumbered to his feet, ducking low to stop his head going through the roof. Grunting, he gave the door a shove and it snapped off like it was made of plywood and clattered across the asphalt. Pan jumped out, standing in the sun, a breeze kicking up her short hair.

"You're welcome, Truck," said Truck, speaking in a falsetto that was still deeper than most men's voices. "I don't know what I'd do without you, Truck. Man, you're so strong, Truck. You're my hero, Truck."

The van rocked wildly on its suspension as he followed Pan. Night was next, taking Truck's outstretched hand as she skipped nimbly onto the pavement. Marlow wanted to go too—the van stank of smoke and sweat, reminding him of what he'd seen outside the school.

Yeah, said his head, *and what was that?*

It had seemed like the end of the world. Something unimaginable—literally, even now, knowing what he saw, he couldn't picture it. When he tried to look back all he could make out was a black hole in his memory, like somebody had gone at it with a pair of shears. He clamped his teeth around the skin of one dirty knuckle, chewing, grateful to the pain for distracting him.

"That was . . . something," said Charlie beside him. When

he turned to his friend now he barely recognized the boy. Charlie's face was drawn and haggard, his eyes so bloodshot they didn't look human. "Please tell me I was high."

Marlow would have laughed if he could remember how. Herc leaned over the back of the seat, studying the girl from the school—who was still out cold—and then them. His scarred brow creased into a frown.

"Please tell me I'm *still* high," said Charlie.

"You in one piece?" Herc asked Marlow. Marlow didn't know what to say, just nodded. As an afterthought he patted his legs, his chest, his crotch, just to make sure. Everything seemed to be where it was supposed to be. Herc coughed, wiping his mouth with his fist. "You know this guy."

"Who, Charlie?" Marlow said. "Yeah, of course. He's a friend."

"Shame," said Herc.

"Huh?" Marlow and Charlie asked together.

"Nothing. Come on." Herc rubbed the back of his neck, grumbling, then he popped open his door and stepped out. Marlow could hear him talking about a helicopter as he strode across the lot.

Marlow stood, gritting his teeth against the pain. He hadn't gone far before Charlie's arm shot out, grabbing his wrist. In the half-light of the van his eyes looked huge.

"Marlow," was all he said, but there was a question there. Marlow put a hand on top of his friend's, holding tight.

"It's okay," he said, then he snorted. "Actually, it's not okay, not even close. I can't explain it, but these guys can."

He helped Charlie up and they crept across the van, jumping down into a small parking lot. His nose told him where he was before his eyes, the instantly recognizable bittersweet aroma of the Fresh Kills landfill. The van was parked by the river, shielded by a platoon of bulldozers and a mountain of warehouses beyond. On the other side of the water were the rolling hills, trees, and wildflowers of the Island of Meadows, and just looking at them made Marlow's chest feel a little looser, like he was standing in the countryside and not on the ass end of Staten Island. He took a deep breath through his nose, held it, then exhaled through his mouth—something his mom had taught him to do when he felt an attack coming on, when he needed to calm down. It sounded a bit like he was playing a kazoo.

Everyone was milling around, a collective unwinding. Pan stood right on the edge of the dock, hands on her hips, staring at the horizon, and even after what he'd seen, even though everything he thought he knew was falling apart, he couldn't help but admire the sight.

"Yeah, now I know how you got embroiled in this mess," said Charlie. The smallest of smiles danced around his mouth, a butterfly looking to land. Marlow felt his cheeks heat up and he waved his friend's words away. Charlie breathed a laugh through his nose. "Always told you chasing tail would land you in trouble, just didn't imagine it quite like this."

"Tell me about it," said Marlow.

"I thought you said you weren't interested," said Herc. He was stooped over against the van, looking even older than he had when Marlow had first met him. Out here, in the sun, each of his scars seemed to glow. There were so many of them that he looked like he'd been sewn together from scraps of other people's skin. "In door number one."

"Please tell me what he's talking about," said Charlie.

"Why don't you?" Marlow asked. "Tell us, I mean. I think we deserve it. Saved your asses back there."

Herc nodded reluctantly.

"Hey, Pan," he said. She didn't reply and he shouted her name again, three times, until she turned and glared at him.

"What?"

"I think we need to talk."

"Yeah?" Pan said, marching toward them. Her face was so full of rage that Marlow took a subtle step back, shielding himself behind Charlie. "About what? About the fact that *he* was there? About the fact that he nearly caught us. Jesus Christ, Herc, what the hell was Ostheim thinking? He landed us right in it just so we could use this scrawny asshole as bait, just because there was a small chance we might catch a fish."

"Wait, *what?*" said Marlow.

She ignored him, jabbing a finger at Herc. "He had no right to do that. You know what would have happened, another five seconds and we'd be finished. We'd be worse than dead, Herc."

She wiped her eyes with her hand, tears leaving trails in the dirt on her face.

"Five more seconds. First Forrest, now this. He's getting dangerous, Herc. Ostheim's risking everything. He's going to send us all to hell."

Herc sighed again, toeing the dirt with his boot.

"Who was he?" Marlow asked. "I mean, what. Or who. I don't know."

"Oh," said Pan, shooting him a look that could have left an exit wound the size of a fist in the back of his skull. "You suddenly decided you want in? Last thing I remember is you clucking out the door like a chicken."

"Yeah?" Marlow snapped back. "Last thing I remember is using a beat-up crossbow from World of Warcraft to shoot some bug-eyed freak in a big-ass evil bubble cloud."

They eyeballed each other for a moment, the anger boiling up from Marlow's gut. His hands hurt and he realized that his fists were balled so tight that his nails were digging into his palms. He wasn't sure whether he wanted to punch the girl or kiss her.

"No you didn't," she said. "You were about to shoot yourself in the foot. Lucky I was there."

Definitely punch her.

"Why do I feel like I'm missing the joke?" said Charlie. "What happened with you guys?"

"No," Marlow said, waving his hands in the air like a conductor. "Just start from the beginning. Tell me the stuff you forgot to mention the other day. I need to know."

Herc and Pan shared a look.

"You sure you're ready?" Herc asked. "You won't believe it."

Marlow laughed, but there was no humor there. After what he'd seen in the last forty-eight hours or so it was impossible to know what he believed. Herc took a step back and looked expectantly at Pan. She seemed about to argue, then her shoulders sagged and she stared back out at the horizon. It took her an age to start speaking.

"What would you say if I told you there was a machine that could grant any wish?"

"I'd say wait right there while I call the DEA," said Charlie. "Because you're obviously smoking something pretty whack."

Nobody laughed. Pan didn't even acknowledge the comment.

"A machine that can do anything," she went on. "That can make you . . . superhuman."

"Come on," said Charlie. "That's bullsh—"

"Truck," Pan yelled across the parking lot. The big guy was leaning against a bulldozer, sipping water from a bottle. "Show them, like they haven't already seen it."

Truck swallowed, replaced the cap on the bottle, then grabbed the bulldozer by its caterpillar tracks and lifted. It tilted up at a forty-five degree angle, the frame groaning in outrage. He held it for a few seconds, then let it go. It crashed back down, swaying back and forth like a rocking chair. Truck wasn't even breaking a sweat, just went back to his drink.

"Got no sense of adventure, that guy," Pan said. "Same deal every time. Hey, Night," she called to the girl sitting on the dock. "Got a sec?"

Night nodded, then in a sudden blur of motion she was right next to them. Charlie actually squealed, staggering back in shock. Even though Marlow had witnessed it in the school he had to clamp his mouth shut to stop his jaw landing on his toes. Here, in broad daylight, away from the panic and the violence, it was just insane. What he was seeing was impossible. Nobody could move like that—the sheer force of acceleration would snap your neck like a twig.

"What?" Night said, panting slightly.

"Nothing," Pan replied. Night frowned, mouthed *whatever*, then sped back to the riverside, a blur of color that reminded Marlow of a kingfisher he'd seen once on television.

"This can't be . . . It *can't* be real, Marlow," said Charlie. He didn't look shocked anymore, or even surprised. He just looked sad, like somebody who's discovered the universe has been playing a trick on them.

"It's real," said Pan, walking to the van, checking on the girl inside, then pulling a bottle of water from a duffel bag. She chucked it to Marlow and he snatched it out of the air, screwing off the cap and taking a deep pull. Only now did he realize how thirsty he'd been, his mouth like sandpaper, so dry that it crackled as the water filled it. He downed three-quarters of the bottle before remembering Charlie, handing the rest to him. He took it but didn't drink, just let it hang by his side as Pan rejoined them.

146

"But how?" Marlow asked, feeling like his batteries had been recharged, the water making everything less fuzzy.

"The truth is, we're not sure," Pan said. "All we know is that this machine, the Engine, it's something older than time, something that . . . that doesn't belong in this world. It was discovered during the war, beneath the streets of old Europe. Nobody knows who built it. To be honest, nobody even knows how anyone *could* build it. So far we've counted over eight hundred million moving parts, and there are sections of the machine we've not even gotten near yet."

"A machine?" said Marlow. "I don't get it."

"Then maybe let me finish?" Pan said. Marlow held up his hands in surrender.

"The Engine . . . It's hard to describe, you need to see it for yourself. There are so many moving parts it's more like a . . . like a creature than a machine. It's almost intelligent." She shuddered and Marlow could see the goose bumps erupt on her arms. She rubbed them away, still staring into space. "It can give you anything. All you have to do is wish for it. Strength, like Truck, or the ability to run faster than sound, like Nightingale there. I've been invisible, I've had the ability to read minds, to *control* them. I've been able to fly." She smiled, obviously remembering something good.

"You've come back from the dead," said Marlow, and her smile vanished like a mouse that's seen a hawk's shadow. She glared at him like it was his fault, then nodded.

"Yeah, it can do that too. It can do pretty much anything."

"But how?" asked Charlie. "How is that possible?"

"Because it's not something human," she replied.

"Alien?" Charlie said.

Pan shook her head. "No. Not that we can work out anyway. Not alien."

"Then what?" said Marlow.

"Something worse," she said. "You ever heard of *Faust*?"

The name rang a bell but Marlow couldn't remember from where.

"Sounds like a player," said Charlie.

Pan shook her head in disgust.

"It's a story," she said. "About a guy who makes a deal with Satan."

"And what's that got to do with . . ." Marlow started, then frowned. It felt like something dark and cold had burst inside his stomach. "Wait, what are you saying?"

Pan kicked the dirt, wiped her nose with the back of her hand. Her eyes caught the sun and there might have been tears there.

"It's what the Engine does," she said. "It lets you make a deal with the Devil."

SHE'S EXPIRING

For a while the only sound was the distant roar of traffic from the expressway and the lazy rush of Fresh Kills River. Then Marlow's friend, the boy called Charlie, laughed. It was high-pitched and desperate, and there was a hint of lunacy in it. Pan knew the sound, she'd made pretty much the same one when she'd first been told about the Engine. She'd also told Herc to go screw himself and various members of his family, then slapped him across the face for wasting her time. She looked at the old guy and smiled warmly. Seemed like an eternity ago that he'd walked into her cell and told her she had choices.

It wasn't easy to hear, though, she knew that much. Marlow and Charlie were staring at her with big, vacant expressions. She knew exactly what they were thinking. She would have felt sorry for them if her heart had been whole.

"The Devil?" said Marlow.

"It's not . . ." How had Herc explained it to her, all those years ago? "It's not the Devil, not the way you think. It's not something you'll ever find in the Bible. It's something older than that, something nobody really understands. The Devil's just a name for it. All we know is that you make a deal with the Engine. You ask it for whatever you want and it grants your wish. But not forever. You get twenty-seven days and change."

"Twenty-seven days," said Charlie. "Random."

"Six hundred and sixty-six hours, to be precise," she said.

"Then what?" Marlow asked. "You lose your . . . your powers?"

If only it were that simple.

"No, you don't lose them, you keep them till the end. Not that they'll do you much good. No, you make a contract with the machine, a contract signed in blood. You get whatever your heart desires for six hundred and sixty-six hours. Then, when the contract expires, you pay up."

"Pay up?" Marlow and Charlie asked together.

"With your life," she said. "And . . . and something else, too."

"There's something worse than losing your life?" snorted Marlow.

"Yeah," said Pan, turning and looking at the river, at the island beyond. It looked like a paradise now, flowers and trees and switchgrass. But she knew that underneath lay half a century of trash and rubble and ruin. *Just like my world,* she thought. *Everything looks okay, but scratch the surface and there are horrors there, things that you could never have imagined.* And once again she thought of Mammon, heaving himself up the road, just too big, too powerful to fit in this universe.

"What's worse than that?" Charlie asked.

"It takes your soul," she said eventually, knowing how stupid it sounded even though she'd almost lost hers so many times. Charlie laughed again, and even Marlow was smiling. A solar flare of anger erupted inside her head but she bit down hard. "Why is that so hard to believe? You've seen them, the demons. You've seen them with your own eyes."

"The things in the parking lot," Marlow said, "they were *demons*?"

"It's just our word for them," Pan said. "We don't know what they are. All we know is that you do not want to let your contract expire, because that's when they come. They can't exist in this world, they can only possess things."

"Like the Exorcist?" Marlow asked.

"Kind of," she said. "But like the opposite too. They can't possess anything living. They can't get inside you or another human or an animal. Not even a plant."

"Yeah, I remember," Marlow said. "They were coming out of the walls, out of cars."

"Not out of them, they were made *from* them." Pan closed her eyes and saw them there, clawing their way from the ground, from tables and chairs, from trucks, from anything and everything. "They can only possess inanimate objects, things without a soul. But that's worse, that's a whole lot worse, because you cannot hide from them. There is no place on Earth you can be safe."

"But you can kill them, right?" asked Marlow. "I saw you."

"No," she said, shaking her head. "Once your contract is up you're finished. You still have your powers, right up until you die, so you can fight them off for a while. But only for a while, no power can keep them at bay forever. Shotguns slow them down, but you have to blast the hell out of whatever they've possessed—*literally* blast the hell. It takes a huge amount of energy for them to form in this world, this plane. They're strong, but only as strong as the material they possess. If you destroy the host, then you destroy the parasite—but only for as long as it takes the demon to build up the energy to cross over again for another possession. You can hold them off for a while, but you're only delaying the inevitable. If your time is up, they *will* take you."

"Take you where?" Marlow asked. Pan shrugged. She'd asked Herc the same question. She'd asked Ostheim too. The truth was that nobody knew, but she had a good enough idea. She'd seen it too many times, the demons dragging you into the molten earth, into the fire. She'd felt it too, the other day when she thought her time had come. A huge, gaping, burning emptiness, the weight of eternity on her shoulders.

"Take you somewhere you really don't want to be," she said.

There was a moment of silence, broken only by a meaty fart from Truck's direction. It didn't do much to relieve the tension.

"So how come you're still here?" Marlow asked. "How come the demons didn't take you the other day? You survived."

"I survived because my contract was broken," she said.

"Broken?"

This was always the hardest part to explain. Pan took a deep breath.

"The Engine is a machine. It brokers a contract. Years ago, centuries, when the machine was first built, the contracts were unbreakable. I mean, there are so many moving parts, so many variables, that nobody would have been able to crack the deal. But things have changed. Technology has improved. We've cataloged the machine, we've made digital maps of every section—well, the sections we use—we have a much greater understanding of how it works and a team of Lawyers who work nonstop to break the contract before it expires."

"Lawyers?" Charlie asked.

"Anyone else hear an echo out here?" she said. "Yes, Lawyers. But not like ambulance chasers or suits. These are more like . . . They're essentially quantum mathematicians. Cleverest guys on the planet, probably. We just call them Lawyers because it annoys the hell out of them."

"And they, what? Take the Engine to court, get a restraining order?" Marlow said.

He turned away and she locked her reply deep in her throat. Arguing wasn't going to help anyone right now.

"You've seen it," Pan said. "You want the truth, just *think*. How else is any of this possible?"

"And what about the thing that chased us up the road?" Marlow asked. "That a demon too?"

Pan sighed. "No, not quite. Mammon is something else entirely, something—"

"Hey!" It was Herc, yelling from the van. He clapped his big hands together. "Enough with the socializing, our guest's waking up."

Pan jogged over, peering into the darkness to see that Brianna was starting to stir. Her blond hair was a mess, her clothes filthy and torn. She sat up, blinking away sleep, and Pan saw the moment of blissful unawareness before her memory clunked back into place. She scooted back on her ass, hitting the back of the van. Her brow furrowed and Pan felt a stab of pain in the left-hand side of her brain. Herc must have felt something too because he unholstered his pistol and aimed it at her head.

"Don't even think about it," he said, clicking back the hammer. "I feel so much as a probe up there and we'll be reading *your* mind when we wash it off the back of the van, understand?"

The pain in Pan's head vanished as the girl nodded.

"Brianna," Pan said. She looked at Pan, a rabbit in the headlights. Truck appeared, blocking out the light. Night was there, too. Pan reached in and grabbed another bottle of water from the duffel bag and offered it to the girl. "Thirsty?" Brianna shook her head like she'd been offered a bottle of poison.

"She's young," said Night. "Too young to be fighting for *them*."

"I'm seventeen," the girl replied, showing none of the confidence she'd had back in the school. "Just."

"Well, happy goddamned birthday," Herc said. "You must know what's going to happen now."

"You're gonna ask me questions," she said, some of that bluster returning. "And I'm going to lie."

"Then we're gonna stop asking so nicely," Pan said. "Where is your Engine?"

"You should know," the girl said. "It's up your butt."

"Where is Mammon?"

"Coming for you," she said, meeting Pan's eyes, not blinking. "He knows all about you, all of you. He's going to end you."

"Yeah?" said Pan. "From what I saw back there he couldn't even get his fat ass up the street."

But something in her expression must have given away her fear because Brianna smiled.

"He'll eat you alive," she said. "I just wish I could be there to see it."

"Why won't you be?" asked Herc. "Got a vacation planned?"

She just shrugged, sadly, and glanced at her watch. It must have been broken, because she rattled it, then looked up and asked, "Anyone got the time?"

"Yeah," said Herc. "Time you woke up, kiddo. Mammon's got his agenda but you don't have to be a part of it. There are other ways of doing things."

"Like *your* way?" she said, looking at Herc as if he were a piece of dog crap she was cleaning off her shoe. "I'd rather die."

"Yeah?" Pan said, resisting the urge to reach for her crossbow and grant the girl's wish. "You guys make me sick. You've got all the power in the world and you live like this, you waste it."

Chaos, bloodshed, rot, and ruin. It's all the Circle cared about.

"All you have to do is give us the location," said Herc. "Last chance."

"She's never going to do it," said Pan. "It won't even matter if she does. She could tell us exactly where it is, longitude and latitude, and we won't find it. How many times do we have to do this dance? Tell us about Mammon. How can we find him, and how do we kill him?"

"You don't need to find him," she said. "He'll find you. I told you, he's going to find your Engine, and when he does this will all be over. Please, does somebody have the time?"

The fuse on Pan's patience burned up and the fury detonated in her gut. She reached out and snatched Herc's gun from his sweaty hand before he even saw it coming, stepping into the van and pressing the weapon against the girl's temple. She hissed with pain but the look she gave Pan showed no sign of weakness.

"Mammon," Pan said. "Now."

"Pan!" Herc said, but she ignored him. Having one of the enemy right here, at their mercy, was a rarity. They had to make the most of it.

"Go on," said the girl. "Do it."

"You're willing to die for him?" Pan asked.

"I'd do anything for him," Brianna said. "Anything to stop you—stop Ostheim—getting what he wants. Now, *please*, would somebody tell me what the time is."

It suddenly clicked, why she was so desperate to know.

"Oh *crap*," Pan said, lowering the gun and hopping out of the van. "She's expiring."

"*Now?*" asked Herc, swearing. He started to back away. "Not in the van *goddammit*."

Pan stood by the door, refusing to believe it. There was no way the Circulus Inferni would let her expire, not like this. Mindreading was an easy contract to break, one of the easiest. The Circle's Lawyers would have no trouble. Mammon was an evil bastard but surely even he wouldn't give up one of his own without a fight. Brianna looked up, her eyes full of a sad, tired resignation.

"You're fighting for the wrong side," she said. "Mammon would welcome you. He welcomes everyone."

"Yeah," said Pan. "I can see how much he cares. He's going to let you expire."

Brianna shrugged.

"Happens to us all, eventually."

"Not like this, though," said Pan, and she had to bite down on her lip to stop the lump in her throat from exploding out of her mouth. "Not like this."

There was a crack of static as loud as a pistol shot, powerful enough to dent the van and rock it hard on its suspension. Brianna let loose a scream, clamping her hand to her mouth. Everyone scattered but Pan held her ground, even as the ground beneath her trembled and cracked. It was like the earth was splitting in two.

"He can't do this," she said. "It's not right."

A bolt of brilliant blue light fizzed past her, a rip in reality that breathed out a blast of hot air. Pan gagged against the stench of sulfur, staggering away and wiping the tears from her eyes. There was another crunch, an invisible fist hammering a crater into the roof of the van. One of the tires exploded, the headlights shattered. Pan looked into the growing darkness, Brianna just a lump of shadow with two diamond-bright eyes. She stared back, full of fear, full of defiance.

"Last chance," Pan said. "You don't have to die for nothing."

"I'm not," she replied, her voice almost lost in a growl of thunder. "I'm dying for *him*. He saved me. He'll save us all."

"He's sending you to hell," Pan said, then she had to throw her hand in front of her face against an explosion of light. A shock wave hit her in the chest like a tackle and she lost her footing, landing painfully on her back and rolling in the dirt. She felt hands under her armpits, dragging her away, and by the time she'd opened her eyes again it was over.

At first it looked like the van was inside a compactor, the metal crumpling like tin foil, shrinking. Then something began to pull itself free of the wreck, a vaguely bestial shape with a head made up of the wheel arch and half a tire, the body formed of the back bumper. It unfolded with an ear-shredding metallic squeal, the whole rear of the vehicle tearing away. The demon shook itself like a dog, gas spurting from the ruptured fuel line and pooling on the asphalt.

Something else was rising from the ground like a corpse dragging itself out of its grave. It looked like a turtle, a shell of asphalt over a body of orange dirt. A metal pipe ran the length of its midsection like it had been speared. It wriggled, its legs thrashing, until the pipe snapped free, then it hauled itself out of the hole, opened a maw of concrete, and screamed.

"Jesus Christ." Pan heard Marlow's voice by her side and glanced at him, seeing the terror etched into his face. He was chewing his knuckles like he hadn't eaten in a month. She ignored him, turning back to the van.

"They won't hurt you," Herc told the boy. "Not unless you get in between them and her. They only want what they're owed."

Her soul.

The metal demon sniffed the air, then darted forward like a scorpion, pushing its snout into the gaping hole at the back of the van. Brianna groaned, jumping out of the door and making a run for it. Both demons howled, like dogs catching scent of their prey—a noise like a thousand fingernails being dragged down a blackboard. Pan slammed her hands to her ears and gritted her teeth against it. Every fiber of her being was telling her to go, to get the hell out of here before the demons discovered she was there. But Herc was right: they wouldn't come for her, not this time.

"Can't we do something?" Marlow said. "Help her!"

Brianna skidded around the front of the van, almost tripping. The concrete demon reared up in front of her, twelve, thirteen feet tall, showering the parking lot with dirt. It swung a fist made of rock and Brianna only just managed to duck beneath it. It struck the remains of the van and sent it rolling across the ground, spraying glass and shrapnel. The girl scrabbled on her hands and knees but she only made it a dozen yards before the van demon caught up with her.

"Please," Marlow said.

"There's nothing we can do," Pan replied, her voice made of ice. "She signed a contract."

The demon clamped a hand around Brianna's chest, hoisting her into the air. The girl tried to scream, batting her hands pathetically against the metal fist. The dirt demon loped over, uttering another hellish screech. Already the ground was growing soft beneath them, the skeletal remains of the van starting to sink into the melting asphalt, the spilled gas bursting into flame.

I'm sorry, Pan said, knowing that Brianna still had the ability to hear her. *It should never be like this.*

Brianna stopped struggling and looked right at Pan with those red-rimmed eyes. She breathed in a long, desperate breath. Then she spoke, and even from where Pan stood, even over the deafening clatter of the demons and the roar of the fire, Pan could hear her.

"I'll see you in hell."

The metal demon's jaws snapped shut around the girl like a bear trap, cutting her in two. The other demon attacked, its gaping maw engulfing her. All three of them were sinking into the earth, the air dancing around them, so hot that Brianna's blood ignited, hissing and steaming. Pan wanted to turn away but she forced herself to watch as the demons fought over the girl, devouring her like wild dogs until all that remained were charred scraps of meat.

Then, just like that, it was over. Brianna vanished beneath the scorched earth. The demons collapsed like marionettes whose strings had been cut, the metal one crashing to the ground, the other one dissolving in a hail of dirt. The parking lot fell quiet, the ground becoming solid once again, but Pan swore she could still hear Brianna, a distant, unending scream as the very essence of her was dragged into the depths.

Only when that, too, had faded did Pan finally close her eyes, and start to cry.

GOODBYES

Marlow couldn't speak. He couldn't move.

He had the absurd idea that he was in an open-air theater, watching some kind of sick show. If he spoke, then the illusion would be over, and the alternative was just too awful to think about. Even though he'd seen it twice now—the demons appearing out of nowhere, each time to murder a girl— he couldn't believe it.

He noticed that he was holding somebody's hand, his fingers locked tight in a sweaty grip. He looked to see Charlie there, pale and drawn, his eyes as wide as moons. His teeth were chattering. Marlow felt awkward but he didn't let go. He thought that if he did, then it would be like weighing anchor—he might just float away. The laws of physics had been well and truly obliterated, after all.

He wasn't sure how long they stood there, the six of them. Nobody spoke, nobody really made any noise at all apart from Pan's soft, desperate sobs. They all just stared at the parking lot. The two mounds of metal and dirt lay still, just bits and pieces of a broken world, and it was almost impossible to believe that they had ever possessed life. The splashes of crimson—the brightest thing in sight—spattered across the ravaged concrete were the only evidence of what had happened, that and the ribbons of torn cloth that drifted across the lot, kicked along by the wind. They looked like they were trying to escape.

It was Herc who broke the tableau. He coughed gently, a noise that seemed to make everybody flinch. Then he walked to Pan's side and wrapped her in his big arms, pulling her head onto his chest.

"Nothing you could have done," he said. "Not your fault."

She pulled loose and gave him an angry shove, wiping away tears with the back of her arm.

"It's *his* fault," she said, spitting. "Mammon just let her die."

"And you're surprised?" rumbled Truck. "You know he'd kill off every one of his Engineers, every one of his Lawyers, if it kept him safe." He smacked a giant fist into a palm and sent a clap of thunder out across the parking lot. It echoed back off the warehouses. "Coward."

"You think Ostheim would have done any different?" asked Night, kicking at a loose stone. "You think he'd risk it?"

"No way Ostheim would let us die like that," Pan said, but even Marlow noticed the hesitation there, the uncertainty.

"You're forgetting that this is a war," said Herc. "We're soldiers, nothing more. Soldiers die."

"Gee, thanks for the pep talk," muttered Truck, turning away and walking to the river. Night followed him, treading in his shadow.

"Marlow," said Charlie, a voice that was broken into a thousand pieces.

"Yeah?"

"This is a dream, right? I'm . . . I mean, this can't actually be happening."

"Kid, believe me," said Herc. "This is about as real as it gets."

Herc turned to them, running a hand through his graying buzz cut.

"So, looks like we're right back here again," he said. "Choices."

"Choices," said Marlow. "Yeah, okay. You mean choose *that*, choose the same thing that happened to her? No thanks."

"Did Pan tell you why we do what we do?" he asked after a moment.

"No," said Marlow. "Just about the Engine, about the—"

"We do what we do because if we didn't, the whole world would look like that."

He jabbed his thumb over his shoulder. Marlow looked at the van, at the pools of blood that were evaporating in the heat. A pocket of dust crumbled free from the dead demon and he jumped like he'd had an electric shock, a wave of nausea rushing over him and leaving him coated in cold sweat.

"What do you mean?" asked Charlie. Herc sighed.

"I don't have time for the whole story. We gotta move, chopper should be inbound." He chewed his lip, his brow furrowed in concentration. "Our Engine, it's not the only one in existence. There are two that we know of for sure. They have one, Mammon and the Circulus Inferni."

"Yeah," said Marlow. "I got that much."

"The Engines, they were designed by the same person, the same force, whatever you want to call it. They both have the same powers, the ability to grant you any wish. They both ask for the same price in return. But we use them for very, very different purposes."

Marlow could make out a very soft rumble in the distance, the throb of a helicopter. Herc heard it too, and when he spoke again it was faster, full of impatience.

"Cut a long story short, Mammon recruits his Engineers to cause havoc, to destroy lives, to kill innocents. His goal . . ." Herc shook his head, his expression full of disgust. "He wants an end to everything, he wants the demons to spill out of the pit and consume the entire world. He wants hell on Earth, literally."

"And the Engine can do that?" asked Marlow. "How?"

The chopper was getting closer, a pulse of noise that seemed to fill the whole sky. Herc glanced at his watch, then over at Truck.

"Prepare for exfil. Pop a smoke." He turned back to Marlow. "Yeah, the Engines can do that. Fortunately for us he hasn't worked out how yet. It's our job to make sure that never happens."

"So, you're basically trying to save the world?" Marlow asked, feeling his eyebrow creep up in disbelief. Herc shrugged.

"Yep, that's us. Goddamned heroes."

Herc walked to what was left of the van, rummaging around inside the wreck. Truck had set off a canister of red smoke, which curled lazily up into the summer sky. Marlow stared at it, mesmerized for a moment, then turned his attention to Pan.

"Is it true?" he asked. "You do what you do to save the world?"

Pan just scoffed. "This world is already screwed, with or without the Engine. But yeah, it's our job to stop Mammon opening the gates of hell and filling the streets with freaks."

A shudder ripped through Marlow's body at the thought of it, hundreds of demons, maybe thousands, *tens* of thousands, tearing their way into the world. *We wouldn't stand a chance.* Herc must have found what he was looking for because he walked back over, a small black pouch in his hands.

"You in or out?" he asked.

"You mean, come fight with you?" said Charlie. "Like her? Like these guys?"

Herc nodded. Charlie turned to Marlow, shrugging.

"Gotta be better than school, right?" he said.

"No," Marlow replied. "No way, Charlie. You got your life on track, you're doing good, you can't give it up."

It was the truth. Charlie had turned his life around in Victor G.—good grades, the promise of a scholarship. He'd put the bad times behind him, had something positive to look forward to if he didn't screw it up.

"Man, you think I can go back after this?" he said. "After what we've seen?"

"You really want to die like her?" Marlow said. "Torn to pieces, dragged to wherever she went. Come on, man, it's my fault we're here, I shouldn't have brought you with me. You can't ruin the rest of your life because of me."

"So what?" he said, squaring up. "You think you deserve this and I don't?"

"*Deserve* it?" Marlow said, not backing down. "Charlie, I got nothing. Kicked out of school, got the police after me. What do I have left? Go live with my mom for the rest of my days, work at the plant slinging cement? You don't understand, man, this is my one shot at doing something good."

"Don't you dare," said Charlie, pointing a finger at Marlow. "Every time, dude, every single time, you just dump me, run off without me. Not again. We do this, we do it together."

Herc was fiddling with the bag, unzipping it and peering inside. He pulled out something long and thin that glinted in the sun. Marlow recognized it straightaway, the sight making him feel sick to his stomach. A hypodermic, probably filled with concentrated alcohol. Charlie was too focused on Marlow to notice.

"Not again, man," he said. "Not this time."

"Got to have an answer," Herc said. The chopper sound was palpable now, a second heartbeat inside Marlow's skin. He looked up to see a black speck against the blue. "Yes or no."

"Yes," Charlie said at the same time that Marlow said, "No, not him, just me."

"Marlow," said Charlie. "Please. You're my best friend, my only friend. I need you, I need *this*."

Marlow's stomach was doing somersaults, something fat crawling up and sitting in his throat. The thought of saying goodbye just about snapped his heart in two but he knew there was no other way. He pictured Charlie being chewed into bloody pieces. No way, he couldn't do it.

"Please, dude," Charlie said. "Let's do this together."

"No," said Marlow. He looked at Herc and nodded. "Just me," he repeated.

Herc stepped up behind Charlie and jabbed the needle into his neck. Charlie yelped, grabbing the wound and staggering back. His expression twisted, his eyes full of disbelief.

"What have you done?" he said to Marlow.

"It's okay, man, it's just alcohol. Just relax, it will be okay."

He walked to Charlie but the other boy staggered away, looking at Marlow like he'd stabbed him in the back.

"You bastard," he said, his words starting to slur. "How could you? You were my friend, Marlow, you were my *friend*. You think they're gonna want you when they find out the truth? Find out you're a coward?"

Charlie stumbled, dropping onto his ass, his eyes losing focus. Marlow ran to him, cradling him in his arms, wondering if it was too late to change his mind. The chopper was almost at them, flying low over the river and blasting out a mind-numbing pulse. It hovered over the parking lot, kicking up a tsunami of dust as it spun around and slowly touched down. Pan looked at it, then at Marlow.

"You really gonna take him?" Marlow heard her say.

"Why not?" Herc replied.

"He'll be a nightmare. You won't be able to control him."

"Funny, Pan," said Herc, replacing the needle in the pouch, "that's what everyone said about you."

"He's a hothead. He'll get somebody killed."

"Yep, they said that about you too."

"He won't do what he's told. I can tell. He'll do the *opposite* of what he's told."

Herc turned to look at her. "Pan, can you hear the words coming out of your mouth?"

"He's nothing like me," she said, glaring at Marlow.

"No, nothing like you," Herc said, turning to the chopper. The door slid open, revealing the moose-faced guy, Bullwinkle. "Absolutely completely one hundred percent nothing at all like you. Come on."

Pan grumbled something else and jogged to the helicopter, Truck and Night following her.

"Time to go," said Herc. "Best say goodbye, you won't see him again."

Charlie kicked at the ground, trying and failing to stand up. He blinked, gulping for air like he was drowning. His eyes swam in and out of the fugue, latching onto Marlow for a second before drifting away.

"You're a coward," he said again, slurred almost beyond recognition. "I trusted you."

"I'm sorry," Marlow said. "Please, Charlie, I did it for you."

Charlie said something else but he was too far gone. Marlow lowered his friend's head gently to the ground, then stood, wishing he could give Herc a different answer. But there was no time. Herc grabbed him by the shoulder, marched him toward the chopper. Strong hands hauled him inside, Herc following and sliding the door shut behind him.

"Plane tanked and ready to go?" Herc yelled to the pilot. The woman nodded, then Herc wiggled a finger in the air

166

and the chopper lifted off, bucking unsteadily. Marlow looked through the filthy port window, seeing Charlie sprawled in the dirt, alone. Then they banked hard and he was gone.

"No going back now," said Pan, sitting beside him on the bench. "Congratulations on making the stupidest decision of your life."

"Pan," said Herc as he crashed down on Marlow's other side. "For once could you please just not be such an evil cow?"

He held out a hand and Marlow shook it limply. Herc squeezed, pumping his arm with enthusiasm.

"Kid, you did the right thing," he said, grinning. "Welcome to the Hellraisers."

PART II
OLD MAGIC

DON'T BARF
IN MY JET

The plane shuddered and Marlow stifled his scream with the back of his hand. It was as if there were a demon about to crawl its way out of the fuselage, tear the jet in two, and send them all hurtling to the ground thirty thousand feet below. It lurched again, and this time he let out a screeching cry that was somehow louder than the roar of the engines. He clutched the sink hard enough to make his knuckles crack, offering a prayer to anything or anyone that was listening.

Please don't let us crash, please don't let us crash. Please—

There was a knock on the door of the tiny restroom, a voice from outside.

"Hey, kid, you okay in there?" Herc asked. "You been a while."

That was an understatement. He'd been locked in here for going on seven hours, pretty much since they'd left the chopper at Linden Airport and bundled into a private jet that was waiting for them on the runway. It had been the first time in his life that he'd been to an airport, let alone on an actual plane, and he'd been giddy with excitement right up until the point they'd accelerated for takeoff and his insides had just about been pulled out his rear end. That hadn't been the worst of it, either—the fact that the whole team had been laughing at him was almost enough to make him open the door and dive into oblivion.

"Don't make me come in there," Herc said. "Seriously, *don't*—I can smell it from out here."

"I'm fine," Marlow shouted back, sniffing the air. True, he'd pretty much unloaded from both ends from sheer terror, but that had been hours ago. "It was . . . something I ate."

The plane vibrated again, like they were inside a washing machine at full spin.

"Is it supposed to be doing that?" Marlow asked.

"What that? No, one of the engines has blown up, we're preparing to crash land, that's why I wanted to speak with you."

"*What?*"

"Calm down, kid," Herc said, laughing. "Don't crap your shorts. Again. It's just a bit of turbulence."

The plane dipped and he felt his stomach hover somewhere in his throat. He squeezed off a shot of his inhaler to try to remove it.

"We're not far off," Herc said. "Got another thirty minutes flying time. Just wanted to let you know. You can come out, we've stopped laughing now."

Marlow held his clammy head in his hands, wanting to throw up again but knowing there was nothing left to eject. He heard Herc's footsteps retreating and exhaled slowly, trying to control the panic. His heart was a woodpecker trying to hammer out through his ribs. He'd seen a lot of crazy in the last few days but surely nothing was more insane than the idea of being inside a small tube as it burned its way through the sky. He glanced at the walls, just a thin sheet of metal between him and nothing much at all, and he felt his bowels loosen again.

But if they were preparing to land soon, then he needed to

get back to the others. There was no way he was going to go down in history as the guy who died in the restroom.

He splashed his face with cold water and stared at his reflection. He didn't like what he saw—not because of the sickly sheen of his skin, the red-veined eyes, like he was a hundred years old. No, he hated it because of what he'd done to Charlie. He never should have left him there, not like that. He wondered if his friend was still there, out cold on the parking lot. What if he'd tried to get away and he'd toppled into the river? His best friend—his *only* friend—might be getting eaten by fish right now, his bloated and unrecognizable corpse found weeks later floating somewhere in Raritan Bay. Of all the cowardly things he'd done in his life, this had to be the worst.

Marlow gagged, reaching for his cell so he could call him, sighing when he remembered it was gone.

"I'm so sorry, Charlie," he said. "Be okay, yeah?"

He took another couple of deep breaths, then unlocked the door, squeezing through. A curtain separated him from the main cabin and he pulled it open to see everyone looking at him. They all managed to hold a straight face for a second or two, then Truck cracked—spluttering out a deep, booming laugh—and the others followed him into meltdown. They howled together, Night actually crying with laughter, slapping her own legs in an attempt to stop herself. Even Pan had a smile on her face, although she was doing her best to conceal it. Betty, the woman who'd patched him up back in the tower, wore a wry smile. Only Bullwinkle and Hope—the guys he'd fought back in the elevator—sat quiet, still wearing the bruises he'd given them.

Marlow's cheeks ignited and he had to force himself to stand there, teeth clenched, rather than run wailing back into the restroom.

"It's . . ." Herc said, wiping a tear from his eye, "it's not you. I promise."

"No, man," said Truck. "No way we'd ever laugh at you. You're one of us now, a member of the team, got a key to the company bathroom and everything."

They erupted again and Marlow sighed, traipsing to a spare chair and collapsing into it. He'd just about gotten his seat belt on when the plane bucked, shuddering violently for what felt like forever. It was as if nobody else even noticed it, and he chewed his knuckles to try to conceal his terror.

"How about Captain Vomit?" said Night.

"Huh?" Marlow asked.

"Nah, I reckon Crapper," said Herc. "It's got a nice *ring* to it. No pun intended."

"What are you guys talking about?" Marlow said, although nobody could hear him over the new round of giggles. He blew out another sigh and looked away, trying to pretend he wasn't bothered. This felt like the first day of school all over again, everyone mocking him about his asthma, pretending to wheeze and choke. Next they'd be taking turns to give him a wedgie. Now, just like then, he wished Danny was here to kick their asses.

The only other thing to look at was the window, giving him a view of the moon-streaked clouds below, the vast blanket of stars overhead. His stomach did a backflip and he had to stare at the floor for a moment to avoid the rush and roar of vertigo.

"I've got it," said Truck, clicking his giant fingers. "Oh man, I've got it. Elvis."

"Elvis?" said Herc, looking about as confused as Marlow felt. "Why Elvis?"

"Because he was in there so long I thought he'd died on the can."

Nobody laughed.

"You know," Truck said. "Because Elvis died on the toilet."

"Too far," said Herc, stony faced. "You don't make jokes about the King."

"Would somebody please tell me what the hell you're going on about?" Marlow said, wondering how much more his credibility would be dented if he just gave in and started crying.

"*Su nombre,*" said Night. "Your nickname. We're trying to decide what it should be."

"What's wrong with Marlow?" he said, feeling the plane dip a little more, making his head spin. How could there be all that space beneath him and nothing holding them up?

"To be honest, Marlow fits just fine," said Herc. "You know, the writer."

"The what?" said Truck.

"Wri-*ter,*" he said, obviously disgusted. "The author. You know, Christopher Marlowe, with an *e*. He wrote a story about somebody selling his soul to the devil."

Truck shrugged. "Like Harry Potter or something?"

"For the love of . . . You guys embarrass me."

There was a soft chime and the seat belt lights pinged on. Marlow grabbed his belt to make sure it was buckled up, pulling it so tight it could have acted as a gastric band. The plane descended, making Marlow's ears ache, and he swallowed to pop them. They sank into the clouds like they were a submarine plunging into an ocean of cotton wool. The plane shook until they dropped out of the bottom, and for a moment Marlow thought they must have been flipped upside down because the world below was a canvas of black felt studded with stars. Then he realized they were lights—houses, streets, cars—and even though the terror still gripped him he couldn't stop himself putting his nose to the glass in fascination.

"Quite something, right?" said Herc.

"Where are we?" he asked as the ground rose up to meet them.

"Prague," said Night.

"Prague?" Marlow had never heard of it.

"It's in the Czech Republic."

"Okay . . ." He wished he'd spent more time paying attention in geography. "Prague. That's where the Engine is, right?"

There was silence behind him and he turned.

"Kind of," said Truck. "Not where it is, but how we get to it. It's complicated."

Marlow returned his attention to the window, the ground close enough now that he could make out trees and individual cars. Were they supposed to be going this fast? He gripped the armrests of his chair, swallowing hard to stop whatever was left in his stomach from finding a way up his throat.

"Don't worry, kid," said Herc. "Landing's not the most dangerous bit." He snorted a laugh. "Just the second most dangerous. We'll probably be fine. You'll be on the ground in no time. Then we head to the Engine."

"Cool," he said, his words steaming up the glass. He closed his eyes, waiting for the crash, for the explosion, for the fire. "I just might need to use the restroom again first."

He was almost grateful that the sound of the plane screeching down was drowned out by another chorus of laughter.

ANOTHER WORLD

It was less like he'd flown to another continent and more like he'd arrived in a whole new world.

Everything felt different the moment he stepped out of the plane door. The sky was bigger, the stars were so numerous and so bright that it was as if the sun had exploded into a billion burning pieces. He took a breath and even that felt strange, the air so crisp, so clean, so cool, that it was like he'd just had a blast on his inhaler. *This must be what it's like not to have asthma,* he thought, and he felt a sudden, deeper rush of hatred for it, knowing that the monster still sat on his back, its fingers hovering next to his throat. The plane powered down, the engines whining, and then it hit him—how quiet it was here. Where were the revving cars, the horns, the shouts, the sirens?

"Gonna stand there all night?" said Pan, barging past him and clattering down the stairs. He followed her.

"No, it's just . . . I'm not used to being away from home."

"First time abroad?" she asked over her shoulder.

"First time abroad, first time out of *state*. Apart from Jersey, obviously."

"Jersey doesn't count," she said, walking across the floodlit tarmac. This couldn't have been the city's main airport because there was only one hangar, a silhouette against the sky, and a cluster of smaller buildings. Not unless things were just smaller in Europe. There were three cars at the side of the runway, two black Land Rover Defenders and a bright blue BMW M6 Hurricane, all with their engines running. Figures stood beside them, shielded by the blazing headlights, just ghosts in the dark. It was so surreal. He rubbed his gut to try to settle it.

"Nothing to worry about," said Truck, rolling up beside him and planting a huge hand on his shoulder. It weighed a ton and Marlow grunted in surprise. "I remember the first time I got here, I freaked. I wouldn't even get on the plane, they had to dope me, Mr. T style."

"How long ago was that?" Marlow asked, grateful to know he wasn't the only one.

"Couple of years now," he said. "Herc pulled me out of an illegal boxing ring in Chicago. Told me I'd be better off fighting for something that might make a difference. And here I am."

Truck lifted his hand and Marlow felt about twenty pounds lighter, stretching the kinks out of his back.

"This is so weird," he said. "Feel like I'm dreaming."

"Believe me," Truck replied, laughing so deeply that it was almost subsonic. "Weird doesn't cut it. Doesn't come close. You haven't seen anything yet."

Truck sashayed across the runway, replaced by Herc. The older man was carrying half a dozen huge bags and he looked pissed.

"Any of you lazy bastards want to help?" he yelled after the others. Nobody replied. Herc swung two of the bags off his shoulder and handed them to Marlow. "Here, make yourself useful."

They walked toward the SUVs and gradually the figures there came into focus. A couple of guys a little older than him, midtwenties he guessed. One of them was so tall and thin and perfectly manicured that he looked like a store mannequin. He was dressed in a sharp suit and was wearing sunglasses even though it was the middle of the night.

"Herc," he said in a voice he could have stolen from Sherlock Holmes. "You're late."

"Got held up," he replied gruffly. "Tends to happen when Mammon chases you down the street."

"Yes, Ostheim told me. He wants to talk."

"He's had all night to talk to me," Herc said, slinging the bags to the other guy, who stuffed them into the back of one of the Land Rovers. "It's late and I'm tired."

The man wearing shades turned to Marlow, an unpleasant sneer creasing his face.

"Another stray dog for your pack?" he asked, and Marlow felt his hackles rising. He took a step forward, trying to make himself look as big as possible. The man just shook his head. "So bloody predictable. Aggressive, impatient, troubled, undisciplined. This one smells, too. A mongrel even by your standards."

"Hey," said Marlow, but Herc rested a hand on his arm, shaking his head. Sunglasses guy turned and climbed into the driver's seat of the blue BMW, slamming the door shut and revving the engine. Herc steered Marlow toward the Defender, speaking in a whisper.

"Ignore Douche Bag there. His name's Hanson, and he's British."

"That explains it," said Marlow. He climbed onto the back seat, asking, "Where are we going?"

"Straight to the Engine, kiddo. Just sit back and enjoy the sights. This particular sack has some of my favorite shades of black."

"What?" asked Marlow. Herc lifted a piece of cloth that

looked like it might once have served as a diaper in medieval times.

"Rules is rules," Herc said. "You need to put this on."

"No way," Marlow said. "It's got . . . stains on it."

"Yeah, all adds to the flavor." He opened it up and offered it again. "It's either this, or I knock you out."

Marlow still wasn't sure which was worse, but he took the hood and gingerly lowered it over his head.

"It smells of ass," he said, his voice muffled.

"Yeah, sorry about that," said Herc. "I think Truck was sitting on it on the plane."

Great.

Marlow heard the door shut, then the engine gunned and they were moving, fast. Herc clapped him on the back, making him jump.

"Just close your eyes and enjoy the ride."

It wasn't exactly enjoyable, but a trip on the back of a drunk, three-legged donkey would have been smooth compared to the experience he'd just had on the jet. The Land Rover took to the streets like a racing car, accelerating and braking with equal force, screeching wildly around the corners. Marlow would have been worried, but not being able to see anything took some of the fear out of the experience. He just settled back in his chair, closed his eyes, and listened to Herc droning on.

"I'd like to take this opportunity to fill in a few of the details," he said. "I'm sure you have quite a few questions. I'm going to do my best to preempt them. First, who we are. We're an organization called the Hellraisers. I don't know where it comes from, we've always been called that. I guess because we raise hell wherever we go. But it's kind of ironic, too, really, given what our purpose here is."

Right . . . Marlow thought. It sounded more like a bad eighties rock group. Lloyd Cole and the Hellraisers, coming to a venue near you.

"Two, how long have we been around? Well, it's complicated. The Engines are old, *very* old. Nobody knows for sure but it might be centuries. Millennia maybe. Our organization, the Hellraisers, has existed for almost as long, but in its current form only since the last century, since the war. There's a lot of history there, kid, that I don't want to bore you with. But for a while the Engines were lost, only rediscovered in the thirties when . . ."

Marlow tuned out, lulled into a stupor by the warmth and motion of the car. He'd not slept on the plane—it was hard to sleep when you were too busy screaming and puking in a tiny room—and the exhaustion was like another hood pulled down over his consciousness. He dozed, waking when he sensed that the vehicle had stopped. The world was a pit of silence, only the sound of his breathing echoing back from the sack. He reached up and pulled it off, seeing that the car was empty. There was nothing but darkness out of the windows, like they'd driven right off the edge of the planet.

"Hello?" he said. "Herc? Pan?"

He fumbled with his seat belt but his fingers didn't work properly, everything moving like he was underwater.

"Hey? Guys?"

"They're lying to you," said a voice from the front of the car, a whisper. Marlow jumped, his heart almost stalling. Somebody had materialized in the passenger seat, staring out of the windshield at the darkness beyond, a face shrouded in shadow. Even his reflection in the rearview mirror was inscrutable, two eyes as black as pitch, unblinking. A crawling sense of unease skittered down Marlow's spine.

"Where are they? Who the hell are you?"

"They're lying to you," said the man again, and his whole body seemed to shake for a second, too fast, the way an image flickers when you pause a VHS.

"Who?" Marlow said, trying to push the button on his belt. He reached for the door handle and pulled but it came off in his hand like a strand of warm licorice, sticking to his fingers. He yelped, trying to shake it off. The whole car was losing its shape, like it was melting in some immense heat. "What's going on? Let me out!"

"It's too late for that, Marlow," said the man. "There is no way out. It knows who you are."

"It?" Marlow was panicking now, feeling his windpipe begin to fill. He coughed, snatching in a half-breath that stank of death and decay. "I don't understand."

The man raised a finger, pointing into the darkness outside the window. Marlow looked but there was nothing there, just an impossible void. Couldn't he hear something, though? A distant rolling wave of thunder. He wheezed in another breath but there was no oxygen in it, like he was drowning. He pulled his inhaler out of his pocket and put it in his mouth, only to feel it squirm between his lips. He screamed, spitting it out, seeing a fat, orange slug writhe in the footwell. Bile burned up from his stomach, choking him.

"No," he said, punching the window, feeling the glass melt around his fist. He was sinking into his chair, the whole car trying to fold over him, smothering him. And still that sound of thunder grew—no, not thunder, but the pounding of hooves, like something was galloping this way, *fast*. Marlow struggled, but the more he moved the more the melting car sucked him in, burying him alive. "Please, stop it!"

The man in the front began to wail, the desperate sob of a dying man. The noise got louder, rising in pitch, becoming a scream, a rattling shriek. Marlow screamed too, the fear filling him from head to toe like ice water. Something was appearing out of the darkness, an impossibly huge shape that bore down on them with gut-wrenching speed. The scream from the front was still growing, so loud now that Marlow felt a gout of blood erupt from his ear, so loud that the car was shaking. The man's head began to turn, rotating as smoothly as an owl's, twisting too far, like his neck was about to snap. His eyes were as big as saucers, dripping black, his mouth a gaping wound, blasting out that ear-shattering howl of despair.

"No!" Marlow shouted. "Nonononono!"

The shape outside rose up in his window, traveling too fast, darkness flooding from darkness, a freight train about to crush them. Marlow held up his hands against it, screaming.

It hit him like a slap, wrenching him up out of the car, out of the dark. He punched the air, kicking, trying to fight it, but the shape was holding him down, stopping him from moving. Gradually the world swam into focus, three faces staring down at him, etched with concern. Marlow struggled for a second more until he recognized Herc, Pan, Truck. He lay there, sobbing with the relief of it.

"Whoa," said Truck. "That must have been some nightmare, bro."

"Nightmare?" said Marlow, snatching in an airless breath. Herc handed him his inhaler and he shook it, feeling how close to empty it was. He took a couple of hits and lay there, his whole body trembling. Already the dream was leaking out of his head, dissipating like salt in water. He was more than happy to let it go.

"Happens to us all," said Herc, offering him a hand.

Marlow took it and hauled himself up, holding on to it for

a fraction longer than he needed to. They were in a narrow cobbled street next to the SUV, quaint, old-fashioned buildings on both sides. A large gate stood open right in front of him, big enough to get a car through. He caught a glimpse of a courtyard beyond, swimming with yellow light. He stood there for a moment, everything aching. His knuckles were sore, like he'd punched a wall.

"Got a pretty good right hook for a scrawny kid," said Truck, grinning. He had a split lip and sucked the blood from it with a noisy slurp. Marlow blushed.

"Oh, hey, man, I'm sorry, I didn't mean—"

"Don't sweat it," Truck said. "If I had to travel all this way with an ass rag over my face I'd wanna punch someone too."

He walked through the gate, laughing, and Marlow stood there.

"The nightmares, they're normal," Pan said, appearing by his side. He looked at her, at the way her face caught the light, hard and yet perfectly soft at the same time. Even though his heart had taken a beating he still felt it wobble. She turned to him, and the look she gave him wasn't quite a smile, but it wasn't quite a scowl either. "It's because we're here."

"Here?" Marlow said.

"Yeah, here," she said. "We're at the Engine."

THE BOOK OF DEAD ENGINEERS

Pan walked into the courtyard of the Nest, feeling like it had been a million years since she'd last been here, not a month. Brick walls that had seen better days surrounded it on three sides. The fourth was made up of a building, one that had once been a church. It, too, was dilapidated, its windows boarded up, tiles missing from the roof, a short, squat tower bent at an angle. Only the door—big and red, perfectly lacquered— appeared new. Pan didn't look at it, though. That door was an evil piece of work.

The courtyard was full of people. Herc was in one corner, arguing with Hanson. Truck and Night leaned against each other, both looking exhausted. Being under contract did that to you, sapped everything except whatever it was you'd traded for. Bullwinkle and Hope sat on a crate, Bully picking his nose so enthusiastically it was like he'd found treasure in there. She started to look for Forrest, then caught herself.

He's not here, is he? Because he's in hell.

The light in the yard came from a couple of halogen lamps and she hated it. It was yellow and sickly, and it turned everyone it touched into walking corpses. Every time she was here she had the impression that she was in a graveyard where the dead had decided to start living again.

"Who are all these people?" Marlow asked. The kid was the color of wet ash, his body stooped and weak, his eyes red-rimmed and raw. Every time he breathed he made a sound like a broken accordion. She still didn't know what Herc saw in him, other than the asthma. It was always easier to turn someone when there was something they wanted. Or rather, something they *didn't* want.

"They're roadies," Pan said, nodding at the guys unloading the cars. "They do the donkeywork. You can trust them."

Marlow nodded. He was still in shock, she guessed. She couldn't blame him, she'd not been right for weeks after she'd first seen the Engine. She watched him as he studied the courtyard, the walls, then the door, and she saw the exact moment it hit him, that *feeling*. He staggered a couple of paces, groaning, thumping into Truck, holding on to the big guy like he was a life raft in the middle of a cold, dark ocean.

"Somebody's getting his first taste," Truck said. "Just ride it out, bro, it gets better, eventually."

"What *is* that?" Marlow said, putting his hands to his ears. Pan knew what he would be hearing, the voices, the sounds, those infernal scratchings. Barks that didn't come from any dog, screams that couldn't be human, a dozen whispered voices tickling the inside of his skull like cold, wet tongues. She could hear them too, although she'd been here enough times now to know how to tune them out. There were smells as well, rotting flesh, excrement, and sulfur, always sulfur. It didn't matter how clean they kept the yard, how many times they scrubbed the door, those smells never went away.

"Ignore it," she said as he reached into his pocket again, taking a blast of his inhaler. "It's just messing with you."

"The Engine?" he asked, wincing.

"Yeah."

He looked like he was going to ask another question but

she didn't have the patience for it. She pushed past him and walked up to Herc.

"Waiting for anything special?" she asked. "Or do you just enjoy standing around like ducks in the rain?"

Herc's eyeballs bulged with rage but he gritted his teeth, swallowing noisily.

"You think we're going to let your new boyfriend in without a test?" Hanson said, leering at her behind those sunglasses. She was grateful that he was wearing them, because she knew what he looked like underneath.

"So test him, then," Pan said. "I'm freezing my ass off here."

"And you're boring mine," Hanson said, walking away.

She wrapped her hands around herself, stomping on the wet ground and cursing him under her breath. She knew there was no way around it. Given that the Circulus Inferni would try anything to find out the location of their Engine, it made sense to ensure that they weren't letting a spy through the door. Marlow looked like a dope, but appearances could be deceptive.

She glanced at him, stooped over in his wet clothes, his brow furrowed and his bottom lip quivering. *Yeah, not that deceptive.*

Hanson placed a hand on either side of Marlow's head and lifted it until he was staring right into his eyes. The boy struggled a little but only the way a beaten dog struggles when it knows it can't escape.

"What's your name?" Hanson asked.

"Marlow Green." He shivered. Hanson always dealt for mind reading—among other things—so he'd know if the kid was lying.

"Are you working for Mammon? For the Circulus Inferni?"

"No," he said. "No way, man, I—"

"Do you have any plans to infiltrate the Engine, to destroy

or otherwise damage the Engine, to cause harm to anyone working for this organization?"

"I'm feeling like I might want to kick you in the balls sometime soon, does that count?" Marlow said, and a spluttered laugh actually escaped Pan's lips before she managed to catch it. Hanson gripped Marlow's head harder, making the boy wince.

"Do you have any plans to infiltrate the Engine, to destroy or otherwise damage the Engine, to cause harm to anyone working for this organization?"

"No," he said. "Of course not."

Hanson tilted his head back, his nostrils flaring like he was sniffing for a lie. He let go, pushing Marlow away and wiping his hands on his trousers.

"He's clean," he said. "Holding a pretty big torch for you, though, Pan. Just about all I could see in that simple little excuse for a mind."

"Wait, no, *what?*" Marlow spluttered, and Pan turned away before he could see her cheeks boil.

"Close up!" Herc yelled to two of the roadies near the gates. They obeyed, slamming them closed and pulling a bar down to lock them. It wasn't exactly secure, but Pan knew they could leave the gates wide open and intruders still wouldn't be able to find their way through that big, red, evil door. This place was protected by something else, something older and vastly more powerful.

"I honestly don't know what he's talking about," Marlow said.

Herc put his hand to his collar mic and yelled, "Crack it."

Pan steeled herself, taking three deep breaths, blowing each one out slowly. This part of the process always sucked. The door uttered a series of clicks, soft and wet and chittering, like there was a giant cockroach on the other side. Then it hit her, a sudden, thunderous chaos of light and noise, right in the center of her brain. She groaned, clenching her fists as hard as she could, trying not to see but unable to switch it off—corpses, toothless mouths twisted open in horror, maggots spilling out of empty eye sockets, limbs flailing inside an inferno, and something else, something worse than the demons, worse even than Mammon. A sculpture of bone and shadow that sat above it all, watching her with a cluster of fat, black spider eyes.

The door clunked again, swinging open, and the images vanished like a projector in her brain had been turned off. She swayed unsteadily, shaking her head like she could somehow dislodge what had been in there. She hawked up a wad of acid and spat, feeling the blood trickle down from her nose into her mouth. *Every frickin' time.* She glared at the door, wondering if—when all this was over—she'd be allowed to take an ax to it, carve it into splinters.

Not that she'd dare.

She marched toward it, her stomach churning. Behind her came Truck, holding Marlow like a sack of groceries. The kid looked close to passing out, his breathing shallow and ragged. It was always worse the first time, feeling the Engine inside your head. She'd thrown up over Herc and Hanson. One recruit had died on the spot.

"Age before beauty," Herc said, flashing his monstrous, gap-toothed grin.

Pan walked to the door, seeing the inside of the church, the rotting pews, the holes in the roof where the rain dripped through, the vines that had taken root and were climbing the pillars. She took a deep breath, then crossed the threshold, feeling that familiar twist and tumble deep inside, her guts protesting as she passed over. Everything fizzed, bolts of bright white agony flashing across the front of her brain. She took another step, forcing herself to, knowing that if she paused here she'd be stuck here forever, in the space between. The pain fluttered away like a startled bird and she was standing in a narrow corridor, shivering against the sudden chill.

She walked a few steps, then looked back, seeing the same open red door, and beyond it a view that never failed to take her breath away—a field of snow, as crisp and unbroken as a blank page, ridgeback mountains faintly visible through the blizzard. A face appeared from nowhere, a yellowing skull, almost invisible against the vista beyond. It pushed into the space, changing, growing a sheen of red, strands of muscle, a layer of skin and hair. Then Truck was in the corridor, Marlow materializing alongside him. The kid stood for a moment, then opened his mouth and retched, a dribble of sick hanging from his chin.

"This way," said Pan, leading them down the corridor, trying to ignore the unpleasant tickling in her skull, the half-whispers that danced against her eardrums. Insignias decorated the walls, recognizable even though somebody had tried to scratch them away. A swastika, an outstretched eagle. They made her stomach churn just as much as the vibes that blasted up from below.

After thirty yards or so the passageway ended at an elevator. The doors stood open, the mouth of a predator waiting for her to walk right in. She did. Truck and Marlow followed, making the elevator wobble, and she tried not to think about how deep the shaft stretched beneath them, the thousands of feet of empty space between her and the pit below.

"Here we go again," Herc said as he strolled inside.

The elevator rumbled, then started to clatter down. The

first time she'd used it Pan had felt like she was on some kind of reverse rocket, one that was blasting down into the earth rather than up into space. Even now, after so many trips, her stomach did loop-the-loops as they picked up speed. She ignored the need to hold on to something, her hands balled into fists, closing her eyes for the forty-eight seconds it took the elevator to slow.

She heard the noise of the bullpen before they'd come to a halt, a clamor of voices and machinery that tripled in volume when Herc wrenched open the gates. He ushered them out into the first level of the complex, a room easily as big as a couple of basketball courts. It had been carved out of the rock, the gray walls and ceiling rough-hewn and uneven—all except for a section above the elevator, which displayed a huge swastika. It had been covered up with a dozen tarps but it still seemed to burn up there, scorching a hole right into the past. Under it, somebody—an Engineer from the eighties, apparently—had painted the words *Nazis Suck, Hellraisers Rule!*

Everything else in the space was brand-new. Banks of hard drives lined the far wall, humming. There were more than a hundred of them, each the size of a fridge, cased in three layers of transparent plastic so the damp and the cold wouldn't get to them. Their lights blinked warily, making her think of caged animals at the zoo.

Next to them was a whole wall of monitors, the two outer ones as big as cinema screens, the other sixteen mounted in between. Each one showed the usual display of numbers and countdowns and infograms, like a NASA control center. One of the big ones, though, was playing a Harry Potter movie. Four women and three men sat on swivel chairs in front of it, rapt, scoffing popcorn from a couple of saucepans. Herc strolled halfway across the room, almost on his tiptoes, waiting until he was close enough before clapping his hands together. The noise was like a rifle shot, echoing off the walls, and the Lawyers just about fell out of their chairs.

"Jesus *Christ!*" yelled Seth in his heavy Austrian accent. Nobody really knew how old he was—sometimes he looked sixty, sometimes eighty. Right now he looked about a hundred as he clapped a liver-spotted hand to his chest. "You would really do this to me, an old man who has had four heart attacks already in his life? You are a bad guy, Herman Cole. You will be the death of me."

"I could never be so lucky," Herc said, walking the rest of the way and embracing the man fondly. They looked like a couple of old crusties meeting in the park, Pan thought, smiling.

"Good to see your mind's on the job," said Truck. "Nice to know you're working hard on cracking our contracts."

Seth waved a hand like he was wafting away a bad smell.

"Oh please, you know I could crack yours as easily as I could crack a fart. You insult me, Gregory, with your pathetic deals. When will you be brave and go for something *really* fun?"

One of the other Lawyers had paused the film and they were all milling around now like they were actually working. Pan ignored them. She knew a little about each of them, but other than Seth she did her best to avoid them. There was something about knowing the person who had to break your contract that made the whole thing scarier, made it more real. It was better to pretend that some nameless, faceless superhero was trying to save your life, not an old guy with a triple bypass, or some geeky mathematicians from MIT who were still young enough to think that ironic T-shirts were cool.

"It's good to see you, Amelia," Seth said, using the name that Pan hated. "We almost lost you then. That was a tough cookie to break. See, Gregory, you should be more like this young lady here, actually giving me some work to do!"

Seth wiggled his huge, bushy eyebrows at her and smiled and she couldn't help but smile back. Until she thought of Forrest, that was.

"You should have broken his contract," she said. "We didn't have to lose another one."

"Cody." Seth sighed. "Yes. We should have. I am sorry, Amelia. Ostheim commanded us to keep your contracts active until your mission was complete. And by that time it was too late. We only just managed to break yours in time."

"Yeah, I noticed," she said, scratching her chest, her ruined heart. Seth walked to her, placed a warm, leathery hand on her shoulder.

"I truly am sorry, my girl. It was not my choice, but it is my responsibility. I should have said no to Ostheim."

Yeah, right. Nobody said no to Ostheim. Pan shrugged him away.

"I will write his name in the book," Seth said.

"Don't," she replied. She steeled herself, walking to the corner of the room. There was a desk there, an old, leather-bound ledger the only thing on it. It was open now, and she ran her hand down the list of names written there in black ink. *Lucy White (Simmer), Beki Smith (Bluebeard), Sophie Hicks (T-Rex), Wesley Adams (Marathon Man), Tyra Jynn (Spitfire), Ryan Hodapp (Hammer), Hannah Wilkinson (Berserker), Leticia Gallardo (Bookworm), Courtney Webb (Captain Obvious).* All the Engineers and their war names. All of them dead. Some of them rotting in the ground, most of them somewhere far, far worse. She did what she always did, flicking back through the book. How many names? A thousand? Those at the front were faded almost beyond recognition, centuries old. And how many more would there be, before it all ended?

Picking up the pen, she wrote *Cody*, then stopped, racking her brains. What the hell had his surname been? The pen hovered and she felt the shame wrap her up, smothering her. How could she forget it? He was dead, and she couldn't even remember his name.

It's better this way, better to forget he ever existed, better to—

Baranowski. It was suddenly vomited back into her head and she scribbled it down, adding *(Forrest)* afterward. Herc had given him that name because he'd always been going on about how life was a box of chocolates. She ran her finger softly over the name, then closed the book with deliberate slowness.

Job done. Time to move on. I will not think of him again.

"And who is this?" said Seth, getting out of his chair and shuffling over to Marlow. "A new recruit? Oh goody!"

"Seth, meet Marlow," said Pan. Seth took Marlow's head in both of his and studied him like a scientist might study a rat. He nodded approvingly.

"Oh, Marlow, how fitting," he said, putting his head to Marlow's chest. "Bit of asthma there, I see. Nothing we can't take care of. A good specimen, Herman, we will have a lot of fun with this one. Have you thought about what you might like, Marlow? Have they filled you in on the possibilities, the endless, wonderful possibilities?"

"Um . . ." said Marlow.

"He can wait," said Herc. "It's been a long day. A long few days. We should rest."

"Balderdash!" said Seth. "You need no such thing. Please, let's work up a contract for him. You don't know how bored I get here. They make me do terrible things, *terrible things,* when you are gone. These films they make me watch, about wizards and dragons and . . . and strange elves with socks. I cannot think with such nonsense in my head."

"He put it on!" said one of the Lawyers, a young woman called Trix. "He's made us watch it four times this week."

"Lies," said Seth, holding up his hands. "See how they slander me. Come, come."

He took Marlow's elbow and walked with him toward the elevator. Pan looked at Herc and the big guy shrugged.

"It's too late and I'm too tired to argue with Seth," he said. "I'm going to bed. You make sure he doesn't deal for something unbreakable, all right?"

"Come on, Herc," she said, wanting nothing more than to crash down on a soft mattress, bury herself in the warmth of her duvet. "I'm—"

"Good night, Pan," Herc said, flashing her a smile. She looked at Truck and he shook his head.

"Bed for me. Good night, kiddo."

"*Buenas noches,* Pan," said Night before she'd even asked her.

She groaned in frustration then spun around on her heels, following the old man and the kid. Already she could feel that maddening itch, the call of the Engine. She pictured it beneath her—its sprawling insanity, an ocean of moving parts powered by unspeakable evil—and her heart began drumming. The truth was she wasn't tired. The reason she didn't want to babysit Marlow was because if she went downstairs, if she saw the Engine, then the desire to forge a new contract would be almost overwhelming. It always wanted her, and she no longer knew how to say no.

"Do not dally, Amelia," said Seth from inside the elevator. "I don't want to be another hundred years older by the time you join us."

She shook her head in resignation, then jogged over to

them. Marlow smiled nervously at her and she almost felt sorry for him. Almost. The truth was he didn't know how lucky he was. Right now he was a wheezing, trembling sack of flesh and bone and worry.

And in a few minutes he'd be a god.

THE ENGINE

Marlow wasn't sure how it was possible that they could go any deeper, but the elevator rattled downward at full speed for another minute before it began to slow. He could feel the vast pressure of the earth above him, a billion tons of rock and soil bearing down, ready to crush him to jelly. The panic was like a cold fire inside his chest and he had to fight the urge to scream, to beg for them to take him back to the surface. He tried to take a deep breath to calm himself down but there was no air here. He panted, fumbling for his inhaler, until the old man put his hand on his arm.

"You no longer need it," he said, patting the back of Marlow's hand like a father taking his son to the first day of school. "It can be a bit much, I know. The moment that everything you thought you knew about the world is proven to be wrong. But it gets better. Come."

The elevator shuddered to a halt and Pan opened the doors. Marlow focused on her in an attempt to blot out everything else—the way she walked, like she owned the place; the way her hips moved, it was almost hypnotic. He kept his eyes on her, so engrossed that it took him a moment to notice there was something in his head, something scuttling around the circumference of his skull, buzzing like a fly. He put his hand to his temple, scratching furiously, but the itch was inside him, unbearable. If he'd had a hammer he'd have gladly used it to get at whatever crawled and feasted in there.

"What is that?" he grunted, using both hands now, feeling like his brain was full of insect eggs, all hatching into needled feet and bulging eyes. "Get it out."

He felt hands on his, looked to see Pan right in front of him, close enough that he could feel her breath on his lips. Even with his head erupting he felt himself melt, like the bones had been pulled right out of his legs.

"The Engine will do its best to mess with you," she said. "You'll feel its touch in your head, in your soul. It's trying to understand you, probe you. It's unlike anything you've ever experienced, and believe me, it will make you feel like you want to die. Ignore it."

"Ignore the creepy magic Engine that's probing my soul with evil stalker fingers," he said, trying to smile and offering what was probably a grimace. "Okay, cool."

Pan studied him for a moment more and he had the almost overwhelming desire to lean forward and plant his mouth on hers. It would be so easy, she was six inches away, and those lips were so full, slightly open . . .

"Do it and you die," she said, reading his mind. She prodded him hard in the forehead and backed away. "Believe me, the Engine is a mean piece of work but I'm worse."

"Do what?" he said as innocently as he could. "I wasn't . . ."

"Sure."

They were in a small room, just the elevator on one side and what looked like a vault door on the other. The walls were made of concrete, and the same Nazi decoration covered two of them. Somebody had painted over the swastikas but it was almost as if the poisonous symbol had eroded the paint, causing it to bubble up like diseased skin.

"What's with all the Hitler crap?" Marlow asked. "There

something you're not telling me? Because I'm really not into all that white supremacy stuff."

"Us neither, Marlow," said Seth, gesturing at himself. "Obviously. No, the Nazis found this place when they invaded Czechoslovakia in 1939. We don't know why, exactly, but the Engines had been lost for a long time before this, almost forgotten. Fortunately for us, the Nazis didn't work out how to use the machine before the end of the war. Things could have turned out very, very different."

"It's why we call it the Pigeon's Nest," Pan said as she typed a code into a pad by the vault door. "Like the führer's mountain hideout they called Eagle's Nest, but this place was full of pigeons when the Hellraisers found it. Dead ones."

The door bleeped and she turned to Marlow.

"Nothing I can say, nothing anyone can say, will prepare you for what you're about to see. There's no training you can do, no way of readying yourself. You could have a thousand years to gear up for your first encounter with the Engine and it would still hit you just as hard. So we're gonna throw you right in. The most important thing to remember is that it cannot hurt you. It will mess with your head, make you feel worse than you've ever felt, make you think things you never thought yourself capable of, make you feel like you're evil, but it cannot hurt you. Okay?"

"Sure," he said, wanting to add, *No, I'm nowhere near okay, please just get me out of here, I don't want to be part of this anymore.* But the truth was he was tired of running. "Sure," he said, firmer this time. "I'm ready."

Pan breathed out a laugh, like it was the stupidest thing she'd ever heard, then she smacked a hand down on the pad. There was a moment of hesitation before the room was full of noise, a siren blasting out the same time as a light began to flash above the door. It felt like they were inside a prison waiting for the gates to release. Why did they need a door this size? Who were they trying to keep out?

Or what were they trying to keep *in*?

The hydraulics inside the door hissed, then there was a clunk as the locks disengaged. It swung open lazily, and Marlow's last fingerhold on the rock of reality popped loose, plunging him into the abyss. The onslaught was overwhelming—a feast of rotting flesh and howling screams devoured every thought. He gripped his head, blinking away tears, feeling exhausted, like he'd been crying for hours. He felt Pan's hand on his arm, and for once her expression had softened.

"Come!" said Seth, pushing past them both. "We must begin, this is so exciting!"

Exciting wasn't the word Marlow would have used, but there was definitely something inside him—past the churning terror, the maddening horror—that made him giddy. Part of him was still convinced that they were all trying to trick him—*They're lying to you,* his dreams had told him—but he'd seen it, seen what they could do.

You've seen the price they have to pay, too.

He closed his eyes, tried to force away the image of the girl Brianna, being torn to pieces, her soul dragged into the burning ground. It was okay. That wouldn't happen to him. They'd look after him.

Right?

Pan led the way through the door and Marlow kept close behind her, his heart pounding so hard at his ribs that it was as if it were trying to break its way loose to be closer to her. A strong, cool breeze blew past him, stinking of something that could have been smoke or rotten eggs. He put his hand to his nose and coughed out the phlegm in his throat. His inhaler was all but empty now but he was trying not to think about it. If he had an attack, he was thousands of miles away from his spares, from his nebulizer. *Deep breaths, calm and steady, just don't panic.*

He stepped through the door and the panic hit him like a punch to the gut.

It was like being on a vessel in the dark heart of space. Beyond the door was nothing, just a vast, black emptiness that took his breath away—literally snatched it from his lungs. It was impossible to get a sense of how big it was because there were no landmarks, but somehow he knew it was vast, something in the immense stillness of the air. He felt as if one more step would send him spinning out into that depthless silence and he'd be smothered by it, swallowed whole.

Gasping, he reached out and grabbed hold of the first thing he could find—a cold metal handrail—clinging on as if his life depended on it. Even like this, rooted in place, he felt as if the entire world might flip upside down at any second, cast him off like somebody shaking a bug from their hand. He screwed his eyes shut, but that only made it worse, made him feel like he was already spinning into oblivion.

There was a distant crunch and he opened his eyes to see a microscopic dot of light in the distance, as tiny as a firefly seen from the top of a mountain. Another one joined it, then a third, a row of lights flickering toward them forming a line that could have been a runway. More lights buzzed to life, sparking, and Marlow's jaw dropped as the size of the space became apparent—bigger even than he'd imagined it, bigger than a dozen football fields, a hundred maybe. The hanging lights blinked on, thousands of them, until the cavern was blazing.

And what they illuminated was almost enough to make him want to shout for darkness, to pluck out his own eyeballs so as not to see.

He stood at the top of a steep, narrow metal staircase that

plunged to the cavern floor. Down there was a ledge the size of a classroom, dwarfed by the rest of the chamber. There was nothing there aside from a rectangular pool filled with something that rippled like water, but which gave off no reflection.

It was what lay beyond the ledge, though, that was surely impossible. It might have been an ocean, but one made of mechanical parts. It was hard to get a sense of it from up there, but he could make out cogs and levers and gears and springs and spindles, hundreds of thousands of them—no, *millions* of them. It looked like a dumping ground for old clocks, for clockwork toys and mechanical oddities. The scale of it made him feel like an insect, something minuscule and insignificant, something worthy only of being crushed. And the thought seemed to make the Engine grow larger still, made it appear to rise up, to tower over him even though it lay below. It was as if a vast wave was approaching from the far side of the cavern, roaring and blasting and thundering toward him.

Then he blinked, and the ocean of parts was once again still, like it hadn't moved in a thousand years.

He suddenly wanted no part of this thing, this vast and ancient device. What had Pan told him? That it had been constructed by the Devil? That was impossible, of course, there was no such thing, *right*? But here now, seeing this abomination sitting fat beneath him, a boundless leviathan of razor-sharp parts, he could easily believe it. It was something that had no right to exist, and he tried to turn, to run back through the door, but found that he couldn't.

Don't you want to know? said something in his head, a warm, sour breath like somebody had clamped their cold lips to his and whispered right into his mouth. He put his hands to his ears, but still the words came. *I can give you anything you want, anything you desire. All you have to do is ask.*

Another image flooded his battered brain, him running

down a track. He couldn't quite figure out why it felt so good until he realized that he wasn't wheezing, wasn't fighting for every breath. It was so vivid that when it dissolved he almost mourned it, until another one took its place—Pan, her hands on his chest, her lips parted as she moved in for the kiss.

All you have to do is ask.

Somewhere out in the vast silence of the machine there was an insect's *click*, a soft mechanical chirrup. Marlow's head was suddenly empty again, his cheeks burning with the sheer power of the fantasy. There was a blissful moment of silence before another one took its place, filling his head like he had a home cinema between his ears. And this one almost made him cry out with joy.

He and Danny, walking up the steps to their house, everything drenched in sunlight as they laughed their way through the front door. His mom, hugging him first and then his brother—smelling of dewberry the way she used to, not a single empty bottle in the sink. Danny turned to him, older now, lines on his face, a patch of gray hair by his left ear, but those eyes so full of life, so full of kindness.

All you have to do is ask, his brother said, ruffling his hair.

And then Marlow was dropped back into the cavern, blinking the sun from his eyes like he'd actually been there. The scent of his mom's moisturizer was still in his nose, his scalp tingling from Danny's touch. Pan had reached the bottom of the stairs and she looked up at him curiously.

"What is it showing you?" she asked. "Money?"

"No," he said, clattering down the steps and standing beside her while Seth shuffled laboriously after them. "No, I saw my brother, Danny. He . . . he died."

Pan nodded knowingly, looking out into the Engine. From down here Marlow got a closer look, seeing that it was even more intricate than he'd imagined. It stretched to the left and right for as far as he could see, a shoreline of needles and prongs, each one perfectly still. Huge cables stretched into the Engine, and unlike the rest of it, these looked brand-new.

"Don't," Pan said. "The Engine tries to control your choices, tries to make you wish for something impossible. If you deal to bring back the dead . . ."

He thought he saw her shudder and she ran a hand over her stomach as if to settle it.

"I thought the machine could grant any wish," Marlow said, his voice feeble, like the vast silence out there was pushing it back.

"Oh, it can," Pan said. "You can wish your brother back and he'll be back. But it won't be him. He'll look the part, maybe even speak the part, but he'll be rotten inside. It's a ghost of a memory wrapped in someone else's dead flesh. We call them wormbags, and they're nasty. Not to mention when you break somebody out of death like that, sooner or later all hell comes after you to get them back."

"And it will cost you everything," Seth shouted down. "Because that's one contract we cannot break. The Engine knows it, too, the damned thing."

Marlow shuddered, but the image of Danny was still etched in his head, as real as anything else in his life.

"Remember, the Engine isn't your friend," Pan said. "It lies, it deceives, that's its purpose. That's what it's been doing for centuries, tricking people into making a deal, signing a contract."

"In return for their soul," Marlow said. "It can't be real, though. How the hell does it take your soul?"

Pan shrugged.

"We don't know," she said. "Nobody does. Not even Gramps there."

"Yes," said Seth as he reached the ledge. "There are things

even I do not know." He stopped, panting for breath. "But Pan is right, you must be very careful what you deal for."

"Listen," said Marlow. "I don't think I should do this, I don't think—"

"It will be fine," said Pan. "Everyone bricks it the first time. You just need to focus, keep your mind clear."

"Yes, know exactly what it is that you want. It is the man who wants everything, and he who does not know what he wants, who lands himself in trouble."

Marlow shook his head, about to give his excuses and leave, but there were suddenly voices from the top of the stairs. A face appeared through the door, the British guy Hanson, still wearing his sunglasses. Next to him were the two guys from the elevator, Hope and Bullwinkle.

"Looks like Herc's Jerks have beaten us to it," said Hanson, galloping down the stairs. "Past your bedtime isn't it, Amelia?"

"Screw you," Pan said. He just laughed.

"One day maybe I'll let you," he said, turning to Marlow. In the harsh light of the cavern he looked older than he had before, lines etched into his face. But without seeing his eyes it was impossible to know for sure. "Gonna throw the new dog in the pool? See if it drowns?"

"Call someone a dog too many times," Marlow said, speaking slowly so he wouldn't trip over his tongue, "and they might just start to bite."

Hanson considered this for a moment, then leaned forward. The lenses of his shades were mirrored and Marlow could see his own face there, greasy and drawn, about as intimidating as a wet blanket. For a second he thought he could almost see Hanson's eyes, too. But he must have been mistaken because they looked like two empty pits in his head.

"Then they get put to sleep," he said softly.

"What do you want, Hanson?" Pan asked with obvious disgust. "If you're not here to make a contract, then just piss off."

"No," he replied. "I think I'll stay. It could be fun."

"Nothing better than watching a new fish cock up his first contract," said Bullwinkle.

"That look in their eyes when they realize they've made an unbreakable deal," said Hope.

Marlow felt sick, felt the asthma start to fill his lungs with gunk the way it always did when he was angry. He coughed, trying not to make it too obvious.

"Just ignore them," Pan said, walking to the edge of the pool. "They're not worth it."

Marlow glared at Hanson for a fraction of a second before turning away. He walked swiftly over to Pan, speaking low. "But maybe they're right. I mean, I have no idea what I'm doing."

He looked at the pool of water, trying to make sense of what he was seeing. It was filled with a liquid that didn't look real. It was as black as tar, and yet ripples danced lightly across its surface—like there was something in there. Even though there were lights hanging right above it, there was no sign of their glow in the pool, and when Marlow leaned over he saw no reflection there. Small silver flecks floated in it, like stars. The movement of the liquid was mesmerizing, sickeningly so, reminding him of liquid mercury. Seth was busying himself with a control panel on the other side of the pool, something that looked like it belonged inside NASA.

"Seriously, Pan," Marlow whispered, "can't we do this another time? Tomorrow?"

His voice must have carried because somebody behind him made a clucking-chicken sound. He blew a wheezing breath out of his mouth, wanting to reach for his inhaler but refusing to look weak. He wasn't even sure if there was anything left in it. Pan looked at him, raising an eyebrow.

"You gonna let these guys get to you?" she asked. "It's your choice, Marlow. I'm not going to force you. Just remember that most people would give anything to be here right now, to have this chance."

"What are you going to wish for?" Seth interrupted. "To be able to breathe without impediment? I would recommend it, we know how to deal with that contract. We had a young woman with terrible asthma many years ago."

Had.

"And something else, perhaps? It seems a bit of a waste to limit yourself to that. Pan, any suggestions?"

"How about making him smell less disgusting," said Hope.

"Give him strength and speed," said Pan. "Start with the basics, have some fun."

"Good, good," said Seth. Marlow felt like he was on a train that was out of control, moving way too fast. He tried to force on the brakes again.

"Look, I'm really grateful for this but I'm not feeling so good, please can we just do this tomorrow?"

"Repeat what you are going to wish for," Seth said, like Marlow's voice wasn't working.

"I don't know what you mean," he said, clawing in a breath. It did little to stem the panic, and this time he did reach for his inhaler, firing off a shot that was full of nothing. He shook it and tried again, breathing hard, swearing.

"Just say it," said Pan. "So it's clear."

"Breathing," Marlow said. "I want to be able to breathe normally."

He thought he heard his words echoing across the cavern but then understood he was hearing something else, the soft, knitting-needle whir of some part of the machine. There were other noises inside his head, too soft to identify, fleshy and wet. They made his skin crawl. There was an explosion of light in the core of his brain, like a firework going off.

"I want to be as strong as ten men," said Pan. "I want to run faster than sound."

"Seriously, I can't," Marlow said. The clicks from the Engine were growing louder, the sound of something huge coming slowly to life

"Say it," she said.

"I want to be able to breathe normally. I want to be as strong as ten men. I want to run faster than sound."

"Again," she said. "Louder."

He repeated the words, then again, then again, until Pan turned to Seth and shrugged. The old man beamed at Marlow.

"You're ready," he said. "You can enter the pool."

"I can *what*?" said Marlow, shaking his head. "No way, man, I'm not going in there."

The liquid rippled and danced, its mottled surface impenetrable, the color of disease. He had no idea how deep the pool was, what else might be in there. It had been so long since he'd last been swimming that he wasn't even sure if he could remember how to stay afloat.

"No way," he said again. "I can't do this, Pan. I won't. I need time to . . . I just need time, okay?"

"Just what I thought," said Hanson. "They all try to be hard, they all fall to pieces. Pathetic."

"This has got nothing to do with you," said Marlow, jabbing a finger at the English guy. "You don't know me."

"I know everything about you." He sneered. "I've seen your kind before, full of bravado, bollocks the size of beach balls, right up until the point it hits the fan. Then you go crying back to Mummy with your tail between your legs."

It was just like being back at school, Caputo telling him he was out of control, waiting to self-destruct. *Screw them.* They had no right to tell him what to do.

"Why don't you—"

He only managed to get three words out before Hanson flicked a finger and Hope broke into a run. She was fast, grabbing one of Marlow's arms with impossible strength. Marlow reached for her with his free hand but it wouldn't move, as if it was bound with invisible ropes—just like back in the elevator. Bullwinkle was stepping forward, and every time his fingers twitched the bones in Marlow's arm seemed to creak. The pain burned through him and he gritted his teeth against it.

"Hanson!" yelled Pan. "Don't!"

He ignored her, walking up to Marlow and clamping a gloved hand around his jaw. Marlow kicked out but Hanson just smacked his leg away with an iron blow. He tried to breathe but his lungs had all but given up, refusing to let the air in. His whole body was a fury of panic, sparks of light bristling across his vision.

"Hanson!" Pan said. "Seth, for god's sake *stop them*."

"You're all the same, Herc's dogs," Hanson said. "I've seen it so many times."

He pushed forward, the three of them just about lifting Marlow off the floor. He tried to look over his shoulder, knowing how close they were to the pool, but Hanson held him tight.

"How many like you have we seen come and go?" Hanson whispered, pulling Marlow close. Once again he could see his reflection in those glasses, the face of a hanged man gasping his last breath. "It will eat you alive, spit you out. But so what. Let it have you."

"No!" Marlow said. But it was too late. Hope and Bull-winkle let him go and Hanson's fist connected with his stomach, a punch that seemed to turn him inside out. He staggered back, spluttering, putting his foot down on thin air.

Then he was falling, only the dancing pool of dead water there to catch him.

DROWNING

It was like falling into death.

The pool stank of open graves, of maggot-infested flesh, worming down his gullet, choking him, pulling him in. He burst out again, grappling for something solid, his legs thrashing into nothing. He found the lip of the pool, clutched at it.

"Not today," said Hanson, grinding a foot down onto his knuckles. He let go, barely able to keep his head above water.

"Pan, help," he said, coughing, wheezing, kicking.

"It's too late," Pan said. "Whatever you do, don't forget what to deal for."

Marlow tried to reach for her but the pool held him like it had fingers. He felt something glide past his foot, an icy grip around his ankle, and he screamed. The darkness took advantage, sliding into his mouth. Something latched onto his arm, like there was an army of corpses beneath the surface, and he fought against it, floundering.

"Do not struggle," said Seth. "It cannot hurt you."

"Oh, it hurts you," Hanson said, one foot on the edge. "It's a nightmare in there. Did they tell you that some people never even make it out of the pool?"

What?

"You're such an *asshole*, Hanson!" Pan yelled. "Marlow,

ignore everything the Engine shows you, they're lies, it will try to trick you."

Whatever was holding him began to pull, tugging hard on his skin as he thrashed on the surface of the pool. He was hyperventilating, his lungs exploding as he tried to take a breath. But nothing was happening. He felt his body begin to slide into unconsciousness, his eyes rolling back in their sockets. The fluid was leaking into them, blades of black light carving up his vision. Through them he saw Hanson grinning. This couldn't be the last sight he would ever see, it *couldn't* be.

"Shut it out," Pan said. "Keep your wishes in your head, don't forget, never forget."

"And whatever you do," Hanson said, leaning toward him, his words muted by the liquid that burrowed into his ears, "don't think about Pan with no clothes on."

The invisible fingers reeled him under, the whole world turning black. He struggled, feeling himself dragged deeper and deeper, faster and faster, the fluid boiling past his head, his stomach in knots. He felt like he was being sucked into a vortex, something that would pull him to the very center of the Earth.

Or even deeper than that, something that will drag you to the very depths of hell.

He opened his mouth and water flooded into his lungs, cold and choking but somehow letting him breathe. A face appeared in the darkness, Danny, a smile blazing out beneath his combat helmet. It was the Danny he knew from the photograph, exactly the same—sunglasses, the armored car, the tents in the background. He'd died eight days after the photograph was taken.

But I don't have to, he said. *Marlow, please, save me. Let me come home.*

Couldn't he do it? Couldn't he do this one good thing? Bring him back?

It's so easy, just a wish, just think it. I want to see Mom again, Marly. Take me to her.

Marlow nodded, then shook his head. There was something wrong with his brother's smile, it was too wide, his teeth like broken glass.

"You're not him," Marlow said. "You're not Danny."

His brother's smile twisted into an expression of horror, his mouth opening too wide. His face began to peel away like old wallpaper, maggots and mealworms squirming out from beneath his flapping skin. Then he was gone, and Charlie was there—or at least a flyblown mass of jellied meat that might once have been him.

You left me to die, he said, one of his lips peeling loose, rolling wetly down the front of his shirt. *You left me to fall in the river and drown. Wish me okay, Marlow. That's what friends do for each other. All it takes is a wish.*

"I'm sorry," he said, and he almost gave in, almost wished for him to be safe back on Staten Island. Then Pan's words blazed back into his mind: *Ignore everything it shows you, they're lies, it will try to trick you.* He reached into his memory, everything so far away, nothing real. But there were words there.

"I want to be able to breathe normally. I want to be as strong as ten men. I want to run faster than sound."

It was stupid, ludicrous, like a kid before Christmas. But he kept saying them, over and over, a mantra that held the Engine at bay. There was another thought in his head, planted there by Hanson—Pan, looking at him and smiling, reaching out and touching his face. She wasn't wearing a scrap of clothing and the sight of her was almost enough for him to forget where he was.

"No," he said, repeating his wishes again, and again, forcing the words from his lips.

Somewhere—it seemed like miles away, but how could it be, the pool was only small—the darkness seemed to be parting, great black clouds billowing to the side. A crack of thunder pulsed through the water, felt rather than heard, like the skull-crushing blast of a depth charge. There was something there, beyond the shadows. It was a figure, one that was surely far too big to fit here, one that might have been as vast as a mountain. Marlow turned away. He didn't want to look, but the invisible hands gripped his head, forcing him to see. There was something wrong with the figure, like it was radiating darkness, waves of invisible black light that broke against Marlow's skull. It was a monstrous bag of bones and skin, peering down at him with a clutch of eyes as watery as egg whites. It seemed to radiate cruelty.

This is what you desire?

There were no words in his head but he understood what was being asked of him. He didn't want this anymore, didn't want anything to do with this thing, but he knew it was too late. *Some people never even make it out of the pool.* Those who changed their minds? Those who didn't wish for anything? He didn't know. He didn't *want* to know. He just wanted out, away from this nightmare and the corpse hands that held him.

"I want to be able to breathe normally," he was almost screeching. "I want to be as strong as ten men. I want to run faster than sound."

And Pan, I want her to love me. His brain added without his permission.

It is done, said the wordless voice in his head. *It is yours, and the price is your soul.*

And with that thought came an unbearable sadness, a huge, gaping, lonely absence that made him feel as if everybody he had ever loved had died. He howled in despair, clutching at his stomach, trying to hold himself in. He realized that his arms were free and he began to paddle upward, desperately pushing himself toward the surface. His lungs were two shriveled sacks inside his chest, empty of everything but pain. He kicked and struggled his way through the liquid, suddenly bursting through the top of the pool into a riot of color and noise.

Hands reached for him, dragging him out, and he clung on to them with everything he had. There was a cry of pain, then he was dropped onto the stone floor.

"Let go, Marlow, let go, easy now."

Marlow released his grip, the world swimming into focus. Seth was there, his face contorted with pain. Pan was next to him, one hand on the old man. Marlow coughed, spitting the last dregs of black water from his mouth. They landed on the floor, wriggling like worms, squirming their way back toward the pool as if they were living things. The sight of them—hundreds of droplets swarming over each other—made Marlow gag. He retched until his stomach was empty. He tried to push himself up but the whole world was swimming.

"Wait there," said Pan. "Marlow, don't move, give us a second."

She looked flushed, the color on her cheeks making her even more beautiful than before. Marlow lay there on the stone, tasting the acid in his mouth. Hanson and his two douches stood exactly where they had before, those crap-eating grins still plastered over their faces.

Marlow turned back to Seth and Pan. The old man was shaking his wrist, still grimacing.

"That's some grip you have there, Marlow," he said.

"What?" Marlow asked, looking at his hand. Nothing had changed, he didn't feel any different.

Wait . . .

He sucked in a breath and he could have been standing at the top of a mountain, his lungs full of crisp, clean, oxygenated air. He breathed out slowly, not wanting to jinx it, then tried again. It was like it was the first time he had ever truly taken a breath and he almost laughed with the joy of it. "I can breathe," he said, grinning. "Holy crap, I can breathe."

"You can probably wrestle a bear too," said Seth, and Marlow understood what must have happened—Seth offering him a hand out of the pool, Marlow grabbing his arm, squeezing hard. He flexed his fingers. It was impossible, right? How could he have the strength of ten men?

"No way," he said, looking at Pan. She was redder than ever, like she was flustered. She stared back at him, biting her bottom lip. She looked different, softer somehow, like her icy exterior had started to melt. Marlow had to turn away, his own cheeks flaring. If he wasn't careful, then he was going to have to throw himself back into the pool.

"How long was I in there?" he asked, pushing himself to his feet.

"A second, less really," said Seth. "You went under and came up instantly. There is no time inside the Engine. My guess is it felt quite a bit longer to you."

"A second?" said Marlow. But he'd been down there for minutes. "It can't be."

"How did you do, doggy?" Hanson said. "What did you wish for?"

"Go on, tell us you brought the dead back," said Bullwinkle. "Time travel, something unbreakable. Make our day. We love seeing the demons eat rookies for breakfast."

"You guys make me sick," said Pan.

"Poor little princess," said Hanson, pouting.

Marlow stepped forward, feeling like a new person, feeling

like somebody had injected him with adrenaline, stripped out everything that made him weak.

"Why don't you do as she says and piss off," he said, his heart drumming like he had an engine of his own. He felt like a machine, like he could do just about anything.

Hanson raised his hands in mock surrender.

"Don't worry, I'm going. This bores me. I'll leave you two together, let the puppy have his bitch."

Last. Straw.

Marlow threw himself at Hanson, feeling the world suddenly slow, like it had run out of momentum. It was as if everybody else had frozen. Only he was moving, sprinting across the stone, his fist balling up. He unleashed a punch, aimed right at Hanson's nose. Only then did time suddenly catch up with itself, snapping back with a sudden lurch.

Marlow's fist connected with Hanson like two cars colliding, the impact so powerful that a shock wave blasted out across the chamber, kicking the surface of the pool into a frenzy. Hanson collapsed onto one knee with the force of it, his glasses splintering into shrapnel and exploding out across the stone.

"Whoa whoa whoa!" Pan said, running to Marlow and grabbing his arm. "Christ, that's enough!"

Marlow looked down at his fist, suddenly afraid of what he was capable of. Hanson shook his head, picking glass from his face, then slowly stood. What Marlow saw there made him stagger back.

He had no eyes. They were completely gone, leaving two red, ragged holes in his face. Somehow, though, they still seemed to burn into Marlow like blowtorches. Hanson straightened his collar and then smiled, the skin around his nose already starting to bruise.

"Hanson, he's new, he didn't know what he was doing," Pan said, maneuvering herself in front of Marlow like a shield.

There was a tremor in her voice that was even more un-settling than Hanson's eyeless death stare. "You were being an ass—just call it even, okay?"

"Like I said," Hanson replied, running a long, pink tongue around his lips, then spitting blood. He blinked, his eyelids flapping wetly, uselessly over the gaping pits in his face. "You two deserve each other. But try that again, dog, and I'll skin you alive."

He studied Marlow a moment more, a fly scuttling out of one of his eye sockets, buzzing up into the dark. Then he turned and walked up the stairs, his two lieutenants sloping after him. Pan waited until they had disappeared through the door before she turned to Marlow, letting out a long, ragged breath.

"Oh god, I thought he was going to kill you," she said.

"I could have—"

"No, you couldn't," she said. "Not him. Not even if he wasn't under contract. Jesus, Marlow, if you'd hit a normal person like that you would have sent their head spinning out into the middle of the Engine."

He looked at his hands, swallowing uncomfortably.

"You're not you anymore," Pan said, fanning her face with her hand like she'd just run a marathon. "You've got to remember that. Hug someone too hard and they'll burst. High-five somebody and you'll snap their wrist." She swore. "Man, maybe we should have thought this through."

"But I don't feel any different."

"You are," said Pan, staring out into the mechanical ocean. It had once again fallen silent and still, its work done. "You've got *that* inside you."

The thought made him feel sick, made him itch like he no longer had veins but pipes, not bones but levers and springs. He closed his eyes, took a few deep breaths—the air sliding into his lungs, crystal clear. When he opened them again he was surprised to see Pan standing right in front of him, squirming like she was uncomfortable, so close that he could feel her breath on his face. His heart flipped in his chest, so carried away that it took it a few seconds to settle back into a rhythm.

"What?" was all he had time to say before Pan leaned in and planted her lips on his, kissing him. She opened her mouth and he felt her tongue dart into his, exploring. He stood there, no idea how to respond, his brain screaming *ohmygodkiss-herbackyouidiot*, and he did, his hands gently resting on her elbows, the lightest of touches, like she was a bird he didn't want to startle.

He wasn't sure how long it went on for. There was no time here either, the moment so unexpected, so incredible, that it seemed to have lifted them out of the world into their own ageless, private universe. Eventually Pan broke free, stepping back, her mouth still open, her tongue running across her own lips. She stared at Marlow like he was the most desirable thing in the world, her pupils so dilated that she didn't look real.

Then her face crumpled into a look of fury. She swung her fist and punched Marlow in the mouth, hard enough to rock his head back. He staggered away, yelping.

"You bastard!" she said. "You wished for it, didn't you? You wished for *me*."

"No!" he said, retreating as she advanced. "I didn't . . . I . . . It wasn't my fault, it was Hanson, he planted the idea in my head, please, I would never—"

She threw herself at him and he did his best to shield his face, only to feel her lips on his again, her arms around his neck, pulling him closer. He couldn't resist, his brain struggling to make sense of what was going on. He kissed her back, then it felt as if an atomic bomb had been detonated in his stomach. He dropped, nursing his groin where Pan had kneed him. It felt like he was on fire down there and he groaned, everything turning into a blur through his watering eyes.

"Enjoy your gifts while you can," said Pan. "But that's one wish that even the Engine can't grant. Seth, cancel that contract *right now*. And you." She loomed over him, a finger jabbing repeatedly into his forehead. "You better not tell a goddamned soul about this."

Then she was gone, leaving him with the powers of a superman but crying like a baby.

NOT MUCH OF A GAMER

Marlow sat in the company rec room, a pint of ice cream resting on his aching crotch. The room was large, packed with sofas, kitchen stuff, and an air hockey table, but it felt even bigger because he and Seth were the only people there. The old man sat by Marlow's side, fastening a watch onto his arm. It had a huge circular face and the only things on it were big, bright, icy blue numerals. They currently read, *665:44:23:59*

Six hundred sixty-five hours and change until they come for me, until they drag me down to hell.

He was so tired that he couldn't take it seriously. The exhaustion kept creeping up on him, ambushing him, making him slide out of reality into the opening scenes of a dream. There were monsters down there in his nightmares, demons and Mammon and worse—the creature he'd seen when he was inside the engine. Every time he dozed off and they appeared he was startled back into wakefulness. He wasn't sure how much longer he could hold it off.

"So," said Seth, tightening the strap. "How does it feel to be a Hellraiser? To join the ranks of the Engineers?"

Marlow just shook his head. What he was feeling right now couldn't be summed up in any combination of words. The expectant silence was awkward, though, so he filled it with a question.

"Why Hellraisers?"

Seth stared into space, frowning. "I cannot tell you, for sure. The history is long lost and Ostheim is the one you need to talk to. He is a scholar, an expert on the Engine. But I do know that it was many centuries ago that the first Engineers came here. Back then the organization was known as Militibus de Inferno Pugno, which can be loosely translated as the Knights of Hell's Fist. The Knights who strike at hell. We do not know much about that time, other than the names of the martyrs in the *Book of Dead Engineers*. They had a motto, those soldiers. *Facilis descensus Averni.*"

He laughed to himself.

"Yeah, we didn't make it to Greek in school," Marlow said when no translation followed.

"Latin," Seth said with a gentle tut. " 'The descent into hell is easy.' It was, for them, *too* easy, because they had no way of breaking their contract. They had twenty-seven days in which to make their powers count, and then they slipped down into hell like a stone falling into a pond." He mimicked the action with his hand, contemplating it for a moment. "It must have been terrible, sacrificing yourself like that, knowing that there was no hope of salvation, that even your god was powerless to help you. But these were men who believed in what they did. They knew that their actions could save the world from a terrible fate. Hence the motto, the descent into hell is easy if you believe it is for a just cause."

"So . . ." Marlow said. "Why Hellraisers?"

"Oh, yes, sorry, my mind is old and weary." Seth cleared his throat. "Everything changed in the last century. The Engines, both of them, had long lain forgotten. We do not understand why, only that perhaps both sides simply ran out of soldiers. They almost consumed themselves into oblivion. It was in the fifties that we started to understand there was a way to trick the Engine, to break the contracts. Back when I was a young man—if you believe such a thing was ever true—we saw that it was possible to save people, to stop them from going to hell. Of course it was another few decades before we made that a reality. These people, this new breed of Engineer—we did not quite raise them from the underworld, but the principle was the same. Hellraisers. Somebody suggested it and it stuck. *Facilis descensus Averni, nisi vos a bonus causidicus.*"

Marlow gave a shrug and Seth's smile grew.

"The descent into hell is easy, unless you have a good lawyer. There," he said, patting Marlow's arm. "Good to go. Wear this at all times, never take it off. It is very easy to lose track."

"But you're not going to let that happen, right?" said Marlow. "I mean, you're going to cancel my contract."

"Yes yes," Seth said, struggling to his feet. "Of course, but you must have some fun first, get to learn your new powers."

Marlow laughed in disbelief, shaking his head.

"Powers," he said. "You make it sound like . . . like I'm a superhero or something."

"You are," Seth said. "For the next twenty-seven days, until we cancel your contract, you are in possession of superhuman abilities. Not just that, but the contract will do a fair job of looking after you. It's inbuilt into every deal the Engine makes. Wounds will heal more quickly, illnesses will pass you by. Better than an apple a day, if you ask me!"

He lifted a cup from the table and passed it to Marlow. Marlow took it and it exploded between his fingers, spraying water everywhere.

"Oh, man, sorry," he said, brushing flecks of china from his shirt. That was the sixth cup he'd broken since they'd ridden the elevator up here. "Maybe I'll just drink out of the faucet."

"A good idea, I think," said Seth, smiling. "How do you feel?"

"Okay, I think," he said. "I mean, no different. Just normal. Tired."

"The tiredness will not go away, I am afraid. Everything in that body of yours is now working to accommodate the Engine. It will make you feel exhausted from the moment you wake to the moment you sleep."

Marlow nodded. It didn't really matter how tired he felt, not when he could breathe like this, when he had the powers he did.

"But how does it work?" he asked.

Seth sighed, easing himself down onto a chair and perching there like an owl. He took off his glasses and rubbed his eyes.

"You really want to hear this now?" he said. "At . . . at half past four in the morning?"

"I'm still on East Coast time," Marlow said, shrugging, seeing how tired the old man looked. "But it can wait, sorry."

Seth sighed. "Actually it can't. Pan will not be happy if she wakes up in the morning and finds she is still infatuated with you."

"Maybe she just likes me," Marlow said.

Seth laughed.

"What? It could happen."

The old man struggled to his feet, shaking his head.

"Yes, I suppose anything is possible. Come with me." He walked to the door, Marlow following him. They were on a level just above the Lawyers' bullpen, a dozen or more doors leading off from the corridor into dorms and restrooms. Seth stopped at one and opened it, revealing a gym full of cardio machines and free weights. "Go, see how strong you are."

Marlow stifled a yawn with the back of his hand. Working out was the last thing he felt in the mood for but he couldn't deny he was curious. He walked to the weight bench.

"What I said before is true," Seth said behind him. "We don't know how the Engine works, we don't know who built it. But we understand the principle behind it. It reprograms the universe."

"What?" Marlow asked, frowning. "How?"

"Rather, it reprograms your particular section of the universe. Everything can be reprogrammed, Marlow. If you are a religious person, then you believe that God programmed the universe. If you are not religious, then look at science. We are now capable of changing somebody's genetic code, turning them into a different person altogether. We can reprogram our own species."

"But that's different," said Marlow.

"Why?"

"Because . . ." He realized he had nothing to say. He studied the rack of weights, huge round iron ones that looked like they belonged in an Arnold Schwarzenegger movie from the seventies. "Because this is physics and stuff. I don't know."

"The simplest way to think of it is like we are inside a video game. You play games, yes?"

"Yeah, of course," said Marlow, feeling a sudden pang of homesickness at the thought of his Xbox. He wondered whether his mom was thinking of him, whether she was worried. He doubted it, he didn't come home for days sometimes, just crashed on Charlie's floor. She'd probably be so drunk she wouldn't even notice he was gone. "Yeah, Call of Duty and stuff, all the time."

"Imagine you were playing this game and you wanted your character to have, say, a faster horse."

"You're not much of a gamer, are you?" Marlow asked. Seth waved the comment away.

"Or a larger gun, perhaps, I don't know, anything you like. If you happen to be a coder, if you happen to speak the language in which the game is written, you simply wriggle inside and change it. You rewrite the program."

"Yeah, but—"

"That is what the Engine does. It knows the code, it knows the secret language of our universe, the language that we ourselves have been written in. And it changes it. Go on, lift one, see for yourself."

Marlow reached down and picked up a weight with 20KG written on it. He wasn't sure how heavy it was supposed to be but when he hefted it up it was like lifting a sheet of paper. It was so surprising that he almost unbalanced himself, the weight flying up over his head. He let go and it crashed down with a *thunk*, narrowly missing his foot.

"I said lift it, not play shot put with it," said Seth, chuckling.

Marlow tried again, but this time he lifted the entire stack—seven or eight weights in total, the lowest two weighing fifty kilos each. He felt it this time, but it was still no more difficult than hefting a small box from the ground. It couldn't be real, could it? They had to be made of plastic, hollow. But when he let go and they crashed back down into their case he felt the floor tremble with the force of it.

"By my reckoning that's a couple hundred kilos you just picked up without breaking a sweat," Seth said. "Maybe a quarter ton. Not too shabby, young man. Come, this is not what I wanted you to see."

He disappeared. Marlow looked at the weights, then at his hands, still refusing to believe it. He jogged after Seth, then stopped, seeing a heavy bag hanging from the ceiling. He jabbed at it and the punching bag ripped free from its mount and cartwheeled across the room, thumping into a treadmill hard enough to knock it over. Plaster dust rained down from the ceiling and Marlow backed away, walking swiftly through the door.

"What was that?" Seth asked.

"Nothing," he replied, steering the old man away. "Definitely nothing. What did you want me to see?"

"This way," said Seth, reaching the end of the corridor and opening the elevator. He pressed the button for the bullpen. "So you see, the Engine rewrites the physics of your particular pocket of existence. It hears what you want and reprograms the code accordingly, granting you any wish."

"And the only price you have to pay is your soul," said Marlow. Seth grinned.

"Yes, once upon a time that was true, for our friends the Knights. Originally you would have had to part with that piece of you, the very essence of your being. It was inevitable. There was no way you could crack your contract."

"But why?" Marlow asked. "What can a soul do? Why is it worth anything?"

"Who knows. I certainly don't. Not one scientist on the planet could explain the nature of the soul, but few would deny we have one. It is one of the mysteries of the human condition. Perhaps one day we will unlock it."

The elevator grumbled to a stop and Seth heaved open the gate, walking into the bullpen. Two of the Lawyers were still there, one of them startled out of sleep when he heard Seth's voice. He jumped to his feet, slapping his face gently to wake himself up. He was a young guy, twenties maybe, and his messy hair and Halo T-shirt made him look more like a surfer than a lawyer.

"Yo," he said. "I wasn't sleeping, honest, just resting my eyes."

"And practicing his nocturnal flatulence," said the woman.

She was his senior by at least a decade, dressed like an old-fashioned librarian. She peered over her glasses at Marlow. "I take it we're repairing some rookie mistakes?"

"Yes, Annie, we had an unfortunate wish, didn't we, Marlow?" Seth said, still smiling. "A certain, ah, unrequited desire."

"You wished for the dish," said the guy. "Happens all the time."

He moved across the room to a storage locker and pulled out a pair of gloves and a helmet, connected to each other with wires. He chucked it to the woman called Annie, who just managed to snatch it out of the air.

"Tim, I really wish you wouldn't treat our equipment with such disregard," said Seth. "You do know how expensive it is, don't you?"

"Sorry, boss," he replied, donning a pair of gloves of his own and pulling the helmet over his head. It looked like a virtual reality set, or something Daft Punk might wear.

"This is quite something," Seth said, pulling Marlow to the edge of the room. Tim snapped his fingers and the huge bank of computers along one side of the room roared to life, a noise like the pounding rush of a waterfall. He clicked his fingers again.

"We need section, um, 808-FR-403.2," he said.

"Correction," said Annie. "408.2."

"Whatever," muttered Tim. He waved his hands like he was a cop guiding traffic. Lights embedded in the walls blazed to life, beaming out lines of white laser as delicate as cobwebs, hundreds of them. They converged in the huge empty space in the middle of the room, taking on the shape of cogs and pistons, chains and gears and levers. It looked like a phantom version of the inside of the Engine and it took Marlow's breath away. Tim moved his hands again and the entire hologram shifted, pushed across the room, new sections appearing as the old ones vanished into the wall.

"It's an exact simulation of the Engine," whispered Seth. "Well, the parts of it that we have documented. This section here, as far as we can tell, deals with what we shall call affairs of the heart."

"We may have a slight irregularity in the eighth quadrant," said Tim, spreading apart his hands and causing the hologram to enlarge. He zoomed in some more and Marlow saw a series of pins lined up together, some raised, some lowered. They reminded him of the arms and needles of a record player. Each one contained a small vial filled with a drop of dark liquid, swimming with flecks of light. "Four and five?" said Tim.

"No," replied Annie. "I don't think so, go north."

He swiped his hands and the floor moved, the hologram passing through Marlow, making him feel giddy. He ran his hands through the light, seeing it dance on his skin, wondering how on earth somebody had managed to think this up.

"There," said Annie, pointing to a clutch of coiled springs, more needles attached to them. "Six, seven, eight . . . the ninth point has shifted."

"Good spot," said Tim.

"What are they doing?" Marlow whispered, not wanting to disturb them. Seth leaned in, speaking quietly.

"The Engine uses those filaments to write your contract. There are millions of them, billions, each one as small as a hair on your head. We're not sure how, but they have the power to rewrite the code, reprogram the universe. When they do, they change position, like that."

"But how the hell do you know if they have?" Marlow asked. "There are so many of them."

"Our computers pick up some discrepancies," said Seth.

"But the computer isn't as sharp as a human mind. These guys are genii, photographic memories. They can identify when something in the machine has changed. And when they do, they reset it, they cancel the contract."

"Like Lawyers," Marlow said, nodding.

"Oh come on," said Annie, genuinely irritated. "Not you, too. We're not lawyers, we're quantum mathematicians. There's a big, big difference."

"Sorry," said Marlow, watching as she walked through the hologram toward the area they were discussing. She reached down, touching one of the filaments with her glove.

"Definitely the ninth," she said. "Confirm."

"Confirmed," said Tim. "This is . . . section 808-FR-408.2, subsection fourteen, and filament nine. You ready?"

"I was born ready," Annie said. She plucked the filament like it was a guitar string and it moved, popping up. There was a rumble beneath Marlow's feet, like continents were shifting deep beneath the surface. Something sharp stabbed him in the side of his head, as if he'd been bitten, and he slapped a hand to his temple.

"That is normal," said Seth. "Especially the first time the Engine is cheated. It doesn't like it, not one bit."

"What's happening?" he grunted.

"This display is connected to the actual Engine, to each and every filament. If they change position here, they change position inside the Engine."

"So that's it then?" Marlow asked. "My contract's broken?"

Seth laughed again, but his eyes were full of a profound sadness.

"If it were that easy, then I would have had three fewer heart attacks and my hair would still be the same color as my eyebrows," he said, shaking his head. "No, that is most certainly not it."

Tim was swiping at the floor, faster now, giving the illusion that they were all sailing down a river of light.

"There, the eighteenth," he said, and they flicked another filament. Something burrowed into Marlow's skull again and he winced. "If the eighteenth is gone, then we'd better check out thirty-six too."

"Every contract is different," said Seth. "Some involve perhaps several thousand filaments. More complicated contracts, such as Pan's last deal, have a total of hundreds of thousands. The more you wish for, the harder it is to locate and repair the filaments. To make it more complicated still, the filaments correspond to the individual. Two people wishing for the same thing would have a very different contract. Somebody of more advanced years, such as me, would unfortunately have a contract involving a million filaments. Which is why old farts cannot make a deal. And when too many people have a contract at one time, it becomes too muddled, impossible to differentiate, which is why we do not have an army at our disposal. Come, Marlow, we must leave them to their work."

Tim and Annie burrowed their way deeper into the holographic Engine, shouting to each other as they navigated his contract. It looked almost as if they were playing some hi-tech sport, virtual tennis—only the prize they were playing for was his soul. He jogged after Seth, pulling the elevator gates shut behind him.

"How long does it take them?" he asked as they rumbled upward.

"For this? Not long. Several hours. It could be longer." Seth saw his expression of disbelief. "Remember, the Engine does not want you to beat it. The contracts are designed to be unbreakable. It is only because of the technology we possess that we even stand a chance. The mathematics here, the equations involved in breaking the simplest of contracts, they are mind-boggling. Some contracts take the full twenty-seven days to crack."

"Couldn't you just, y'know, make a contract to know how to break a contract?" Marlow asked, feeling like a genius himself for even suggesting it. Seth shook his head as the elevator came to a halt.

"We tried it," he said sadly. "The Engine knew we would. It was an impossible contract to break. We lost an Engineer, right here. Would you, please? My strength is not what it was."

Marlow opened the gates and Seth stepped out, walking to the third door along the corridor.

"This is where you will sleep," he said. "It is not a five-star hotel, I am afraid, but it is comfortable. You should rest. If you do not feel tired, then by all means use our gymnasium, or sit in the recreation room. But whatever you do, please stay inside the complex. The Engine is powerful, but secrecy is our most important weapon. The fewer people who know about us, the less likely it is that the Circle will discover our location. We fly far beneath the radar, so close to the ground that our bellies are scratched by the trees."

"Seriously?" Marlow said, raising an eyebrow. "Since I've met you guys you've blown up a hospital and taken out half a block in a city of eight million people. You don't so much fly under the radar as blow the hell out of it."

Seth hissed out a dry wheeze of a laugh.

"Nothing to do with us," he said, waving a hand and winking. "The events you talk of are terrorist attacks, gas explosions, terrible car accidents, catastrophic and tragic building collapses, midair collisions, riots and stampedes. These are the events that make the news, yes? And surely the news does not lie."

"But—"

"Enough, Marlow. I must go, or you will be carrying me to my bed. Just remember, do not leave this place."

He shuffled away to another door.

"Thank you, Seth," Marlow called after him. The old man waved, then disappeared, the door closing behind him. Marlow stood there for a moment. He was tired, no doubt about it. He didn't think he'd ever been so tired. But he knew there was no way he could sleep, not now, not with so much power inside him. He set off toward the gym, wanting to test himself, wanting to see exactly what he was capable of. He was halfway there when Bullwinkle stepped out of the door, wiping his sweating face with a towel. They both almost jumped out of their skins when they saw each other, and Marlow was the first to recover.

"Not so tough now, eh?" he said.

Bullwinkle straightened, but he looked afraid. The guy was under contract—Marlow's arm still ached from where he'd been held by phantom telekinetic fingers—but he knew that if he punched him now the way he'd punched Hanson downstairs he could tear him in two. The thought made him feel sick and he unclenched a fist he didn't even know he'd made. Bullwinkle saw it and he took a step forward, lobbing the towel back into the gym.

"You shouldn't be out wandering the corridors, *mutt*," he said. "Isn't it past your bedtime?"

"Isn't it past yours?" Marlow replied. He knew it was probably the lamest comeback that had ever been uttered but he had been too tired to think of anything else.

"You better be in the dorm before Hanson catches you," Bullwinkle said. "There are rules. You shouldn't be pissing around out here. What were you trying to do? Find Pan's bed?"

"I wasn't—"

"I'm telling you to go to your dorm, rookie," Bullwinkle said. "You understand me? That's a direct order."

Bullwinkle walked past, barging Marlow with his shoulder. Marlow stood firm and the big guy bounced off, grunting.

"Disobey me and you'll have Hanson to answer to," he grumbled as he walked into the shower room. "And give up, she doesn't want you."

Marlow heard the rush of water from inside. He sighed and took a couple of steps toward the gym. Then he stopped. He'd rather eat his own crap than take it from Bullwinkle and his eyeless freak of a boss. Besides, Bullwinkle was right. It would do him good to get away from Pan for a while, try to fill his head with something else.

He turned and walked back to the elevator, quietly shutting the gates before pressing the button for the top floor— the way out.

Time to have some fun.

DOUBLE DOUBLE DOUBLE CRAP

Pan wanted nothing more than to be able to sleep, but Marlow was making that impossible.

He was the only thing in her head, invading every thought. She tried to fight it, but he was a tick burrowing into her skull, impossible to dislodge. She thought about how annoying he was (*how beautiful he looks when he smiles*). She tasted his breath, a hint of vomit from when she'd kissed him (*but his lips are so soft, so warm*). She tried to focus on all the negatives, on how much she hated him, but then she'd see him there, grinning at her, moving in for another kiss, and she felt her heart melt into a warm, gooey mess, her stomach doing loop-the-loops.

She cursed, turning onto her side. She knew it wasn't really Marlow's fault (*nothing could be his fault, he's perfect—oh, god, shut up, brain!*). It was Hanson. He'd known exactly what he was doing, planting that image in Marlow's head right before he went into the tank. He'd done it before, the first time Truck had brokered a contract—although luckily Truck was of another persuasion and it hadn't worked. Hanson was just an asshole, but he was one of Ostheim's favorite Engineers so there wasn't a damn thing any of them could do about him.

Except Marlow. He stood up to him, punched him in the face. So brave, so strong.

She growled, pulling the pillow over her head. Marlow stared back at her from the darkness, moving in for a kiss, and her mouth was open, ready . . . She threw the covers off and sat up, her heart drumming, her skin cool with sweat.

"Goddammit!"

"*¡Silencio!*" said Night from the other side of the dorm. "Some of us need our beauty sleep."

Pan crashed back down, thumping her fist against her forehead to try to knock out the Marlow images. She knew it was just the Engine messing with her thoughts, but it felt so *real*. She loved him. She wanted to shout it from the rooftops, *I love Marlow Green!* But it couldn't be true because she'd sworn never to fall in love, never to give anyone that power over her. Not again. Not after what had happened last time.

She saw him now, the guy she'd met when she'd been taken into foster care, the guy who told her she was special, told her he wanted her more than anything else in the world, wanted to own every little piece of her. And she'd believed him, right up to the point he'd tried to take those little pieces for himself. She'd just turned thirteen and she hadn't even known she was capable of violence until that point, until she'd snatched up the only thing she could find—a cast-iron lamp by her bed—and beaten him to death with it.

If only Marlow had been there, he'd have saved you.

"Oh shut up," she told her head, the rush of emotions—love, hate, love, hate—churning inside her stomach, making her feel sick. No, she was never going to put herself in that position again. The day Herc had marched into her holding cell, the day he'd given her a choice about who she wanted to be, was the last time she would ever let somebody else control her head, her heart, or any other part of her.

Apart from them, of course, Herc and Ostheim.

She wasn't stupid. She knew they had manipulated her. That's what Herc did—picked the troubled kids, the ones in care, the ones who'd been kicked out of school, the ones shivering inside a cell. She knew why, too. These were the guys who had nothing to lose, the ones who'd run right out of choices.

Marlow fit the bill perfectly. They'd run a background check while he was out cold in the Manhattan tower—minor criminal record, just been expelled—he was a model candidate for an Engineer. Herc would have recruited him on the spot if he hadn't wanted him to escape, to become bait. *But thank god he did recruit him, otherwise I wouldn't be in the same building as him now, wouldn't be so close to him, wouldn't be able to sneak out of my room right now and find him . . .*

"Traitor," she whispered to her brain.

He was cute, though. Marlow. Too young for her, obviously, and annoying as all hell. And his breath stank, and he was a pretty awful kisser, and his hair was truly atrocious. She sat up again, probing her thoughts, picturing Marlow. She screwed up her face, nothing there but distaste.

"Thank god," she said, scrubbing her lips with the back of her hand, a sour taste on her tongue. The Lawyers must have cracked this part of Marlow's contract. Maybe now she'd finally be able to get some rest. She closed her eyes, her thoughts blissfully empty, sleep wrapping itself around her like a warm, comfortable blanket.

The alarm ripped its way through the beginning of a dream and Pan shot up, her heart just about catapulting through her throat. Night was already out of bed, a blur as she bolted to the door. Pan struggled into her pants, buttoning them as she went. It was rare that the alarm went off but not unheard of.

Usually it was a contract that was nearing expiration and needed emergency work, other times it was a drill. Plus Herc had set it off at least twice trying to smoke a secret cigarette in the toilet.

He was there now, standing outside his room looking like somebody had just dragged him from his grave.

"No rest for the wicked," he mumbled, rubbing at his stubble. "Any idea?"

She shook her head, running to the elevator, bundling in alongside Herc and Night and Hope. It was an uncomfortable ride down to the bearpit, and when she opened the gates she saw Hanson there, wearing a new pair of sunglasses. He looked pissed and he jabbed a hand at Herc.

"You happen to know where your latest mongrel is?" he said.

Oh crap.

"Herc, you have Marlow, right?" blasted a voice from hidden speakers. Pan straightened to attention when she recognized Ostheim's accent. "Tell me he's inside the complex."

"He's inside the complex," Herc said.

"No, Herc, he's not," said Ostheim. "He breached the door."

Double crap.

Herc stormed across the room to one of the monitors. It was the security feed from outside the door, but it wasn't the courtyard entrance. A streak of light burned across the image, just a second.

"Again," Hanson said. "Slower."

The clip replayed at a fraction of the speed and Pan saw Marlow running across the street, a goofy grin plastered over his face. The tape ran on and Pan saw Marlow reappear next to Hanson's shiny blue BMW—the same one he kept in every city connected to the Red Door. He looked like he was scratching something into the hood with a rock.

"What is that?" Pan said. "Looks like a rocket ship."

"Why the hell wasn't anyone watching him?" Hanson said.

"I left him with Seth," Pan said. "He—"

"That old git wouldn't know where to find a turd if he'd just laid it," Hanson said. "Jesus Christ, Herc, this is a total clusterf—"

"Keep your knickers on," Herc interrupted. "We'll just go get him."

"You'd better make it fast," said Ostheim. "And I mean fast, Herc."

"Why?" he said. "What's the hurry, all he'll do is mess around for a bit. How much damage can he do?"

Hanson sucked his teeth, pointing at another monitor. It was filled with data, the type used to identify fluctuations in the code, and at the moment it was going wild. Herc stared at it for a second and turned three shades paler.

"Because we've got Engineers in the city, Herc," said Ostheim. "Enemy Engineers."

"In Prague?" Pan asked.

"The door didn't let him out in Prague," said Hanson. "It dumped him in Budapest. That's where we're watching him."

Double double crap.

"For the love of . . ." Herc said, his cheeks blazing. "So there are Engineers in Prague, right?"

"No, Herc," said Ostheim. "Wake up, they're in Budapest, five hundred clicks from Prague. And if they get to your boy before we do, then he could lead them right back here."

Double double double crap.

HOW THE HELL DID WE GET TO BUDAPEST?

This. Is. Awesome.

Marlow couldn't stop grinning as he ran into the night. He didn't feel like he was going particularly fast, but as soon as he started to run everything else dissolved into slow motion. The raindrops falling from the sky became almost stationary, defying gravity, hanging like jeweled ornaments. Cars slowed from silver bullets to snails, slow enough that he could climb over their hoods, could look in through the windshields and see the drivers, oblivious to him. Every time he ran a shock wave rippled out from him like a gunshot, kicking up dust and dirt and making windows rattle in their frames.

I want to run faster than sound.

The Engine had given him what he wanted.

There weren't many people out at this time of night, in this weather. And to those who had braved the streets Marlow was a ghost. He ran up to them, the slow-motion world only starting to spin again when he stopped. It must have looked like he'd appeared out of nowhere because they always jumped back, screaming, scared out of their skins. Then he'd bolt and the world would grind almost to a halt, turning the people into statues with startled faces. He laughed at the sheer joy of it, the impossibility of it, as he broke into a run once again.

He had no idea where he was. He hadn't emerged in the same courtyard he'd entered through but rather on a quiet road facing a river. He'd had a sack over his head en route to the Engine so none of the streets were familiar, but he didn't care where he was going. It just felt so good to be moving, to be the fastest thing in the night.

He sped around a corner, dodging a slow-moving couple and careening across a cobbled street. He slipped on the wet asphalt, momentum throwing him toward a parked car. He reached out to stop himself and his hand left a crater in the metal side panel of the vehicle, the window glass shattering. The vehicle rocked hard on its suspension, the alarm sounding like it was drenched in syrup—slow and deep—until time pinged back to normal.

Whoa. He looked at the dent in the car, then back across the road to the startled couple. They stared back, jaws almost on the floor, eyes bulging, trying to figure out what had happened.

Marlow ran, everything blurring, stretching, like he was entering warp speed. He crossed the street in a heartbeat and stopped again, seeing the couple stagger away, shouting to each other in shock. In their eyes he must have just blinked out of existence. He left them to it, sprinting down the street, over a moving car. He kept thinking he'd have to stop soon, kept reaching down to his pocket to make sure his inhaler was still there, but his lungs were working at what felt like 200 percent of their capacity, like someone had ripped them out and replaced them with a carburetor.

He sped up, just a blur as he crossed onto the sidewalk and wove his way between the streetlights. He couldn't remember a single time in his life, not one moment, where he'd felt this exhilarated, this *free*. Every time he opened his mouth the laughter spilled out, cool and golden. He couldn't remember the last time he'd laughed like this either. It felt like it might never have happened before.

He ran through a group of guys, all of them drunk, specks of their spittle hanging in the air like dewdrops. He was close enough to one that he grabbed the bottle of beer from his hand, zipping around a corner before slowing. He peeked back, seeing the man lift his hand to his face, the moment he realized his drink had gone, the confusion as he studied his hands and the concrete behind him. Marlow collapsed against the wall, snorting with laughter.

The beer was cool in his hand and he lifted it to his lips. The smell hit him hard, made him think of his mom, sitting at home cradling her Bacardi. It was a world away from this moment, tearing through the streets, faster than time. He pulled back his arm and lobbed the bottle down the street, watching it spin in a perfect arc, dropping earthward. Then he ran, catching up with it in an instant, snatching it out of the air. Man, if he could keep these powers he'd be a millionaire, a football star, the only person ever to play as quarterback and wide receiver on the same team—for the same pass.

He slam-dunked the bottle and darted into a park, sprinting between the trees, leaves dancing weightlessly in his wake. Taking a deep breath, he jumped onto the roof of a van, using it like a springboard, crossing the whole street in one bound before crunching down on the opposite side. Facing him was a hill, covered in green. He bounded up a set of stone stairs, climbing, climbing, climbing, feeling like he was scaling a mountain, feeling like he was running right into the heavens.

Only when he ran out of stairs did he collapse onto his ass, out of breath but not in the *clutching-his-throat-feeling-like-he-was-about-to-die* kind of way that he was used to. He had no idea where he was but a city was laid out beneath him, studded with light, a fat, lazy, moon-drenched river splitting it in two. He sat there for a moment, the cool, fresh air rushing into his lungs like they were bellows. This was insane, totally insane. It couldn't be real. But he could smell the city, dust and grease and the faint aroma of the river. The warm touch of a summer night prickled his skin, the stone beneath him was cool and damp. The air was full of distant engines, a siren, and the hesitant chatter of the first birds who dared break the silence of the night. It was real. It was all perfectly, beautifully real.

"Marlow?"

The voice came from nowhere and his scream lodged in his throat like a fish bone. He jumped up, just trees behind him, the darkness in between them so profound that nothing might have been there at all, like you could step between those trunks and find yourself obliterated from existence.

"Who's there?" he asked. Probably Herc or Truck, right? Come to bring him back. Maybe it was Pan. Maybe she missed him.

"Marlow, don't run, please."

He suddenly recognized the voice, but it couldn't be.

"Charlie?" he asked.

The foliage rustled, a shape gliding from the gloom twenty yards away. Charlie stepped into a pocket of moonlight, looking like a ghost. His clothes were torn, his face pale and smudged with bruises and blood. His nose was bent at a strange angle, like it had been broken. Marlow moved toward him but Charlie held up his hands, a set of handcuffs rattling.

"Don't," Charlie said, sounding like he was chewing toffee. "Please. Move and they'll kill me."

Marlow's heart went into overdrive. He looked to the side, trying to make sense of the darkness between the trees.

"Who, Charlie?"

Somebody else emerged from the shadows, treading carefully, keeping Charlie between himself and Marlow. It was the guy from the school, Patrick.

"Who do you think?" he said. "You figure we'd just pack up and go home? I told you I'd come for you."

Patrick wrapped a fist around Charlie's throat, squeezing. Charlie struggled.

"Let him go," Marlow said, taking a step forward, ready to run at them. He was fast now, could reach Charlie, could knock Patrick's head off with a single punch. But before he could take another step a third figure strolled from the trees. It was a young woman dressed all in black, like a cat burglar. She had red hair and she brushed it out of her eyes with one hand. In the other she was holding a pistol, pointed right at Charlie's head.

"You're fast," she said. "We've been chasing you all over the city. But you're not faster than a bullet. Go for me and Patrick snaps your friend's neck. Go for him and I pull the trigger."

"They will," said Charlie. "They beat the crap out of me trying to find out where you went."

"But you didn't know," Marlow said. "I didn't tell you."

"No, you left me."

"I wanted to *protect* you," Marlow said, trying to ignore Charlie's bitter smile.

"Yeah, Marlow, that worked out great."

"So how did you know we were in Prague?" Marlow asked.

"Prague?" Charlie gasped for air. "This is Budapest."

How the hell did we end up in Budapest?

"You've got one chance to save your friend's life," said Patrick, lifting Charlie off the ground. He kicked at the air like a hanged man, batting pathetically at the vise-like grip around his throat. "Where's the Engine?"

"I don't know what—"

"You've seen it," said the girl. "You've *used* it. Where is it?"

"I don't know," Marlow said. "Please, I don't . . . They put a bag over my head, wouldn't let me see."

"And what about tonight?" Patrick said, lifting Charlie higher. "Where's the door?"

Marlow desperately thought back, seeing a street, cars, a river. He'd been running so fast he hadn't been paying any attention to where he was or where he was going.

"No idea. It was just a street," he said. "But the door, it's red, like bright red. That's all I know, I promise."

Patrick and the girl shared a look. Charlie's face was a mottled shade of purple, his eyes starting to roll back in their sockets. *Do I go? Do I stay?* Marlow bounced on his heels, the panic like a straitjacket.

"Please," he said. "Let him go. He's dying."

"Like you let my sister go?" Patrick said. "How long did you torture her for?"

"I didn't. *We* didn't," Marlow said, wondering when he'd become part of the "we." "Her contract expired, we never got the chance. She didn't tell us anything. *Please.*"

"He's useless to us," said the girl. She put her hand to her ear. "Negative on the new fish, tell the scouts to search for red doors, east of the river." She listened for a second, then nodded. "Disposal authorized."

Disposal?

She pulled the trigger before Marlow could so much as blink, the bullet thudding into Charlie's stomach. He groaned, his chained hands dropping to the wound, trying to hold himself in.

No!

Marlow started to move but he was too slow. Patrick grinned at him, then pulled back his arm and launched Charlie into the air. His strength was phenomenal, his friend spinning up and over the edge of the hill, a fan of blood trailing after him toward the city below.

"That's for Brianna," Patrick said, moving in. "And this is for you."

FREE FALL

Marlow watched Charlie spin over the edge of the hill, dropping toward the river. He couldn't let him die, not like this. There was still time.

He ran, the world slowing to a crawl—slow enough that he could see droplets of Charlie's blood suspended in the air, almost perfectly still. He'd only taken a few steps before something materialized in the air before him, scraps of bone and skin winding themselves around the rain, flesh knitting itself together until Patrick was standing there.

Marlow skidded to a halt, ducking beneath Patrick's swinging fist. He managed to straighten in time to see the boy fire off an uppercut. This one connected with his ribs, the force of the punch lifting him off the ground in an explosion of pain. He spun head over heels, landing on his back. Patrick 'ported again, reappearing right next to him.

A gunshot tore through the night, a bullet gouging the rock next to his head. He rolled up, scrabbling into a run as the girl fired off another shot. A slow-motion plume of fire crawled from the barrel of the gun, the bullet sailing out after it, carving a path through the air.

Marlow sensed a shape pop into existence beside him, Patrick there again, his face feral. Marlow lashed out, a lucky shot that connected with the boy's chin, catapulting him toward the trees. He didn't stop to see where he'd landed, just turned and ran through the frozen night, a shock wave of sound pulsing out before him like a cannon blast. It was too dark to see much, even with the moon grinning down at him, but wasn't that Charlie there, a silhouette against the city, falling in slow motion?

He propelled himself off the side of the cliff, leapfrogging rocks and railings, almost losing his footing in the dark. He was fast, yes, and strong, but he knew that if he fell here, if he tumbled over the rocks to the streets below, he'd be as dead as any mortal. He slowed a fraction, seeing Charlie's flailing body drop toward the river. He could still reach—

Something thumped into his back, as hard and fast as a train, and he tumbled. He rolled down the hill, Patrick next to him, pounding at him with fists of concrete. One connected with his nose and the world went white, a supernova of light detonating right in the middle of his head. The pain followed almost instantly, an inferno inside his broken nose. He tried to fight back but they were rolling too fast, bouncing off rocks, their fall out of control.

There was a sudden lurch, then nothing at all—no rocks, no steps, just free fall. Marlow's stomach exploded and he saw the ground rush up at him, a parked car. He landed on the roof, crushing it, groaning as he rolled off. There was a sudden rush of air behind him as Patrick 'ported onto the street, but Marlow ignored it, running faster than he'd ever run, the world almost stationary around him. The river was up ahead, a bridge, buildings. Marlow scoured the sky, no sign of Charlie. Was he too late? Was his friend smeared over a street somewhere?

There, level with the rooftops, a dark shape dropping. Marlow leaped over a fence, then onto a car, propelling himself into the river. He prepared himself for the cold, but when his foot hit the water it was spongy, almost solid. He ran across it, Charlie almost in reach, so close, hanging in the air like a phantom. Marlow jumped, reaching out for his friend, tackling him in midair. His momentum punched them both toward the riverbank and they rolled to a halt on the grass.

Marlow snatched in a breath, leaning over his friend. Charlie was in shock, his eyes open but unseeing, blood dripping from his mouth. His T-shirt was drenched and when Marlow pulled it back he saw a gaping hole. He pushed his hands against it but the blood leaked through his fingers, as hot as boiling water.

He was going to die.

"Oh god, Charlie," Marlow said, tears burning his eyes. "Man, I'm so sorry. I never should have left you."

Charlie opened his mouth but all that came out was a bubble of blood. Marlow looked around, the windows dark and lifeless, the street empty. He wanted to call for help but it would bring Patrick much more quickly than an ambulance. He had to carry him, get him to a hospital. Marlow reached down to scoop up his friend but something big smashed into the grass a couple of yards away, showering him with dirt. It was a bollard, rooted in a half ton of concrete, rolling past him like a wrecking ball before crunching into the side of a building.

He scanned the sky, saw another one sailing across the river like it had been launched by a catapult. Patrick was on the other bank, ripping a third bollard from the ground.

Marlow managed to get to his feet, the slab of concrete hurtling right toward him. He threw a punch at it and it exploded into shrapnel, a bolt of pain lancing from his fist to his armpit. He blinked the dust from his eyes, only just managing to get his hands up before the next bollard struck. He caught it, the impact driving him back, his heels gouging trenches in the dirt. He recovered his balance and lobbed the bollard across the river, as easy as if it were a beach ball.

It was a wild shot, nowhere near its target, thumping into the side of the bridge with a sound like a church bell. Patrick vanished, reappearing almost instantly on this side of the river. But Marlow was already running right for him, everything slowing. He slammed into the boy, both of them dropping into the river.

Time snapped back and he hit hard, sinking, the cold like a kick to the gut. Marlow tried to breathe and inhaled a lungful of freezing water. He kicked upward, bursting out of the surface in time to see Patrick swing a punch. It connected with his temple and for an instant there was nothing but black. When the world swam back he realized he was beneath the water again, hands on his head, pushing him down.

Something dark and cold was creeping into the edge of his mind—nothing to do with the river. He choked, lashing out, but the water slowed him down, made it impossible to see where to punch. The hands on his head were squeezing so hard he felt his skull creaking, about to splinter, his vision sparking. He would have screamed if there was anything left in his lungs.

Distant pops, then something streaked through the water like a shaft of sunlight. More followed, one coming so close to Marlow that he felt a cold burn on his skin. He heard a thud, then the grip on his head came loose. He clawed his way to the surface, snatching in as much air as he could. Patrick was there, clutching his shoulder with one hand, looking like he was struggling to stay afloat.

More gunshots, bullets tearing through the water, too close. Marlow looked toward the bank to see a cop there, an old guy, a pistol in his shaking hands. He was yelling something that Marlow couldn't make any sense of. He fired again and Marlow heard the whistle as the bullet seared the air beside his ear.

He swam, trying to make the world speed up again. But he

couldn't get his feet on the ground, couldn't *run*. Patrick was panicking too, too tired to 'port, both of them trying to get to the opposite side of the river. The guy was hurt, though, blood oozing from the wound in his shoulder.

The cop was shouting, over and over, squeezing off more rounds. Then his head erupted into a fan of crimson and he crumpled to the ground. The girl with red hair dropped casually from the bridge, turning her gun out into the river.

"Patrick?" she yelled, barely audible over the rush of water. "Where are you?"

"Here!" came a reply from the darkness. "He's that way, by the bridge."

Pop pop pop, more bullets tearing into the water. Marlow snatched in a breath and dived into the murk, paddling manically, the current dragging him along. He was a sitting duck out here. He swam for as long as he could, until he felt the slimy riverbank. Bursting back out he clung to it, choking, snatching at anything he could to try to root himself in place.

A hand. He snatched at it, holding as tight as he could, silently yelling, *Please please please, pull me up!* Because there was nothing left in him.

Then Patrick's head appeared above the hand, pale and exhausted but still smiling.

"Beat you," he said, then he pushed Marlow back beneath the surface.

PROTOCOL CAN KISS MY ASS

"Follow the sirens, sounds like World War Three out there."

Truck was driving the Defender, Herc in the passenger seat bellowing out orders. Pan, Night, and Hope were crammed in the back, clutching at each other every time the car skidded around a corner. They didn't have a mobile tracking unit with them but it wasn't hard to guess where Marlow was— gunshots and explosions ringing out from the direction of the river.

"Can this piece of crap go any faster?" Herc yelled again. "Come on, Truck, put your fat foot down!"

They shot across a junction so fast Pan thought they were taking off, narrowly avoiding a police car traveling the other way. It squealed to a halt, its tires smoking as it spun after them. Truck hand-braked around a narrow corner, the SUV demolishing a bus shelter as it bounced off it. Pan could see the bridge, and beyond it the walls of the capitol building. The whole area was swimming with red and blue lights, at least six squad cars parked along the far bank.

"For the love of all things holy," Herc growled. "Could this be any more messed up?"

Apparently it could: a SWAT van was now skidding from a road ahead, accelerating hard toward the chaos.

"Take that out," said Herc. Truck stomped on the gas and

they roared up behind the van, pulling alongside it. Truck waved to the startled cops inside, then punched through his window, giving the SWAT vehicle a massive shove. It tipped onto two wheels, balanced perfectly for a moment, then crashed down onto its side, the cop car smashing into the back of it. Truck wiggled the wheel until the Defender settled, Pan just about ready to barf up her internal organs.

"We gotta get him fast," Herc said, stating the obvious. "Park it, and *find him*."

Truck slammed on the brakes and the SUV skidded to a halt. Pan popped her door and jumped out, seeing the river through a break in the buildings. She didn't have a contract but she had her crossbow, a fresh load of bolts taken from the armory inside the Pigeon's Nest. The cops were mainly on the far side, yelling as they fired randomly into the water. It was too dark to see if there was anything there. She followed the flow, making out a figure a few hundred yards downstream. He was crouched at the water's edge looking like he was reaching for something.

Reaching for something, or drowning something.

She ran, Truck bounding along by her side, grunting like a bear. Night was a streak of light blazing past them, heading right for the shape. He must have sensed her coming because he looked around, his face catching the moonlight.

Patrick.

He 'ported and Pan hefted her crossbow, just in case he appeared right next to her. Truck stormed past, crouching down by the river and fishing for something in the murky flow. A second later he pulled out a limp bag of rags, laying it gently on the path. Pan ran to it, recognizing Marlow.

"He breathing?" she asked, crouching down beside him. Night appeared, panting, her eyes darting left and right.

"*Hijo de puta*," she said.

Pan put her fingers to Marlow's neck, feeling a faint pulse.

"Hold his arms," she said to Truck. He did as he was told and she slapped Marlow on his face, hard, then again, and again, until his eyes opened and he vomited water all over himself. He struggled, his unnatural strength matched by Truck's.

"Calm down," Pan whispered. "And shut up, we've got to go."

"Charlie," Marlow spluttered. He shook free of Truck's grip to point toward the far bank, the one the cops were lined up on. "Charlie, he's over there, *they* had him."

"What?" Pan stood. This was bad news.

There was the crack of a gunshot, closer this time, and Truck suddenly reeled back, clutching his arm. A spray of blood misted over Pan's face and she gagged, wiping it away. Another shot, a bullet grazing her head. This time she saw the muzzle flash, a redheaded girl on the bridge.

"Get her!" Pan yelled, passing Night the crossbow. Night took off, becoming a blur of color that snaked up the steps and along the walkway. The girl unloaded the rest of her magazine but Pan knew Night would be too fast, the bullets like paper airplanes to her. Night snapped back into real time and leveled the crossbow at the girl's chest. There was a flash as Patrick appeared on the bridge, popping into existence for long enough to grab hold of the girl and 'port them both away. The crossbow bolt carved through the space where they'd just been and embedded itself in the metal of the bridge.

Dammit.

"You okay?" Pan asked Truck. He nodded, obviously in pain. "We need to go."

"Charlie's over there," said Marlow. "He's hurt, we have to help him."

"No way," said Pan. It was too risky, too many cops.

254

He sat up, groggy, saying, "Let me go, I can get him."

Marlow didn't look like he'd be able to fetch a stick, let alone a person. Pan offered him a hand, helped him to his feet. The cops must have spotted Night on the bridge because some were running her way, shouting at her in Hungarian. Somebody fired off a panicked shot and it ricocheted off the railing beside her. She ran, reappearing beside Truck in the blink of an eye.

"I saw him," she said, panting. "Your friend. He's over there on the grass. They're trying to help him, looks like he's hurt bad."

"He won't live," said Marlow. "He's nearly gone. He needs the Engine."

Pan shook her head.

"Please, Pan," Marlow said. "I don't want him to die. He *can't* die."

"You have to let go," she said. "These things happen."

"No," he said, giving her a shove. He must have checked his strength but it was still like being charged by a bull. She staggered back, watching him go, swearing under her breath. She turned to Night.

"Can you grab his friend?"

The other girl smiled, handing back the crossbow. "Do you even have to ask?"

"Go," Pan said. "I'll get them back to the car."

Night became a streak of light, her footsteps drumming across the river, churning up plumes of water behind her. Pan ran after Marlow, grabbing him.

"We'll fetch Charlie, you come with me."

An engine growled, the SUV gunning around the corner and up onto the grass. Herc's face grimaced behind the wheel as he squealed to a halt beside them. Pan wrenched open the door, ducking when she heard another shot, something pinging off the roof of the car. She wasn't sure if it was the cops or the redhead, and she wasn't interested in finding out.

"Get in!" she yelled at Marlow. He looked like he was about to argue and she raised her foot, booting him in the ass and sending him tumbling into the rear footwell. She climbed in after him, the vehicle groaning as Truck got in too.

"Where's Night?" Herc asked, the SUV tinkling as bullets tore into it. Pan ducked down, cradling her head as chunks of glass rained down into her hair.

"Just drive!" she screamed at Herc. He slammed his foot on the gas and they lurched forward, the car rocking as they bounced over a flower bed and through a barrier. They swerved around a corner and Herc pulled on the hand brake, bringing them to a halt. He looked back.

"Where's—"

Something hammered on the window, making them all jump. Night looked exhausted, holding Charlie by the scruff of the neck. Pan reached over Truck and opened the door and together they wrestled the boy in. He already looked dead, drenched in blood and encrusted with dirt.

"He took a pounding on the way, sorry," Night said as Herc floored it again, the acceleration pushing everyone back in their seats. "He was too heavy for me to carry so I had to drag him."

That obviously hadn't helped, the boy's clothes torn to shreds, the skin beneath ripped and raw. Pan tried for a pulse, didn't find one, tried again, found something fluttering in his neck, as weak as a butterfly's wings. Marlow pulled his friend's head onto his lap, weeping openly.

"I'm sorry, I'm so sorry," he sobbed. Then, to her, he said, "We can save him, we just need to get him to the Engine."

She opened her mouth to argue, then snapped it shut. It was a moot point anyway, the odds were the boy would be stone-cold dead before they got there. Herc must have thought the same because he leaned back, yelling over the roar of the engine.

"We'll do what we can with him but we can't go straight back. It might be a trap, they might be following us. There's protocol to follow." They screeched around a corner onto a wider road, the sound of gunfire fading. "Your choice, kid, you wanna drop him off at a hospital or you wanna hold on to him?"

Pan sat back, grateful that the call wasn't hers. It's why she didn't like to make friends, why she tried to keep her emotional distance from Truck and Night and the others. In this line of work, sooner or later, your friends got shot, or stabbed, or pulled to pieces. How many had she already lost? She didn't have enough fingers to count them, but she'd already filled too many pages of the *Book of Dead Engineers*. Marlow had his hands over the gaping wound in Charlie's stomach. The blood had slowed to a trickle but there were other things coming out, the car full of the sickening smell of ruptured intestines.

"Please," said Marlow, his expression so full of love, so full of fear, that something began to swell in Pan's throat. She turned to face the broken window, the wind whipping at her hair, at her face, drying the tears before they could fall. "The Engine can save him, right?" he said. "He can wish for his injuries to heal, right? Pan?"

"We'll do what we can, Marlow," said Herc. "Just keep him breathing."

They were on a highway of some kind now, Herc keeping them at a steady eighty, weaving in and out between the other cars on the road. She could hear sirens but they were distant, over to the east where the molten dawn was just starting to spill over the horizon.

"Hang in there, Charlie," said Marlow, holding the boy's hand, his thumb stroking gently. There was blood everywhere.

Two police cars blazed past on the other side of the road but they didn't look over, didn't slow.

"Everyone else okay?" Herc asked, easing off the gas.

"Um, *hello*," said Truck. He had his hand to his shoulder but there was just a trickle of blood. "I got *shot*."

"Oh shut up, Truck," said Pan. "You probably didn't even feel it through all that blubber. Anyway, your contract will patch you up."

"I'll have you know it stings," he grumbled, poking at the wound with a giant finger. "A little bit. It might get infected."

Pan and Night rolled their eyes at each other. Herc was speaking again but he must have had Ostheim on the line.

"Yeah, we recovered the lost dog . . . He's okay, two enemy agents, possibly more." He looked into the rearview mirror. "Nothing obvious but they might be tailing us from the sky. No way of knowing . . . Yeah, okay, let me know, boss. Oh, and we recovered another lost puppy, hurt bad, requesting directives . . . Yeah, they pretty much finished him off, left him to die . . ."

They passed a freeway sign and Herc slowed, squinted at it. He pulled off at the next exit, heading down the ramp. Pan looked back—no headlights following them. Patrick might have chased them for a while, but this was too far for anyone to 'port—he'd blitz himself right out of existence.

"Your decision, Ostheim," Herc said. Then he nodded, sighed loudly, and killed the call. "Hanson's gonna meet us about a mile away, we'll zigzag back to the Nest. Looks like we're clear, though."

"That easy?" Truck said. "Not like them to give up a chance to pop one of us."

"They didn't give up the chance," said Pan. "They shot you, nearly drowned Marlow. If we'd got there one minute later we'd be dragging him home in a body bag."

"Least I'd have gotten out of my contract," said Marlow, hissing a laugh through his nose. Pan frowned at him.

Whoops.

"Oh, yeah, I might have forgotten to mention something," she said. "Dying doesn't release you from your contract. If you die, they come collect you. Sorry."

She wasn't sure if the look he gave her made her want to laugh or cry. He shook his head in disgust, looked back at his friend, stroking his hair. And once again she was grateful that she had no friends, no family, nobody to love. Because wasn't that one of the indelible truths of life? If you love someone, sooner or later they end up bleeding out in the back of a car while you drive away from demons.

Or maybe that was just *her* life.

She turned to the window, not laughing, not crying, not *anything*—just watching the world slowly turning from black-and-white to color as the sun seared its way through the dying night.

YOUR MISSION, IF YOU
CHOOSE TO ACCEPT IT . . .

Marlow paced back and forth in the dorm, utterly exhausted. His head was a storm of dark clouds, thick with fog. He couldn't sleep, though, not until he knew Charlie was okay. Not until he knew that he hadn't murdered him.

He checked his watch, no time there just those numerals, *659:34:15:52*. The power of the Engine still thrummed inside him but it no longer felt good. It felt more like a poison, something slipped into his drink—a toxin that would take twenty-seven days to turn his insides to rot. He wanted to snatch up a knife and drain his tainted blood. His skin was raw where he'd scratched at himself, like he could scour away the stench of the machine.

It was hopeless, though. It was inside every cell, every fiber of his being. It was inside his soul.

He walked back and forth, his feet drumming on the floor. Truck was asleep in the far corner of the room, his snores and snorts sounding like drum and bass through a subwoofer. It had taken them hours to get back, zigzagging across half of Budapest before Herc was confident they weren't being trailed. They'd entered the Nest through a red door that was identical to the one in Prague—*literally* identical, it was the same door. This one had been set into a section of the ancient city wall, but it still made Marlow's guts feel like they were being tumble dried as he stepped through.

Marlow wasn't sure where the others were now—he hadn't exactly been Mr. Popular on his return—but he knew they'd taken Charlie down to the Engine. Hanson had thrown a hissy fit but he'd been overruled. Not that there was much point, of course—Charlie had been unconscious for the last thirty minutes of the journey, and, as Pan had pointed out, the Engine didn't work unless you were awake.

"Come on, Charlie," he said. "Please be okay."

He sat on his bed, chewing his knuckles. He'd spent over an hour in the shower—most of which curled up beneath the spray sobbing his eyes out—but he could still smell blood on his hands. He pushed himself to his feet again, pacing like a caged animal. That wasn't too far from the truth, he supposed. He'd been ordered not to leave the room. Truck had been left to watch over him and Marlow supposed he could sneak out now, just run for it—he was faster than sound, after all—but where would he go? And who would he get killed this time? No, better he just stayed here, that way nothing else would turn to crap.

Truck farted extravagantly, rolling over in his sleep, muttering something about a monkey. The bullet that had struck the big guy had gone straight through, in and out, and he'd been patched up. It was already close to healing, the contract seeing to that.

The sound of footsteps rose up outside and the dorm door opened. He was hoping to see Pan but it was Hanson who entered. He strode forward holding a cell phone.

"How's he doing?" Marlow asked.

"Do I look like I care?" Hanson said. "He never should have been allowed in. For all we know he could be working for them."

Marlow scoffed. "Yeah, sure, and I'm Hugh Hefner's jockstrap. Please, tell me how he is."

"I take it you're the one who gouged a rocket on my pretty little BMW?"

"Me?" said Marlow. "No way, man, I'd never deface something that belonged to such a nice guy. Anyway, it looked like a penis to me."

Hanson squared up, close enough for Marlow to see those gaping sockets behind the tinted lenses. He smelled of something sweet—too sweet, like fruit that had started to rot.

"You know how long I've been doing this?" he said. "Over forty years."

Marlow frowned. There was no way he could be that old, he looked like he was still in his twenties—haggard, yes, but young.

"I've seen more people die than you could imagine. Friends. Enemies. It doesn't matter. Death is death. And I do what I do because it matters. Because we save more lives than we destroy. If it wasn't for us, this world would be hell, literally. You have no bloody idea how stupid you were tonight, leaving the complex. If you knew the danger you'd put us in, if you knew what was at stake, you'd put a gun to your head right now and blow your brains out."

Marlow knew the Brit was right, but he still felt his hackles rise, felt the fury pounding in his stomach, like something trying to claw its way out. He shrugged like he didn't have a care in the world.

"Maybe you should put some windows in, then," he said, hating himself for it but unable to stop the words spilling out of his mouth. "Get an Xbox or something. It's as *boring* as hell in here."

262

Hanson ignored Marlow and shoved the phone at him. "Ostheim wants to speak to you."

Marlow took the cell. He wasn't sure if he wanted to speak to the man, he knew he'd only get another shellacking. Hanson walked out the door, turning back to say, "And, *dog*, don't talk to him like you talk to the rest of us. He will end you."

Marlow swallowed, waiting for the sound of footsteps to fade before lifting the phone. For a second he thought the call must have dropped because there was no sound there, not even the static hum of background noise. There was just a profound silence, like he'd gone deaf in one ear. He flexed his jaw, the deafness seeming to spread into his skull, making the side of his head feel numb.

"Marlow," said a voice, and he almost screamed. It sounded like the man was inside the room, whispering. His voice was high-pitched, his accent unfamiliar, European. The silence dropped back over him like a weight and Marlow opened his mouth to reply, only so he wouldn't feel smothered by it.

"Hi," he said, his own voice so weak, so insignificant. He coughed, speaking louder. "Ostheim, right?"

"At your service," said Ostheim. "And call me Sheppel, please. It's nice to finally meet you. I hear you almost got us all in a heap of trouble tonight."

"It wasn't my fault," Marlow said. "I didn't know I wasn't supposed to leave the Nest." The lie seemed to hang in the air like a bad smell and he paced away so that he wouldn't have to breathe it back in. "Look, I—"

"All's well that ends well," Ostheim interrupted. "Truth is, there's no real danger, it's just protocol. They can't get inside our Engine, we can't get inside theirs. They only open from the inside. It's just a dance we do, each side trying to weaken the other. Do you know what a war of attrition is?"

Marlow shook his head, and Ostheim must have guessed.

"It's a prolonged period of conflict where each side gradually seeks to wear out their enemy through a series of small-scale actions. In other words, it's tit for tat, we kill one of yours, you kill one of ours, over and over and over. For a long, long time, Marlow. For hundreds of years. Two of the most powerful machines ever created and we use them to slap each other around the face."

"But why?" Marlow asked. "Why don't you work together. Man, you could rule the world, could, like, be rich and stuff. You could be the most powerful people on the planet. I don't get it."

"Power and riches. You sound like them, Marlow. Is that what you want?"

Duh, he almost said, but bit his tongue. Ostheim's voice was quiet, gentle, almost soothing, but there was something there right beneath the surface, something dark and dangerous, like the shark-filled depths of a quiet ocean.

"No," Marlow said. "I mean, it would be cool. But what else is there? What are you fighting for?"

"We're fighting for everything. And I mean everything."

"The world," Marlow said.

"More than that," Ostheim said. "Much more. If the Circulus Inferni have their way, then they will open up the gates of hell, fill the world with demons. Do you have any idea how thin the walls are between our worlds? Do you have any idea how close we are to the other side, and to what inhabits it? They are there now, all around us, dimensions separated by the merest fraction of space, the stitches held together by old magic, by the first laws of the universe. All it takes is one snip and the whole thing will unravel. Demons will flood our world, and we will all be prey."

Marlow rubbed at the gooseflesh on his arms, sitting down on his bed. His legs didn't feel quite strong enough to hold him. He pictured it, those things peeling themselves from walls, from the floor. The world would be an island of sundered flesh in an ocean of blood.

"Not just that," said Ostheim. "It's not just death that we're talking about. Demons don't care about blood and bone. It's your soul that feeds them. Do you understand, Marlow? If the gates are opened, then every single person on Earth will lose their inner self, their essence. They will burn for the rest of time."

Marlow wiped the sweat from his forehead, had to close his eyes against the sudden wave of nausea and vertigo. Every single person—his mom, Charlie, Pan, *him*.

"Do you understand now why it's important to listen?" Ostheim asked. "Why we have rules?"

"Yes."

"Good. But as I said, no harm, no foul. I also heard that you fought well tonight, that you nearly took out an enemy Engineer."

"No," Marlow said. "Not unless 'nearly taking out' is the same thing as almost being drowned by."

"But you're still here to tell the tale, and that's no mean feat when you're fighting somebody like Patrick Rebarre. Herc did well recruiting you. He saw something in you. He saw that you are a brave man. Yes?"

Marlow felt his cheeks burn, stared at the floor. A brave man? No, he was the opposite of that. How many times had he tried to run? How many times had he abandoned and betrayed the ones he loved to save his own ass? He was Marlow Green, and he was a coward.

"You may not know it," Ostheim said, once more seeming to pick the thoughts right out of Marlow's head. "But it's there inside you, and I need it. I need brave men, Marlow. Can you help me?"

"I guess . . ."

"Good. Then I have something I need you to do. A mission. We think we've managed to track Patrick. He's running but he's hurt. We need you to go after him."

"Okay," said Marlow, his pulse drumming in his ears.

"Pan, Truck, and Night will be going with you. Marlow, I don't need to tell you how important this is. If we get to Patrick, then we may have a way into their Engine."

"Okay," Marlow said. "What happens then? If we get inside?"

"We destroy it," Ostheim said. "We take it to pieces and sink them at the bottom of the ocean."

"Then we win," Marlow said, nodding. "Is that what they want to do, too? Destroy our Engine?"

"No," said Ostheim. "They need our Engine. If the two Engines are united, then they will possess the key to tearing down the barriers between our worlds."

A bolt of fear tore through him, followed by a sudden rush of emotion, too powerful to identify. It was almost *excitement*.

"Then can't we just, y'know, destroy our Engine? Stop them getting it?"

Ostheim breathed out a laugh, the sound as soft and sharp as a knife through steak. "We could, but that would be like giving up your nuclear weapons in the hope your enemy will do the same."

Marlow nodded, still feeling that itch, that unbearable tickle of excitement in his chest.

"Ignore that sensation, if you can," said Ostheim. "It's easy to forget that this is why the Engines were designed—to bring about a union of worlds. Can you hear it? It's what the Engine wants you to do, unite it with the other infernal machine. Do not listen to it, and it will fade."

Marlow *could* hear it, a soft whisper that seemed to be coming from inside him, scratching at his skull.

"Go now," Ostheim said. "Be brave. Return when your mission is done and know that you played a part in keeping this world safe. You are an Engineer. The fate of this world lies in your hands."

Marlow nodded. He could be brave.

He *could* be brave.

"Now, go see your friend. He's out of the Engine and he's still alive, but only just. His fight is far from over, but he is on the right path."

"Thank you," he said, a wave of cold relief washing over him, but the call had ended, that immense silence cutting out and replaced with the quiet hiss of an empty line. He kept the phone to his ear for a moment more, then tossed it onto the bed.

An Engineer. He still had so many questions, there was so much he didn't understand. But at least he had a better idea of his role in the war, and what he was fighting for. And at least Charlie was out of the woods.

He jogged from the room, out into the corridor. Hanson was waiting inside the elevator and he closed the gates behind Marlow before pressing the button.

"What did he say?" Hanson asked as they rumbled down.

"He told me to tell you you're fired," Marlow said.

Hanson bristled but didn't reply, just waited for the elevator to come to a halt before opening the gates. Marlow walked out into a corridor he hadn't had a chance to explore yet. Only one of the doors was open and he walked toward it, turning into a room that could have belonged inside a hospital. There were six medical beds, and in one of them lay his only friend—battered, bruised, and asleep.

"Charlie?" he said, running to him. He noticed Pan sitting beside the bed. "Is he okay?"

She shrugged.

"We managed to wake him up with a shot of adrenaline to the heart," Pan said. "He was conscious, and aware, when he went in. He knew what to do. Ask me, it was a stupid move. He could have dealt for anything."

"What did he deal for?" Marlow asked, sitting on the edge of the bed. Charlie was looking better than the last time he'd seen him, which was one good thing. He still resembled a sculpture of bruises and broken bones, sure, but he was breathing evenly, and the heart monitor that bleeped by his bedside held a strong rhythm.

"To stay alive," Pan said. "He repeated it back to me a dozen times before we let him in."

"So why is he still out?"

"I don't know." She sighed. "He was right there, on the edge of death. He might have been too close. Bad things can happen when you use the Engine to prolong life. He might have been better off dying."

Marlow started to argue, then understood what she was saying.

"The Lawyers can break it, right?" he said. She didn't reply. "*Right?*"

"They're looking at the Engine now," she said. "They're doing their best. This is a tough one to break, and they don't even know if it's all he brokered for. It could be anything, they don't know where to start."

Marlow swore. Not only had he dragged Charlie into this crapstorm, not only had he nearly gotten him killed, he'd also damned his soul to hell for all eternity. He took Charlie's hand, the boy's skin cold, clammy, like he was already a corpse.

I'm so sorry, he said without saying.

"You spoke to Ostheim?" Pan asked. He nodded. "Then you know we have to go."

"I can't leave him."

"There's nothing you can do for him," she said, standing up. "They'll do everything they can."

"Just give me a sec, okay?" Marlow asked. Pan nodded and walked out of the room.

"I'm going to get a new contract," she said, sighing. "Meet me in the bullpen. Don't be long."

Then she was gone. Marlow held Charlie's hand for a moment more.

"Just hang in there, okay?" he whispered, stroking Charlie's hand with his thumb. "I can't do this without you, man. I can't do any of it."

He stood, preparing to go, only to feel Charlie's fingers tighten around his own. The boy's eyes were open a crack. He licked his blistered lips, croaked out something that might have been a word or a breath.

"What is it, Charlie? You need water? Some morphine or something?"

Charlie slowly shook his head, licking his lips, swallowing noisily. He was obviously in a lot of pain, grimacing as he tried to shape the words.

"Careful . . . Marlow . . ." he said.

"What?" Marlow leaned in, so close he could feel the next words against his ear.

"Be careful . . ." Charlie said. His eyes had closed, the heart monitor thumping along at a faster rate.

"It'll be okay, man," Marlow said, walking to the door. "I promise you, it will be okay. I'll get the doc."

Charlie didn't open his eyes, but his whisper reached Marlow across the room.

"They're lying to you."

PART III

WHEN WORLDS COLLIDE

HOMECOMING

Pan hated touching down in America. It was always too much like going back in time.

The plane's engines powered down and she popped the clasp on her belt, stretching like a cat. She'd slept for most of the journey—they all had—and despite the fact she'd been playing leapfrog with time zones for the last couple of days she felt relatively awake, just the familiar ebb and pull of the Engine making her ache. She flexed her fingers, careful not to think too hard about what she'd traded for this time. One sideways thought and she'd take out the plane and everyone inside it.

Not to mention a good chunk of the airport.

She peered out the window as the plane taxied toward the small tower. This was the point she always dreaded—the cop cars screaming around the corner, the chopper descending. She'd been a felon the first time she flew out of the airport, and Herc had turned her into a fugitive by busting her out of her cell. She was still wanted for her original crime and it wasn't like she'd been lying low since. She'd lost track of what she was guilty of now in the eyes of the law: *arson*, check; *theft*, check; *assault*, definitely; *GTA*, many, many times; *murder* . . .

That was one she hadn't lost count of. She knew exactly

how many lives she'd taken and each one burned a hole in her dreams every night.

All in the name of duty though, *right*? At least that's what she told herself when they came calling, the dead faces of those she'd shot, stabbed, run over, and those who had been ravaged by demons because she'd been too slow to save them. It's what she told herself when the guilt made her want to scream herself to death. If she didn't do what she did, then the world would fall. Each of those deaths held the gates of hell closed. That knowledge was the only thing that kept her sane.

They jolted to a stop and Pan walked to the door, wrestling with the lever until it popped open. The stairs descended automatically and she hopped down them into the heat and smog and noise of a sweaty Jersey afternoon. Ostheim would have already put the word in, greased the palms of the airport officials. It was pretty hard to get into the U.S. undetected, but it wasn't like the Hellraisers were short of money—turned out that trading the Engine for a small fortune was one of the easiest contracts to break. And even the most anally retentive official was willing to turn a blind eye if you stuffed enough cash in his pocket. No, their route out of the field was guaranteed.

"I wish they'd find a way to put a Red Door over here," said Night, massaging her back with both hands as she strolled down the stairs. "I mean, how hard can it be?"

Rerouting the pathways that accessed the Engine, rewriting the old magic that kept it out of space, out of time. It was just about the hardest thing you could attempt to do. Night had a point, though, sticking a Red Door in the middle of Manhattan would be a hell of a lot easier than a nine-hour plane trip between contracts.

At least this way, though, you didn't have to walk through pure evil to get where you were going.

Night skipped lightly down the steps and Truck followed her, almost too big to get out of the airplane door. He stomped down, heavy lidded, still half-asleep. The big guy was *always* half-asleep.

"You just take your time," Pan said to him, tapping her foot with impatience. "Mosey on down at your leisure. Not like we're on a mission or anything."

"Keep your hair on, Pan," Truck said, swaying down the steps. He glanced at her short locks and snorted. "Oops, too late."

"Sides, splitting," she said, feeling too exposed here in the airport, feeling like she was back in the past, blood on her hands and the cops on their way. "Seriously, we need to go. And would somebody get Marlow out of the goddamned toilet."

The safe house was a walk-up in Hoboken and it obviously hadn't been used in a while. It was like stepping into a mausoleum, thick with dust and dark, the heavy drapes drawn tight against the heat outside. The only piece of furniture in the combined living room was a couch, still in its plastic wrap, and Truck shouted "Dibs!" before launching himself at it. Pan was amazed that the pair of them didn't disappear through the floor into the apartment below. She waited for everyone to step inside before closing the door and turning the dead bolt.

"Why do these places always have to be so dreary?" Night said, tugging at the drapes. The light flooded in like a dam had been breached, waves of dust billowing out. Pan was pretty sure she saw some mice darting into the skirting. Yeah, the Hellraisers might have been richer than Croesus but they were stingier than Scrooge McDuck. It's not like a room at the InterContinental would have broken the bank.

She coughed out a lungful of dust and walked to the kitchen, slinging her bag onto the counter. Through the greasy window she could see another building, a mirror reflection of their own. Past that, across the Hudson, lay Manhattan, drenched in sunlight. She wondered what would happen if she just walked down the stairs, crossed the river, disappeared into the heat, did her best to forget about the Engine and Ostheim and the dead. She checked her watch. *654:32:20:11.* It would be twenty-six days of bliss, then an eternity of hell. It was one of the rules—go AWOL during a contract and the Lawyers won't break it.

Not worth it, Pan.

Besides, it really did look like they had a chance to catch Patrick. The fight in Budapest had injured him, but this was something else. He thought they were responsible for his sister's death and it looked like it had driven him insane, looked like it had forced him to go renegade. If Patrick was gunning for revenge, then he'd be alone, and thoughtless, and all of that would make him easier to find. Maybe this would be the mission that ended it all, the one that set her free. She opened her bag, blinking sunlight out of her eyes. The laptop was state-of-the-art and she booted it up, connecting with the Pigeon's Nest through a secure satellite connection. Herc's face appeared, and he didn't look so hot.

"Sorry, must have the wrong number," said Pan. "I think I've connected to an old people's home."

"Pan," said Herc.

"Is your grandson around? His name's Herc, white hair, face like a dog-chewed catcher's mitt—"

"Pan, it's late, and I'm tired, and I will gladly murder all of the Lawyers in this place and leave you to the demons if you don't quit it."

"Sorry, Gramps," she said, unable to stop the smile from spreading. "We've arrived, you got anything?"

"He's in Manhattan," Herc said, rubbing his stubble. "We've been monitoring all channels and he's uptown. He isn't hiding, Pan."

"Any sign of Mammon?"

"Nothing, but keep your eyes open. That bastard snuck right up on us last time."

"Will do, boss. You rest up, get your slippers on, put something nice on the gramophone."

"Go fu—"

She cut the connection, stretching in the little pool of sunlight by the window. It truly was filthy in here, reminding her of the apartment she'd grown up in, a hellhole in Queens. The memory made her skin crawl and she turned her back on it, walking into the sitting room. Night and Marlow were staring out the window, chatting quietly. Truck looked like he'd fallen asleep. She almost smiled at the sight, then she remembered the others—the fallen, those who'd been murdered right in front of her eyes, and those who'd been dragged kicking and screaming to hell. You couldn't have friends in this line of work. You couldn't get attached.

"Herc's going to let us know when they've zeroed in," she said. Marlow turned to her, just a silhouette against the glowing city.

"How long will it be?"

"Not soon enough," she replied, walking to the sofa and kicking Truck until he grudgingly made room. She collapsed, her leg jiggling impatiently. The waiting was always the worst part. "Just get some rest. And Marlow?"

"Yeah?"

She gave him the fiercest look she could muster.

"I don't wanna see you do your vanishing act again, okay?"

He grinned at her.

"Sure."

DOING THE VANISHING
ACT AGAIN

Being back on Staten Island felt like waking up from a dream, and it was a good feeling. Walking out of the ferry terminal into the cool, golden evening, Marlow found himself wishing that the events of the last few days were some kind of hallucination. A machine that let you play with the fundamental laws of physics? Demons that came after you when you did? It was insane. Maybe he'd fallen asleep on the ferry, lulled into nightmares as it swayed across the upper bay. Here, now, with people bustling past him—tourists snapping pictures, suits heading home from late nights in the city, tired children yelling—there could be no such thing as monsters. It was just him, in the place he'd lived his whole life.

Then his new cell buzzed for the fourth time and he saw Pan's text there—*Get your stupid ass back here, Marlow, last chance*—and the world flipped upside down again like a stunt plane. Of course it was real. He'd seen it, felt it, been beaten half to death by it. He could still feel the power of the Engine thrumming inside him, knew that he only had to start running and time itself would slow down to accommodate him. He checked his watch, those numbers counting down relentlessly, thought about what would happen when it reached zero, what would come after him.

Yeah, there were *definitely* monsters.

He batted back a quick text, *wont be long*. Then he pocketed the cell and set off. Technically he hadn't disobeyed Pan, she'd said she didn't want to see him disappear, and she hadn't—she'd been fast asleep on the couch when he left. Besides, he needed to go home, needed to check on his mom.

He could have taken a bus, but at this time of day it would be quicker to walk. It was farther than he thought, though, and by the time he reached his street the sun was hovering over the rooftops, nesting in the trees, making it look like the island was on fire. His legs were grumbling as he walked up the steps to his house, but there was a song in his heart he hadn't heard for what felt like forever. He was smiling as he pushed open the door.

"Yo, Mom," he said, walking into the cool interior. "Donovan, here boy!"

There was a familiar scrabble of claws on wood, a gentle *ruff* from the dining room. Donovan skittered around the corner, tongue dangling, tail wagging, and Marlow dropped to one knee, slapping his legs.

"Come here, D, I missed you."

The dog stopped, his tail dropping like a guillotine blade. He took a few clumsy steps back, cocking his head and whining from the darkness at the end of the corridor.

"Hey, stupid, what's up?" Marlow said, scooching closer. The fur on the dog's neck began to rise, the skin around his mouth pulling back to reveal teeth. Donovan whined again, then barked, twice, the kind of bark usually reserved for yappy dogs in the park.

Or for strangers.

"Hey, dude, it's me," Marlow said, patting his legs again. When he disappeared for a couple of days Donovan usually had him on the floor by now, that pink tongue trying to lick his face off. The dog's eyes were huge and white and there was a definite growl throbbing in his throat. Marlow stood up and Donovan flinched, retreating to the wall, that growl like a generator. He barked again, white foam flecking his mouth.

"Better get out," came a voice from the back of the house, his mom, her words slurred. "Dog'll tear you a new one."

"Mom, it's me," he yelled. "It's Marlow."

Footsteps, soft and slow. The dog looked to the side, whined, licked its lips. Then his mom was there, squinting around the corner. There was a glass of Bacardi in her hand and she was swaying like they were at sea. But it was good to see her. Marlow smiled, taking a step toward her, but Donovan barked again, his hackles fully raised.

"Jesus, Mom," he said, trying to laugh it off. "What you been feeding him?"

His mom didn't answer, just stared at him, studying him like he was a TV show with crappy reception. The only noise in the house was that pulsing growl from Donovan's throat.

"Mom?" Marlow said, his gut churning. She leaned forward, her face screwing up.

"Marly?"

"Yeah," he said. "It's me. What's going on? I'm sorry I went away. I've been somewhere. I've got a . . . a job. I should have called but you wouldn't believe—"

"Not him," his mom whispered, the words almost lost beneath Donovan's growl.

"What?"

"You're not him," she said, jabbing her glass at him so violently that some of the alcohol slopped out over the dog's head. Donovan didn't even notice, padding forward on those big feet, barking wildly. Marlow took a step back, crashing into the door. "You're not my son, you're not my Marly."

"Mom, *please*," he said. The dog was still advancing and Marlow scrabbled for the doorknob. "Donovan, boy, it's *me*."

The dog was running now and Marlow ripped open the door, tripping out and pulling it shut behind him. Donovan thumped against it, his claws scraping at the wood. Marlow crawled back on his ass, almost rolling down the steps. By the time he'd found his feet again he could hear his mom behind the door, screaming.

"What have you done with him? What have you done with my boy?"

He backed away, out onto the street, clamping his hands to his ears.

"You're not him, you killed him, you killed my Marly."

It *couldn't be* real.

"You killed my boys, my boys."

He turned, blinded by tears, not caring where he was going. He just had to get that voice out of his head, that awful, fear-choked, desperate cry.

"My Marly! My Marly! You killed him!"

A horn blared, tires screeched, and he looked to see a car next to him, the red-faced driver throwing him the bird. Marlow lashed out before he even knew what he was doing, a thumping blow that flipped the car into the air like it was made of tin foil. It crunched down, riding a wave of sparks along the street before finally grinding to a halt. Marlow stood there, shaking his head, wondering whether he should go help. Then another car pulled up, somebody yelling at him. Doors were opening along the street, a woman's voice yelling for somebody to call the cops.

Marlow ran, knowing for sure now that there were monsters in the world.

And knowing that he was one of them.

CONFESSIONS

"Try this one," said Pan, pointing up the hill.

Truck steered the stolen car around the corner, honking the horn at a delivery van blocking both lanes. Tired of waiting, and not wanting another Budapest incident, they'd driven to Staten Island in search of Marlow. She was planning to throw him in the trunk as soon as they found him, keep him there till this whole thing was over. Luckily Marlow wasn't exactly clever or subtle. She figured he'd probably head straight home.

"You guys found him yet?" Herc barked in her ear, speaking through the open channel from the Pigeon's Nest.

"Dammit, Herc," she spat back. "Do you have to ask every thirty seconds?"

"That him?" Night asked, leaning between the two front seats and pointing. Pan looked to see Marlow up ahead, staggering down the hill, his expression vacant.

"That ain't Marlow," said Truck, pulling the car to the curb. "That's a zombie."

"Truck," said Pan, "I seem to remember that when you got your first contract you were so upset you ran away and broke into the Empire bakery."

"Nope," he said, shaking his head. "Not me."

"Yeah, we found you curled up in the corner, crying like a baby."

"Must have been somebody else," said Truck, squirming in his seat.

"You'd eaten fourteen doughnuts."

"It was eighteen doughnuts," he grumbled. "And it still wasn't me."

Pan popped the door and stepped into the cool evening air.

"Circle the block," she said. "I'll talk to him."

"Just try not to kill him," Night said as they drove away.

Marlow stomped toward her, his eyes red and puffy, his chest heaving. He was close enough to touch before he noticed her, and when he did he turned away sharply, wiping his face.

"What do you want?" he asked, sniffling like a baby.

"Came to check on you," she said. "See if you needed your diaper changed."

He spun back, fists clenched, and she took a step away. Marlow could probably knock her head clean off right now if he wanted to—and if she defended herself she'd turn half the street to dust.

"You don't know what it's like," he said.

"Oh yeah, I've never, *ever* been in your shoes." She tried to swallow the rest of her sarcasm, taking a deep breath and blowing it out slowly. "Marlow, we've all been here. Come on, let's get off the street, we can talk."

"Yeah?" he snapped back. "Talk about how my mom doesn't recognize me, how my dog tried to chew my throat out?"

Count to ten, Pan, she thought, reaching five before she ran out of patience. She grabbed Marlow's arm and pulled him into an alleyway between two rows of houses. The sun had all but disappeared, just a smudge of dirty orange against the horizon, and there were no lights down here. Marlow was two dark, sad eyes blinking in the twilight. He shrugged himself free and stood sniveling. There, in the darkness, he could have been any of them. He could have been *her*. She almost hated him for it.

"Look, Marlow, it's part of what the Engine does, it doesn't—"

"I might have killed them, Pan," he blurted out.

"What? Killed who?" she asked, keeping her voice to a whisper. Somebody in one of the houses flicked on an upstairs light, casting a sickly yellow glow across the alley.

"Some guys, in a car. I . . ." He sniffed, scuffed the ground with his sneaker. "I didn't mean to."

"Anyone see you?"

"What?" He looked away and she took that as a yes. *Dammit.*

"Any cameras?"

"No, no I don't think so. How the hell would I know?"

"Because you could use your eyes?" she said, biting her tongue too late. "Look, you know the first rule, Marlow. Nobody can know."

"That's all you care about?" he said. "Nobody knowing. Christ, Pan, I could have *killed* somebody."

"Look, Marlow, I know what it's like, how *bad* you feel."

"Yeah?" he shot back.

"Yeah." She took another deep breath, then opened her mouth and let the words tumble out before she could stop herself. "I was in care, a few years back. Some guy decided he liked me, *wanted* me, and there was nobody around to make him stop. So I made him stop. I made him stop everything." She choked, remembering the soft, brittle crack of his skull, remembering the way his eyes had filled with blood, the way his whole body had twitched like he was being electrocuted. "I killed him, because it was the only way of making it end."

Marlow was studying her intently, the alleyway suddenly quiet and still, as if the whole world had frozen. She gripped the fence, clutching the wire so hard she could feel it biting into her skin. Better to feel pain there, though, than the crushing agony in her chest.

"I know how much it hurts," she said.

"Guy was a creep," Marlow said after a moment, chewing his knuckles. "Had it coming. Not them, though. I didn't even know them. I shouldn't have lashed out."

"You shouldn't have," Pan said. "But you did. And you can't take it back, but you can make up for it."

He looked at her and she could see the desperation there, the need to make everything right. Marlow was a mouthy, rebellious idiot, no doubt about it, but he had heart.

"Herc chose you for a reason," she said. "What we're doing, it's about more than just saving one life. We're trying to save everybody. *Everybody*. If it wasn't for us—for me, you, Truck and Night, Herc, Ostheim, every single Hellraiser, even that turdblossom Hanson—then there would be nobody left. The Engines will be united and the whole world is on a fast train to hell. You get that?"

Marlow nodded, taking a deep, shuddering breath.

"One life, Marlow. It sucks, but it's done. You know the best way to get over it? Save a million more. A billion. We're the only ones who can."

"Yeah," he said, sucking in a ragged breath. "We're the good guys."

The alley lit up as a car pulled to a halt at the end of it, the engine purring.

"What about my mom, though?" Marlow asked. "What happened to her?"

"Not to her," she said, pressing a finger against Marlow's chest. "To you. It's the Engine. When you use it . . . you change.

You've got to remember, Marlow, got to remember what it is. You made a deal with the Devil, or at least something as old as the Devil, as old and as evil."

She closed her eyes, seeing the pit inside the Engine, the darkness, the creature who sat there, watching, every time she made a contract.

"It's inside you now, and it changes you. In good ways . . ." She looked at him, shrugged. "And bad ones too. Sometimes it's worse than others. Some people feel it more, especially if they know you, if they *love* you. Animals too, like your dog. Their senses are a lot sharper than ours. But it does go away."

"When the Lawyers break your contract?" he asked, his face full of hope.

"Yeah." Truck flashed the high beams and she looked away, blinking smudges of light from her vision. "Y'know, provided they *can* break it."

"Oh, yeah, sure," Marlow said, almost smiling. "Provided the demons don't get you first."

The smile took her by surprise and her face ached as she tried to clamp her jaw shut around it. She punched Marlow hard in the shoulder.

"Ow," he said, pouting. "You don't have to be such a bitch."

"You don't have to be such a baby," she said. He grinned at her.

"As sweet as this is," said a voice in her ear, making her jump— Herc, on the open channel, she'd completely forgotten about him. *"Can you two get your asses in the car? We've found him."*

"Where?" she asked, putting a hand to her ear.

"St. Patrick's, Fifth Avenue."

"The cathedral?" Pan said, walking to the car.

"No, the strip joint," Herc said. *"Yeah, the cathedral. Get a move on, we can't risk losing him."*

Pan didn't think that would be a problem. She had the awful feeling that Patrick wanted to be found.

"He alone?"

"You'll find out, won't you, if you ever get there."

Pan muttered beneath her breath, opening the car door and letting Marlow enter first. She clambered in next to him and he looked at her.

"We're the good guys?" he said. She nodded.

"Yeah, Marlow, we're the good guys. Now let's go do what good guys do." Truck floored it, the car burning rubber before lurching away. "Kick some evil goddamned ass."

UNFINISHED BUSINESS

"That's it."

It wasn't like Night needed to point it out. St. Patrick's Cathedral stood across the street like a corpse at a party. A sculpture of bone, Gothic towers stretching up into the night sky like skeletal fingers. It was dwarfed by the glamorous glass-and-steel office towers around it and the vast bulk of Rockefeller Center across the street, but somehow the building looked like the biggest one here, a kind of gravity that made it feel as though even the tallest skyscraper was bending down to pay its respect.

It was also pumping out one hell of an evil vibe.

"Anyone else getting that?" Truck asked. "Feel like a horse has just kicked me in the sphincter."

It was a good way of putting it. Pan's whole body felt itchy inside, as if her blood had been replaced by feathers. If they hadn't already known that Patrick was inside the building that shared his name they would now, the presence of the Engine sending pulses through the night, making it tremble.

The normals felt it too, because this section of Fifth Avenue was all but deserted. The crowds that would normally have swarmed the street had thinned to a trickle, and those few souls who trotted past moved quickly, one woman even breaking into a run until she'd crossed Fiftieth Street, clutching her stomach and looking back with fear in her eyes. It was human nature to avoid evil, a warning signal in the blood, and right now that warning was blaring like a siren.

"He's not even trying to hide it," Pan said. And that was a bad sign, because the only reason you'd want to advertise yourself to the enemy was if you were trying to lure them into a trap.

That, or you were just spoiling for a fight.

"Wants us here," said Truck, nodding.

"Herc," Pan said, talking into her collar mic. "You sure there's no sign of Mammon? Any other Engineers?"

"No Mammon, for sure," came his reply. *"Hard to read the rest. You know what consecrated ground does to the readings. Patrick might not be alone, so tread carefully."*

Pan nodded, flexing her fingers and feeling the charge, like she'd plunged her hands into a bucket of ice-cold, boiling-hot water. It was hard to believe the power there, coded into her own genes by the Engine. One twitch could put a hole in pretty much anything. It was exciting, but it was pretty unsettling too, like holding a live grenade with the pin pulled out. She hadn't brought the crossbow this time—holding a weapon like that when you had a power like hers was just asking for trouble.

"And, guys," said Herc. *"For god's sake try to keep a lid on it, okay?"*

"Sure," she said.

"Oh, yeah, no worries," added Truck. "You know us, quiet as country mice."

Pan had one foot on the street when Marlow grabbed her arm.

"Wait," he said, eyes as wide and bright as the moon. "I don't know what we're doing. I don't know the plan."

"The plan?" said Truck, clapping one giant fist into his palm. "Crush his ass."

"No, you don't," said Herc. *"You take him alive, so we can ask him some questions. We need him to try to get to their Engine. You hear me? Alive."*

"Sure," said Truck, forming air quotes with his fingers. "Alive."

"I saw that," said Herc, even though there was no way he could have.

"Just keep your eyes open," Pan said to Marlow. "Patrick's pissed because of what happened to his sister. It'll make him angry, but it'll make him stupid, too. Anger does that. Wait for him to expose a weakness, then move in."

"No way," Truck added. "Not gonna wait for nothing. Gonna crush his ass."

"Truck!" Herc yelled, so loud that it hurt Pan's ear.

"Yeah, but what's the plan?" said Marlow. "What do we do?"

"Like the big guy says, crush ass. Oh, and don't die."

"Crush ass, don't die?" Marlow said, shaking his head. "Great."

He was still grumbling as they crossed the deserted street. Somewhere in the distance a summer storm was brewing, thunder and lightning stomping the hell out of the Bronx to the north. It was hot here, her skin prickling. It was *too* hot, like some of the layers between this world and theirs had peeled away. For a second she wondered whether she should turn around and go. There was *always* a second where that thought crossed her mind. Then she flicked it away. She'd made a choice, long ago, a choice to do the right thing.

This *was* the right thing.

Besides, where else was she going to go?

"You wanna find a way in through the back?" Night said.

Pan shook her head, marching toward the steps that led to the huge bronze doors. They stood open, a soft light trickling out from inside.

"Nah," she said. "Asshole wants a scrap, let's give him one."

She climbed the stairs and looked inside. There were no lights on in there but there must have been a thousand candles blazing in the main body of the building, making it look like the cathedral was on fire. Even though it was night, light from the sleepless city streamed in through the huge windows. Pan couldn't see a single sign of life, although with the flickering candlelight it was hard to be sure.

He was here, though, she could feel the presence of the Engine like a knife in her soul.

She stepped over the threshold, a cold sweat breaking out on her skin. Sickness squirmed in her stomach the way it always did when she crossed onto hallowed ground with the Engine in her blood. Every time it happened she half expected to burst into flames, but thankfully it didn't work that way. The cathedral opened up around her, above her, far bigger than it had any right to be. It was like a cavern, the vaulted ceiling lost in shadow, the columns like some vast, primeval forest. The silence was so profound it was almost a physical force and she flexed her jaw to make her ears pop.

Glancing back, she saw the others on her heels. Night nodded to her, moving off to the side, flanking a row of long wooden pews. Truck went left, his big sneakers padding on the polished stone, the only noise in the building. Pan walked straight up the middle, slowly, her heart thrumming like a plucked string. Up ahead in the middle of the cathedral was the raised platform of the sanctuary, shrouded in a cold, gray half-light. Was that a figure there? A pocket of black? Pan blinked, trying to make sense of the gloom.

"Patrick?" she called out, her own voice so loud that it scared her. It echoed around the empty space like a trapped bird.

"You sure this is a good idea?" Marlow whispered, so close behind he was treading on her shadow.

"Patrick," Pan said, ignoring the kid, "we know you're here."

A fluttering up ahead, something that might have been hushed laughter. Pan glanced to her sides to see Truck and Night creeping through the dark.

"We've got unfinished business, you and me," she said.

Something popped at the far end of the cathedral, like bubble wrap. A wave of warm air rippled past her and she recognized the shock wave a 'Porter made when they rematerialized. There was definitely a silhouette up there, standing in front of the altar. It moved, and Pan saw that it wasn't just one silhouette but two. She stopped, flexing her fingers, wondering if she should just attack now, while she still had the chance, burn them both to ashes. She didn't, though. Orders were orders.

"Unfinished business," said a voice from the twilight dark. "Yeah, I'd say that's a good way of putting it."

Patrick walked down the steps and stood stooped and weary. He looked like he'd not slept for a decade. He was wearing the same clothes he'd had on in Budapest and they were covered in filth. When he looked up his eyes were two pockets of darkness in his face, but they burned into Pan with an intensity that made her want to run. She stood her ground, swallowing hard, sensing Truck and Night and Marlow around her.

"You gonna come quietly?" she asked. "Make our lives a little easier?"

Patrick smiled, a lunatic half-moon of teeth. Then he shook his head.

"So you can torture me too," he said, "like you did my sister? So you can murder me and send me to hell?"

"Come on, Patrick," Pan said. "You know the game. You make a deal, sooner or later you pay the price. You can't cheat the Devil forever."

"No, you can't," he said, then breathed a long, sad sigh. "You shouldn't have taken her, though. She wouldn't have died if you hadn't taken her."

"Your Lawyers should have broken her contract," Pan said. "Don't you dare blame us for that."

"Yeah, let her live so she could tell you how to find us." Patrick took a step forward, jabbing a finger. She flinched, fear squeezing a spark of lightning from her finger into the marbled floor. The static crack echoed around the cathedral, acrid smoke rising into her nostrils. Patrick was unimpressed. "Brianna was never strong," he said. "She would have talked. We had to let her go. You cannot know the location of our Engine."

"You can't hide it forever," said Pan. "We'll make you talk. And if you don't, somebody else will. Sooner or later, we *will* find it."

"Maybe," Patrick said. "But you won't be there to see it. None of you will. It's over for you. For all of us."

"This is boring," said Truck from the aisle. "Let's just crush his ass."

She opened her hand, feeling the charge building up.

"He's got a point, Patrick, we didn't come here to chat."

"No," he said. "You came here so you could pay for what you did to her."

"That's what this is?" Pan asked. "You brought us here to avenge her?"

"Not me," he replied, looking over his shoulder to the second figure on the altar. "Brianna," he called softly. "Brianna, it's time."

Brianna?

The figure behind Patrick made a noise, a low, throaty growl like a bear. It moved, or at least it was *trying* to move, its limbs as shaky as a puppet's. It twitched, its whole body spasming hard for a moment before staggering into the light.

Oh god.

It was Brianna Rebarre, Patrick's twin. But there was something wrong with her. Her face was a patchwork doll's, badly stitched together, one side bulging grotesquely. Her body was bent and broken, like she'd just been pulled from a car crash. She was naked, but her skin was so burned and so scarred that she looked like she was clothed in a corpse's flesh. Her hair had all but fallen out, clumps hanging down in thin, greasy strands. Her eyes were glassy and blind. Dead eyes.

"Oh, Patrick," said Pan, stumbling back, grabbing a pew to stop herself from falling. The last time she'd seen the girl she'd been bitten in half, dragged into the fire. "What did you do?"

She knew exactly what he'd done. He'd traded for her. He'd made a deal to bring his sister back from hell. It was one of the first rules, one of the things you could never ask for. *You cannot bring back the dead,* Ostheim had told her on Day One. *It is impossible.* All you could do was conjure up a memory of them, a wormbag stuffed with rot and jelly, something cold and old and *wrong.*

And you definitely, *definitely* couldn't bring back the dead from hell. Because when you did that, they brought something back with them.

"It was the only way," Patrick said, smiling. His own eyes had a glassy sheen, the look of somebody pushed way over the edge. Only Mammon would be sick enough to let somebody make a deal with the Engine in that frame of mind. He'd just condemned his own Engineer to an eternity of suffering.

"You know they can't break it," Pan said. "That contract, it's too hard. You're screwed."

He shrugged, watching Brianna as she shuffled down the stairs. She missed one and went sprawling, landing with a sound like a garbage bag exploding on the curb. Slowly, painfully, she picked herself up.

"Life doesn't mean much without her," Patrick said. "We came into this world together, I guess we'll leave it together."

"You'll spend the rest of time in hell together," Pan said. "Just so Mammon can have his way."

"Better than the alternative," Patrick said. "Better than what you and Ostheim are proposing."

"Sure," said Pan. "End of the world, so much better."

He looked back at her, those oil-black eyes blinking.

"You don't get it, do you? You're so blind to the truth that you can't even see what you're fighting for."

"Don't you dare," she shot back. "You're the bad guy in this equation, not me. Ostheim has only ever tried to do the right thing."

Patrick laughed, shaking his head.

"All this time, fighting for the wrong side. You should have joined us, Pan. The things we could have given you."

"Yeah, a dead sister and a one-way ticket to the Devil's playground." She snorted a humorless laugh. "Man, I totally messed up that decision. Just tell us where we can find your Engine. Least that way your last few minutes on Earth won't be spent with me beating it out of you."

"It's too late," Patrick said. "You'll never know. You'll never know how wrong you were."

Impatience was gnawing at Pan's soul and she took a step forward, energy crackling between her fingers, her whole body fizzing. That was the thing about dealing for electromagnetic abilities, it was as uncomfortable as a suit of electric wire.

"Yeah," she said. "How'd you figure that? Four of us against you and a wormbag. Seems like pretty good odds."

Patrick just smiled at her. Brianna had stumbled to his side, almost doubled over, her eyes looking like they might roll out and shatter on the floor. Even now Pan could see that they were twins, although Brianna was like a mirror image that had rotted, a twisted shadow that had torn itself free from Patrick's feet. He seemed to know this, because he looked at her with an expression of profound sadness.

"I didn't just bring her back," he said, quietly. "I made her something terrible."

Brianna straightened like an old lady, the sound of breaking bones echoing around the cathedral. She uttered that throbbing growl, then without warning she threw her head back and shrieked. The noise was so loud it was a physical force, a fist that punched into the darkness of the ceiling, terrible and unending. Dust and rubble rained down as Pan staggered back, hands to her ears, that scream like a tornado as it churned up the air. It cut out, and Brianna's head snapped down again. Her eyes were burning, literally sizzling in their sockets. The cathedral was full of the smell of cooked meat and sulfur.

"I made her a monster," Patrick said, wiping tears from his own eyes. "They're yours, Brianna. Take them."

Brianna screamed again, and hell arrived.

CRUSH ASS, DON'T DIE

Marlow screamed.

It was the only thing he was capable of doing. The girl's shrieking howl ripped up the floor of the cathedral, marble and stone rising like a vast wave. The vibrations threatened to shatter his bones, the noise unbearable. He had time to see Pan throw herself to one side, a slab of brick crunching off her skull, then it was on him, a tsunami of dust and debris that thundered forward.

Something thumped into his side, the tackle sending him skidding across the floor. He covered his face with his hands.

"It's easier to fight with your eyes open," said Night, and he looked to see her there, crouched beside him. Behind her the wave of debris rolled into the wall where he'd been standing, making the whole building tremble. A groaning howl rose up above the crash and it took Marlow a moment to realize the church organ was collapsing, the pipes blowing out curdled notes as they clanged to the ground.

Night helped him to his feet and he had to clamp another scream in his throat. In the middle of the cathedral, Brianna was a statue of fire, burning from head to toe. She didn't seem to notice, taking a step forward and thrusting out her arms. A jet of blue flame tore out, engulfing the first few rows of pews in an explosion of wood. A shock wave of heat burned through the air, hot enough that Marlow could feel his hair sizzle even from thirty feet away. He lifted his hand over his face, blinking away tears.

When he looked again he saw Pan crawling away from the fire, her clothes singed, her head bleeding. She rolled onto her back and shot something at the girl, a bolt of forked white lightning that crackled upward, missing its target and shattering one of the windows in a rain of stained glass. The building shook again, moaned in protest, a crack of thunder almost splitting Marlow's skull open. Brianna reached out, another fountain of liquid fire shooting from her hands. Something slapped into her, a streak of light that could only be Night. The impact knocked the burning girl back, her flames spitting and spluttering like napalm, so hot that it was setting fire to the stone.

Marlow started to run, time crawling into silence, the fire burning in slow motion, almost beautiful as it curled upward, dancing on its own heat. He dodged pieces of plaster and mortar that hung suspended in midair, sprinting down the center aisle and stopping when he reached Pan. Time snapped back with a sickening punch, the sound and fury blasting back on.

The heat here was insane, blistering his skin as he grabbed her under the arms. There was something electric in her, like holding on to a live wire, but he clung on, dragging her back. She fired off another deafening pulse of lightning, this one hitting Brianna in the chest and sending her cartwheeling back through the cathedral.

"No!" Patrick yelled, vanishing with a soft *pop*.

"Watch—" was all he heard Pan say before the air ruptured next to Marlow and Patrick appeared. He threw a punch that connected with Marlow's gut, launching him up. The world spun and he landed on a pew hard enough to crush it to splinters. It was like Patrick had reached in and grabbed his lungs because when he tried to breathe he found he couldn't. He whined like a beaten dog, clawing at the air until his solar plexus started working again.

What the hell was he doing? He was going to die.

Hands on him, wrenching him off the ground like he was a toddler. Then he was airborne again, slamming into one of the stone columns and dropping to the floor. The pain was like nothing he had ever felt, carving through him like a circular saw in his spine. He pushed himself to his feet just as Patrick 'ported back into the world, the boy's teeth bared, his eyes full of a madness that made Marlow want to scream again.

"Got you," Patrick said, wrapping a hand around Marlow's throat. Marlow swung his fist but Patrick dodged the punch. He tried again, squirming in the iron grip, darkness starting to creep in at the edge of his vision.

Something exploded against Patrick's head and he released his grip, staggering away. Truck was there, the big guy holding a twenty-foot pew like it was a baseball bat. He swung it again and it broke in half against Patrick's back, sending him tumbling down the aisle like a bag of bones. Marlow didn't hesitate, grabbing a pew of his own. It was solid oak but as light as a feather and he swung it in a wild arc toward Patrick. It was longer than he'd thought, glancing off the side of a pillar, jarring his spine so hard he thought it had been ripped out of his back.

He lifted the pew again for another strike but Patrick 'ported. Marlow spun around, waiting for him to appear. The cathedral was ablaze, a curtain of fire almost hitting the ceiling. Brianna was back, striding through the flame, her whole body shimmering in its burning shroud. A black hole opened up in the furnace of her face and she screamed again, a physical force that blasted through the church, lifting pews from the ground and scattering them.

Marlow couldn't see Pan anywhere in the ocean of smoke and was halfway to calling her name when a forked branch of lightning exploded from the far end of the building, hitting Brianna and knocking her back. She lay on the floor, writhing and twitching. Pan was striding out of the coiling smoke, a face like murder. She pulled back her hand like she was going to pitch a baseball, then thrust it forward, grimacing. The whole cathedral lit up like it was dawn, Marlow shielding his eyes with his hands to stop from going blind. The noise was incredible, a million firecrackers going off at once.

"Come on!"

Truck grabbed his arm, dragging him across the church to where Brianna squirmed. Marlow coughed smoke out of his lungs, blinking tears and light from his vision, trying to see where he was going.

"Take that one!" Truck yelled, pointing to a column. He ran to the next one along, charging it like a defensive tackle bringing down a quarterback. It split on contact, a crack running all the way up to the ceiling. Marlow jogged to his and punched it, his fist blasting through the stone, sending shrapnel flying. The ceiling above them groaned, sagging. He punched again and the column broke, crumbling earthward and bringing half the roof with it. Truck barged his way through the wall to avoid the falling stone. Marlow ran too, the world spinning slower. He dodged falling rocks as he sprinted across the cathedral, tripping on a broken pew and sprawling back into real time. Dust and dirt rained down on him, the ceiling disintegrating overhead.

A chunk of wood and stone the size of a car broke free and crashed earthward. Pan aimed her power up, lightning tearing off a second piece, even bigger, which landed on Brianna with a dull crunch. Smaller pieces followed, burying the girl alive— or dead, or whatever the hell she was. Pan stopped firing, shaking her hands like they were hot, her face a mask of pain. There was a cry from across the aisle and Marlow looked to see Patrick, his expression so full of hate and anger that he looked demonic.

"Not again!" he screamed. "Not again! Not again!"

Then Night was there, blocking the view, saying, "We should go, whole place is gonna collapse."

Marlow took her hand and pulled himself up, every cell in his body aching. Pan stumbled to them, her hands so black she might have had them on the barbecue. She smelled of summer storms and Marlow reached out, propping her up, her skin hot against his own. She opened her mouth to say something, then stopped, staring at the pile of rubble where Brianna had fallen.

It was moving.

Something pushed up from the mess, a thin, red stalk that could have been a plant. It stretched farther and Marlow saw that it was an arm, stripped to the bone, scraps of flesh hanging off it. Five mangled fingers extended like petals, swaying back and forth almost as if they were waving. Patrick's sobs had become something else, a lunatic laughter that rose above the roaring flames, above the ringing in Marlow's ears.

"Not good," said Pan.

That was an understatement. The mountain of debris was shaking, and with a bone-jarring crack it split in two. Brianna appeared in the gap, her body broken beyond recognition. Her skin had split in a dozen different places, slick purple organs poking out and swinging gently as she moved. Her head had been crushed, the top of her skull missing, hollowed out. But that didn't stop her scuttling out on all fours. Her toothless jaw hung like a broken branch and she gargled through it, a single bloody word that might have been her brother's name.

Pan stretched out her fingers and a bolt of cold light ripped out, but Brianna was faster, scampering spider-like to the side as the ground blasted into dust behind her. She vanished into the smoke but Marlow could still hear her hands and feet pattering wetly on the rock, moving fast, circling them.

"You're all dead!" yelled Patrick, still laughing. "You're finished!"

"You guys, go shut him up," said Pan, wiping her face and smearing soot over it. Her voice trembled but her eyes were clear. "I've got the wormbag."

Marlow nodded, taking a deep breath and walking toward Patrick. He'd never felt this tired in his life, never been in so much pain. Death was stalking him, hovering over his shoulder, just out of sight. And death was the least of his worries, too. Because where he was going the fires burned way hotter than this.

"You're finished!" Patrick screamed, filling the air with lunatic howls. "You're finished!"

Yeah.

Marlow had a bad feeling he was right.

GODDAMNED WORMBAG

Pan ran, stumbling over the loose stone. The ceiling was still raining chunks of plaster, the whole thing coming to pieces. Worse still, she could hear sirens from outside, closing fast. The place would soon be flooded with cops and firemen and Herc would be chewing her a new one.

If she lived, of course.

She heard shouts, glanced to the side to see Marlow and Night bursting in and out of real time as they attacked Patrick. She left them to it. She had bigger things to worry about. The back of the cathedral was a wall of flame, like the building had been sculpted from fire. She had to squint at it because it was so bright, holding up her hand against its heat. Something shimmered there, a shape scuttling across the broken ground. She opened her fingers and felt the energy build up, the air crackling as she fired off a painful burst of electrostatic discharge. It thumped into the fire, fighting it, creating a storm of light and flame. Brianna had long gone, moving impossibly fast on those broken bones.

"Where are you?" Pan muttered beneath her breath, ignoring the agony in her hands. Sweat dripped into her eyes, blood too, although she didn't remember getting cut. She wiped it away, moving sideways across the width of the cathedral, trying to make sense of the fluttering shadows behind the remaining pillars. Brianna was a wormbag, the worst of the worst. She was capable of anything, but she had no soul, no mind. A madness of cruelty and horror that Patrick had wound up and let loose.

There. Something scuttled between pillars and Pan ran for it, vaulting an upturned pew. The shape reared in the shadows, stretching up, too tall to be human. As Pan got closer she saw that Brianna's body was unraveling, her spine stretching. The girl's skin tore, her top half ripping free, rising like a cobra out of a basket of ribs. Guts slopped to the floor, the stench of ruptured intestines making Pan gag.

Brianna screamed and Pan threw herself to the side as a solid fist of noise blasted past. She rolled to her feet, dodging to the side, keeping the pillar in between her and the girl. Brianna's crushed head peered around the side of it. Her neck was a snake's, four times longer than it should be, the skin pulled taut and torn in places to reveal the slick cords of muscle beneath. Her drooping jaw shook and fragments of words dropped like spilled teeth. Her eyes had been burned out, just gaping holes in her ruined skull, but she still looked right at Pan.

"Yeah, make the most of it," Pan said. "You're going right back to hell."

Brianna's top lip—what was left of it—curled up, the closest thing she could manage to a smile. There was definitely life in those eye sockets, but Pan understood it didn't belong to Brianna. Something else was looking at her, something much, much worse than a wormbag.

Pan jabbed both her hands out. Lightning burned from her fingertips, carving through the pillar, so bright that even though she screwed her eyes closed the world still blazed white. She kept it going until it felt like her fingers had been burned to stubs, then she snapped it off, staggering back.

305

There was a hole in the side of the cathedral, darkness pouring in through the gap. She could see the street outside, the gaping hole in the building opposite. Sparks flew from ruptured cables, brick dust crumbling. There was no sign of—

Something moved overhead, a spider clawing over the remains of the ceiling. Brianna was missing one leg but she was still quick, a tangled mass of sinew and skin that spasmed toward her.

And dropped.

She landed on Pan, a wet, stinking bag that thrashed and squirmed. Pan grunted, pushing against it, feeling Brianna's fingers drill into her chest, into her neck, feeling the girl's flapping jaw rub against her face. Something sliced through her stomach and the world was suddenly made of cold fire. The stump of Brianna's leg bone was lodged in her flesh, pushing deeper. Her fingers, too, had pierced the skin of her chest, like the girl was trying to climb inside her, trying to wear her like a coat.

"No!" she grunted, punching up. Her fist ripped off a loose fold of cheek skin and it stuck to her knuckles, but Brianna didn't notice, her body rocking, her bones grating against Pan's.

She placed her palm against Brianna's face and unleashed a burst of energy. There was a sound like a watermelon exploding and Brianna's head vanished in a spray of blood and bone. Her body twitched violently, a spasm rocking through her. Pan pushed it away, shrieking as the girl's dagger bones ripped free of her flesh. The one in her stomach stuck and she grabbed it with both hands, pulling it until it came free with a sucking sound.

The Brianna thing was a mound of flesh, twitching its way toward the hole in the cathedral wall like a headless chicken. Pan pushed herself up, trying to get to her feet. The world spun and she dropped to her knees, blood leaking out of her wounds, pattering to the ground and steaming on the hot stone. She backed against a pew and sat there, trying to find her breath. The fire was everywhere now. Death couldn't be far away. At least the demons would feel at home when they came for her.

"Bring it on," she told them, wondering if dying in a cathedral would give her soul a fighting chance in hell, knowing that it wouldn't make the slightest bit of difference. She put her hand to her ear. "Truck?"

Nothing.

"Night?"

Nothing but static. *Dammit, why do I have to do everything?* The wormbag was almost out and something else was happening to it. The remaining scraps of skin seemed to be bulging, like somebody was inflating Briana's corpse with a pump. A wet, red bladder was pushing its way out of the stump of her neck, a clutch of pus-filled eyes bulging open in the mess. Pan swore, gritting her teeth as she staggered to her feet. She held her stomach like she was holding in the last few scraps of life, wondering if she had it in her to make it outside, and knowing what would happen if she didn't.

"Come back here, you goddamned wormbag," she said, wiping the blood from her mouth. "I'm not done with you yet."

WE SHOULD PROBABLY
KILL IT

Marlow was airborne again and he didn't even know how. He managed to raise his hands before he hit the cathedral doors, crashing through them and landing hard on the street. He thought he felt something inside him snap, his ribs suddenly made of molten lead. He rolled to a halt next to a car, looked up to see a cop staring right at him, the man's jaw almost on the floor.

"Hi," Marlow tried to say, but it came out as a groan. The cop was wrestling with his sidearm, tugging it out of the holster, and Marlow opened his mouth to try to explain himself, to tell him they were fighting on the same side.

Then Patrick was there, 'porting out of thin air. He swiped his arm and the cop went flying. Patrick grabbed the squad car and hefted it over his head, his fingers gouging holes in the metal like it was made of butter. Marlow rolled out of the way just as the car came down, crumpling next to him, cratering the asphalt. He scrambled to his feet and bolted past another cop—this one falling back in slow-motion shock, looking like he was sitting on thin air.

The pain in his ribs was too great and he had to stop, time snapping back. There was a grinding crunch of metal as

Patrick lobbed the same car across the street. Marlow raised his arms just in time to deflect it, the impact knocking him back. By the time he'd recovered, Patrick was gone.

"Where'd he go?" Night said, materializing next to him. She looked exhausted, putting her hands on her knees to catch her breath. "Oh, there he is."

Marlow looked to see a fire truck grating toward them on a wave of sparks. Marlow threw himself on Night, pulling them both to the ground as it bounced over their heads, close enough to touch, uprooting trees and signs before slamming into the side of the Banana Republic store. Patrick flashed into sight next to it, relentless, grabbing the truck and spinning it around in a wide, deadly arc. Marlow tried to move but he wasn't quick enough, the truck driving into him and catapulting him over the street. He lay there, everything spinning.

"Get up, lazy ass!" Truck yelled, barreling past and grabbing Patrick in a bear hug. Night was there too, laying into him like he was a speedball in the gym. Patrick grunted and popped away, appearing again in an instant on the opposite sidewalk. He staggered, bracing his arm on the cathedral wall, looking about three steps away from death. Then Truck was on him again, launching the fire truck like a spear. Patrick didn't 'port this time, just threw himself to the side as the truck hit the cathedral. It was like a wrecking ball, too much for the burning building, half of St. Patrick's falling into itself like a wave-washed sand castle.

"Don't let him out of your sight," said Truck, his whole body jiggling as he crossed the street. But it was too late, the dust clearing to reveal an empty space where Patrick had been.

Marlow's head snapped left and right as he tried to pinpoint where he'd 'ported to. *There*, movement to the side of the cathedral, something creeping out of the smoke. He squinted into the dark. Whatever it was, it wasn't Patrick. It couldn't

309

even be human, could it? The space where its head should have been was just a ragged hole, something grotesque bulging from the stump.

"What *is* that?" said Night, leaning on him for support.

The creature crawled onto the street, a mangled mess of skin and bone that looked as if it had lost a battle with a wood chipper, a blast furnace, and a steamroller all at once. It was shaking, struggling to stay upright on its severed limbs. And something was definitely happening inside it, impossible shapes pressing against the remaining scraps of skin.

"I don't know," said Marlow, trying to swallow his stomach back inside. "But we should probably kill it."

The bulge of the creature's neck stump was ballooning outward, a mass of leathery flesh mottled with dark veins. There were eyes there, a whole bunch of them, as big and as watery as cracked eggs. A hole opened beneath them, a gaping, toothless maw that snatched at the air. It uttered a foghorn groan so loud and so low that Marlow didn't so much hear it as feel it in the soles of his feet.

"Yeah, we should *really* kill it," he said, gritting his teeth against the pain. "You do it."

Something burst out of the creature. It was a fat, jointed limb that had to be six or seven feet long, sliding loose alongside a gout of black blood. At the end of it was a hand that looked half human and half reptile, topped with a mix of stumpy fingers and blade-like claws, dozens of them. Another followed, tearing out of the jelly of Brianna's demolished rib cage, a limb of muscle and sinew. They were expanding impossibly fast, swelling, the skin stretching to accommodate them.

The creature's torso was growing too, like something had hatched inside the corpse of the girl. It bulged out, as black and shiny as a tick's shell. It was as big as a horse now, even more limbs sprouting from it. The beast tottered unsteadily, unable to control its bulk, its mouth lolling open, gumming the sky, its eyes straining, bulging.

"No, it's okay," said Night. "You can do it."

"No, really, it's all yours," Marlow said.

The world burned white and he threw his hands up against the force of it. Bolts of lightning scorched their way from the cathedral, turning the air to cold fire as they sliced into the beast. Its insect hide crackled and spat and it reared up on its stunted back limbs. Black hairs—no, *spikes*, as big as javelins— were erupting from its hide, bristling like a porcupine's.

Another burst of electrostatic discharge, forks of lightning slicing through the night. They whip-cracked against the creature's rear end and it howled, a cannon shot of sound that tore into the air. It broke into a run, the whole street trembling with the force of it.

Night dived to one side as the creature pounded their way. Marlow threw himself in the other direction but not quick enough, the beast's ass-ugly face butting him as it passed. It was like being hit by a subway train and the world flipped in wild circles until he thumped back down again.

It took him a second to work out where he was, the world so dark that he thought the impact might have blinded him. Then he looked up to see a sliver of firelight, and the panic was drenched by a wave of relief. He groaned into a sitting position, noticing that he was inside a shop—he'd been thrown right through the wall. He offered thanks to the Engine for keeping him alive—*please, please, please don't stop now*—and pulled himself up.

The street was a war zone. The fire from the cathedral was spreading, gushing out like lava. The other side of Fifth Avenue wasn't faring much better, the statue of Atlas crushed and a massive hole torn into the lobby of Rockefeller Center's International Building. Truck was running toward it, Pan too. She scanned the street and saw him.

"Any chance of you actually *helping*?" she yelled.

He clambered out, brushing dust and rubble from his hair. Farther down the street the cops had formed a perimeter, mobilizing fast. There was still no sign of Patrick but the douche bag had to be around here somewhere. Marlow broke into a run, then stopped, clamping a hand to his ribs. Something was grinding around in there and every time he took a breath he felt like he'd been stabbed. He limped toward Rockefeller Center.

"What *was* that?" he asked Pan.

"A wormbag," she replied, rubbing her blackened hands on her pants. "A nasty one. That's what happens when you bring people back from hell."

Something exploded inside the building, and a fire alarm was blaring too. Screams fluttered out of the hole in the wall, first one or two, then so many that it was like a second alarm ringing into the night.

"Where's Night?" asked Pan. Marlow glanced around, shrugged.

"Think she's inside," said Truck. "Think it's gunning for her."

Pan swore, taking a deep breath, then climbing through the demolished wall. Marlow followed her, seeing a ruined lobby, cables sparking and water pipes spraying. There were what looked like torn sacks on the floor, but as they scrabbled over the rubble Marlow saw that they were people, trampled into mush against the marble. He put a hand to his mouth, his nose full of the stench of the dead.

"There," said Truck, pointing. Not that he needed to, the creature had put a hole in the other side of the lobby, and the wall after that, a tunnel of destruction that cut through to the street on the other side. Marlow could hear the building above him rumbling in outrage, struggling to stay standing with its legs cut out from beneath it. There was another noise, too, a thundering of giant footsteps, getting louder, closer.

Night suddenly streaked into sight. She slowed to a jog and then collapsed onto her knees. She was bleeding heavily from a cut on her head and she looked so pale she might have been halfway drained. She looked up and saw them.

"It's—"

Coming, Marlow guessed, but she didn't have time to finish before a second hole appeared in the far wall and a tsunami of flesh tumbled through. The beast seemed to have doubled in size, as big as a subway car, its cavernous mouth vast enough to swallow them all whole. It charged like a rhino, roaring, those fish eyes bulging wildly.

Pan unleashed an arc of lightning that hit it in the neck but it didn't even seem to notice, lowering its head like a bull and carving a path through the lobby. Truck put his shoulder down and charged, hitting the beast with a bone-jarring crack that deflected it right toward Marlow.

Oh sh—

He sidestepped at the last second, reaching out and grabbing hold of the first thing he could. It was a fistful of soccer-ball-sized eye and it popped in his grip, warm gunk exploding over his fingers. He was jerked off his feet and he clung on to the socket, punching at the creature with his other hand, each blow leaving craters in its shell. It roared, trying to shake him off, bursting back out through the front wall of the building. Bricks detonated against Marlow's face and he let go, spinning back to earth. It felt like a hand grenade had been set off inside his chest.

The thing that had once been Brianna skidded to a halt, its hand-claws gouging trenches into Fifth Avenue. It was still expanding, swelling. It turned back to Marlow and snorted, looked like it was going to charge again. There was a series of pops and its skin rippled, gunfire tearing into it. Police were moving down the street, dozens of them opening fire.

They didn't stand a chance.

The beast moved again, its whole body trembling as it threw itself at them. Marlow watched the first two cops pounded to meat before he turned away, fury igniting inside him. He felt a hand on his shoulder, saw Pan there, a face like grim death.

"What the hell do we do?" he said.

"I don't know," she replied. "I've never fought anything like this. Damn thing is invincible. I can't even get through to Herc or Ostheim, something has taken down the comm."

"We've got to do something," Marlow said, hearing the screams of the cops, the sick glee of the beast as it howled into the night.

"Yeah?" she snapped back. "And what, Marlow? What do you suggest?"

She was looking at him like he was the world's biggest idiot, and he didn't disappoint her, letting his gaze drop to the floor like he might be able to find an answer in the dirt.

"Nothing we can do," said Truck. "Just hope it stays distracted long enough for us to get away, find some help."

There was a flash in the middle of the ruined street, Patrick standing there inside a cyclone of dust. He struggled to stay upright, a trickle of vomit leaking between his lips. Then he turned and looked their way.

"Brianna!" he yelled weakly. He took a breath. "Brianna! They're *here*!"

"Not good," said Truck.

Patrick called out again and this time the beast that had once been his twin sister answered with a bellow. The wormbag bouldered down the street, each footstep like a gunshot, that train wreck of a face zeroing in on Marlow.

"Run," said Pan as it charged toward them. Marlow didn't need to be told twice, ignoring the pain in his ribs as he turned and sprinted. The world slowed into blissful stillness and silence, but only for a moment. Then he ran out of steam, his system completely drained, plunging him back into the chaos. He stumbled along the side of the building, ducking around the corner onto Fiftieth Street. He barely had time to catch his breath before the wall next to him erupted outward in a hail of stone and glass, the beast howling past him, shaking pieces of Rockefeller Center from its bulk.

There were people here, Marlow noticed, streaming from the buildings—tourists and staff and late-night workers. The wormbag tore into them like a fox in a chicken coop, its car-sized paw-claws grinding them into the dirt. It uttered another sound, one that was even more terrifying than its howl— a deep, throaty *uh-uh-uh* that could only be laughter. It was unbearable.

No more.

Marlow sucked in a breath and leaped onto its back, grabbing fistfuls of its flesh to haul himself up. It bucked beneath him like a giant bull but he clung on, balling his fist and punching through the skin. It was like a bag full of sewage, bursting at his touch, a flood of rancid black gunk splashing into his face, into his mouth. He ignored it, reaching in, grabbing anything he could and wrenching it out.

The creature roared, the noise a dragon might have made, loud enough to shatter the windows in the building opposite. It shook itself and Marlow lost his footing, grabbing onto the wound he'd made, swinging in midair as the creature bucked and twitched. It was too much, though, his fingers slipping out of the mess. He dropped, managing to land on his feet, his arms wheeling to keep him balanced.

Truck appeared, armed with the metal pole from a streetlight. The big guy swung it, the makeshift club cracking into one of the creature's arms. The wormbag recoiled, whimpering, and Truck swung the pole a second time, smacking it hard in the face, again, and again, driving it back.

There was a blast of light as Night streaked up the creature's back, one of the beast's eyeballs erupting in a fountain of pus. She was moving too fast up there for Marlow to see her but she was making a mess of its face, more of those eyes popping out, gallons of fluid splashing to the asphalt. It lifted one of its hands to knock her away but she was too quick, throwing herself to the ground and rolling. The creature towered above her, above all of them, stamping down hard enough to split the street in half.

Pan was right. It was indestructible.

Truck jabbed the pole into the creature's flank like a spear. He fought to pull it free but Marlow stopped him.

"No! Leave it!"

He ran to the sidewalk, grabbed another streetlight, and wrenched it out, taking a run-up and launching it like a javelin at the creature's torso. It wasn't a straight shot, and the streetlight wasn't exactly sharp, but the force of the throw punched it into the beast's side. It howled like a speared mammoth, tumbling onto its side, writhing there. Marlow had already pulled another post free and threw this one just as hard, puncturing its throat.

"Pan!" he shouted, looking around. Where the hell was she?

A blinding flash of light blistered the air, fingers of lightning crackling into the beast. Pan strode out of the side of the demolished Rockefeller Center, grimacing as she unleashed hell. She must have read Marlow's mind because she was aiming the attack at the spikes in the creature's skin, millions of volts burning their way through its guts like it was a skewered chicken.

The beast shuddered, trembling so hard that its skin was splitting, more of that rancid dark water flooding out. Marlow hopped onto the sidewalk to avoid it, hearing it gush down the drains. Smoke was billowing from its wounds, great clouds of it boiling into the sky.

Pan stumbled and the stream of lightning cut out. She took a breath then lifted her hands, firing again. The light was weaker, duller, like she was running out of charge. Marlow noticed that her shirt was soaked with blood. He had no idea how she was even standing.

The wormbag was on its belly, its claws scratching at the ground, at the air, its blind eyes blinking wetly. It uttered a soft, pathetic whine, one that almost made Marlow feel sorry for it.

Not sorry enough, though.

He ran to the next streetlight and uprooted it like a tree, a root-ball of solid concrete. Then he doubled back, ready to perform the coup de grâce, ready to splatter its infernal brain all over Fiftieth Street.

No . . .

The wormbag was pushing itself up, grunting with the effort, hauling itself onto its feet. It wrapped a claw around one of the poles in its flesh and wrenched it free, pulling out blackened chunks of organ and muscle. It tore out the other two, then broke into a run, retreating down the street, bulldozing its way through the wall of the Rockefeller tower.

Pan flexed her fingers but she was too weak, producing nothing but a fistful of sparks. She dropped onto all fours, breathing hard. Marlow jogged to her side, Truck and Night arriving at the same time. They were all bleeding from a number of different wounds, panting, swaying like the whole of New York was a boat sinking fast. The power of the Engine was holding them together, but for how much longer?

"What now?" Marlow asked.

"Bitch is . . . too strong," Pan said, her voice the sound of dry leaves kicked down the street.

A dozen windows in the tower shattered, dust pouring out of them. People streamed from it, a tide of screams and sobs.

"Can't we cancel its contract or something?" Marlow said. "Get the demons after it?"

"It's not an Engineer," Pan said, spitting out a bitter laugh. "It made no contract. That thing's escaped hell, and there's nothing . . ."

She cocked her head, her eyes scrolling back and forth, thinking hard. She held out a hand and let Marlow pull her up, then she leaned over and kissed him on the cheek. Of all the injuries he'd suffered, this was the thing that almost stopped his heart dead.

"That's it, that's what we need to do." She was grinning. "For a stupid guy, you're a genius."

"What?" Marlow said as she set off, limping down the street. "I don't get it. What did I say?"

More crunches from inside the Rock, the groan of a sinking ship. Marlow set off after her, clutching his ribs.

"What?" he repeated.

"We can kill it," Pan shouted back. "We can send that gal right back to hell."

And Marlow almost had time to smile before she added, "But one of us will have to go with it."

FINISH HER!

Pan was running on fumes. She felt like she was dissolving, like the electrostatic energy she'd been blasting out all night had hollowed her out inside, left her an empty husk. She knew she couldn't go on much longer—the Engine could work miracles, but even it had its limits. Much more and she'd lightning herself right out of existence.

But she couldn't stop now. That wormbag would turn the city into a ruin of bone and blood.

She limped on, feeling a hand under her arm. Marlow. The kid looked in a bad way, wincing every time he took a step. But he'd fought well, there was no denying it. She started to shake him off, then realized she'd be on the floor. She leaned on him instead, the four of them crossing the street to the Rock, following the path of carnage.

"Anyone got a line to Herc?" she said. She'd tried her radio twice since leaving the cathedral but it was dead. No sign of Herc, no sign of Ostheim.

"Everything's down," said Truck. "Haven't heard anything since we entered St. Patrick's. Probably the satellite feed."

She hoped that was all it was—they'd never lost connection before.

"If you're listening, Herc, you owe us one hell of a pay raise after tonight."

Not to mention a retirement party.

They reached the gaping wall of the Rock. The skyscraper was living up to its name, the tower scratching the heavens. She focused on the hole in the wall, like the mouth of a cave. The lights inside flickered, strobing on and off, revealing bodies plastered to the floor. There was no sign of the Brianna-bag, but Pan could hear it, those demonic howls shaking the building to its foundations.

"What did you mean?" Marlow asked as they clambered over the wreckage. "Why does somebody need to go to hell with it? Who?"

That was a good question, and the answer was inevitable. *Me,* she thought, and suddenly stopped, looking back into the night, aware that this might be the last time she felt fresh air on her skin, saw the moonlight. Her heart was suddenly a ton weight slipping loose in her chest, sinking fast.

You knew it would happen one day. You play the game, you take the pain.

Yeah.

She took a long, shuddering breath and carried on, slipping and tripping on the loose stone, on the blood-slicked ground. At one point she lost her footing, her hand plunging into something warm and wet. She snatched it loose, a snarl throbbing in her throat at the horror of it. And for a moment she didn't think she had it in her to get up again. Better to just lie here, listen to the dying night.

Then Marlow and Truck were there, grabbing an arm each and hauling her to her feet.

"What's the plan, Pan?" Truck said. "Better let us in on it just in case next time you fall you drop right out of life."

She opened her mouth to answer but was cut off by a howl from farther up inside the building. The wormbag sounded hurt. Pan thought she could hear something else, too, a voice above the storm. The next time she spoke it was in a whisper.

"Herc told me once that there's only one thing the demons want more than an owed soul, and that's an escaped one." Something ran out from behind a mound of rubble, a woman covered in blood, her eyes full of madness. One of her arms was missing, the other hand clamped over the gushing wound as she shuffled toward the street. "That wormbag got free," Pan went on. "Patrick pulled his sister's soul right out of hell, and that pisses the demons off big-time."

"So you're saying we need to get the demons here," said Night. "Show them where to find their missing prisoner."

Pan nodded.

"And therein lies the problem," Truck said. "Because the only way of getting them here . . ."

"Is for one of our contracts to expire," Marlow said, and Pan could see the understanding blossoming in his expression. "Or for one of us to die."

Bingo.

The ceiling of the lobby had been torn away, a drooping hole that stretched up for what must have been four or five stories. Dust and debris rained down, and when the wormbag bellowed again it came from somewhere up there. This time Pan could definitely hear a voice, although it was too soft for her to make out what it was saying. She flexed her fingers, trying to drum up a little more juice. She didn't even know if the plan would work. The demons were pretty single-minded when they came for you. Who's to say they would even notice that Brianna was there.

What was the alternative, though? Let it rampage across Manhattan? And then what? A wormbag like that could take out the whole East Coast if it wanted to. How many would die? She couldn't live with that on her conscience, in her soul.

Not that it would be her soul for much longer.

She kicked her way through the chaos to the stairwell, clattering up to the third floor and peeking out the door. There was a hole in the ceiling here and she climbed again, reaching the next level. This time, when she opened the fire door, she could see movement up ahead in the darkness of the tower. She held up her hand, motioning for the others to be quiet.

". . . do it, I had to." That voice was up ahead, and she was pretty sure it belonged to Patrick. "They deserved it, we need . . ."

A roar, like the wormbag was answering back. How much of Brianna was still in there? Pan wondered. How much was her, and how much was the festering madness of hell?

"I want you to do it, Truck," she said, looking up at the big guy. It took him a moment to understand what she was saying and he shook his head.

"No way, no way, Pan. I'm gonna take the bullet on this one."

"Truck, you couldn't take the bullet because you'd just try to eat it," she said, managing a half smile. "Just do it, okay? I'm tired of it all, anyway. Crush my head. One punch. I don't want to see it coming."

"Pan . . ."

She rested her hand on his arm, met his eye, gently shook her head.

"It's okay, I'm ready for this."

"Nobody's ready for this," he said.

Marlow reached them, both hands wrapped around his stomach. Even though his asthma had been canceled he was still wheezing.

"Don't feel too good," he said.

"Poor diddums," Pan spat back. "You wanna stay here while I call your mommy?"

She didn't wait for an answer, just walked through the door into the shattered remains of an office. The noises were coming from the other side of the space, behind the wall of the elevator shaft. She clenched her fist, feeling the energy building up, bracing herself for another fight. Truck could do the deed now but she wanted to make sure it was definitely Brianna up ahead. Nothing would suck quite as much as being dragged to hell, then realizing that the wormbag was nowhere nearby.

She eased her way around a desk, hearing Patrick more clearly now.

". . . be okay, I'll look after you, we can still do this, just—"

Something crashed to the ground behind her and a scream slipped between her lips before she could stop it. She spun, ducking down, seeing Marlow standing beside a desk, a computer monitor lying in pieces by his feet.

"That wasn't my fault," he said, his words almost drowned out by a bone-shaking roar from the other side of the room. There was the sound of galloping feet, then the elevator shaft detonated like it had been packed with C-4. The wormbag pile-drived through, its mouth the size of a house, its fleshy back dragging against the ceiling, its eyes hanging loose and useless.

"Ah, screw this," she heard Truck say, seeing the big guy running at it. He bent low like he was going in for the tackle, slamming into the beast like two trains crunching into each other. They careened into the outside wall together, punching right through it, both of them tumbling out into the night.

"No!" Pan yelled, running to the edge of the building in time to see them hit the ground. The Brianna thing burst, its rotten guts exploding over Rockefeller Plaza. There was no sign of Truck.

"Brianna!"

Patrick shuffled around the ruined elevator shaft. He moved like the living dead, limping, bleeding heavily, his eyes still full of lunatic hope. Pan had her hand up, ready to unleash a burst of energy, to fry the asshole for good, but he passed her like she didn't exist, moving to the window. For a second she thought he was going to fall out too. Instead he looked down, the wind snatching at him like it was trying to finish the job.

"Brianna," he was sobbing. "Nonono." He spun, jabbing his finger at her. "You did—"

Pan flinched against his attack, a burst of electrostatic burning from her fingers, whip-cracking against him. Too late she realized that he wasn't attacking but 'porting, half of him already erased, like he was a phantom. The lightning snapped around his ghost-like body, leaving just a coil of smoke where he had been standing.

Something fizzed in the plaza, an echo of her strike, a crackle of lightning down below. Then Patrick screamed—a noise so shrill and so full of pain that Pan had to clamp her hands to her ears.

"Come on!" yelled Night, heading back the way they'd come. Pan started to follow but felt herself scooped up, Marlow's arms beneath her like he was carrying her over the threshold on their wedding day. He stepped through the window and they dropped, Pan clamping her mouth shut to stop her stomach flying out of her throat. They landed hard but Marlow cushioned her, putting her down gently. She braced herself, building up another charge, ready to fight.

The wormbag was lumbering to its feet, its sides literally split, tar-colored organs slopping out of it and splashing on the ground. Truck was underneath and Pan almost cried with relief when she saw the big guy sit up. Patrick screamed again and the Brianna thing cocked its butt-ugly head, whining. Pan scanned the plaza, found Patrick. And even after everything else she'd witnessed tonight, this was the thing that made her double over, made her empty her stomach over the ground.

Patrick's upper body grew from the plaza like a stunted plant, a flagpole protruding from his shoulder. Half of one foot stuck out from the stone, twitching. There was no blood. It was like he was fused there, a statue that had come to life. And that's what had happened, she realized. Her strike had thrown off his aim. She'd made him 'port right into the ground. Patrick's whole body shook, the horror dripping from his eyes. He opened his mouth and shrieked, somehow the loudest noise Pan had ever heard. She put a hand to her mouth to stop a scream of her own from spilling out.

I didn't do this, I didn't do this.

The wormbag lumbered across the plaza but it wasn't coming for her. She stepped aside to let it through, the creature moving toward the screams of its onetime brother. It sniffed him, uttering a low, grief-filled whine. Then it collapsed beside him, dwarfing him, its blind face nuzzling his body. One of its feet, bigger than a car, pawed at Patrick, like it was trying to pull him loose. He screamed again, holding on to one of the finger-like digits.

The air hammered as a chopper flew across the plaza, the sound of sirens filling up the whole city. Pan ignored it. They had time. They had to see this through.

Patrick was dying, fast, the color all but drained from his face. He coughed out blood, gargled as he tried to breathe. It made her sick to see him there, pinned like a butterfly. But he deserved it. He was one of the enemy. The thing that had once been his sister lay next to him, panting like a dying horse. He held on to her as a drowning man would hold on to a float, staring at Pan with a look of pure fury.

"Last chance," she said. "Just tell us how we can access your Engine. Just do the right thing before you die."

Patrick spat out a noise that might have been a laugh. His hands dropped to his sides and he seemed to give up, resting his head on the wormbag's paw.

"Least I don't have to crush your head," said Truck. He was drenched in wormbag guts, steam rising off him into the night. The relief that hit her—the knowledge that she didn't have to die—was as painful as it was sweet. She could take no joy in this. There was a definite scent in the air, over the smoke—that same sulfurous stench as before. She scanned the street, waiting for the demons to pull themselves loose, to come collect what they were owed.

"Please," said Night, "just tell us, and it can all be over."

"It's already over," said Patrick, a dry wheeze that Pan could barely hear. His face twisted into something that might have been a grin. "We found your Engine."

The world stopped spinning. Pan was suddenly drowning in silence. Her heart stuttered, stalling for what felt like an eternity before revving back to life. She lost her balance, only Truck keeping her standing.

"Yeah, sure," she said.

"Try to . . ." He paused, coughing up blood. The smell of sulfur was getting stronger, burning up her nostrils. "Try to contact them. You can't, can you?"

"What's he talking about?" Night said.

"He's talking crap," Pan replied. "Not for much longer, though. They're coming for you, Patrick. Can you feel them?"

"I don't care," he said, a tear winding its way down his face, cutting a line into the dirt and the blood. "I did my part. *We* did. And at least now we get to go together." He stroked Brianna's hand. "We can look after each other."

"You did your part?" Pan said. "What does that even mean?"

He started fitting, shaking so hard that his skin was tearing loose from the ground. There was a ripping sound, his upper body coming loose. Beneath was an impossible mix of concrete and flesh, infernally bound.

"We only had to get you here," he whispered. "To distract you. The others took care of the rest. They opened the door."

"Don't even bother," Pan said. "It's not true. It can't be. Nobody gets in to the Engine."

"Not unless you let them in," said Patrick. "Not unless you open the Red Door from the inside."

"What are you talking about?" she said, her fingers a mass of crackling light.

Somewhere overhead there was a crunch of rock, dust raining down. She could almost see them, the demons, teeming just behind the skin of reality, frantically tearing their way through so they could claim Patrick's soul and reclaim Brianna's. She took a step back. Patrick turned to Marlow, his eyes slipping in and out of focus.

"Thank you," he whispered.

"What?" Marlow stuttered. *"Why?"*

"You ended the war," Patrick said. "You made it happen."

Marlow raised his hands, shaking his head.

"I swear, I have no idea what he's going on about. I didn't make anything happen."

"Not you," Patrick said, his words barely louder than a breath. "Your friend. Charlie."

Pan felt as if time had stopped, everything slowing to a nightmare singularity.

"No," said Marlow. "He'd never . . . It's impossible."

"He opened the door," said Patrick. "He let us in."

"It's not true," he said. "He wouldn't do that."

But Pan could see the uncertainty there, the doubt. She swore, terror rising up inside her like a cold, dark wave. Patrick reached up, spoke into his collar radio.

"It's done," he said. "Tell her. Please. I want to see the look in her eyes before I go."

Her earpiece fizzed, then a voice she knew all too well. Bullwinkle.

"Pan." He was sobbing. "Oh god, Pan, he let them in, he let them in, they're all—"

A pistol shot, so loud that she had to dig the receiver out of her ringing ear. She called Bully's name, holding the earpiece there, trying to make out what was going on. But there was only static. She looked at Night, the girl's eyes big and white and laced with horror. Even Truck was scared, the big guy shaking. Pan looked at Marlow, ready to rip his head off, but the kid seemed about ten years old, his hands held up defensively.

"Here's what's going to happen next," Patrick said, stroking his sister's paw. "They're going to cancel your contracts. Then they're going to come for you. You won't be able to fight them, you'll be defenseless. Mammon will pick you off one by one. Not you, though." He looked at Pan. "You get to keep your contract. I want you to think of Brianna. I want you to think of her for however many hours you have left. I want you to think of her when they come for you."

She looked at her watch. *649:43:20:18.* It couldn't be happening. It *could not* be happening. More crumbling dust from up the Rockefeller tower, a faint, distant, demonic scream. The wormbag lifted its head, sniffing the air, uttering another mournful groan. Patrick held his sister tight.

"And when they come for you," he whispered, "we'll be waiting."

IN HELL

This couldn't be happening.

The Circulus Inferni had found their Engine. They had breached the Red Door. They were *inside*.

"We'll be waiting," Patrick said again, then his eyes closed, his hands dropping limply to his sides. The wormbag sniffed him with its giant face, pawed his half-body hard enough to peel him from the stone like a piece of chewing gum. It opened its maw and howled its monstrous grief into the sky.

Brianna's howl was met by a shriek from the top of the Rock. There was something up there, pulling itself free of the building, a creature made of brick and glass. It was just a shadow against the night but it was moving fast, scrabbling down the side of the building. The demon opened its mouth and uttered a squeal like sheared metal.

"Go!" yelled Night, vanishing in a streak of light. Pan backed away, seeing a demon claw its way down the front of the building. Another was pushing up from the rubble, this one made of paving slabs and pipes and electric cables. It shook itself like a wet dog, then pounced, landing on the wormbag, laying into it with its claws. The Brianna thing bayed, shaking as it tried to bat the demon away.

More demons were appearing, a dozen now, two dozen maybe—more than she'd ever seen. The plaza was dissolving as they teemed out of the ground, out of the street, out of the buildings. They swarmed toward Brianna, as thick as ants as they clambered onto her thrashing body. The ground was already getting hot, the flagpoles of the plaza wilting. Pan staggered back, her shoes sticking to the melting stone. She could barely see the wormbag now, lost beneath the demons, so many that their claws and jaws looked like some nightmare machine.

Some had spotted Patrick, and were spilling off and scuttling over his cooling body. The ground was glowing so hot now that Pan had to look away, like she was staring into the heart of a volcano. She could still hear the twins, though, a pair of voices screaming as they were dragged into the pit. And she had to hold back a cry of her own, thinking it might have been her. Thinking it was *so close* to being her.

And knowing that it *would* be her.

There was a sudden roar overhead, a chopper riding into the plaza on a wave of heat and noise. It banked hard, the air splitting as somebody inside started firing a machine gun. The demons burst into dust and dirt, the bullets punching holes in the soft, glowing ground. But it was too late, most were dropping dead anyway, their job done. They collapsed, just chunks of stone and rock and glass and metal sinking into the molten earth.

A couple fought back, launching themselves at the helicopter. The pilot panicked, the tail rotor clipping one of the ruined Rockefeller towers. The helicopter bucked clumsily to one side, crunching down onto the street. The rotor churned up the asphalt for a second before tearing free, and the helicopter cartwheeled toward Fifth, plowing into a line of cop cars on the corner. Gas was spraying everywhere from the chopper's ruptured fuel line, dangerously close to the inferno.

Oh crap.

Pan bolted, seeing Marlow up ahead near the end of the

street. She followed him, *please, please,* almost there when the world turned white. The blast ripped her off her feet. A concussive wave of sound followed, an explosion that threatened to turn every bone in her body to dough. She hit the ground and rolled, everything going dark for a moment.

It's over. You're finished. The voice in her head might have been Patrick's, might have been her own. *Just die, because otherwise it will be twenty-six days of waiting for the inevitable.*

"No," she groaned, everything shaking. Somebody grabbed her, strong arms hauling her up. Marlow, slapping the flames from her back—*oh god, I'm on fire*—and leading her away.

"Come on," Marlow said.

Night and Truck had somehow made it out of the carnage and were up ahead, waving them on. They passed Radio City onto the Avenue of the Americas together, holding on to each other like children in the woods. Every window in the street had been shattered and the air was full of clanging alarms. The lights, too, were dead. People still streamed out of the buildings, the handful of cops down here trying to manage the flow in the dark. Pan ran into the stampede, slowing to a walk and grabbing her gut to conceal the wound there. They blended into the crowd as best they could, herded across Fiftieth. There were more people here, milling on the sidewalk, filming the scene with their cell phones. Incredibly, some of them were laughing.

Only in New York.

Pan felt like laughing too, like opening her mouth and howling until she was empty, until her lungs stopped working. She clamped her teeth shut, trying to hold it inside, trying to hold everything inside, knowing that if she started screaming now she would never, ever stop.

"Where do we go?" said Night. "Oh god, what do we do now?"

Nothing. Patrick was right, it was game over. At least the

others would have their contracts canceled, at least their souls were safe. She looked at her watch again. Six hundred and forty-nine hours and they'd come for her.

"This way," said Truck, leading them over toward Broadway. Two cop cars blasted east, heading to the cathedral, but neither of them stopped. Another helicopter was hovering overhead, this one higher, out of harm's way. They were halfway down the street before Pan remembered to take a breath. It was as if the air were on fire, her chest burning. She collapsed against Marlow and he lowered her down onto the wall of a flower bed. He was struggling to breathe too, snatching in small, noisy gulps of air. He looked like death, like he was the one who had been dragged to hell.

"We gotta find Ostheim, he'll know what to do," said Night, pacing back and forth.

Ostheim. He'd probably kill her on the spot when he found out what had happened. But Night was right, it was the only thing they could do. And fast, because if the Circle really did have both the Engines, then it would only be a matter of time before they found a way of uniting them, opening the gates permanently. Then the whole world would look like midtown Manhattan, drowning in blood and fire.

"First things first," Pan said. "We need to get off the island. Truck?"

"On it," he said, lumbering across the street to a parked car and punching through the window.

"I'm sorry, Pan," said Marlow, clawing in another breath. "I had no idea. He was my *friend*."

"Marlow, just shut your mouth until we figure out what happened."

The Lincoln's engine gunned to life as Truck hot-wired it. Pan stood, shakily, not wanting Marlow's help but pretty sure she wouldn't be able to cross the street without it. Together they clambered into the back of the car, Marlow slamming the door behind them. Truck floored it, the car accelerating smoothly up Sixth Avenue, hooking west on Fifty-first. Truck honked and ground his way through traffic across town, to Ninth Avenue.

They swung left, heading downtown to the Lincoln Tunnel. Pan spotted an old pay phone on the corner and leaned forward, slapping Truck's arm.

"Pull over a sec."

He did and she climbed out, grunting against the pain. She dialed the operator, giving her name and asking for a collect call to a cell phone in Europe, a number she knew by heart.

The phone rang. And rang. And rang. *Please, Herc, please pick up, please be alive.*

"Do you want me to continue?" asked the operator.

"Yes," Pan snapped.

Ring. Ring. Ring.

He's dead. He's dead. He's—

"This better be you, Pan." Herc's voice was like a golden ray of light cutting through the night. It cracked the floodgates and Pan broke down, sobbing, just so relieved to hear him, so relieved. *"Pan?"*

"I have a collect call from Pan in New York City," said the operator. "Do you accept the—"

"Yes, dammit, piss off," growled Herc. *"Pan, Jesus, I thought you were dead."*

"What's going on?" she said, barely able to fit the words past her choking sobs. "The Engine . . ."

"It's gone," he said. *"The bastards had a Trojan Horse, Charlie. He must have dealt for something immense when he used the Engine because we couldn't stop him, none of us. He opened the*

door and Mammon was there. We couldn't fight them, not without you."

"It was a lure," Pan said, wiping her eyes. "Patrick baited us away so we couldn't fight it. Jesus, Herc, how did we miss this?"

"You guys okay?" he asked. "Any casualties?"

"We made it," she said. "Patrick's dead. Brianna too, again. Where are you?"

"I got out," he said. "Just. It was chaos. They're dead, Pan."

"Who?"

"All of them. Bully, Hope, the Lawyers. Mammon butchered them. I think Hanson made it out, but I lost him."

"Oh god." She had to cling on to the phone to stop herself collapsing. Her whole body was shaking. "No."

"I can't get hold of Ostheim," he said. "And they're after me, Pan."

"Where are you?"

"I don't know. The Red Door spat me out somewhere, I didn't have time to see where."

A car drove past, full of guys, huge beats blasting from the stereo.

"Herc," she said quietly. "They've got both Engines, they're going to unlock the gates."

"We can stop them," he said, although his words sounded hollow. "We've got time, Pan."

She checked her watch, those digits counting down relentlessly, plunging toward zero.

"Actually," she said. "I don't."

He grunted, a noise that might have been a sob. She heard the sound of his feet pounding, the click of a door, and when he spoke again his voice was a whisper.

"I gotta go, Pan. Get out of the country, head back to Europe, if you can. I'll get hold of Ostheim, we'll figure out what to do."

Shouts from the other end of the phone, a pop that might have been a gunshot.

"*I gotta run,*" Herc said. "*Pan, be okay. I . . . Just be okay.*"

Then he was gone.

She stood there for a moment, listening to the static on the line, wishing she could reach through and grab him, drag him into New York.

Be safe, she thought, then she replaced the phone in the cradle and turned back to the car. Truck, Night, and Marlow were leaning against it, all of them watching her.

"That sounded like bad news," said Night.

She opened her mouth to lie to them, to tell them it would be okay, but the sobs were like caged birds finally being set free. She couldn't stop them. She wasn't sure who it was who carried her back to the car, who sat with her in their arms. She just leaned into them and cried, hugging them with everything she had, her body no longer hers but a broken machine that heaved and sobbed and shook as they drove out of Manhattan.

BETTER THE DEVIL
YOU KNOW

The stone he sat on was cold and uncomfortable, slick with algae. A few bright stars burned through the permanent smog of light that hung over New York. Even though it was summer, the air had cooled. The truth was, though, that Marlow had never felt more relieved to be anywhere in his life. Compared to the molten heat of a soul being dragged to hell, cold was good. And he was just grateful that he could still feel anything at all. After the day he'd had, that was no small mercy.

But the relief was short-lived. He couldn't believe what had happened, what he had done. It couldn't have been Charlie. Surely he wouldn't have done that in a million years. *Not unless they got to him, not unless they forced him.*

He shivered, chewing his knuckles for a second before the taste of blood and dirt made him spit. They were sitting by a small wooded lake somewhere west of New York, somewhere quiet. Truck had driven them through the Lincoln Tunnel and then gunned it for Pennsylvania, although Marlow had no idea where they were now. Truck and Night were off scouting for another car. Better safe than sorry. The blast doors had slammed down over Manhattan and the surrounding boroughs, Homeland out in force. They'd listened to the radio on the way down and it had been full of terror—a series of coordinated attacks on St. Patrick's, on Rock Center, on Staten Island. Everybody was shouting terrorists. Even witnesses to the scene spoke of bombs exploding, gun battles in the streets. Nobody mentioned demons, or people with superpowers. No, it was much easier to believe in a convincing lie than an impossible truth.

Better the devil you know.

Pan sat a short distance away, lobbing stones into the unsettled water. Even in the bruised dark he could see how broken she was. The physical wounds were clear enough. Her body was wrapped tight in linen bandages that Night had looted from a drugstore downtown, but blood still seeped through her chest and stomach, turning her into a Rorschach inkblot. Marlow kept staring at it, wondering what it would tell him about himself. Nothing he didn't already know, he suspected.

It was the mental wounds that were most obvious, though. Before today, Marlow had thought Pan's emotional core had been iced over, her tear ducts frozen shut. But she'd wept for the whole journey, over an hour, her racking cries softening to soft sobs, then hitched, whimpering breaths. Although she was quiet now, her face was deeply lined and she chewed her nails like she hadn't eaten in a month. Every other second she checked her watch and Marlow knew what she was thinking. The demons were coming for her, and there was absolutely nothing she could do about it.

He had injuries of his own, too. His chest radiated pain and he was drenched in blood. How much of it was his, though, and how much belonged to other people, he had no idea.

Still, what was it people said? Scars were just proof that you were stronger than whatever tried to kill you.

Pan sniffed, her chattering teeth the loudest thing in the night. Marlow stood up, then lost heart and sat down, then stood up again, stumbling over the loose shingle and sitting next to her. He had no jacket, but he pressed himself against her, putting an arm around her shoulder.

Smooth, Marlow.

She pushed him away, almost hard enough to knock him off the rock.

"Sorry, you sounded cold," he said, knowing full well that the night had nothing to do with it. These were the shakes you got when life sucker-punched you.

"I could be sitting naked in the Arctic and I still wouldn't want you near me," she said, hugging herself. "You did this. I'll never forgive you."

"I didn't," he said, the guilt like a knife sliding into his stomach. "I didn't know, Pan. I don't get why he did it."

Charlie. It was still impossible to understand what had happened. The Circle must have brainwashed him, used some kind of mind control. It was the only explanation, right? And he saw Charlie lying on the ground near Fresh Kills, injected with alcohol, pleading with Marlow to bring him. Pan was right, this was all his fault.

I'm sorry, Charlie, he thought, wrapping his arms around himself, against the tremors that rocked his own body, against the night, against the world.

"What happens now?" Marlow said. "We find it, right? We find our Engine and we take it back."

Pan shook her head.

"It's impossible, Marlow. We'll never find it."

"They found ours," he said. "It can be done. If I can just get hold of Charlie, if I can just speak to him."

"Don't you think you've done enough damage?" she spat at him. "They're dead because of you. I'm dead too."

He swallowed down his reply alongside a mouthful of bile.

He coughed, his airways still held open by the Engine. Not for long, though. Once the Circle had canceled his contract the asthma would be back, and somehow he knew it would be worse than ever—the way a cell seems smaller to a prisoner who has escaped for a while. The monster would have its claws well and truly around his throat again.

"I want to help," he said. "I need to. I know Charlie, I know he wouldn't do this unless he was forced to. I can find him, Pan."

She reached down and grabbed another stone, but instead of throwing it she held on to it, looking at it like it was engraved with the answer to everything.

"Did he say anything to you?" she asked.

"Charlie? No, nothing."

Wait, didn't he? Marlow thought back, Charlie in the infirmary bed, the last words he whispered.

They're lying to you.

"No," he said again, the word surprising him. He wasn't sure why he was keeping it to himself. "How long do we have until the Engines are united?"

"I don't know," Pan replied. "Nobody has ever done it before. Nobody really knows how it works."

"So that's a good thing, right?" he said. "They might not figure it out."

"They will," Pan said. "It's Mammon. He'll figure it out."

"Then we find him before he does," Marlow said. "I promise you, Pan, it will be okay."

"Okay?" she said, spitting out a bitter laugh. "It's over, everything is finished. You've seen it, when you were in the machine. You've seen *him*."

Marlow could see him now, a mess of rot and decay who watched the world with insect eyes. Something so horrific that he made the wormbag look as harmless as a hamster. He could almost sense that longing, the desire to be unleashed. Whatever was down there—Devil or not—it wanted to be free. And what then? Marlow thought of Staten Island, pictured his mom at home with the dog. Saw his neighbors, his classmates. Saw them trying to fight the demons when they tore through. It was too much and he had to force the image from his mind before he drowned in blood.

"He's there, Marlow," Pan said. "He'll take us all."

This time, when he put his hand around Pan's shoulders and pulled her close, she didn't resist. He held her tight until the soft purr of an engine rose up behind them. Marlow turned to see an SUV trundling down the path, its lights off. It pulled up to them and Truck rolled down the window, leaning out. He looked tired but he was doing his best to smile.

"You two wanna get a room?" he said. Pan grumbled something under her breath and pushed herself up. Truck beamed. "It's no trouble, there's a Motel 6 up the street."

"Shut it, you perv," Pan said as they walked to the car. But Marlow thought he saw a glimmer of a smile there too. That was the weird thing about life, he thought. No matter how bad the injury was, laughter could fix it. It had powers of its own, laughter. An Engine of a different kind.

"You know where we're going?" Marlow said.

"There's a private airfield outside Bethlehem, Pennsylvania," Pan replied. "We head to Europe, find Herc and Ostheim."

"And then what?" Night asked. She was curled up in the passenger seat like a bird in its nest.

"And then we take back the Engine," Marlow said. "We take ours and we take theirs and we end this war for good."

"You're forgetting something," said Truck.

Marlow paused, then nodded. "Yeah, we crush some serious ass."

"My man," said Truck with a fist bump.

Marlow waited for Pan to climb in the back, taking one last look out across the lake. For a moment he thought he saw a silhouette against the water, a blurred shape against the drifting dark. For some reason, he thought of his brother, long dead, and his stomach loop-the-looped. In his tired mind's eye Danny lifted his hand in a salute. Marlow smiled, feeling the prickle of tears in his eyes. He saluted back but the illusion had gone, the water just water, full of night.

Miss you, bro, he said. *Wish you were here.*

Yeah, right, Danny replied in his head. *Chasing the Devil while demons try to devour my ass. Sure, Marly, I'd love to be there.*

And Marlow was laughing to himself as he climbed into the car. He slammed the door shut behind him.

"I'm glad someone finds this funny," said Pan. She was glaring at him from the other side of the car but it somehow made her look even more attractive. That was one good thing, he supposed. At least he got to spend a little more time with her. She may have hated his guts but surely the thought of being dragged to hell in twenty-five days or so would make any girl lower her standards.

"I just know we can do this," he said. "I think things will be okay."

"Wish I shared your optimism," said Truck, putting the car in drive and rumbling slowly out of the park. "Four of us—three without powers once the Circle cancels our contracts—against two Engines."

"They'll be recruiting more Engineers, too," said Pan. "They'll be gunning for us."

"And Mammon will be there," added Night. "Maybe another wormbag or two."

"And the demons," said Truck, turning left onto the deserted parkway. "Don't forget the demons."

"So, the four of us against all the armies of hell," said Marlow, nodding. "Why wouldn't we be optimistic?"

Pan leaned over and thumped him on the shoulder, but she was smiling now, the sight of it like the first golden rays of dawn peeking over the horizon. Smiling and laughing, all of them laughing, like birdsong as they drove into the night.